SECONDS

LOIS WYSE

SECONDS

CROWN PUBLISHERS, INC. NEW YORK

Grateful acknowledgement is made to Macmillian Publishing Company for
permission to reprint an excerpt from "Lullaby," by William Butler
Yeats, from *The Poems of W.B. Yeats: A New Edition,*
edited by Richard J. Finneran.
Copyright 1933 by Macmillian Publishing Company, renewed 1961
by Bertha Georgia Yeats.

Published by Crown Publishers, Inc.,
201 East 50th Street, New York, New York 10022

CROWN is a trademark of Crown Publishers, Inc.

Manufactured in the United States of America

Book design by Shari deMiskey

Quality Printing and Binding by:
Berryville Graphics
P.O. Box 272
Berryville, VA 22611 U.S.A.

*For two men who
believed in these women:
Edward J. Acton
Freddie Gershon
and
for the extraordinary friends
who shared stories, time, and love,
who gave advice and warm support,
my grateful thanks.*

BOOK ONE

*"Our passions do not live apart in locked chambers, but . . .
bring their provisions to a common table and mess together."*

GEORGE ELIOT

1

H ER PALE YOUNG EYES WERE LARGE WITH FEAR. LIFE, WHICH
had beckoned like a never-ending road just hours ago, was now
reduced to the minutes at hand.

"Don't," came her sharp cry. "Don't. Please don't."

There was the low repeated rumble of thunder, and for the
moment her words were lost in the sounds of heaven.

Then the thunder stopped, and her words came sharp and clear
and unbelieving. "No, you can't.

"No, no, no," she repeated, but with each *no* the voice grew
fainter.

≡

Sienna lay quivering in bed waiting—waiting for that sound,
that last faint *don't* that would end her recurring nightmare and
silence that voice, stop those words that took her back in time and
place.

At last it came. "Don't."

Sienna strained to hear the faint cry before it trailed into a
whisper on the wind.

How many years now had this vision come back? Always it was
preceded by an angry rumbling in the sky. Sometimes there was
lightning that followed, sometimes not. But each time there was the
sound of that first clear, strong warning, each time there was the
chance to go back. Yet each time Sienna remained motionless, just
as she had then, and each time, just as she knew that the last
unheeded warning would galvanize her return to life, she knew the
unheeded warning also ensured the repetition of this nightmare.

Did the others hear it, too? Did the voice come back to them?
That was the question she never asked. After all, the sound came to
her only with the thunder, and life was sunshine now—well, wasn't
it? So why think about the things you couldn't change, those things
that might spoil the fairy tale?

Sienna opened her eyes. The rain beat heavily on the terrace outside her bedroom, and from under the bed she could hear the whimpering of Puff, her small terrier. No surprise. She knew it would be raining. Even before she heard Puff, she knew from the long anguish of that repeated dream that she would awaken to the sound of rain.

But why today? she wondered. What gods conspired to give her dreams and rain today, today when the three golden girls—Sienna, Anne, and Bronwyn—were speaking at Hargrove College, when the three young consorts of the kings of commerce were going to tell of triumph over trial, emphasize the importance of education while downplaying—what was it they were going to downplay?

Was it their bad dreams or their husbands' bad deals?

And who would really know the difference besides Virginia? Virginia Payne North, their mentor and guide, the knowing hand that shaped them each to live this rich, royal life.

Sienna reached for a terry robe. It didn't matter that her closet was filled with silk and lace peignoirs. When she was alone, she still liked best the coziness of her old terry robe. "It's my security blanket," she'd told Peter. And as she'd said it, she knew it was true.

The funny thing was that Peter thought she looked sexy in it anyway. Even under the bulkiness her tight, disciplined body moved to a self-imposed, lithe rhythm. "Damn you. You were born with good posture," Anne always complained. "I had to be an athlete to learn how to move my body." It wasn't Sienna's body that Bronwyn noticed, however; it was her unlined, unmarked face. Poor Bronwyn. She'd never really gotten over the anxiety of her acne-scarred skin. And now, despite the medications and treatment, she still tried to hide behind her makeup.

And me, Sienna wondered, what is the shield between me and reality? Peter, she said to herself. Peter. Yes, Peter. Now she said it aloud. There. That did it. Every time she said her husband's name aloud she planted herself firmly in the moment.

Yes, she was Peter's wife. Peter Marvell, brilliant businessman, major contributor to presidential campaigns, rumored to be in line for an ambassadorship. That was reality. And today it was raining. That was real, too. Just an ordinary rain. Would it delay Peter? No, there was his car now pulling out of the garage.

She didn't have to look at a clock. It was 7:03. Peter's life was lived by a self-imposed clock. She wondered if he would have had that same slavish devotion to time if she had been his first wife, or was that minute-by-minute discipline his way of dealing with that other wife who—never mind. Forget it, she chided herself. The other wife is gone, and you're here. Back to the present, Sienna.

At 7:05 Peter would walk out the front door, step into the car, and be driven to the city. She did not have to see him walk out the great oak door through the sheltered portico to get into the car. She knew by the clock he had left.

Good.

She would go back to bed and begin her day. She smiled as she moved. Virginia had shown her how days begin in bed. Sienna rang for Hedda. "Everyone has a maid," Virginia had said, "but you really need more than a maid. You should have a secretary, and then let staff report to her. She will hire your maids, cook, butler, valet."

Sienna had listened eagerly. She liked anything that put her two steps ahead of her mother. Her mother had always had a personal maid, but never a secretary. In Hunting Valley, the Cleveland suburb for the horsey set, only husbands had secretaries.

And so Hedda had joined the household, the secretary-confidante of Madam. At first she'd called Sienna Mrs. Marvell, but over time and shared secrets, the Mrs. Marvell had been replaced in private by Sienna.

"Good morning, Sienna." Hedda stood at the door with a breakfast tray, the newspapers, and a date book. "There's a story about a battered wife in the *Tribune*. I've marked it because you may want to send a donation. I think it would be a good idea; it makes people know that you have a human side. You know, not just the glitz-and-glitter stuff. I think you have to show that you have a conscience now that Washington has an eye on your husband. Also it would work well if you mentioned that in the speech you're giving this afternoon. You remember, I'm sure, that today's the day that Virginia is introducing you and Bronwyn and Anne at Hargrove College to show coeds the choices that nineties women have."

Hedda put down the tray, handed the morning papers to her boss, and then, even though she was square-built and fifty-three, walked with a quick, light step to pull a chair next to the bed, should Sienna want to begin with the morning dictation.

When Hedda had first come to her, Sienna had been intimidated, but now she found that her life was moving with a new kind of energy. It was really wonderful having a secretary. She couldn't imagine why everyone didn't have one. Today, however, she wished Hedda's energy would move her, too. She felt that strange discomfort that always came with the rain and the sounds of that old, infecting dream. She wanted to reach out to Hedda and be comforted by her, but their relationship, while good, was not that intimate. Sienna knew she seemed remote today. She didn't want Hedda to think it her fault, so she tried to smile. Yes. She'd attempt a little easy banter. "Hedda, I think you'd make a better me than I do. I don't know what I would do without you."

Hedda shrugged. She had worked for years for a team of lawyers and had learned not to take overpraise or overcriticism with too much emotion. "I'll tell you what you'd do first without me. You'd learn to make coffee."

Sienna nodded, wrapped her robe tighter about herself, and slid her body to an upright position, two pillows behind her back. Her long dark hair was still tousled from the night's sleep.

Hedda turned and looked at her boss. Her pale skin was almost translucent, and her large violet eyes were heavily circled. She was sitting up in bed, but her arms were crossed in front. Hedda had never seen Sienna look so vulnerable. She was strangely touched by this woman for whom she had never felt any kind of pity. She wanted to ask her something, but she was not sure what. She paused awkwardly for a minute and then asked, "Did you sleep well, Sienna?" Although the two dealt daily with household and money matters, this was the most intimate question Hedda had ever asked Sienna, for Hedda, who was accustomed to viewing the world through the small cracks in other people's lives, had just been permitted her first real glimpse of her employer.

"I look terrible, don't I?"

"Not terrible, just tired," Hedda reassured her quickly.

Could Hedda read her secret dreams? Maybe this was the time to confide in her secretary. Yes, tell the real dreams so the secret nightmares would fade. "Well, I'm going to tell you a secret, Hedda. I am tired. Now don't say a word, but I think I probably am pregnant."

Hedda felt a small shock. Pregnant? Yes, Sienna had talked about becoming pregnant; Hedda had even made appointments with the gynecologist—a Dr. Palmer on Park Avenue—but Hedda had assumed that her appointments were the usual checkups. Why would she want children? Why would he? After all, the two children by his first wife were already grown. Weren't second wives supposed to be partying partners, rich men's trophies in the marital wars?

"Maybe you have indigestion," Hedda volunteered.

"And we'll name this indigestion Peter Junior."

"Well, if that is what you want—" Hedda said. She had already heard more than she wanted to know.

Sienna nodded. "I think so, and I really want to be."

Hedda stood. She'd have to say something, but she wasn't sure what was an appropriate comment. She made a stab. "Well, if you want to have a child, you'd better get pregnant soon. You don't have much time."

Sienna bristled. "I'm only forty-one."

Hedda flushed. She hadn't meant to say it quite that way, but wasn't every magazine these days full of warnings about the biological time clock? Now embarrassed by her gaffe and aware that jobs like this did not exactly grow on manicured hedges, she said quickly, "Well, I hope you're right. If you are, you'd better take care of yourself. Not so many late nights. No drinking. Maybe not even coffee." In her nervousness she issued her warning as she poured a cup for Sienna.

Sienna did not seem to notice. "I'm not much of a drinker. But then none of my friends really drinks."

Hedda wanted to ask, "What about Bronwyn?" but she had said quite enough for one morning. Instead she raised her steno pad and asked, "Do you want to go to work now?"

Mercifully the telephone rang. "Mrs. Marvell's line," Hedda answered gratefully.

The crisp, cultivated voice of a receptionist announced, "Dr. Palmer calling."

Hedda handed the telephone to her boss. "It's Dr. Palmer," she said as she began to walk from the room.

Sienna smiled. "Stay," she advised. "He's going to tell me I'm pregnant." She took the phone eagerly.

Only the steady sound of the rain could be heard as Sienna listened, her large violet eyes concentrating on a distant place on the wall.

Sienna listened, and then her face contorted with disbelief and pain. "Don't," came her sharp cry.

Hedda looked in fright at her employer. There was a desperation in her face. What was he telling her?

"No," Sienna insisted. "No, there must be something you can

do. This just cannot be. We'll pay anything. Aren't there some treatments? I heard about Switzerland. What do you mean, 'Money can't help'? There must be something I can do, somewhere I can go. 'Accept the inevitable,' you say? Doctor, I have never accepted the inevitable. No, I tell you. No. No."

Sienna put the phone firmly back on the hook, leaned forward in her bed, and began absentmindedly to twist the telephone cord. The corners of her mouth were turned down, her eyes narrowed.

Hedda took a step back. The beautiful, vulnerable woman she had seen just minutes ago was now on fire with a kind of determination Hedda had known only in men of power.

"No," Sienna said to no one. "No," she repeated, her voice louder. "No, no, no." Now her voice was growing shrill with anger and frustration.

She turned to Hedda. "I told you I want a baby, and that doctor says I'm never going to have one. And it's me. It's because of me. It's not because of fifty-eight-year-old Peter. It's because of me. Me. I threw away every chance on those abortions years ago, and nobody can do anything about it now. Isn't that rich? I'm the one who's sterile. I can't even have a test-tube baby. I can't be pregnant. I can't ever be a real mother. Hedda, I can buy houses and art and planes. I can even buy people, but I can't buy what I want the most."

Outside thunder crashed, and lightning zigzagged across the black sky.

2

THE FORWARD CABIN OF THE REVAMPED 737 WAS SET UP AS AN office, and Anne had her papers spread across the work table when the bolt of lightning blazed through the right aisle window and danced crazily across the aisle. Anne clenched her teeth. Lightning. She hated lightning more than anything, but she said nothing. She bit her lip, dug her ballpoint pen into her paper, and held her breath until that instant that the lightning flashed back into the skies through the left window. She felt the moisture in her palms, but she did not utter a sound. Not that anyone would criticize her if she did.

How could they?

After all, the people here were paid to listen to her screams, answer to her call, and cater to her whims.

This was her plane, her command, her world.

And she was Mrs. Casey Burrows.

Casey Burrows. His name was so well known it was used to describe others, as in, "Who does he think he is? Casey Burrows?" Or, "That's some deal. That's a real Casey Burrows."

Anne looked around. She could stop most of the world, but she couldn't stop this damned storm, and she couldn't stop the plane. Not now. Not at thirty-six thousand feet. High enough to look down on the world, but not high enough to stop the fear every time she heard that thunder, saw that lightning. You'd think that with all of Casey's toys—the house in the south of France, the hotel in London, the fleet of planes—you'd think life was a sandbox where nothing would scare her. That's what they all said, all those people who were sitting here waiting to serve her. The pilot. The copilot. The steward. The secretary and the hairdresser. The nanny and the children. All of them here for the beautiful, blond Mrs. Casey Burrows. And beautiful, blond Mrs. Casey Burrows was still afraid of the storm.

But no one saw the fears. Not even Sienna and Bronwyn. For a moment, just for a fleeting second, she wondered if the lightning frightened them. And if it did, would they admit it any more than she would. They were all so positive and strong now. "Three little maids from camp are we," they had once sung together.

And of the three, Anne was certain she had done the best. Sienna's husband, Peter Marvell, was rumored to be as rich as Casey. But she'd always found Peter stuffy, too sure of himself. If he were made an ambassador, which was the rumor going around, Anne was sure he'd become a pompous prototype of the rich American. Now he was only a medium-rare bore.

As for Bronwyn's mate—the poor rich Harold Ashter—he was so anxious to have everyone think him as great a deal maker as Casey that he had even hired Casey's public-relations firm. It made Anne laugh.

No, there was no question about it all. Anne had done the best of the three. Her husband was the handsomest, the richest, and the best liked of the trio.

Still it was only right that she have more than the others. She looked tougher and stronger than they, acted as if she were afraid of nothing and no one. "What do you want?" a reporter had asked her once. And she had answered with her now-famous line, "Just what any ordinary, everyday woman married to a billionaire wants: everything."

Everything. That was the word, the thought that always centered her, brought her back to reality. When the lightning was too crazy, the thunder too loud, the thought that now she had everything—the money and the power—reminded her that storms were temporary. Life lasted.

Her life anyway.

And just look what she had made of a life that could have been ordinary.

At forty-two Anne Burrows was obviously very blond, to some very beautiful, and to all very tall. At six feet one inch she stood head and shoulders above all the women she knew. She used her blondness and her size to make herself noticed, and she coupled that with the kind of voice that issued commands even when she was not in command. She was not in command of the 737 in which she was a passenger at the moment, but that didn't matter. Only thirty minutes earlier, the copilot of the plane had stood in front of her, summoned from the flight deck. "Lucky we have some time before takeoff," she had said to him in her firm, loud voice. "I want you to look at these ridiculous seats that were just put in here. Only a first-class dummy would put seats like these in my plane," she'd announced. "These chairs give me no support when I want to work. Don't these idiots know that I'm an athlete?" She had not paused for his response. "I understand the human body. Now I want that stupid designer to put some chairs in here that are meant for working. No more of her reclining seats designed especially for men with big behinds and no forehead. Tell her she's not working for some man she wants to have an affair with. Tell her she has a real job now; this is the main office of a woman who works."

"Yes, Mrs. Burrows," the copilot said meekly.

"Does my husband know about these chairs?"

"He ordered them."

"Casey ordered them?"

"Yes, Mrs. Burrows."

"Well," she said, "he's a fantastic businessman, but fantastic as he is, this just proves he can make a mistake every once in a while."

The copilot had opened his mouth to speak, then, suddenly remembering his two children and pregnant wife, he had closed his mouth and returned to the flight deck.

"I hope he flies better than he talks," Anne snapped to no one in particular. Her male secretary, Wilfred Bilmont, quick always to interpret her commands, both spoken and unspoken, said, "I'll send a memo to the designer and see her about the chairs."

"All right," Anne said petulantly. "Just make sure Casey doesn't see her. He doesn't need any female designers at the moment."

Wilfred opened his alligator notebook, took out his slim gold pen (a Christmas present from Anne's children, ages one, three, and five), and made a notation.

Even watching her secretary do her bidding gave Anne a sense of triumph. Her long road to high places had begun from the moment she realized that she lived in the finest apartment house in New York not because she was the daughter of the owner, but because she was the daughter of the maid. And from that time she was determined to rewrite her past and invent her future.

Her official biography now referred to her father as a long-dead officer in the Hungarian uprising, and her mother, a God-fearing Polish immigrant, had become a Romanoff. It was all very easy to do. Her father had never challenged the facts, for he had never known that she existed. He had been a waiter at a party given by the family that had employed her mother, and her mother—new to the country and young at love—had believed him when he took her to the roof of the apartment where they were working, and told her in a variety of Italian phrases, none of which she fully understood, that she was about to do something very American.

The result of that language lesson was Anne, who was named Svetlana Crossetti by her hapless mother, who nevermore looked at a man lest she again be cursed in the same way.

When Anne's mother died, the last vestiges of Anne's true story were buried, and her biography became even more melodramatic. She went from being a very good swimmer who had practiced at public pools and attempted to train for the Olympics to an Olympic swimmer. Her eight credit hours at Columbia University were now translated to a degree from Radcliffe and interrupted study at Harvard Business School. And her one swift attempt to enter a beauty contest had become the basis for the biographical note that mentioned her as a Miss Texas finalist in the Miss America pageant.

Wilfred Bilmont cleared his throat as he always did before he announced something unpleasant to Anne.

She, now accustomed to his habits, looked up. "Now what?" she demanded.

"The children are frightened. Nanny thought you might want to comfort them."

She sighed. Of all her jobs, motherhood was the most boring. Still, Casey wanted those children, and she knew that no matter how far he might wander, the thought of three heirs and the concern over what she could get in a New York divorce brought him home each time.

"Tell them I'll be right with them. And then let's get my notes ready for the talk. I wish I hadn't told Virginia I'd do this today. I wish—forget it, Wilfred. Forget what I just said. You know," she said, her now-famous smile directed at her stone-faced assistant, "I love my life."

3

BRONWYN OPENED HER EYES AND REACHED AUTOMATICALLY FOR the tabloids before she reached for her coffee. What were they saying about her today? What item had Harold had planted in the last twenty-four hours? It was from the papers that she'd learned he was buying a chain of specialty shops, selling a plastics company, and merging two airlines. It was also in the columns that she had found she was spending the summer in France, was buying a new co-op on Fifth Avenue, and was considering a horse farm in nearby Bedford. When she reminded Harold that Sienna and Peter owned the largest horse farm in Bedford, he'd quickly switched deals and bought instead the largest oceanfront property in Southampton. "My friends can do better than me," he'd said gruffly, "but your friends better not."

So he moved her summer and weekend activity to the Southampton house, where she entertained nonstop for what she knew was a passel of people who wouldn't have looked at her if her husband hadn't been her best accessory.

"Did you see the papers?" Harold was asking now. He was wearing a dressing gown and walking toward his study, where Cargill, his valet, would have his English-tailored size 48 suit at the ready. Harold's awesome mounds of flesh were reduced to rolling ripples by his clever tailor, but no tailor could cover his baldness. Instead that was the job of his barber, and with his barber's help, Harold had found the way to grow his hair long at the sides, then comb it across his hairless dome. Bronwyn thought it looked ridiculous, but the first time she had ever told him she liked bald men, he'd answered, "Then marry your father. He's bald. I still have my hair."

Harold's voice with the words, "Did you see the item?" came to her through the pages of the paper.

"Now what did you do?" she asked, her voice full of concern.

"The Driscoll deal went through."

"Which means?"

"It means your daughter will never have to marry for money." He laughed.

Bronwyn bit her lip. That was typical of Harold's humor. Gwyneth was three, the daughter born to them three months after their marriage. When Harold's grown children—the products of what he called "the usual stupid first marriage"—horrified by both Bronwyn's youth and obvious pregnancy, asked their father to pay off the mother-to-be and get her out of their lives, he'd decided to marry Bronwyn. "Anything those kids think is bad for me must be good," he'd reasoned.

Still the marriage hadn't been bad for Bronwyn. The best thing about it was Gwyneth. She adored the little girl with a streaked ponytail that matched hers, a tiny body almost like a miniature of Bronwyn's own size 2. But most of all she loved Gwyneth's smooth baby skin, the skin Bronwyn never had, never would have. No, despite the pumice and the prescriptions, despite the treatments and promises of miracle cures, nothing had really worked. Nothing had ever removed the traces of that early acne and given her the smooth skin she dreamed of having.

Every morning Bronwyn stood at the mirror in her bathroom— the marbled modern spa that was her redone bath in Southampton, the painted, gilt boudoir that had been designed for her in New York, or the blue-and-white bath Harold had built for her on the yacht that they kept off the coast of Bimini. "Why Bimini?" she'd asked. "Listen, kid," he explained, "you never know when you need to move a boat to make a deal. Got it? Maybe I want to do something that I don't want registered in the United States. So what do I do? Move to Switzerland? Hell, no. Just move the boat, and make the deal. Remember this, baby. You don't tell me how to move my boat, and I don't tell you how to move your—"

She didn't listen to the rest of the sentence. It would end with a vulgar reference to some part of her anatomy. Most of Harold's sentences did.

Still this life was a lot better than growing up over a drugstore in the Bronx. That's where it had all started. And if she hadn't spent that summer of '61 at the Peabody School in New Hampshire, if she hadn't met Anne and Sienna, she'd probably be some druggist's wife just as she'd been some druggist's daughter. And furthermore she still wouldn't have skin like Gwyneth's.

Bronwyn looked around her white bedroom. That was the thing she loved about the Southampton house. It was all so—so white. It had a pure, antiseptic look, the kind of scrubbed look she wanted for everything in her life. The white canopy bed stood in the middle of the room. "I like big beds," Harold had said, so Binkly & Bobbers, the society decorators of '89, had done the room around the bed. Of course, if they had done the house the year before they never would have used B & B. "Remember this about me," Harold had told her. "I'll cut a guy for the last nickel on a deal, but when it comes to the way I live, nothing's too good for Harold Ashter."

I hope, Bronwyn thought, that means Gwyneth and me. Bronwyn had expected Harold to be wildly excited about his daughter. She didn't think he'd approach fatherhood in the same perfunctory manner as Casey Burrows did because—well, even though Anne was Casey's second wife, those children were his first, and she'd noticed that rich men took first-marriage children for granted, a kind of necessary appendage to wedlock. But Harold wasn't much interested in Gwyneth. He still preferred deals to daughters.

And he preferred his houses to all other houses. Bronwyn knew that each time Casey bought Anne a dress, a house, or a plane, every time that Peter and Sienna took a trip or acquired art, she knew that Harold would not be far behind. It always began with his same line, "Did you see the papers?"

So, by reading the papers each morning, Bronwyn was spared

the usual wife's complaint of not knowing what was going on in her husband's life. The papers not only advised her of his current activities, but based on the reports of other rich men, she could predict her own future.

"What's in the papers today?" Bronwyn asked.

"It says you and your girlfriends are talking at some college group. I forgot about it. I think my office arranged the whole thing."

"I don't think so. I think Virginia did it."

"How come?"

"It's her charity."

"She really runs you girls, doesn't she?"

"Harold, nobody can run me except you."

He smiled. "You're right, kid. And don't forget it."

"Virginia's invited us all for dinner—with husbands—tonight."

"Where?"

"Her house at eight."

"Who's going to be there?"

"Sienna, Anne, and us. Oh, and someone she says knows us."

"You mean some fag that knows us will be there for her?"

"I wish you wouldn't talk like that."

"Well, what does she go out with besides fags?"

"I hate that word, Harold."

"That's how I talk, kid. It's about time you got used to it. But listen, I'm not complaining about going there. After all, I'm in the papers, too, today with the Driscoll deal."

"What does that mean?"

"You own the shop where you and your girlfriends buy your clothes."

"Oh, is Polly's on Park part of Driscoll?"

"Sure is. Any designer you want is yours, kid. Wholesale."

"What difference does that make? I go up to designer showrooms anyway and get my clothes at a price."

Harold Ashter, never one to leave a room without having the last word, said, "My price will be better than your price."

As he spoke a bolt of lightning struck the tree outside the window. Bronwyn screamed. Outside gardeners, estate managers, and assorted help ran to aid the stricken tree.

But inside, inside the house where Bronwyn now lay sobbing helplessly, no one came.

4

THERE WAS A TIME WHEN VIRGINIA COULD LIE IN BED AND LISTEN to thunder with the same exquisite anticipation as she did the sound of a lover's footstep on the stair outside her door.

But that was long ago, back when the sheltering arms of the man she loved blocked the view of storms, when the love in her bed matched nature at its wildest. Now she had learned to turn her back on storms and wait for sunshine that was sure to follow.

The storm raging outside her window would turn to sun soon. How could a storm like this last for long? No, soon the sun would come, filter through the blinds, and cast a shadowy pattern over the white duvet that covered her. She loved this bedroom. In palest peach and white, it occupied the northeast corner of the seventeenth floor of East House, New York's best apartment house, a fact never acknowledged by the people who lived there, a group of rich, accomplished people famous for not being famous, Manhattan residents who in the safety-conscious, publicity-shy fashion of the moment pretended that it was really nothing to buy, redecorate, furnish, and maintain an apartment that cost more than most American families earned in a lifetime of hard work.

Virginia Payne North loved this room because it contrasted so sharply with a life that had not always been a bed of white duvets— or even white quilts, white comforters, or white blankets. Black was the color of her childhood, the choking, unforgettable black of coal dust and poverty. She did not look back in triumph; she looked back in wonder. The little girl from West Virginia had come a long way. It was no easy rags-to-riches story; it had been work. And the hardest part of the work had not been the career but rather the marriage. These young women today seemed to think that corporations deserved the talents of women, but the truly smart ones knew what Virginia knew, that the real power of a woman was defined not by her job but by his. So long as men had the biggest jobs in the country, a woman's biggest job would be at a man's side.

She sighed. How many times had she heard the women of the seventies and eighties proclaim their liberation because they were "free"? Free indeed. Free to hold two jobs and feel guilty about both.

No, the truly smart women now were waking up to what she had always known. The best job for a very smart woman was marriage to a very successful man. Such marriages, of course, took great care to develop. They might begin with a woman's skills in bed, but only her artfulness in arranging and directing a rich man's life would guarantee her continuing in her job.

Sex might get a man, but only style could keep him.

And Virginia had been the best practitioner of the stylish, successful marriage. Yes, marriage to Calvin had been successful in all the old ways of measuring. He had been rich and semifamous; she had been beautiful, young, and smart enough to help him become very famous. Then, just when it was all going so well, just when they both knew enough to treasure their love and measure their moments, just when they began to take the time to watch the patterns on the duvet each morning, that was when he had the heart attack. One morning he was there; the next he was gone.

In the beginning Virginia slept only on her side of the broad king-size bed they shared. She never ventured beyond that narrow strip of marriage that she and Calvin knew was hers alone. The chasm between her and the wall came to symbolize the rest of her life stretching bleakly ahead. And then one morning, a day she later recognized as her epiphany, she moved to the center of the bed. That was the day she agreed to join two volunteer committees, the day she knew that she would stop pretending to be alive and begin to live, the day she could again begin to look at the pattern the filtering sunlight made across the white duvet.

Always a woman to live the judged life, she now asked fresh questions of herself.

Was there a time past love?

Could there be love past love?

And over the months and then the years she found that friendship could be that love past love. For friendship now offered her the best of marriage without the most troublesome parts. Friendship provided an outlet for love without requiring constant judgment and intensity, the most difficult part of marriage—and in return she was rewarded with fierce loyalty, deep respect, and daily caring, the best parts of marriage.

Her friendships with the old crowd stayed intact. Then slowly, almost imperceptibly, the crowd changed as the money changed. That was what the Old Guard never really understood. Those well-born women never totally understood that it was money that moved New York. They still thought it was family. That was why when she had joined them as a newcomer they had been stiff and fearful. Now she was old enough to be safe, smart enough to be in the vanguard of the next society. But as she moved to that new place, the Old Society women, fearful for their own roles, greeted the change with chill. Too bad for them, Virginia thought. They refused to understand that New York charity no longer mobilized for unwed mothers and foundling homes. Now the beat went on for AIDS and a plethora of disease-come-latelies. Juvenile diabetes had replaced infant mortality, and infantile paralysis was taken over by spina bifida. All good causes, Virginia reminded her friends. But they chose to cling to the old groups. Not Virginia. Her relationships with her women friends were enhanced by the fresh strong winds of the dynamic new women, and among them were the tough, brash second wives of the power men. In particular there were her three protégés, Anne, Bronwyn, and Sienna.

Virginia welcomed them with open secrets. She shared her masseuse, her butcher, and her caterer—three indispensables for a new wife making her way in a husband's world. Now Virginia found herself waiting to hear from them each day. The Seconds had taken form with Virginia's shepherding of Sienna. Not that Sienna was exactly a poor little rich girl. Sienna was the daughter of a Cleveland lawyer, a well-to-do man Virginia had met along the way. But being the child of some wealth in the Midwest did not help a very rich woman know the ways of New York. She'd met Sienna at the Industrial Age Museum and realized immediately that Sienna was going to need some help with both the Old Guard and the New Trophies. So Virginia became the adviser, the consultant to this bright young woman as she worked her way into the fabric of the City.

Sienna had brought Anne to her, and in turn the two had brought her Bronwyn. Strange how connected the three were. Perhaps not so strange. They needed one another, these three, these overachieving women who made it look as if they needed no one. And they needed her. Virginia knew where the bodies were buried, where society laid its booby traps for the unsuspecting. The Seconds was how she thought of them all. The Second Wives. The Second Chance. Yet each acted as if she were creating marriage, motherhood, and women for the first time. They were not just a community of women in New York; they were becoming New York. There wasn't a week that passed that one of them wasn't getting or giving an award, being saluted as Person of the Year, Woman of the Year, or chairing a charity dinner. But of course none of that was surprising or unplanned. No, it had taken careful orchestration, and Virginia was a master of fine orchestration. She had made the Seconds resound with the artistic authority of first-string players.

Indeed, who could instruct these young, eager-to-learn women better than Virginia Payne North, a woman who ran society without being born of society? The challenge made life a game again. How could she make three young women pass "Go" and collect the rewards of life? How could she ripen them for blossoming in the appropriate seasons of life?

"My new best friends," she laughingly called them in the beginning. But now they were long past the beginning. Now they truly were her best friends, these strong young women, these Magna Cum Laudables, who were—well, why not admit it? They were her. They were each a part of Virginia Payne North.

They had Virginia's determination, her sense of duty, her appreciation of beauty, her willingness to work hard at the marriage game.

Oh yes, they had the well-publicized Virginia Payne North attributes, the virtues catalogued carefully in the style pages of the papers.

But if these women were truly her, then where was the dark side?

Each time she saw them she wondered. Today she would see still more of the public side of the Seconds. Tonight, as a reward, she would invite them all to dine at her home. It would be the kind of dinner Virginia specialized in giving: The Little Weeknight Dinner, where she would toast her Seconds for giving time and talent to her alma mater, Hargrove College. Yes, they would go there today, and each would talk to the seniors about the responsibilities of women of the nineties.

Sienna, the wife who runs million-dollar charity events.

Anne, the wife who runs a real-estate empire.

Bronwyn, the wife who runs shopping malls.

And Virginia, the woman who showed them how to run their lives.

Incredible, wasn't it?

Virginia was a woman of the nineties. Once she had been a woman of the forties. Where did the years ago? Would they speed so for her Seconds, too?

Her lovely Seconds. What had been their firsts?

Didn't they ever lie in their marriage beds and think of other men, dream of other times?

Didn't they ever wake awash in fear lest someone find out about them, learn the truth they tried to reshape with the latest diet, redress with the newest fashion, rewrite with this season's big novel? Were they only sunshine and smiles? Virginia was no cardboard cutout. Why should they be? Virginia had known desires she still remembered but no longer admitted. She had reined passions best forgotten, hidden secrets she prayed were too old to matter now.

But still there had been something to hide. Even now at sixty-seven, inside the young-feeling, well-exercised body there still was something to hide.

With these women, her sweet confidantes, her eager dreamers, where and what was the hidden part that could one day come forth and either save or ruin them?

5

PETER PUT HIS FEET UP AND SETTLED BACK IN THE CHAISE IN HIS wife's dressing room to watch and wait as she applied the makeup he didn't think she needed. He loved to watch her beauty ritual. It was so feminine and sweet, so different from Judith's. Who was it who said men kept marrying the same woman? He smiled to himself. No, no man ever had two wives more different from one another. Judy, that was his first wife. At least she had once been Judy. Later, much later, when she went back to school, she used her full name, Judith, and after she won her law degree she went into practice with her maiden name on the door, but it was written as J. R. Marshall. By that time she had stopped wearing makeup, insisted the children call her "Judith," and created her own unisex world. In the office she affected trousers and jackets, pulled her hair straight back, and wore low-heeled shoes. Still Peter held his tongue. After all, there were two children, and in his own fatherless home he had dreamed of the day he would be a father in his house.

Judith believed in teaching her children and her husband the true meaning of total equality. In the early servantless days, the days when he was just a stockbroker, she washed half the dishes and he washed half the dishes. She named their children so that their sex would not be communicated; their daughter was Sidney and their son Gene. Still Peter did not complain. He said nothing even when she insisted that he initiate sex half the time and she the other half. But when his initiations were refused and her initiations were nonexistent, he began to wonder if there was someone else—male, female, or sexless. It turned out to be the latter. Judith left him for her career. As she explained, "I cannot feel important next to you. You take up all the air in the room." He didn't know how he could take up all the air when she was almost six feet tall, three inches taller than he.

He looked now at Sienna and smiled. Sweet. That was always the word he used when he thought of her. She looked sweet; she tasted sweet; she treated him sweet. Sienna was curvy and sweet and fragile, even a little frightened. He'd married her six weeks after meeting her, never knowing exactly what she was about, only that her father had been a very good trial lawyer from Cleveland named C. N. Craig, and she was named for C.N. Her father was dead and her mother had remarried—more than once. Sienna had bounced around like all kids in the sixties, had spent some time in California—he tried to put that part of her past out of his mind, tried to pretend it had never happened—because Sienna had a truly generous spirit. That was why Virginia's guidance through the intricacies of the New York charity scene had been so good for—well, for both Peter and Sienna. It certainly couldn't hurt for a would-be ambassador to have a wife known for her good deeds. It rather complemented a man known for his deals.

And that was some deal he was putting together now. It would all be pulled together before any appointment, of course. He smiled in happy anticipation of the sound of it. The Marvell Fund. The Marvell Fund, created with his own billion dollars this time, his own money that he'd raised. This would be a good one to—

"Peter." He thought he heard Sienna's voice.

"Peter." Now she sounded cross.

Had he been dozing? Had she been talking?

"I've told you twice, and you haven't said a word."

"Sorry, darling. I guess I had my mind someplace else."

"Well, come home from the office."

"I wasn't thinking about the office," he said half truthfully. "I was thinking about you."

"Me?"

"You're the best deal I ever made."

"I wasn't a deal," she flashed back with the trace of annoyance that crept into her voice every time he came too close for comfort with his version of their love story.

"Okay then," he said, switching conversational gears with the adroitness honed in boardrooms and back rooms billions of dollars ago, "tell me why I'm wearing black tie and you're painting faster than Picasso."

"We're going to Virginia's for dinner."

"Special occasion?"

"It is for me."

"It's not your birthday," he said quickly.

"Good catch, Peter. No, and it's not our anniversary." She turned to look at him. "Peter, someday you're going to learn that everything in the world is not about you." The minute she said it she regretted her words. Everything really was about Peter. His money, his house, his children. That's one of the reasons I want a baby so much, she thought. I want something that's mine, or at least ours.

"Are you angry?"

"No," she assured him. Why was she so edgy? The rainstorm had done it to her once again. Yes, that was it. And how nice of Peter to notice that she just wasn't making her usual effort. She'd have to do better. He deserved her best because even though she'd heard and read that he was tough—some called him ruthless—in business, she never saw that part of him. With her he was always questioning his actions and her feelings. He was still the little boy seeking approval. Most of the time she remembered to respond to that side of him with more warmth and understanding, the kind she knew he never had in that miserable first marriage.

She spoke again, this time with more patience in her tone. "Anne and Bronwyn and I spoke to a group of undergraduates at Hargrove College today. We drove to some town in New Jersey near Princeton, and there was this pretty little college—well, it's Virginia's pet place, you know, and to thank the three of us she's having a dinner in our honor."

"At East House?"

"Of course. Virginia doesn't approve of restaurants for entertaining at dinner."

"Who'll be there?"

"Small-ish, I guess. Maybe just a couple of other couples."

"Didn't she give you the guest list?"

"You know you can never ask Virginia. She's too perfect for words. She just does it, but you're not supposed to ask how and with whom."

"For a woman who doesn't work," Peter said quietly, "she works harder than any man."

"But not harder than Anne—if you ask Anne." Sienna smiled. "Listen to this one, Peter. During a question-and-answer period at the seminar today, someone asked Anne how she managed to run the real-estate business and deal with the unions and the contractors who never do well with women, and when this naïve college girl asked Anne, 'How do you get the respect of men?' Anne just stood there, all six feet of her, and answered, 'They have no choice.' To tell you the truth, I think Anne's beginning to believe that she and God are partners in creation."

6

AS ANNE BURROWS PUT ON HER MAKEUP, SHE CHECKED THE door of her dressing room to make sure Casey was not standing there, for if Casey were there, she would know that something was wrong, really wrong. Only three times in their five years of marriage had Casey Burrows come into his wife's dressing room while she dressed, once to tell her of the October 19 stock market plunge, once to tell her of his father's sudden death, and once to tell her that one of their planes had crashed. The small French clock on her dressing table—pretty but unreliable, just like the French maid she had brought back from the same Paris trip—said seven o'clock. Where was Casey? Virginia's dinner was called for seven thirty, and Virginia was so fussy about punctuality. In tonight's traffic it would take fifteen minutes to get all the way east. There were some nights when it just didn't pay to live on Central Park South. Still it was nice having the hotel penthouse. She hadn't been that enthusiastic when Casey had bought the Dome. Although it was the newest of the Central Park hotels, it didn't have the grande dame elegance of the Plaza, but it did have modern plumbing, and to a maid's daughter who'd grown up sharing her mother's Spartan bathroom in a Park Avenue apartment, good plumbing covered a lot of unborn elegance.

Of course she had taken the Dome apartment to an unexpected grandeur. There were the wonderful pieces of French furniture, the porcelains, and, most of all, the paintings. Anne had raised the ceilings of her rooms to eighteen feet simply by taking the top four floors of the hotel and creating two floors. She then filled the rooms with museum-quality paintings chosen with the help of museum curators throughout the world. "Anne alone," Casey announced proudly one night, "has raised the price of art on the world market by thirty-seven percent."

No one argued. That was the smartness of Casey. Who could fight a number like 37 percent? He always sounded so authoritative that everyone assumed he was right.

As for Anne Cross Burrows, she had her own standards in a world of anything goes. Her primary standard was the gold standard. She dealt in gold, in pounds, in dollars, in marks, and in yen. She watched the international money markets because she was convinced that money was the only thing that mattered, and she wanted to be certain that in a multitongued world her money always spoke the right language. Today the dollar had gone up—and just when she'd bought against it. She should have known. Anne frowned. Why had she done anything in the markets today when the day began with that damned lightning and thunder? She shuddered and looked up, half afraid that Casey might be standing there.

No, it was Miss Patch. Miss Elvira Patch had come to them with recommendations from New York's best families, families whose children she had carefully nursemaided from infancy to college. Now she was in charge of Cissy, Fudge, and Kip, the children Casey called the Pride of the Fleet. Some pride, Miss Patch sniffed to herself. She'd worked for famous parents before, but these, these parents never even looked at their children. And such sweet little ones they were. Cissy, the five-year-old, had been christened Anne. When her sister was born two years later, young Anne became Sister and then Cissy. But Cissy in her baby talk could never pronounce Fudge's real name, Virginia. She had been named for Virginia Payne North. The baby, "a son at last," Casey had said, was named Casey III and promptly called Kip.

"Mrs. Burrows," Miss Patch said in a tone that indicated she expected to be refused, "shall I bring the children in now?"

Miss Patch was not to be disappointed with the response. Anne shook her head quickly. "No, no, we're late now. Have you heard from Mr. Burrows?"

"No, ma'am."

"I thought he might have stopped in to see the children."

"No," Miss Patch intoned, and then to give more weight to her negative word, she added slowly, "the children have learned not to expect their parents more than twice a week."

Anne turned back to her dressing table, then stood.

Where was Casey? It was always possible that he was stopped in the lobby by—yes, by whom? By somebody with a deal? A Wall Street pal? Another deal-maker? A blonde? A movie star? Casey was bigger than television itself. Hadn't the latest polls shown that he was better known than the mayor of New York? Well, he was certainly better liked. Anne would bet that girls didn't stop the mayor in the lobby of the Dome and offer to show him their knickers. Well, that was the price of fame.

Still it wasn't the same with women. Here she was, every bit as famous as Casey, every bit as photographed, yet men didn't gravitate to her the way women did to Casey. It really was a man's world. No matter what women did, men still owned the best of it, including the women. Wasn't she really owned by a man? No, not really. She turned slowly to look at herself in the six-sided mirror. Another signature dress—a white satin dress that hugged her lithe body, a dress made in the thirties style she loved so much, just a long satin sheath indented at the waist, this one with a halter neck to set off her year-round suntan. Yes, she was the perfect accessory for Casey Burrows. Still, she got her licks in when she could. As Anne had said in her last interview—"Of course my husband and I get along very well. Wouldn't you get along well with your wife if she delivered a million dollars a week in profits?"

Veronique, Anne's maid, rushed in and pushed past Miss Patch, who was slowly backing out of the dressing room.

"Madam." Veronique was breathless. "Mr. Burrows just called

from the car, Madam. He will be downstairs in eight minutes to take you to Mrs. North's house."

Anne looked down from her chalky heights. "If he called from the car, Veronique, didn't he ask for me?"

Veronique promptly bent her head as if to share the shame of the Ice Goddess's unresponsive husband. "Never mind," Anne continued calmly, "we both have other things on our mind. Miss Patch," she said brightly, "kiss the children for me, and tell them that Mummy will play with them sometime tomorrow."

7

"IF YOU CAN'T BE BORN BEAUTIFUL, YOU'D BETTER BE BORN WITH a will to work," Bronwyn had told the young women at Hargrove College just that afternoon. "I am the perfect example of a woman who understood that her face wasn't her fortune and that if she wanted a fortune she'd have to figure out how to get one for herself."

Yet even as Bronwyn Corcoran Ashter assured the young women that it was indeed possible to be rich even if one was not beautiful, she did not admit that she had been—and still was—ashamed of her looks. Although Bronwyn was barely five feet tall, weighed less than a hundred pounds, and had to have most of her size 2 dresses custom made, she did not aspire to Anne's awesome heights. Nor was she envious of Sienna's long dark hair and violet eyes. What she wanted and would never have, no matter how many Driscoll deals her husband closed, no matter how many colleges invited her to speak, no matter how many hit shows she produced in the two theaters she now owned, no matter how many successful shopping centers she created, what she would never have was an unmarked complexion, a perfect face with perfect skin. When other women talked of facelifts, Bronwyn grew her streaked hair another inch to cover more of her face. When other women had facials, Bronwyn had yet another peeling, another attempt with pumice, another try for a small miracle.

Bronwyn never truly believed that people were impressed by her accomplishments.

Bronwyn mistook the awed silence of her audience for boredom as she told that portion of her now-laundered, well-rehearsed story that had been published so often. She explained that she had translated a talent for numbers into a series of small jobs in her Bronx neighborhood, parlayed that experience into a summer as a teacher's helper at a school in New Hampshire, used that credential to help her get a scholarship plus the jobs she needed to see her through her education. At the end Bronwyn believed the audience was with her when, in a few moving sentences, she cautioned the young women that life could not be all work. Bronwyn told how, at the New Hampshire school, she had met her friends, her best friends, the women now standing here with her, Anne and Sienna. "Don't be too busy to make friends, for friends last longer than grades," Bronwyn said softly.

What Bronwyn did not confide to the eager young women, however, was that in those days when she met her friends, they were not the poised, finished women of today. She did not explain that back then Sienna was an unhappy rich girl from Cleveland, and Anne a proud, poor girl from New York, who was in the process of inventing herself.

Nor did she mention the Event.

That was how she always thought about that day and night of horror. It was now simply the Event. Sienna and Anne and she never talked about it after that day. Yet they knew they were bonded forever. They knew that the fate of one was the fate of all. It was not her own determination so much as their conspiracy of silence, their nonspoken agreement to forge a pact, an unwritten partnership to guarantee their loyalties to one another, their mutual protection.

There were two names that none of them had ever spoken aloud again, two names that each knew came back in their dreams again and again, two names that rang in tempo with thunder and flashed frighteningly in lightning.

Rosabelle.

And Gregory Sawyer.

Virginia had made it easy to forget the bad parts of that summer; she had been a way for each of them to build new memories, the kinds of memories you could talk about at dinner parties and colleges. And their friendship with Virginia gave them lovely reasons to see one another regularly, for through her original friendship with

Sienna—and with Sienna's help—Virginia had moved each of them into the circle where meeting a very rich man was not only possible but inevitable.

"The rich marry the rich," Virginia had said. "At least that's the way it used to be. Now," she explained, pausing between words in order to emphasize their importance, "the rich marry for the fun of it."

Virginia had taught each of them how to be a wife to the man she married. It was strange, but of the three of them, only poor little Bronwyn had been a multimillionaire before her marriage. Indeed her annual income exceeded one million dollars as she bought and sold Manhattan commercial property in the high-rolling 1980s. It was while she was negotiating a long-term lease in midtown Manhattan that she found the two theaters she bought. And it was after marriage to Harold that she had the money to produce the plays she wanted.

"The perfect life for you," Virginia had said. "He may not be the ideal husband, but you are getting the child you wanted, and you can be paid to make believe. Isn't that a dream life?"

Now Bronwyn waited for the elevator in her Fifth Avenue house. She stood tiny but elegant in her bottle-green dress. Across the hall her most precious possession, Gwyneth, lay sleeping. Only fifteen minutes earlier her perfect little face had been tear-streaked because Mommy was going away. So she had stayed with her until she fell fast asleep. Harold was still waiting in the limousine downstairs. That was all right. He would be on the telephone or reading yet another financial journal. Bronwyn would keep the world waiting for Gwyneth. Yes, even Virginia could wait. Nothing mattered, no one mattered except that exquisite sleeping child.

She breathed a small sigh as the elevator came, smiled at the attendant, and went down to get into the limousine and resume the very social life of Mrs. Harold Ashter.

8

I N 1952 WHEN MR. AND MRS. CALVIN FORBES NORTH MOVED TO East House, it was already too far east for those who walked and taxied to their New York lives. It was, however, the perfect location for those who owned chauffeur-driven limousines and hired dog-walking butlers. East House, with its cul-de-sac abutting the East River, its large rooms, superb view, and excellent in-house club, quickly became home to a noteworthy collection of powerful people known only to one another. In the shabby gentility of their homes, they quietly entertained old roommates, old friends, and old family. It was the cozy world of "we," the old rich. "Them" referred to Irish, Italians, Jews, and anything "new."

The 1960s marked the breaking of social barriers. Still the "news" did not invade East House. "News" were so new that they felt they had neither the money nor the derring-do to invade the self-appointed upper-class digs of New York.

By the 1970s, however, the fiscal resurgence of New York and the making of the new corporate class made East House a much-sought-after address for this new breed of New Yorkers, those corpo-rate hires who, after years of nose-to-the-grindstone diligence in Midwest iron, steel, and automotive hierarchies, were rewarded with temporary custodial power of large corporations, new kinds of jobs with perks that included an apartment in New York, a house in Connecticut, use of the company plane, and a golden key to a retirement package.

By the 1980s the introduction of junk bonds lowered the gates and raised the prices in East House and like apartments. The new billionaires wanted any apartment that didn't want them. Their new young wives quickly learned that New York was for sale, and they found that all it took to make the deal was the ability to make the right friends, give the right parties, and announce it all through the right columnists.

Virginia Payne North had lived through each of the decades. She had survived the snobby fifties, overcome the dark days of her widowhood in the sixties, courted the corporate types of the seven-ties for her charities, ascended to the throne as one of the reigning queens of the egalitarian eighties, and was now poised in a power position for the nineties.

For Mrs. North was a part of New York's delicious handful, the sophisticated widows with their interchangeable escorts (the Reigning Dress Designer, the Reigning Public Relations Man, the Reigning Friend of the Famous, the Reigning Interior Designer) who were able, with less than twenty-four hours' notice, to assemble New York's best for a little at-home. Indeed that was the kind of entertaining that Virginia most loved, a smallish dinner that let her display her best china, her best silver and—most of all—her best ability at mixing and matching people and creating the atmosphere for conversations that could change corporations and influence history.

"There is a formula for parties," Calvin had taught her. "Always make sure that you have at least one person who will impress someone there. It works better than caviar when it comes to social success."

Tonight was a night that would make Calvin proud of her. From the large dressing room adjacent to the bedroom of her duplex, she came slowly, deliberately down the curved staircase to double check her tables.

She nodded as she looked at the two round tables of eight each set with the linens from Venice, the silver from London, the china from Paris.

The candled wall sconces were ready to be lighted; more tiny candles had been placed strategically at each table. The soft pink glow would flatter both women and food.

Yes, the dining room looked wonderful.

And enough names had been collected to impress even the most blasé. Which magazine was it that had called her dining room the New York White House?

Tonight she would prove again that a woman alone could command the world. How lovely that her three young friends understood that, too.

≡

At seven thirty Holmes, Virginia's long-time butler, brought the first guest into the library. Virginia knew who it would be. She had orchestrated the evening well in advance. She stood to greet Gregory Sawyer.

"Thank you for coming early," she said.

Gregory Sawyer bowed without moving his body. Virginia was not sure just how he did it, but she was sure that the man standing before her was no ordinary man in her life. The men in her life were, for the most part these days, a series of sixty- to seventy-year-old homosexuals. Gregory Sawyer was not more than fifty-five, suntanned, muscular, and decidedly male. The first good-looking real man, she thought, since Calvin.

Virginia sped through the amenities, his drink order, the dreary weather, and the cross-town traffic. She was in a hurry to reach her destination before the others arrived. "How do you know my girls?" she asked.

"I met them all when they were teenagers."

"All of them? Anne and Bronwyn and Sienna?"

"You know they met the summer of 1961."

"I knew they knew each other, but I never was quite certain when or how they met."

"In those days I ran a special school, a summer school for boys and girls who had trouble adjusting during their teens."

"Anne and Sienna and Bronwyn had trouble?"

"Well, the sixties were a time of trouble for both boys and girls, just as it is today. You're one of those people who is aware of the terrible destruction drugs cause. Indeed, if you weren't aware, then we'd never have met the way we did last week—at the Coalition for New Yorkers Against Drugs."

Virginia nodded. She knew how she'd met Gregory. Now she wanted to hear more of her girls. "Go on," she suggested in that carefully cultivated tone that made small suggestions imperial commands.

He nodded graciously and continued. "You know, of course, that Sienna comes from a wonderful family in Cleveland, but her parents couldn't really handle her in 1961. There was her mother's nasty divorce, and that mess when her mother ran off with their estate manager. It was a little like Lady Chatterly, you know. In the end he abused her, but these were the early days of that romance, and Sienna had a difficult time imagining her mother in a love relationship."

"How did Sienna know Anne?"

"She didn't—until they came to the school in New Hampshire. But dear little Anne . . ." He laughed indulgently. "She's the best

self-creation I've ever seen. She's taken her patchwork life and
turned it into a satin quilt."

Virginia nodded with interest. She was going to hear some very
good stories in the weeks to come.

"And poor little Bronwyn," he continued. "I always think of
her as poor little Bronwyn, although she's older than the others. In
fact, I used Bronwyn as a teaching assistant. She's terribly bright."

"How interesting," Virginia said, looking away.

But Gregory Sawyer knew that she was hooked, totally and
completely hooked. He sighed deeply. "Since it's all so long ago,
I don't imagine they'd be sensitive about it any longer, Mrs.
North—"

"You must call me Virginia," she answered quickly. Yes, indeed
he must. She had plans for Gregory Sawyer, and it would not do to
have him think of her as an untouchable older woman. She wanted
a different kind of relationship for a change.

"Virginia," he repeated. He said the name with a kind of tender
caress that made Virginia look into his eyes. Blue eyes they were.
Deep blue eyes that made her forget the assorted histories of her
three girls and think with a sharp stab of sweet remembrance of Lake
Como and the summer she was eighteen.

"You're a very attractive man, Mr. Sawyer."

"My name is Gregory. We're going to be very good friends,
Virginia."

"Because of the girls?"

He laughed. "Despite the girls."

"Do you still run this school, Gregory?"

"Unfortunately, no. I think there's a real need for it again,
however."

"We must discuss it. Perhaps we can get the girls to talk about
it."

"Yes, with us," he added softly.

Virginia raised her glass of bottled spring water. "With us," she
toasted.

Gregory lifted his perfect martini. "To us," he responded.

Holmes came quietly into the library. "Some of your other
guests are arriving, Madam."

———

The elevator opened directly into the apartment and deposited Linda Strong-Harrison, the queen of the eleven o'clock local newscasters, along with her current beau, the Secretary of the Treasury, Carter Mack.

Minutes later the others arrived. Sienna and Peter came up on the elevator with the Detweilers, Don and Judy. Don was the editor of *The American*, New York's most influential newspaper. As soon as the elevator doors closed, Peter knew he would like the party. Don Detweiler was someone he needed at the moment. The paper had to stop running those damned liberal editorials; those senators in Washington thought Don's editorial page was the Holy Bible whenever they wrote about mergers and acquisitions.

Virginia made the introductions of the newcomers, and when she preceded the introduction of Gregory to Sienna with a sweet speech about "out of your past," she sensed immediately that it was not a past that was remembered with affection.

Sienna turned to Gregory and stammered. "H-h-how did you get here?"

"The same way you did," Gregory answered. "On the elevator." He turned. "And this must be the famous Peter Marvell."

Sienna nodded and said simply, "An old friend of mine, Peter." In the unspoken language of long-time partners Peter understood that Sienna was letting him know that this man was a nobody, and he could focus on the Detweilers. Peter took his drink and headed toward Don Detweiler once more.

From the corner of her eye Sienna could see Bronwyn and Harold Ashter come into the library. Bronwyn, her streaked hair long—always in the hope that it would hide her scarred face—was wearing a long bottle-green dress. The neck was high, the back low. Poor thing, Sienna thought. She thinks if we look at her back we'll never see the front. Harold, even in formal dress, had a perpetually rumpled look. Harold, the unmade bed, she had always called him. But the look of Bronwyn and Harold was not what disturbed her. Bronwyn must not collapse with fear when she saw Gregory. She had to warn Bronwyn. She went into the hall. "Bronwyn, I thought you were so touching today," Sienna said. "I loved what you said about—" Then she buried her head in her friend's ear as if to whisper some girlie-girl secret. "Don't panic, Bronwyn. I'm going to ask you to come to the powder room with me. Just come."

Bronwyn shrugged. "I'll be back in a minute, Harold."

Sienna took Bronwyn down the long hall with its Hudson River paintings and into the little peach-and-pearl powder room. She closed the door behind them, took a deep breath, and said quietly, "Gregory Sawyer is here."

Bronwyn reached to touch Sienna's arm. "I don't believe it. How did he get here?"

"He's here with Virginia. I think he's about to become her new escort."

"How can you tell?"

"It's written in his beady blue eyes."

"Are we safe?"

"As long as we stay together," Sienna answered quickly, almost automatically. It was an answer not just from her heart; the words came from every ounce of her. It was bred in the bone, something she knew because she knew. *As long as we stay together.*

Bronwyn leaned weakly against the wall; she felt the hollow pain of fear.

"You mustn't panic," Sienna warned.

"Nothing lasts forever, does it, Sienna? Well, thank God I brought a Valium. That'll get me through tonight, but what do we do next?"

"We'll do a Scarlett O'Hara," Sienna answered grimly as she walked out. "We'll think about it tomorrow."

During Sienna's absence, the rest of Virginia's guests had arrived. Obviously Anne and Casey had already seen Gregory. But there was nothing to worry about with Anne. She could tackle polar bears—and in her white satin dress it would be hard to tell the players apart.

The foreign guests—Virginia always had at least two non-Americans—were Lady Diandre Devon and her cousin, the British banker Freddy Fenmore. Dr. James Butler, the famous Texas heart surgeon, was there with his wife, HoneyBee.

Sienna went to Gregory, now standing with Judy Detweiler. "It's been a long time, Gregory." She turned to Judy. "I'm sure Mr. Sawyer has told you that he works with—ummm, with young people."

"Oh, do you?" she asked ingenuously. "I'm on the board of Quincy House. It was a foster care house and then when social needs changed, we became a drug center, and now we're a place for children of the homeless. I really admire anyone who works *professionally*"—she said the word with awe—"with the young."

Linda Strong-Harrison, eager to leave the eleven o'clock local news for the muddy waters of network news, advanced on Judy Detweiler. The hot skinny in TV circles was that Judy Detweiler was the power behind the pen of her husband, Don, and the best way to get good press in New York was to ingratiate one's self with Judy and let pillow talk rule the world.

"Judy," Linda interrupted, "I hear you do a lot of good work in this town, and—"

Judy was all eyes.

"And I think it would be terrific if we could do one of our feature pieces on the eleven o'clock news on you and Quincy House."

"Wonderful," Judy said, and then she turned to Gregory. "Why don't you do a piece on a lot of us who are committed to the young? Gregory Sawyer here is involved, too."

"What do you do?" Linda asked.

Gregory threw back his head and laughed heartily. "I always heard that that was the first question you were asked at a New York party."

"Well, I am a reporter," Linda answered defensively.

Judy broke in. "Relax, Linda. We're all here for a good time. I think I'll go and say hello to Anne."

Linda, unwilling to stand with Gregory after a faux pas she didn't quite understand, walked over to talk to Carter Mack. Sienna, seeing Gregory alone, approached him from behind.

"You have no shame, have you?" she asked quietly.

Gregory turned. He had forgotten how beautiful Sienna was. Somehow her actions, her determination on that day made him forget that she had that look of breeding he always found so attractive, so rare. Now, twenty-nine years later, she had perfected that early quality. She had been born to rooms like this, and it was obvious. Even now the other women were wearing the trendy looks of the day, the inverted lampshade dresses, the fringe-on-fringe tops, but Sienna was covered by a short black dinner dress that was all lines and quality fabric. He was sure it was by a very famous designer.

"Sienna," he said in a low tone to match hers, himself poised to play the big game, waiting to see if he could frighten her still, "*shame* is not quite the word I'd use for you. How does *guilt* fit?"

She was trembling as she walked away.

There was no question in her mind. None of them was safe now.

Anne had two vodkas before dinner. "Aren't you celebrating a little too much?" Casey asked, his face creased with disapproval.

"Mother's milk," she retorted. "All of us Romanoffs drink vodka for good reasons and bad reasons."

Casey ran his fingers around the collar of his shirt. There wasn't anybody at this party he needed. God knows he had all the publicity he wanted at the moment. Forget the Detweilers and Linda Strong-Harrison. The Treasury bastard was on the way out. He'd already had the word from both New York senators. The doctor would only want to hit him up for a few bucks for his hospital. Peter Marvell would be trying to connect with more people and more money for his latest fund, and wacky Bronwyn's screwball husband, Harold Ashter, would either be so depressed he'd consider jumping off a building or so up that he'd think he could take over Casey Burrows and his empire. That left only the British banker and that lady—Lady Something or Other. Casey looked at his watch. Maybe he'd call Tokyo just for the hell of it. The markets were open there, and it would be fun to see what they were doing.

"Dinner is served," Holmes announced, and the sixteen carefully selected guests, matched by the computerlike mind of their hostess, walked into the peach dining room.

Some hostesses had advanced to the custom of seating couples together, but Virginia preferred to mix her guests. The two tables, therefore, had married couples seated separately. At the round table where she herself was, Virginia had put Gregory to her left and Don Detweiler to her right. Virginia called it the media table. She also had TV reporter Linda Strong-Harrison and Anne, who loved nothing more than the media. Sienna was on the other side of Don Detweiler, and Dr. James Butler was between her and Anne. She could count on Sienna to let the famous surgeon recount cases stitch-by-stitch and return to Houston confident that he had conquered New York once again. Carter Mack was seated between Linda and Anne.

Casey Burrows looked at the table where his wife was seated, checked the other guests there, and knew immediately he had been put at the second table. He was furious with Virginia. Look what she'd done now. Put him between Lady Somebody from London and a southern wife named HoneyBee. He couldn't believe it. Couldn't he at least have had the TV broad or a power wife? He'd show them. He wouldn't talk to anybody. It was easy to keep his silence during the first course, artichokes—God, artichokes. That was the New York test. If you were served an artichoke and knew enough to cut the heart out of it, you could advance to the next party and your next deal. If you can cut the heart out, you can survive. Casey attacked his artichoke. He hated these society bitches. He thought for a moment about Lola Potter. Lola. A tiny little brunette. Sort of the Sienna type. Lola was just another New York divorcee with nothing to do when he'd met her. That was at Virginia's, wasn't it? Anyway, he'd gotten her the decorator card and then told her to go ahead and furnish the airplane. He'd been to bed with her on the plane, never on the ground. "You sweep a woman off her feet," she'd said. "Naw," he'd answered, "I screw where it's convenient." Casey looked around the room. It would never be convenient here. This place was so perfect even the artichokes looked bored. And look what Virginia had done. She'd put him at the husbands' table. Casey, Peter, and Harold all at the same table. He should have said he was doing a deal, taken the plane and Lola, and gone out of town.

"Mr. Burrows, you are positively attacking that poor artichoke." He stopped, knife and fork in midair. If that was an English accent, he'd turn right; southern, left. He replayed the words. It was English. He kept cutting and turned right. "Americans always attack artichokes," he said.

She leaned toward him. "I've learned Americans always attack."

Casey looked at her and smiled. That was a very sexy answer, and he knew it. So did she. This might be fun. Maybe Virginia wasn't so bad. She'd given him Lola. Now this one. Who was it? Lady Somebody? "What'd you say your name was?"

"I didn't say."

"Somebody told me."

"Probably your wife."

"My wife is great, absolutely terrific."

"I can see that, Mr. Burrows."

"My name is Casey. You know, Casey Burrows. The *London Times* did a story about me last year. You probably saw it."

"Probably not. I read different kinds of stories."

"You don't read the business pages?"

"No real lady does."

"And you're a real lady?"

"You'll see."

"I will?"

"Well, dinner doesn't last forever, does it?"

"How can I see you?"

"I'm staying at the Wingate Hotel."

"I own it."

"How convenient."

"No, my wife's office is there."

"I thought you said she was great."

"She's fantastic, but—listen, how would you like to have lunch with me tomorrow?"

"Perfect. Where shall we go?"

"A little place by the water. You'll like it. It's mine. By the way, it's in Bermuda. A car will pick you up at the Wingate tomorrow morning. Be ready and downstairs at ten."

"I will."

"One more thing," he asked as he pulled out a small black note pad and gold pencil, "what's your name?"

≡

Anne twisted uncomfortably in her chair. Casey was at it again. She knew every time he talked to a pretty woman, every time he pulled at his ear, every time he took out that black pad and gold pencil he was off—off to the races with the next lady of the moment. Well, why the surprise? Hadn't she met him that way? And she was smart enough to let him have a long leash because it was the only way to keep him, and after tonight it would become more important than ever to keep him. Now that Gregory Sawyer was back in their lives. Funny, but today had been such a good day. It started badly with that thunderstorm, but the sunshine did follow, and the storm was quickly forgotten. She wanted to see that as an omen. But now, who knew what would happen next. This was going to be an endless night. She closed her eyes and wished it were twenty-four hours from now. Anything, anything to get her out of here. For the first time in years she was afraid for her life. What was going to happen to her? For so many years now she had felt invincible. Each time she put on a white satin dress, *her signature dress* the tabloids called it, she felt invincible. She called it her shining white armor, and each time she wore a white satin dress, she found that her dreams turned out as she had dreamed them.

But now as she sat at a table where she had always been comfortable, nothing seemed the same; she felt the chill winds of change. She felt the slight tipping of power, the turning of tables in the direction of the man who sat across from her now, the man who raised his glass of red wine and silently toasted her. She looked at Gregory Sawyer, raised her glass tentatively, opened her mouth to sip, and watched in horror as the red wine cascaded down the front of her white dress.

Anne's eyes filled with tears of embarrassment and fear. "Soda, get soda and pour it over you," Linda said loudly. "We had a show about it. Listen, there are two things I'm good for, spots on tables and the Heimlich maneuver."

Dr. James Butler cleared his throat. "If there's a medical problem, I think your answer may be at this table, Linda."

But Anne did not hear them. She fled the table, ran down the hall to the powder room, closed the doors, and for the first time since she was a little girl, she wept uncontrollably.

At the next table Bronwyn turned to Freddy Fenmore, the British banker who was her dinner partner. "Freddy," she said quietly, "will you please ask the waiter to bring me another vodka. I don't think I can handle wine."

By the time coffee was served in the living room, the world had changed. Sienna wondered if anyone knew it except Anne and Bronwyn. It was amazing to her to see how Gregory Sawyer, who had been—what had he been?—a small-time opportunist, a man who recognized a problem and with a smattering of gobbledygook psychiatric terms turned others' problems into his solution, how he now had matured.

Now Gregory Sawyer stood in one of New York's best living rooms, his back framed by the wide windows that looked out over the East River, and he was waiting.

Waiting to strike, Sienna thought.

Who will it be?

Bronwyn? Anne? Me? Virginia? Or all of us?

9

PETER LEANED BACK IN THE LIMOUSINE. "THIS," HE SAID TO HIS wife as he reached for her hand and patted it affectionately, "is my favorite time, the time when we can leave and go home and be together. I really didn't want to go to Virginia's tonight, dear."

"Ummmm . . . yes . . . well . . . sure," she answered.

"Did you hear me?"

Now she turned and faced him. "What did you say?"

He put her hand down and pulled away. "So what's the next thing you're going to tell me? You have your own agenda? Remember I've heard all those lines. Your mother probably had a headache when she didn't want to make love, and you have an agenda just like Judith."

"Oh, Peter." Sienna looked at him with concern. He was such a precious addition to her life. How could she tell him that it was fear that was causing her to forget that Saturday was a night he wanted to make love. She put her arm on his to try to reassure him. "I'm sorry, darling. I was just trying to think about the evening; you know—" She paused for a moment and then decided to take a small risk. "I sense I've seen that man—what's his name?—the one with Virginia—"

"Gregory Sawyer."

"I think I've seen Gregory Sawyer before. Have we ever met him?" she asked lightly.

"You had a slightly checkered career before I came along," Peter answered tersely.

Now she slid her hand through his. "You weren't my first, Peter, but you are my last. And I saved the best for last." She looked at her small diamond-and-ruby watch. "If I could read the numbers on this watch, dear, I'd tell you at exactly what time you'd be out of the shower and on my side of the bed."

He smiled. "Maybe I'll skip my shower tonight."

"Oh no," she said quickly. She needed that time; she lived her life by his schedules. "You told me when we were first together that you were a three-shower-a-day man, and now I'm used to it. I need that time to—damn, darling, it's none of your business." She squeezed his hand.

"I really don't like to upset my schedule," he said. "The first shower wakes me up. The second shower gets me ready for the evening, and the third one gets me ready for you."

Sienna patted his hand. "Take your shower, and then you're going to find out I really am ready—and waiting—for you."

≡

When she heard the water in the shower, Sienna made the first call. She dialed Anne's private bedside phone.

Anne answered on the first ring, something Virginia had taught them never to do. "If you answer at the first ring," Virginia had explained, "you're like a horse at the starting gate. Be cool. Always be slightly unreachable, wait for the third ring; that's just long enough to make people think they've interrupted you, and it gives you an immediate advantage in any conversation."

Anne said hello quickly and with an agitated edge to her voice. Was it fear?

"Only me," Sienna said. "I wondered, Anne, did you get the wine out of your dress?"

"Yes, the stain came out," Anne answered, small deliberate pauses between each word as if to let Casey know who was calling.

Sienna spoke quickly now that she knew Casey was probably at her side. "Whatever you have tomorrow, cancel. I think you and Bronwyn and I should have lunch together at my apartment. One o'clock."

Now Anne put a little energy into her answer. "I almost forgot about that date with you tomorrow. Thanks, Sienna, for reminding me."

"Sweet dreams—"

When Bronwyn heard the phone ring, she knew through the fog of fear, the haze of too many drinks and just a few pills, that it must be Gregory Sawyer, never mind that the call was ringing on the phone that was unlisted, the phone with no extensions, the phone that only she could answer, the phone that she had put in knowing that one day she would need it. She heard the ring and her heart pounded *Gregory.*

Like Anne, she answered on the first ring.

But she was not prepared to hear Sienna, a lilt to her voice. "Wasn't it a wonderful night, Bronwyn? I just wanted to say I had a great day and remind you about our lunch date tomorrow—"

"Sure. Yeah . . . shwell."

"Bronwyn." Sienna's voice now had a crisp edge. "Don't panic, Bronwyn."

"Yesh . . . lunch . . . you . . . got it."

"Bronwyn, go right to bed, and don't worry about a thing. Look, dear, we'll all be all right. Not to worry."

"Gwyn—Gwynish—the baby—"

"She'll be all right," Sienna assured her. "One more thing, Bronwyn, don't drink anything. Just go to bed. Now—oops. I have to go. I just heard the water in the shower shut off."

10

SIENNA RANG VIRGINIA AT EIGHT O'CLOCK. NOTHING MUST change today; there must be no variance to the visible rhythm of their lives.

"Good morning, dear," Virginia said, her reassuring, mother-like tone making this seem like just another start to yet another day. "Where are you? Did you go back to the country last night?"

"No, we're in town."

Virginia did not have to be told what "in town" meant. She had helped Sienna find the perfect triplex on Park Avenue, had insisted that she use Martha Morgan to decorate her apartment instead of the season's hot interior designers, Binkly & Bobbers. "B and B gets you into the house magazines, but you don't want that, Sienna. You grew up with money so you must stay low profile. That's all part of your mystique. With Bronwyn we need to show that a woman can have whatever a rich man can have today. Don't you understand, darling, you're very different women, and we have to make sure that New York never confuses you with her or Anne."

Yes, Sienna understood. Sienna understood more than she admitted to Virginia. "I called to thank you for that wonderful dinner last night. I thought your toast was so generous—"

"As was your response," Virginia interrupted. "I want to ask you something. I sensed something amiss last night among the three of you. Have my dear little Seconds had second thoughts about one another?"

"No. Whatever gave you that idea?"

"Bronwyn seemed to go a bit overboard with drinking last night, and Anne, who is usually my idea of the original Ice Queen, was so rattled that she spilled wine—"

"Oh, that. You know, we all had a hectic day. It began with the rain, and transportation was so difficult. We all felt we'd spent the whole day in transit. Your party, I think, was just the moment to relax for all of us, kind of simmer down—"

"If you say so, dear. By the by, how did you like my new friend who is your old friend?"

"You make a very handsome couple, Virginia," Sienna said, testing her mentor's reaction.

"It's nice to have a real man around," Virginia confessed, a young trill to her voice.

"It *would* be," Sienna answered. Virginia never noticed that Sienna's response was conditional.

"We're going to see a lot of Gregory."

"*We* are?"

"All of us."

"Oh?"

"To be honest, Gregory's just the kind of person I've wanted in my life for a long time. He's attractive, bright, the perfect person to be a fourth at a lot of things in my life."

"A fourth?" Sienna was startled. "You always seem so complete to me."

"I don't to me. Widows are different from divorcees, you know. I don't mean to sound sad or strange, but there is a difference no one talks about. If I go somewhere without an escort and just one other couple, I'm the odd one out, and my widowhood forces people to come face to face with their own mortality. When people see a divorcee, they know they are confronted by the possibility of life choices. But a widow reminds people that all life is lived by chance. And so people, who ten minutes before shot verbal arrows at one another, begin to speak in softer tones. They even hold hands. I know that by the next morning their bows will be arched for the next round in the undeclared marital wars, but for the moment—just for the moment—they are lost in that grief before grief, that awareness that all life ends, and someone is alone." Virginia was quiet for a moment. "Strange, dear, but I don't think I could have said that if we were talking face to face. Sometimes the telephone releases me. Please forgive me."

"There is nothing to forgive," Sienna said, her heart beating wildly. Forgiveness was not hers to give, not to anyone.

≡

Anne was the first to arrive. "How long will this take?" was her question even before she said hello to Sienna.

"It's taken us twenty-nine years to get here, so who knows? Maybe it will take another twenty-nine years to get out," Sienna answered.

Anne bit her lower lip nervously. "I'm supposed to meet the 747 at three o'clock. Casey had some business thing in Bermuda so he took the GIII. Then he'll bring it back to New York, meet me at Butler Aviation—"

Hedda came into the room. "Excuse me, but Mrs. Ashter is on her way up."

"And let's hope that this time she's taking the elevator," Anne added. "She looked as if she were flying on her own last night."

Sienna silenced her with a look, nodded to Hedda, and said crisply, "When she comes, take her to my dressing room." She turned to Anne. "We're having sandwiches on trays there. No servants, no one but us. I thought it would be such fun to do just a girlie-girl lunch for a change."

"Yes," said Anne, "I think every thirty years we should let our hair down and call things as we see them."

Sienna waited for Hedda to leave and then said to Anne, "Remember, Bronwyn is quite fragile, and nothing is going to work

unless we all stay together. We still have to keep her strong enough
to continue her life."

"Without interrupting ours," Anne reminded her.

"On to the wars," Sienna said as she grasped the cherry banister
that once graced the stairs of a grand hall outside London, and
together the two women went to meet Bronwyn.

≡

Through the years the old Park Avenue apartments had their
rooms redefined, reformed, glassed, glazed, paneled, and mirrored
depending on the mood and mode of the current tenants.

Sienna's dressing room had originally been two guest bedrooms.
When the original owners, after forty years of tenancy, died and left
the apartment in their estate, it was bought by a middle-aged Wall
Street couple who were not, as Sienna later said, "into decorating."
The next owner, a young couple whose marriage was programmed
by their very rich and generous parents, proceeded to rid the apartment of its traditional moldings, fireplaces, and parquet flooring.
They painted all the walls white, turned the triplex into their pur-
view of a downtown loft, and, as if that were not antiestablishment
enough to shock their parents, they next divorced and sold the
apartment to a rock star. Because New York real estate was at a low
point, the board permitted the headline-making star to move in. But
as his records decreased in popularity, so did his need for a splashy—
and now mirrored—triplex. Virginia, her contacts firm with the
leading real-estate woman of New York, was the first to know that
the apartment would come on the market. It was exactly the sort of
apartment that she decided would suit Sienna. "You'll redo the
place, darling, and give it tradition, but you must also give it your
own stamp. Since Peter's bought you that little art magazine, why
not make your home a statement? Do a revolving show with artists
you feature in your magazine. You do have the advantage, dear, of
not being a parvenu, so put a few of your own family photographs
around, add a few portraits of your relatives, and you will be an
instant success in New York. Just remember the old saying, 'There
is no success like excess.' "

"Who said that?" Sienna asked.

"I think I did," Virginia assured her.

Bronwyn, her long mane of streaked hair in a ponytail, was

looking at the moisturizer, two shades of makeup, and blusher on Sienna's dressing table. "Hi," she said when the others came in. "Hedda sent me up here. God, Sienna, you don't even use makeup, do you?"

"What do you call that stuff you're looking at, chop suey?"

"Oh, come on, I mean, this is kid stuff."

"You seem better today," Anne interrupted. "We were worried about you, Bronwyn."

Bronwyn put the moisturizer on the dressing table and looked at them. Her usual makeup, while heavy, seemed even thicker today. "Don't worry. I'm still me. As soon as I leave here, I'm going to have my driver take me to a supermarket in Brooklyn where I can get some real buys on apple juice."

"Apple juice?" Anne asked.

"Of course," Bronwyn explained. "Anne, don't you know your children drink apple juice out of those little boxes with the straws? If you buy that apple juice in Manhattan you pay a dollar twenty-nine for three. In Brooklyn I can get a brand that's just as good and pay ninety-nine cents for three. So if I buy a case—"

"Bronwyn," Sienna said, closing her eyes in utter exasperation, "aren't you ever going to stop being a kid from the Bronx who grew up over her daddy's drugstore?"

"Maybe if you'd had to earn money—"

"Stop," said Anne, "that's not what we're here for. I have a plane to catch. You all have things to do. We're just putting off what we really have to say. I'll go first. I'll say it. Why did Gregory come back? What does he want? I've never even heard of him since—"

"The Event," added Bronwyn.

"No," said Sienna slowly, "let's give it a real name now. Let's call it the Accident."

The other two nodded. The Accident.

That would be a good name.

Their sandwiches untouched, the three women looked at one another, and knew that after twenty-nine years the reappearance of Gregory Sawyer was leading them all back to the same memory.

BOOK TWO

"Accidents will occur in the best-regulated families."

CHARLES DICKENS

11

I N 1961 THE UNITED STATES WAS STILL A NATION WITH A FIFTIES conformist mentality, a nation madly in love with its young, popular president, its young, popular first lady, and the first couple's marks of power, which included touch football, Hyannisport, Palm Beach, men's jackets slung over one shoulder, pillbox hats, Courrèges clothes, good manners, and good times.

Sienna Craig was twelve years old that summer of 1961. She bought her first pair of short shorts as she danced to Elvis records and imagined that her hips and his—oh, never mind, she knew what she imagined. So did her mother. And that was where her problem began. "Sienna's getting some ideas I don't like," Peppy (short for Priscilla) Craig told her husband, C.N., one night as they dressed for dinner at the Hunt Club.

"What kind of ideas?"

"Boys, dear. She's twelve, and in case you haven't noticed how she's grown these past months, the boys all have. She has very large breasts, and she seems proud of them. You know, in my day—"

"Please," C.N. interrupted, "I don't want to hear about this. What am I supposed to do, Peppy? Give her no-grow hormones? If you don't like the way she displays her—her body, then talk to her. I'm not going to. It's not a proper topic for fathers. I mean—my God, mothers are supposed to talk to daughters about sex."

Peppy threw up her hands. "Don't think I haven't tried to talk to her. I've told her girls can get into trouble by acting as if they—you know, as if they want it. Boys are just waiting to do it to girls. You know that yourself."

"I don't know any such thing."

"Well, I can't deal with her anymore. She's willful, and she seems to think that her bra size—"

"Stop that," C.N. commanded.

"Then let me send her away for the summer. I heard about this place called the Peabody School. It's supposed to be very good, and it's in New Hampshire, darling. Far from the madding crowd and that sort of thing. Frankly, Sienna wants to stay here in Cleveland this summer, and she'll probably put up a bit of a fuss with you if you say she can't, but if she stays here, I can see her getting into a lot of trouble. It's hard to supervise a girl with a body like that. Let's send her up to the woods and let her cool off a bit. The Peabody program lasts for eight weeks. Look, it can't hurt her, and I think it will give her some much-needed discipline."

"How do you know about this Peacock—"

"Peabody," she corrected. "The Peabody School. I heard about it from Tippy Cummings, who rides with my group. It's put together by someone she knows. Her cousin, I think."

"All right, then. Let's send her."

"Good. You tell her tonight."

"Why me?"

"Because if I tell her she must go, she'll say that Daddy wouldn't send her to a place like this, that Mummy just wants her out of the way. Oh, darling, don't you understand? Sienna's at that terrible age for daughters, and that makes it a worse age for their mothers. Fathers are—well, fathers are the ultimate, the final word. You know very well that when a man says something, it's just—well, truer than when a woman says it."

C.N. thought for a moment. "You're right, of course," he agreed.

≡

"I thought, my dear, that this year you might enjoy it if we were to book passage on the Italian Line. Although it's late in the season to make summer plans, I think we can still sail on the *Michelangelo*," Duncan Masters said to his wife, Hester, as they dressed for dinner on April 23, 1961.

"What a lovely idea," his wife said, adjusting the diamond-and-sapphire clip that had been in the Masters family for four generations.

"I think it would be comfortable for you if you were to take Svetlana with you. She's the best maid you've ever had."

"So she is, but you know she adores that little girl of hers—"

"Not such a little girl," Mr. Masters said, chortling as he put the male-counterpart jewels, the sapphire-and-diamond cuff links, in his dress shirt.

"Duncan," his wife chastised.

"Little Svetlana is at least a foot taller than Big Svetlana," he reminded her.

"Yes, she is a tall child."

"Did you ever figure out who her father might be?"

"I think her mother does truly believe that it was immaculate conception. So far as I can see, that mother never looked at a man, never had a date. No one was more amazed than I when she was pregnant thirteen years ago. You know, she was so naïve that she just thought she was getting fat; she didn't even know the facts of life, didn't understand what was happening."

"Too bad. If you'd known sooner, we could have sent her over to Dr. Amanson for one of his special psychological abortions."

"Duncan!"

"Well, at least we wouldn't have had the brat underfoot just to keep a good maid."

She smiled. "I don't disagree, but meanwhile if I want Big Svetlana to go—"

"For God's sake, stop calling that little woman Big Svetlana. Give the child another name. And then find some kind of camp or school to send her to this summer, at least for the eight weeks we're away."

"Yes, of course."

≡

"Do you think we could afford to send Bronwyn to some summer school this year?" Margaret Grace Corcoran asked her husband.

"What's wrong with the Bronx? I grew up here. You grew up here. Why can't Bronwyn?"

"Charlie, Bronwyn's a gifted child."

"Cut the crap, Maggie. She's a nice kid who's not too good-looking, so I'm glad she's smarter than most."

"What kind of thing is that for a father to say?"

"It's the truth as God is my judge. I spent my whole life rolling pills, Maggie. I'm nothing but a druggist, but you and I have a daughter with a good mind. But since her pa is a druggist, she won't have a lot of chances to improve herself. So let's be careful. Don't let her go too far or see too much, or, first thing you know, she'll be dissatisfied with our kind of life and think there's something else out there for her. Be careful, Maggie. You show that child too much, and she could be hurt for life."

"Fine father you are. I say she's smart, so let her experience things. You say she's smart, so don't show her anything. I want her to see the better things of life. I don't want my only daughter living over a drugstore like her ma."

"Cut the melodrama. This isn't Edward G. Robinson time."

"Charlie, let that girl out of the Bronx this summer."

"If I do, she'll be ruined for life."

"If you don't," Margaret said, "you'll ruin our life. You give in to me this once, Charlie, and I'll never fight you on another thing again."

"Promise?" he asked as he punched her affectionately on the arm.

"Try me, you old coot." And then she added with a twinkle in her blue eyes, "If you can, that is."

≡

Rosabelle Bonnier came home from school, put her books down on the kitchen table, and immediately opened the refrigerator door.

"That you, Rosabelle?" her mother called. "Close that refrigerator door. Eating between meals makes you fatter than you already are."

Rosabelle's shoulders drooped in despair; her mother had some kind of extrasensory perception that made her know when Rosabelle came home. Still, Rosabelle consoled herself, Mama was probably the source of her powers. Mama had this antenna that worked at all times, and Rosabelle had inherited it—but she had it to a degree that she hadn't yet explained to her parents.

"Come in and tell Mama about your day," she called.

"In a minute, Mama."

"Every minute you wait is another pound, Rosabelle."

Rosabelle lumbered into the sunroom. A big, old-fashioned room with windows on three sides, it was the solarium where her mother spent her afternoons. With gin? With lovers? Rosabelle wondered often if her mother were another Tennessee Williams character or an original.

"Look at you. Just look at you," Charlotte Bonnier chided. "No other girl in New Orleans looks like that. How come everybody has a pretty daughter but me?"

Rosabelle said nothing.

"Mary Lou Charpentier called today. Said you were blackballed by the Triples. I don't understand you, Rosabelle. Triples is the best junior-high club in this town. All my friends' daughters are in it. But those girls look like something. Just look at yourself. A big lump of a girl. Fat and homely as a mud fence. I can't even have the fun of buying cute clothes for my daughter."

"Mama, I got an A on the science test today."

"And another thing, I hear there's a big party over at the Wickhams next weekend. Even though you're only twelve, a lot of the preteens are going. So you just butter up little Cindy Wickham, and you get yourself an invite. You hear?"

"Mama, those people hate me."

"Nonsense. Your daddy and I are pretty well known around here, and those people don't hate you. They'd welcome you. At least they would if they could ever see you. But a lump like you—well, I should have known. This is what comes of marrying a man who's smart. Your daddy is so smart he's dumb. Know what I mean? All these years he's been tutoring you and filling your head with nothing but facts—well, all this time there's been a whole world getting itself together. You think brains are all that matters? Then look at the Kennedys. You think old Joe Kennedy could have put his son in the White House if he'd looked like your father? Well, I'll tell you the answer. The answer is no. No. Absolutely no. You're just not like other girls, Rosabelle. I don't know what will ever become of you. Rosabelle, you don't even *think* like the other girls. I mean, when I go up there to clean your room, I can't believe what I see. Those black candles and that cape—"

"No, Mama, I guess I'm not like other girls. I like reading about things that are a mystery to me. I'm reading now about witchcraft. It's really fascinating. The mind is so much a part of this. Don't just think about the witches of Salem. You see, you have to remember that witches can charm people."

"Then why can't you cast a charming spell on some of the people your own age? Why can't you be popular?"

Rosabelle sighed. It never did any good to explain. Better just to agree and find Father. "I'll try. Really I will."

"I think the best way to get you in shape, Rosabelle, would be to send you away this summer. I saw an ad for a camp—"

Now Rosabelle looked at her mother in surprise. She wouldn't be pushed around this way. At least in the summer she ought to enjoy herself, do something interesting, something intellectual, something worthwhile. "I won't go to camp. I'm not athletic."

"Well, what will you do?"

"Do I have to do something?"

"Camp is what girls like you do, Rosabelle."

"Mama, there are no girls like me."

"All right, then what do you want?"

Rosabelle thought for a moment. "I want to go to school."

"School? In the summer? I don't know what's open here."

"I don't want to stay here. I want to go east, Mama. I want to meet new girls."

"Well, Rosabelle, no one ever said you weren't smart. That sounds like a good idea to me, and a school would be more agreeable to your father. Yes, that's what we'll do. I'll call a few people and find you some special kind of school, some kind of place where a girl who's smart in school but dumb as a toad about being a girl can learn how to get along."

≡

In real life the Peabody School, like most camps and schools, bore little resemblance to its beauty as depicted in the glossy, four-page brochure sent to prospective students and their parents.

The "gracious setting on a lovely pond" turned out to be two long barracks-type cabins next to the marshland of a pond some two hundred feet away.

The "all-weather tennis court" was green hard rubber matting marked with white lines.

The "healthful diet" was simple food prepared with whatever the local A & P had on special sale that week.

Still, despite the school's flaws, each of the students usually found the one thing she needed most: a vacation from her parents.

The "trained staff" was headed by Dr. Gregory, one Gregory Sawyer, whose doctor title was a self-designated honorific bestowed after one summer at Columbia University summer school where he audited two courses in psychology.

The Peabody School had been built as a camp in 1928, promptly went under after the fall of 1929, and remained unused until 1940, when it was again resurrected as a camp. During the war years, the difficulties of travel forced the camp to close, and the grounds themselves were left to weeds and vagrants. In 1953, Gregory Sawyer needed a remote hideaway after a small scam involving a widow and three thousand dollars, so he'd answered an ad to be a counselor at Camp Igewama. When the camp fell into receivership, Gregory—a list of potential campers now his—bought the camp, changed its focus, and resurfaced in the slick world of "schools for children having difficulty coping."

That meant everything from children with dyslexia to those with weight problems. Mostly it meant children whose parents wanted or needed a dumping ground for their offspring who, for one reason or another, were going to be in the way for the summer. Whatever the reason for attending, the Peabody School seemed to suit both parents and children.

Dr. Gregory assigned four girls to each cabin. He looked for geographical balance and closeness in age, and, although the girls did not realize it, one girl in each bunk was there on scholarship. Always she was slightly older than the others, and her role was to serve as an assistant, to help Dr. Gregory with behavioral problems. Each barracks room was eight feet square with two sets of bunk beds on the north and south walls. The east wall held a drawer unit with four drawers, two for each of the north-wall sleepers. The west-wall drawer unit was for the south-wall sleepers. In the middle of the room was a bench, a place where all four could sit at once to put on shoes, throw down tennis rackets. A scarred desk was in "commons," the ten-foot common room at the end of the barracks, and it was there that each of the girls was urged twice a week to send a letter home.

Sienna was the first of the girls to arrive in her cabin. Immediately she took a lower bunk on the north wall, the one closest to the faraway pond, and unpacked her Gucci loafers, the short shorts she had sneaked in her bag, shorts, shirts, and underwear. She had also brought a hair dryer, her favorite shampoo, hair bands, ponytail clips, and suntan lotion.

When she finished unpacking, she sat on the bed and waited to see who would come next.

Her heart sank when Rosabelle walked into the cabin. Rosabelle was the most disgusting-looking girl she had ever seen, even more repulsive than the fat girl who had just come into her grade at Laurel School.

"Hi, my name is Rosabelle Bonnier, and I'm from New Orleans."

"Hi."

"What's your name?"

"Sienna," she mumbled.

"I didn't hear it. It sounded like Sienna."

"Well, aren't you smart? It is Sienna."

"I never knew anyone named Sienna."

"I never knew anyone named Rosabelle."

Sienna walked outside. She had to get away from that monster in her cabin, that big girl. Yech!

Things had better improve or she'd run away.

Inside Rosabelle was chattering, "Sienna, do you like music? I brought my records with me."

Records? That girl was so weird she probably listened to classical music. Sienna walked angrily toward the pond. Damn you, Peppy, she muttered. Damn you. This place is all your fault. I could be at home with my friends, but no, I have a mother who wants me out of the way so I won't see what she's doing—you're not fooling me.

Half in anger, half in frustration, Sienna looked back at the cabin she knew she would hate. And that was when she saw her walk in.

From that first moment, Sienna knew she would like Anne. She would like that long-legged lean look. She would like that stick-straight shoulder-length blond hair. She would like that easy loping walk, that air of self-confidence. It was a look Sienna always wished she'd had. Sienna's hair was dark, her legs too short for that look of elegance. No, Sienna told herself, I can see by looking that this girl is the real thing, my sort of girl. She walked slowly, then faster, to meet the new girl.

She wanted to get to her before Rosabelle. This girl could take a look at Rosabelle and leave school. She needed to see her to let her know they weren't all like Rosabelle. But she was not in time; the girl had already walked into the cabin, and Rosabelle was already saying, "Want to see my records?"

Suddenly Sienna felt foolish. What if the new girl decided

not to like her? Sienna hung back for a minute.

But the new blond girl smiled a warm smile when she turned and saw Sienna. "Hi," said the new blond girl.

"Hi," Sienna said.

"Which bed is yours?" Anne asked Sienna, ignoring Rosabelle.

Rosabelle looked at the two. In an instant they'd formed a bond, a friendship that would never include her.

Sienna, from years of camping experience, pointed to the lower bunk. "That one."

"I suppose you took that other lower bunk, Rosabelle."

Rosabelle hadn't taken any bunk yet, but she nodded. Evidently that was what she was supposed to do.

"I'll take the one on top of yours," Anne said to Sienna.

Sienna breathed a sigh of relief. She liked her. The new blond girl, Anne—yes, Anne liked her.

"Want to walk over to the pond?" she asked Anne.

"Yes," Anne said. She left her trunk for later. It was more important to have a new friend. And she had to test her new biography on someone who looked as if she had a biography of her own. Yes, over the past weeks, from the moment she was told she was going to school this summer, she had decided to invent a whole new self. She would have a new, mysterious, well-born background. Her father, her unknown father, would now become an artist who died in Paris, and her mother—her hard-working, naïve mother—would become a Romanoff. When Mrs. Masters first told her that they were sending her to a fine school for the summer, she had asked to be enrolled under an easier name. "Let me Americanize Svetlana Crossetti," she had begged Mrs. Masters. In truth, Mrs. Masters, knowing her husband's irritation with "Little Svetlana," thought it a splendid idea.

And so Anne Cross was enrolled at the Peabody School. And today, her very first day as Anne Cross, she had already made many decisions. She had decided she would be a stewardess like the pretty one on the plane. She also decided that she would be rich, rich enough to travel all the time—not once in a lifetime—and definitely not as somebody's maid. These rich girls would learn to respect her.

Now she would try out the new part on this girl, Sienna. Plenty of time to unpack. This was her big rehearsal. She flashed a radiant smile at Sienna. "Let's go."

"Wait!" Rosabelle called eagerly in an awkward try to woo

these girls. "I'm almost finished unpacking. I'll go with you."

"Stay and finish!" Anne called. She couldn't play her act for two people yet. She wanted one at a time. "We'll be right back."

"I can tell we're going to be best friends," Sienna said.

Anne smiled, a new kind of strength filling her body. A good athlete always, she had come to Peabody with physical strength, but at this moment she was feeling the strength of equality. She would never be a maid's daughter again. She was new. She was Anne. And Anne had a best friend Svetlana never could have met.

≡

Bronwyn arrived at school an hour later.

She came into the bunk room and saw Rosabelle, still sitting on her bunk. Rosabelle looked up in satisfaction. The new girl was not pretty the way the other two were. This one had acne, and she was wearing more makeup than Rosabelle had ever seen. Maybe she could be her friend. She made the first attempt. "I'm Rosabelle," she said with forced cheer. She dropped the last name. That didn't seem to be the thing to tell.

"Hi, I'm Bronwyn Corcoran."

"Bonnier."

"What?"

"That's my last name."

Bronwyn shrugged. She looked at Rosabelle. Well, what could she expect? Bronwyn was here on scholarship, here to help, here to look but not to touch when it came to friendships. She was the outsider, and all these kids were supposed to have some kind of difficulty, so naturally they'd put her with the weirdos, the uglies, the fatties, the stupidos.

"Bronwyn, you're sleeping above me, that bunk," she explained, pointing ceilingward.

"Okay. That must mean the others are here."

"Yes," Rosabelle said, eager to tell this new person everything. "One is Sienna—"

"What is she? Spanish?"

"I don't think so . . . and the other is Anne."

Bronwyn started to unpack an old battered suitcase that seemed to be full of more makeup, pills, and potions than T-shirts and shorts.

"Will you be my friend?" Rosabelle asked suddenly.

"Sure," Bronwyn said halfheartedly. "We'll all be friends."

12

IN THE BEGINNING IT WAS ANNE AND SIENNA, SIENNA AND ANNE.
Bronwyn was as much outside their cozy friendship as was Rosabelle. Anne stole food from the kitchen for Sienna; Sienna sneaked into town and brought back cookies for Anne. They were the school's bad girls, and everyone wanted to be bad, just like them.

At night, after the "lights out" signal, Sienna and Anne would write notes using their flashlights under covers. Since they were the bad girls, they decided to make their pairing the worst in school history. Each day during meditation they plotted new mischief. They confused Rosabelle with a pie bed. They harassed Bronwyn by hiding her precious skin ointments and lotions. And one night, just to prove that they had the run of the school, they took the keys to Dr. Gregory's car, then stuffed their mouths with Kleenex to keep from laughing when he called the school together to ask who had taken the keys from the kitchen hook. He explained that there might be an emergency one day, and what would they do if they had no car?

"What if he gets mad and sends us home?" Anne asked Sienna.

"Don't worry. He won't. Can't you see? He wants our parents' money."

That hadn't occurred to Anne. She didn't yet know all the things that people did for money, the indignities they accepted, the fools they suffered—but she was learning each day. The trick was to let people get away with anything, to turn your back and pretend not to see—so long as they let you get what you wanted. Anne was learning lessons she would never forget.

Rosabelle knew she could never be a part of the Sienna-Anne bad-girl friendship. She knew she was too hopeless to be bad, but she continued to pray that Bronwyn, unattractive Bronwyn with her mask, might befriend unattractive Rosabelle.

It was not to be. Bronwyn busied herself with the responsibility of monitoring a small group of younger students throughout the day. Only at night did she take any part in the talk among her cabinmates. Sienna and Anne, while put off by Bronwyn's determined use of makeup, were somewhat awed by the older girl in their midst. Their age difference was just enough to give Bronwyn an authoritative mystique. Bronwyn had just turned fifteen. Anne was already thirteen—her birthday was in April—and Sienna would celebrate her entry into her teen years in September, but Rosabelle would not be thirteen until the following March.

In an effort to romance the older girls, Rosabelle tried many ploys. At night when the lights were out she had told them mad tales of Mardi Gras in New Orleans.

"Really?" Sienna would ask. "Really, do men dress up like that?"

"You saw them do it, really do it to each other? Men? Really?" Anne wanted to know.

"Keep quiet," Bronwyn would admonish when the talk got too explicit, too wild. After all, Bronwyn was fifteen, and she had access to all that medical literature in her father's drugstore. She knew Rosabelle was making things up . . . wasn't she?

But sensing that she was finally making headway with the bad girls, Rosabelle, determined to make an even greater impression on her small group of bunkmates, said one night, "Do you believe in ghosts?"

"No," Bronwyn said, "and keep quiet."

"Tell us a ghost story," Anne said.

"Yes, let's hear a ghost story," Sienna added.

"Well, this one is really about witches," Rosabelle said.

"Witches? You are weird," Sienna said. "There's no such thing as witches."

"Sure there is," Rosabelle answered.

Anne giggled and leaned over in her bunk to look down at Sienna. She mouthed the words "Ask her if she's a witch."

"Are you one?" Sienna dutifully inquired.

"Maybe," Rosabelle answered.

"There is no such thing as a witch," Bronwyn said in her role as school assistant. Bronwyn knew that she had just enough years to be the true-or-false expert in the cabin.

"Yeah, there's no such thing," Sienna taunted.

"I am a witch," Rosabelle said in a voice that was thick with mystery.

Sienna laughed, but she was the only one laughing. "Don't you think that's funny, Anne?"

Anne said nothing. Hadn't she just spent days convincing herself she could be anything she wanted? If she could, why couldn't Rosabelle? She felt a small, disquieting chill race up her back. Was that witchcraft? Had Rosabelle made Anne's strong body betray her?

Sienna, sensing something strange and new—this wasn't like the Mardi Gras stories—sat up in bed and said with authority, "Number one, there's no such thing as a witch, and number two, all witches are old and skinny. Rosabelle's too young and too fat to be a witch."

Then she lay back on her lumpy mattress, her heart beating wildly. What if Rosabelle were a witch?

"Quiet or I'm telling Dr. Gregory," Bronwyn threatened.

The four girls were quiet, but none of them slept easily.

≡

For the next twenty-four hours all three girls treated Rosabelle with new respect, but by the end of the second day they had assured one another that there were no witches in New Hampshire who came from New Orleans.

Bronwyn considered telling Dr. Gregory about Rosabelle. Maybe this girl needed some real help. Bronwyn had seen people who did. Plenty of really strange people, a lot of nuts with real and imagined problems came into her father's drugstore, but her parents had usually sorted out the phonies for her. This, however, was the first time she'd ever heard a girl tell anybody she was a witch and make them wonder—was she? Did she really have supernatural powers? Bronwyn wasn't sure. She knew Rosabelle had some black candles in a drawer. She'd seen them one day when Sienna and Anne, playing their bad-girl roles, had hidden her skin lotions. Bronwyn had opened every trunk and drawer in the cabin searching. She hadn't told the others what she'd found, but now—well, now it might be interesting to confide this tidbit. Sure, the girls were young, but maybe they'd be scared enough to stop acting so silly and dumb.

The news only excited the other two, and now Bronwyn felt herself pulled into their conspiracy. "We have to prove she's a witch and get her out of here," Anne said.

"No, no," Bronwyn said.

"Let's try to do something and make her prove she's a witch," Sienna suggested.

"What?" Anne asked.

"I'll think of something," Bronwyn said, in the hope that she would put their pranks on ice for the moment.

Rosabelle knew she had her cabinmates wondering. And she was aware enough to realize that they would never ask Dr. Gregory about witches; they wouldn't talk about something like that to a grownup who would just laugh at them.

The more the girls wondered, the more bizarre Rosabelle's behavior became. Normally messy, she now seemed to take over the room with both her physical bulk and her unending trail of dirty socks and underpants.

But even Bronwyn did not complain. It kept the other girls from their stupid pranks; they really seemed to believe that Rosabelle's witchcraft could harm them.

≡

"If you really want to see me do witchcraft, I will do something black and mysterious the night of the full moon," Rosabelle promised.

"When's the full moon?" Sienna asked.

"Next week," Rosabelle told her.

That whole week the three girls were kind to Rosabelle. Now she was included in their walks around the pond. Now she even joined them in one of their pranks—mixing up all the socks in the laundry—and, as Anne said, "We'll never get caught; we have a witch on our side."

Rosabelle sent happy letters home to her parents. She loved school. She had wonderful friends. This was the best time of her life. There was a lilt to her letters, a sound of joy in her life that her parents had never before heard from her.

Rosabelle wished she had made no promises under the full moon. She would have liked life to go on just as it was.

But the night of the full moon Rosabelle knew she would have to make her first stab at witchcraft. At midnight she sat upright in bed, her arms out in front of her body. She shivered and shook so much that Bronwyn thought the bed slats would come tumbling down. Rosabelle whispered magic words that no one could hear, and then her body slumped forward.

"Is she dead?" Anne asked.

"Hush," Bronwyn whispered.

Rosabelle raised her upper body slowly. "I have done it," she hissed. "My cat is now a pumpkin." No one knew that she did not have a cat.

She lay back on her bed and feigned a deep sleep.

Sienna began to cry. "She's crazy."

"Oh, shut up," Bronwyn said harshly to mask her own doubts.

"Do you think she did that to her cat now, just this minute? I mean, is her mother going to walk into a room and all of a sudden see this pumpkin?" Anne asked.

Rosabelle sat up slowly in her bed and, like an actress whose audience calls for more, said, "If you think this was something, wait until the first lightning storm, and you will see what I can do to you. Wait. Wait."

The three girls said nothing. What would she do to them?

To forestall the effects of the spell, each girl tried her own kind of appeasement. At dinner the next day, Anne gave Rosabelle her piece of chocolate cake. Sienna took a short after-supper walk around the pond alone with Rosabelle and whispered a secret about boys, babies, and s-e-x. Bronwyn reached into a zipped pocket of her jeans and offered a Valium to Rosabelle.

The next four days there were cloudless skies, and the sun shone brightly. Each girl felt her own sense of satisfaction. Each was sure she was the one responsible for the perfect weather. She had done it; she had thwarted the gods.

Rosabelle, happy that she did not have to put her powers to the test—and too bewildered to decide how she would prove herself a witch if lightning struck—was the most relieved of all.

But the four girls did not say a word about their smug sense of relief to one another.

The conspiracy of silence had begun.

≡

But the fourth night after Rosabelle's pronouncement about her cat, the air became heavy, and the sky darkened ominously at eight o'clock. By eleven the flashes of lightning began. The four were in their cabin when at eleven thirteen Rosabelle sat up in bed and with her pale gray eyes luminous as a cat's, she began to howl like a mad wolfchild.

Anne trembled and felt again that small disquieting chill. Would Rosabelle turn all of them into pumpkins tonight?

Sienna hid under the thin blanket. She had hated storms even before this night.

Bronwyn shivered. What medicine would her father give to a witch? Maybe a couple of Valiums. Bronwyn had pilfered a summer supply from the drugstore before she came here, but if Daddy knew she had picked them up, he wasn't saying anything.

Only Rosabelle slept that night, but the next morning the three bunkmates were strangely silent in their classes. They had a witch in their midst, and they knew they would have to do something about it.

≡

At first they giggled nervously as they discussed and rejected a dozen different ideas. They would send her a letter from a dead relative. No. How could they? They didn't know if she had any dead relatives. They would take her to the cemetery. How could they? They didn't know where the cemetery was, and even if they did know, how would they get there?

Finally they came up with the plan.

One of them—was it Bronwyn?—had once read about a magician called Houdini who used to be tied up and put in wells and at the bottom of the ocean and somehow always managed to escape. "If she's a witch, she'll escape, and if she isn't, she'll stop scaring us," Sienna said.

The others agreed.

"We'll wait for a big storm," Anne said, her sense of drama heightened by the promise of terrifying Rosabelle as much as she had terrified them.

"And then we'll take her," Sienna said.

"Let's not wait for a storm," Bronwyn said. "It'll be easier if it doesn't rain."

"Any midnight would be good," Sienna said.

"Yes, at exactly twelve o'clock." Anne giggled deliciously. Anne had never had so much fun. Finally she was just like other girls. And no one here asked about her parents.

≡

At midnight on the Saturday before Parents' Visiting Day, Sienna's tiny alarm clock rang. The three sat up in bed, silently pulled on their jeans, took stockings Sienna had bought in town, put them over their heads to create masks, and crept up the ladder to Rosabelle's bed.

Rosabelle opened her eyes, those large, pale cat eyes, and looked at the three masked girls.

"The Peabody witches are here, and you are powerless to stop them," Anne cackled.

Rosabelle opened her mouth. Was she going to scream? Laugh? They never knew. Bronwyn jammed a sock in Rosabelle's open mouth, and the other two girls commanded her, in the name of the Peabody witch code, to get out of bed and go outside.

Anne, the tallest, blindfolded her, while Bronwyn took a scarf of Rosabelle's and bound her hands behind her back. Sienna led her to Gregory's car.

"Who has the keys?" Bronwyn whispered.

"I do," Sienna answered. "The idiot still keeps them on the kitchen hook. I think he wants us to steal the car."

"With these masks we could," Bronwyn said. "Take them off," she said, pulling hers off and screwing her face into a ghoulish grimace.

The three began to laugh hysterically, the nervousness and excitement mounting with each step they took.

"I can't open the door," Bronwyn said.

"It's a different key," Sienna said. "Don't you know? I drive my father's car around the driveway all the time. There's one key to start the car and a different one for the doors and trunk."

"Let me do it," Anne said.

"I'll do it," Sienna said. "I know about cars."

It was not easy to open the two-door car, but Sienna finally opened the passenger side, pushed the seat down, and prepared to help guide the blindfolded Rosabelle into the back. "Yech," she exclaimed in utter disgust.

"What is it?" Anne asked in a throaty whisper.

"The floor of this backseat," Sienna answered. "He's got all kinds of cloth and junk all over the floor."

Bronwyn pushed forward and peered into the back. "What is this stuff?" she muttered, raking through the mess. "Rags?"

"Look again," Sienna said.

"Wow, it's clothes. Women's clothes."

Rosabelle squealed. She wished she could speak and look, too.

"Don't let the witch see," Anne cautioned.

"Oh no, it's clothes—women's clothes," Sienna gasped.

"Jeez," Bronwyn said. "Jeez. Jesus H. Christ," she whispered, her father's favorite expression.

Stuffed on the floor between the back and front seats were high-heeled shoes, dresses, and wigs.

"What're they for?" Sienna asked.

"A play or something?" Anne asked.

Bronwyn shook her head. "Don't you guys know anything? Look how big this stuff is. This stuff is as big as—as big as Dr. Gregory."

"So?" Anne asked.

"Don't you guys know anything?" Bronwyn repeated. "This is probably Dr. Gregory's stuff. Oh my God, Dr. Gregory dresses up like a woman. Dr. Gregory's queer. Oh my God, what'll my parents say?"

"What do you want to do? Go back and call them now?" Anne said, her voice dripping with disgust. Then, taking control, she directed the others. "Just take the stuff out of the back and put it under the tree. There's no room for Rosabelle and all that junk, too."

"Okay. Under the tree," Sienna said. The shock of the discovery had paralyzed her momentarily. She was glad to be doing something.

"Maybe we should keep some of the dresses and stuff for little pillows for Rosabelle," Bronwyn said.

"No. She's so fat she doesn't need—" Anne responded in quick annoyance, but the sentence trailed as she looked up. Clouds were covering the moon. Was this a storm coming up? The small chill moved slowly up her back.

"Thunder. That's thunder," Sienna said fearfully.

"Hurry," Bronwyn said. "Let's get the hell out of here."

"Don't say *hell*, it might make Rosabelle work a spell," Anne cautioned, totally forgetting that the purpose of their mission was to convince themselves and Rosabelle that she was incapable of working spells.

Grunting and pushing together, they put a fighting Rosabelle in the back of the car, and then Sienna slid behind the wheel. She was frightened; she wished this night would end. Why couldn't it be twenty-four hours from now? Why had she made driving her parents' cars around the driveway sound like such a big deal?

Anne moved in next to Sienna, and as she was about to close the door, Bronwyn pulled it open and jumped in beside her.

"I don't want to sit three in front," Sienna said. "I can't drive that way. My father never lets us sit three in front."

"Fine. Then I'll stay behind. Just the two of you go. Go ahead," Bronwyn said angrily. She stood outside the car, her arms folded.

"You look dumb standing there in your jeans with that stupid pajama top over them," Anne said. "Come on, you're in this with us."

"You're only driving down the hill to the pond, so—" Bronwyn said as she went back into the car. She was holding the door and trying to close it when the first zigzag of lightning flashed overhead. At that moment the ignition turned, and the thunder that followed masked the sound of Rosabelle's first muffled scream.

When driving around her father's driveway, Sienna had never encountered any kind of rain. Now the heavens opened, and the rains came, that kind of blinding torrential downpour that floods the mind as well as the earth.

Sienna began to cry.

Anne put an arm around her. "Don't be frightened. We're all together."

"Yes," Bronwyn said as she tried to pull the door shut.

The car lurched forward. "I can't see," Sienna cried out as she opened the window. The rain poured in.

"Get to the pond. It's over there. Just get to the edge of it!" Anne screamed over the pouring rain.

"Just the edge," Bronwyn instructed. The car was inching forward. "Stop," Bronwyn said, exasperation and fear in her voice, "it's not straight ahead. It's back there."

"No, no, it's not," Anne contradicted.

"For God's sake, which way?" Sienna cried.

"Don't say *God*," Bronwyn reminded her.

There was a crash of thunder, and Sienna, her hair falling over her face, her pajama shirt sticking to her wet body, sobbed, "I don't know how to back up the car."

"There's something called reverse," Bronwyn said quickly.

"How do you do it?"

Bronwyn paused. "I think my father puts his foot on something first. Wait. I'll come around and look." She opened the door to face the rain once more, and as she did Sienna found the gas pedal, pressed on it with all her strength, and the car shot like a missile through the air.

Bronwyn, hair matted, body soaked, was clinging to the door and swinging wildly for her life as the car seemed to take wings.

Moments later Bronwyn knew she was in the water. She was in the filthy, marshy pond. That was when she realized that the car had sped directly into the water, and now they—all of them—were slowly sinking.

"Get out, Anne!" Bronwyn screamed. "Get out. My door's open. Get out!"

"Sienna!" Anne called. "Sienna."

But Sienna's head had cracked against the steering wheel and was oozing blood. "Sienna's dead!" Anne screamed.

"Pull her out. Let's give her first aid!" Bronwyn shouted.

Anne, the strong athlete, pulled Sienna from behind the wheel into the relative safety of the pond.

The cold water revived Sienna. "Rosabelle," she mumbled. "Get Rosabelle."

Bronwyn swam back as the car continued to sink. Now they could hear the voice, the thin voice of their cabin witch. "Don't!" came her sharp cry. She must have loosened the sock in her mouth. She was a witch; she did have the power to escape!

"Don't. Please don't," Rosabelle repeated.

Bronwyn tugged with all her might. "I can't get the seat down. Honest, I can't. Oh, Rosabelle, save yourself. Rosabelle, come out of the car. Rosabelle, be a witch. Come out!" Bronwyn cried.

There was the low repeated rumble of thunder, and for the moment Rosabelle's words were lost.

Then, as the car went under came Rosabelle's words, sharp and clear and unbelieving: "No, you can't."

"Cut the scarf; get her hands free!" Anne screamed as she kept her arm around Sienna.

"How? Where?" Bronwyn cried in the night.

"No, no, no," came the sound from inside the car, but with each *no* the voice grew fainter.

"I think this must be quicksand!" Bronwyn shouted. "Let's get out fast or we'll all be dead."

The girls swam and floated to the shore, rolled onto the grass, and before they could tend to Sienna's bloody head she urged them all to go back and try once more to free Rosabelle.

"The car's sinking," Bronwyn whispered. "I can't get her."

Sienna, pale and limp, tried to comfort the girls. "But we tried," she said. "We really tried. Now maybe we should go back and get some help."

"What will we say?" Bronwyn asked.

"We had an—an accident," Sienna said.

"How was it an accident if we stole a car?" Bronwyn asked.

"We didn't really steal a car," Anne said.

"Yes, we did," Sienna said, overcome by guilt and shame.

"What's to become of us?" Bronwyn asked.

"We're in it together," Sienna said.

"Together," Anne repeated.

BOOK THREE

"That odd American astuteness which seems the fruit of innocence rather than of experience."

EDITH WHARTON

13

WHEN THE TELEPHONE RANG, THE THREE WOMEN IN THE dressing room froze, their thoughts suspended, their lives so secure just yesterday—

Anne pointed to Sienna, her hand trembling. "Answer it." The shakiness was in her voice, too.

Sienna put her hands up and pressed them against her ears.

R-r-r-ring.

Sienna knew she could not block out the summons. "Who knows we're here?" she asked.

R-r-r-ring.

Bronwyn's hands flew to her hair. She pushed it even farther over her face. "I didn't even tell the nanny I was coming here," she whispered.

Sienna looked at Anne. Anne shook her head. "Nobody knows."

R-r-r-ring.

Sienna picked up the phone. "H-hello," she said in a voice that sounded as young and frightened as it did that night twenty-nine years earlier.

There was a pause before Virginia said, "Oh, darling, I've interrupted something. I can tell by your voice. You sound so—so strange."

Sienna opened her mouth to speak, but no words came through her parched lips. Thank God it wasn't Gregory there to haunt them, to taunt them.

"Sienna, are you there?"

She made a small gurgling sound.

"Listen, dear. I have the most marvelous news ever. Gregory and I are at lunch, and I just had to call and tell you. Guess what! We're—I mean he's going to start the Peabody School again, and now for the absolute best part. I've persuaded him to let you and Anne and Bronwyn head the drive for funds. At first Gregory wouldn't hear of it. He said it would be a terrible imposition, but I begged and begged—"

"But I have so many other obligations this year—"

"Philharmonic? I put you on that board. I'll just reduce your fund-raising responsibilities. Ballet? Forget it. There's a darling little divorcee with nothing to do, and she'd like a few ballet masters to escort her to the charity balls this fall."

Sienna was defeated, and she knew it. "Then I guess there's nothing to say, is there?"

"Just one more thing. Gregory wants to speak to you."

"Sienna, dear," he crooned into the telephone, "who would ever believe we'd find each other again? Just to see each another in a simple little unplanned way."

And as she heard his words, she remembered those unctuous tones, that slippery manner. Unplanned? This meeting with these three rich women and their mentor was unplanned? Hardly.

Yes, her antennae were back up. The blood was racing through her veins once again. She'd have to be alert. It was instant-recovery time. "Seeing you after all these years is more than I expected," she said dryly.

He laughed softly, and as he did Sienna remembered the last time she had heard that laugh, that terrible time, that terrible laugh—

"I can't wait to work with you girls again," Gregory said. "You are such an—" He paused. "An inventive group." Now his voice took on a new confidence. "I do know that you girls want to see me succeed. After all, who has a greater stake in my success than Sienna and Anne and Bronwyn?"

Sienna replaced the phone slowly.

"What did he say?" Anne asked.

Sienna took a deep breath. "Well, he's come back. Virginia wants us to help him reopen the Peabody School."

"No." Anne's eyes were wide with disbelief.

"I don't think we have a choice, Anne," Sienna answered.

Bronwyn began to cry. "It's like Rumpelstiltskin. He's coming to take my baby. I know that's what he wants."

Anne and Sienna exchanged glances.

"Hold the line, Bronwyn," Anne coached, her years of athletics always bringing her to sports terms in times of crisis.

Sienna put her arms around Bronwyn, but despite the protective embrace, Sienna could feel her shivering. "I promise we'll all make sure nothing happens to Gwyneth," she assured her.

Bronwyn moved from Sienna's embrace and reached for her handbag. "I think I need a little something—"

"Yes," Sienna continued, "a little lunch. Here, dear. Have a cucumber sandwich."

Again Sienna and Anne exchanged glances. It had been hard enough keeping Bronwyn together, watching the pills and monitoring the alcohol, without Gregory Sawyer back in their lives. But now? How could they be strong enough to keep their own lives intact and keep Bronwyn quiet?

"I just can't tell Peter," Sienna said fiercely. "Can't you see what would happen if this story got out now, just when he could be appointed ambassador?"

"Oh, the papers would have a field day with this one. Three socialites—not one, not two, but three. You're right. This could not only ruin us; it could ruin our husbands. So when it comes to protecting me, I can forget about everything. Harold wouldn't help," Bronwyn said disconsolately.

"Casey wouldn't even hear; he'd pretend it was about somebody else," Anne admitted, shrugging her broad shoulders. "But how did this happen? I mean, it's been *years,* a lifetime for all of us. Where has Gregory Sawyer been all this time?"

"Why didn't he come sooner? Before Gwyneth," Bronwyn mumbled.

"Why now?" Anne insisted. "What do we have that he really wants?"

"Of course," Sienna snapped. "I know what he wants. Gregory Sawyer wants Virginia."

Bronwyn gave a nonamused laugh. "Whatever for?"

Anne nodded. "You just may be right. Didn't you see how she looked at him last night?" Then she paused. "Do you suppose she thinks—"

Sienna felt anger and disgust mingle in her throat. "He can't think we'd encourage Virginia to think—" she began.

"We're the key to Virginia," Anne said, shaking her head in disbelief at the words she was saying.

"But we've got to protect Virginia," Sienna cried.

"What if she doesn't want to be protected?" Bronwyn asked. "Maybe this is what Virginia wants. Do we have a right to tell her she can't have it?"

"I think we must," Anne insisted.

"I never thought we'd ever talk about Gregory Sawyer again," Sienna said.

"It was always a question of time," Bronwyn sighed. "But if we're going to protect Virginia, are we going to help him open the school with her?"

"Yes," Sienna announced firmly in order to bolster Bronwyn's confidence. "Yes, we'll help even if it kills us."

"Kill?" Anne asked reflectively. "Kill? Ah, my friends, what if it kills him?"

14

DIANDRE DEVON WAS NOT WAITING WHEN CASEY'S MERCEDES came through the pillared entrance of the Wingate Hotel. The driver, feeling the beginnings of an anxiety attack—wet palms, churning stomach—stopped and asked himself calmly if he really thought this kind of aggravation was worth that kind of money. It did not take long for him to assure himself that yes, yes it was worth the cold sweats and the hot words to be a part of the Great Man's life. The Great Man was what he always called Casey, both to his face and when speaking about him, but there was no sarcasm in the title. Until Casey Burrows hired him, Bellamy had been a cabdriver, a bouncer in a SoHo club, and a bum panhandling in his own spot at Grand Central Station. Driving for Casey was not only his best job; it was his best life.

So the no-show lady made Bellamy nervous. He was sweating profusely by the time he called Casey's office, and—to mask his own fears (was he at the wrong place? Was this his fault?)—he barked belligerently at the secretary, who didn't know what appointment he was talking about; there was, she assured him, no Lady Diandre Devon listed on Mr. Burrows's calendar.

Bellamy stopped cold. "Sorry," he said, "my mistake." Now he understood. The Great Man himself had given him the assignment. This must be top-secret stuff. A deal. Or a broad. Whatever it was, the Great Man had meant to keep it just between them. Lady Diandre Devon was so important she wasn't even on the calendar. Bellamy went up to the desk and quietly, very quietly, told the man in the formal clothes working there to call Lady Diandre's suite and tell her that her car was waiting.

The smiling clerk, who was paid fifty dollars for every tip he gave to one of the New York paparazzi, did as he was asked, and then as soon as Bellamy went toward the car he made a second phone call. Hand cradled over the phone to mask his voice, he half-whispered, "Lady Diandre Devon of London is staying at the Wingate Hotel, and Casey Burrows's driver just picked her up. She's been here four days, goes out each day with Freddy Fenmore. Right. The banker. Supposed to be her cousin. Beautiful? I guess you could say that. About twenty-five. Great red hair. Married? I don't know. Are ladies married?"

Casey Burrows, on the telephone as usual, was seated in a leather chair behind the desk in the forward cabin, a room outfitted as an office, when Lady Diandre Devon came on board. He looked up, saw her, and with a sweep of his hand indicated the chair opposite his. She sat, waited a moment or two for his conversation to end, and tried to avoid eavesdropping. But there was no avoiding it. Indeed Casey seemed like an actor. This was his stage, and he was playing his customary starring role. "Get the word out now," Casey commanded. "Of course I know I don't have to say anything until I own five percent—" Now Casey made a circular motion with his arm, the engines revved, the plane moved down the runway and lifted off. Still the conversation on the telephone went on uninterrupted. "—So you got it now? I want the guys with the big bucks in the funds to start buying. Once they smell a Casey Burrows deal, you won't be able to keep the institutional money away. Got it? Hang in there for a few weeks. Buy a little, keep saying I won't talk, let the deal seesaw for a few weeks—you know, let the fat guys with the pencils, yeah yeah, the financial reporters—let them play with it. They like stories. They don't get many, so we'll give 'em some to make up. Remember, through all this I don't talk. I don't say yes. I don't say no. I go to a lot of parties. You know, Anne's charity crap. I go to all that, and pretty soon the gossip columnists are in on it, and they want to know will I get KWG? Won't I get it? Still we keep quiet. And the day they stop asking, it takes about three weeks, we bail out. By that time, if we don't get the company, we'll still be okay. I figure we should make a hundred mil. An easy hundred mil."

Lady Diandre took a deep breath. So this was the American style at work. This was the famous Casey Burrows. How could a woman ever compete with the excitement of making one-hundred-million-dollar phone calls?

She opened her handbag and took out a mirror. She'd better check her marketable assets. She touched her hair and moved her head so that the sun coming through the cabin window might add to the red glints. Her hair, the color of old copper, was the feature everyone always remembered about her. Even as a little girl the long red hair had turned heads. It was still its natural color, and she wore it as she always had—long and full. "The mane," her father had called it, and he had tried to buy her a horse almost that very color. She lifted her head slightly. No, there was no mistaking it. Twenty-six years old, and already there was the beginnings of a double chin. Well, she'd been given her father's good looks, and those same genes had arranged themselves to give her father's two chins as well. The beginnings of the chins made those ten extra pounds on her five-foot-three-inch frame seem like even more. And no matter how hard she tried, no matter how many times she decided to forego her favorite English trifle or strawberries and cream, still the ten pounds never went away. Sometimes they even crept up to fifteen or seventeen, but those pounds never seemed to lose themselves. Lady Diandre sighed. She was going to be a plump English matron in a few years if she wasn't just a touch more careful.

Casey waited a few minutes before he put the telephone down. Had she heard what he'd said? Was she impressed? Did she understand what a coup he was planning? Maybe he should have said the names of the divisions. He kept calling the company KWG. Maybe he should have referred to it by the name of the coffee they made. Or the chocolate.

Now he looked out the window as he addressed her. "You just heard a very private conversation," he said. "Don't tell anyone about it."

She put her mirror into her bag, snapped it shut, and dropped it next to her chair. "And that conversation," she said quietly, "is not even as secret as my being on board this aircraft."

He wheeled around in his chair and looked at her. No dumb

bimbo this one. He smiled. "I love the way, you know, the way you talk."

"That's my English accent."

"Love it."

"How nice. Tell me, Mr. Burrows—"

"Casey. You have to call me Casey."

"Casey, am I sitting in Mrs. Burrows's chair?"

Casey rubbed his chin. "Well, yes, Anne usually sits there. Why did you ask?"

"Oh, I just wondered what it was like to sit in the power seat."

"The power seat?" he snapped. "*This* is the power seat."

Lady Diandre shrugged. "It's just that I've read everywhere that Anne Burrows is so competent. And I couldn't help but think how inadequate I am by comparison. I'm sure that if Anne Burrows were sitting here, she'd have given you good advice on that conversation. She'd have followed it all."

"What makes you think you know how Anne works?"

"Oh, I read a story about her in one of the magazines that said she really was the power behind the—"

Casey pounded the desk. "Stop that power crap. She's smart, but she's not the power. I am, and don't you forget it."

"I'm just saying what I read."

"Well, I'm just saying how it is."

"She's so smart and slim—"

"But I make the decisions."

"Of course."

"And the deals."

"I can see that. No need to be angry, Casey."

"I'm not angry."

"Good. I don't think you should eat when you're angry, and since we have a lunch date, I'm looking forward to drinking and eating happily."

"You mean you don't eat a spinach leaf and drink herbal tea for lunch?"

"I'm a strong English girl with a very healthy appetite," she said with a smile. "I like my gin, my beef, and my sweet."

"What a relief. All American women ever do is tell you how fat they are, and they all weigh about six pounds. Anne and her girlfriends keep going to gym class and having their own trainer come in and eating like butterflies—"

"Not me." She patted her stomach, a gesture that for some reason he found the sexiest movement he'd ever seen a woman make.

"Let me feel that, too," he said hoarsely, but as he started from his chair, the telephone rang. He sat down again and picked up the phone, but this time his conversation was over within ten seconds. All he said was, "I'm busy now. Call you back."

"Does your life stop when the telephone rings?" she asked.

"No. Wait a minute. Yeah. Yeah. I guess it does. I never thought about it before." Now he came around the desk and stood over her. "A woman like you is going to make me think about things."

"I'll make you think about yourself," she said. "You know, you're a very attractive man, but the one I really read about the most is Anne."

Now he walked away from her, thoughts of her sexuality dissipated. He picked up a pencil on his desk and jabbed the air as if to make the points of his conversation understood. "Then you don't read financial magazines. I'm all over the financial pages. You can't get a job with a financial paper anywhere in the world unless you know who I am."

"I thought it was Anne who was the real power—"

Casey threw the pencil on the floor. "Damn her. Ever since she got her own public-relations company, she's been putting out stories about what she did, she said, she wore. I don't give a damn if she gets publicity about her clothes, but she's not going to get credit for my deals."

"No, she shouldn't," Diandre agreed.

"You know . . ." Now Casey paused, his hand in midair. "What did you say your name was?"

"Diandre Devon."

He shook his head. "Look, I'm from New Jersey. The girls in my class weren't named Denny—"

"Diandre," she corrected patiently.

"I have to give you a name I can say."

"My name is Lady Diandre Devon."

"D.D. That's it. Your new name is Deedee."

"Spell it," she commanded.

"D-e-e-d-e-e."

"No. I want it to be D-i-d-i."

"Come here, Didi," he said, pulling her to her feet. "Now that I know your name, let's go to bed. There's a room back there."

She looked at him. This was make-or-break time. She waited a full minute. "I was invited to lunch, Casey," she said slowly. "I wasn't told I had to pay for it."

Casey threw his head back and laughed. "Okay," he said. "Okay, you're my kind of girl, Didi. I don't like anything I can get right away. I like to keep everybody guessing. I'm glad you do, too. But I'll give you a little warning. Don't keep me guessing too long."

≡

Bellamy was sitting in the car waiting for the plane to return when the car phone rang. He frowned. Nobody but the Great Man and the Missus had the car number. Bellamy got out of the car and looked up in the sky. Naw. The Great Man wouldn't be calling to check on him. He knew Bellamy would be waiting.

It was the third ring now.

Bellamy bit his nail. Better answer. But if it was the Missus, what should he say when she asked for the Great Man? He'd say the Great Man was out to lunch. Yeah. Good answer. He laughed and picked up the phone.

It was her. It was the Missus.

"Yes, ma'am."

"Bellamy, I need you to do something for me."

He knew from the urgency in her voice she didn't want him to pick up her dress at the dressmaker or take the kids to the circus. Oh, please, Bellamy prayed, don't make her ask me to rat on him.

"Yes, ma'am."

"Can you keep a confidence, Bellamy? I think you can. You keep them for my husband——"

"No, no I don't," he rushed to explain. Now she was going to ask for him. How did he know where his boss was this minute?

Anne talked quickly and disregarded the concern she'd recognized in his voice. "Bellamy, I hear you have a few sources around town who can get information for me. Well, I want some information."

"Yes, I'll try, ma'am."

"I want to know everything you can find about a man named Gregory Sawyer who ran the Peabody School in New Hampshire in 1961. Who is he? Where's he been? What's he been doing? Everything since 1961. Got it?"

"Spell it, ma'am."

Slowly and carefully Anne spelled the name she had thought she would never have to say again.

"I'll get back to you, ma'am, as soon as I find out something." A smile played on Bellamy's mouth.

Wasn't that something? A woman like that, a woman who had everything, and now she was out looking for guys. That was your proof. Never trust a woman.

15

IT HAD BEEN A WEEK SINCE GREGORY HAD COME BACK INTO HER life, a week since the name Rosabelle rang once again in her ears, a week since Bronwyn could see her fear shimmering in the mirrored hallway as she walked to her daughter's bedroom each night, her heart pounding with the unspoken question, Would Gwyneth be there? Would her darling daughter be fast asleep, tucked into her world of sweet dreams and party shoes? And then each night that deep sigh, that wordless expression of relief, when she knew that yes, yes, Gwyneth was there, still there. But the carefree life Bronwyn had so diligently planned for her child was gone.

Each day Bronwyn sat longer than usual at her dressing table staring at her face, her unmasked face. On the eighth night after Gregory's reappearance, she was startled to see something new, the first signs of recurring acne. There was no mistaking them, for these were not the old faded blotches on her skin where she had been treated, nor the dark patches where early treatment had failed. No, now there were red streaks and small pustules in the shadows of her nose and on her forehead where the acne was returning. This had happened once before, but that time she had called it her scarlet letter. For then she had been Harold's girlfriend, not his wife, and then she had been desperate that he would never leave the first wife he professed to despise, never leave the dreary children who seemed interested only in his money, and never give her the child she wanted so much. She still remembered the night of her fortieth birthday, the night she'd made her decision. She had thrown away the birth control pills she'd promised Harold she'd always take, and two months later she'd found herself pregnant. Harold had shrugged when she broke the news; he had just bought the tallest building in Chicago and was in one of his up moods. "So. Get an abortion and go back to work." He'd laughed. Angered by his attitude, she had refused to discuss it further. She'd wait him out. But two months later he was still laughing, still unwilling to believe she'd do anything so dumb as have a child. That was when he'd told her to go away and have the baby and then come back and tell everyone that she'd adopted a child. "Look at me, Harold," she'd said firmly, a new authority in her voice. "I have a baby in here, and I am keeping this baby. It's a girl. I found out, and this is my chance at life. You will not take it from me." That marked the first time he'd seen her toughness outside business. Sensing her determination, he'd tried to dissuade her for practical, business reasons. "It's bad for me, Bronwyn," he'd tried to explain. "Here you are making real-estate deals all over the world for me; you're getting all the tenants for my shopping centers and buildings. How can you walk into a meeting looking like—like—oh my God. It's disgusting." But the only part of pregnancy that disgusted her was the early nausea. She was relieved when it disappeared as she entered her fourth month. It was replaced, however, by acne rosacea; red streaks flared on her forehead. *The Scarlet Letter.* She prayed her child would not be marked as she was. Meanwhile her small body seemed almost grotesque as her pregnancy advanced. When she entered her eighth month, she went to Harold. "I want to give our child your name," she'd said calmly. "What will my wife say?" he'd asked. "It's too late to wonder, Harold. I've really been your wife for four years. I listen to you bitch about deals and advise you, and I make a lot of money for us both. I want this child, and I want our child to have your name. I think you ought to get a divorce, a quickie one, and you know how to do it. You worked out her settlement years ago; I know the papers are ready and waiting." He had looked up in surprise. She wasn't fooling; he'd better stop her now. "Hey, cut the crap, Bronwyn. You've got all the money you want. Why do you want a kid? They're no damn good. Believe me, I've got two, and I know." When Bronwyn heard those words, she knew for certain she'd never get him to marry her for her needs, so she dropped her atom bomb. "You have thirty days to marry me, and if you don't, then I'm taking the Italians, the Germans, and the Japanese with me to Casey Burrows and let him set up—" That was when he held up his hand. "I'll do it," he'd said. The red streaks disappeared the day they went to City Hall and were married. By then she was six weeks from Gwyneth's birth but still doing real-estate deals. Harold was willing to take a lunch hour for the nuptials, but the wait for the judge was so long that Harold couldn't take time for a wedding lunch. The witnesses were two court attendants. Only after the wedding did Harold call his children to tell them he was married to his pregnant girlfriend, who was two years older than his daughter and two years younger than his son. Bronwyn called Anne and Sienna. Anne took her call, explained that she was in a meeting, wished her well, and went back to work. But Sienna said, "I'm going to give you the best wedding present in the world. I'm going to introduce you to Virginia Payne North."

If it hadn't been for Virginia and her advice about the Fifth Avenue house and the Southampton house, Bronwyn knew they'd probably have ended up living on the yacht off the coast of Bimini. But Virginia showed her how to convince Harold that New York–area real estate was important to all his deals, and Virginia guided her through the first years of rich wifehood and showed her how to make a quick splash in the social waters. "It takes money," Virginia had cautioned, "and you know that you have a lot of big money competing with you. So just open your purse and shut your eyes, and you can own New York. What you have to do is have a big house grandly done by the decorator of the moment. In your case, you will also need a Southampton house. While you're doing all of that and concentrating on your new baby, I will put you on every important charity committee. One more thing," she whispered behind her raised hand, "clean up your husband a bit, dear. See if you can get him to lose weight, and urge him to smoke those cigars only with gentlemen after dinner. In New York the well-bred no longer smoke in public."

Harold refused to bend to Virginia's ways, but Bronwyn was a ready pupil. Not for me, she told herself, but for my daughter am I doing all this. She'll belong. She'll be one of them. That was

Bronwyn's justification for spending hours going to committee meetings for benefits whose causes meant little to her. Her cause was not the charities; Gwyneth was her cause. Still she had a business to run. So, to accommodate her busy life, she set up her dressing room with a fax machine, a computer, and two telephones. One of the telephones was the unlisted one on which she made outside calls; the other was on her office switchboard, so that her business calls could be taken at home. With the help of modern electronics and three trained associates, she still handled, with her accustomed professionalism, the leasings of Harold's properties as well as properties for some of her own clients.

≡

Now, nine days after Virginia's dinner party, Bronwyn, seated at her dressing table, stared in fear and wonder at the new outcroppings on her face. Silently and numbly she reached for her bottles and jars and carefully applied, layer by layer, her cosmetic coverup for this most recent evidence of a life gone wrong.

When the telephone linked to the office switchboard rang, she knew she had to pull herself out of her despair; by the fourth ring she felt sufficiently transformed to speak with her usual crispness.

"Excuse me, Ms. Corcoran, but there is a gentleman here who insists on talking to you." In business she and Harold had decided that it was politic to keep her maiden name.

"Who is it?"

"He'll only tell you. Here he is."

"Ms. Corcoran," said the unfamiliar male voice, "I'm here in your office trying to persuade your secretary that you are the Bronwyn Corcoran who lived in the Bronx and went to the High School of Arts and Sciences two years ahead of me and that you were the smartest kid in a school of very smart kids, and she doesn't believe me. Come on, Ms. Corcoran, tell her I'm right, will you?"

The smartest kid in the class? Sure, she had been. But who talked about that kind of thing anymore? Bronwyn took the phone and held it away from her ear. What a happy kind of surprise on a dark brown day. Bronwyn laughed a tinkling little laugh she used only with Gwyneth. "I didn't think anybody would remember," she said, a seldom-used girlish edge to her voice. "What else do you remember?"

"That you have brown hair and you wore it sort of flopped over your face, and I always wished I could talk to you."

"Well, now that you're getting your wish, what's this all about?"

"Do you still love books, and do you still love to read?"

"Yes," she answered quickly. "But I don't know the last time anyone asked me that kind of question. Usually people want to know how I figure a deal."

"That's part of it. Look, Ms. Corcoran, I'm in your office. Will you be coming here? I need to talk to you. It's about business, but it's really more than business. It's passion, my passion, but one you share, I think, the passion for books."

"Can we talk about it now?"

"No. I really have to see you. I'll see you anywhere, anytime you want. I'll meet you at your office, go to your home, whatever you say—"

Bronwyn began to say no; she began to protest; she wanted to say to this unseen man that he should see her associates, but there was something so compelling, so—so neighborhood—yes, that was it. It was a voice from the neighborhood, friendly and familiar. Through his words came the remembered cadence, the speech patterns of a time when life itself was a warm blanket. How reassuring it was to hear a voice from this part of her past, an easy past instead of a black past. Suddenly she knew she would see this man, whoever he was.

"I'll meet you at my office." She looked at the carefully crafted gold-and-silver clock on her dressing table, a clock that cost as much as the tuition for her first year of college. "I'll be there in one hour. But I'll tell you now that I'm on my way to a luncheon date, so I'll only have about fifteen minutes to spend with you. Will you wait?"

"Of course," he said, "for I learned long ago that 'all human wisdom is summed up in two words—wait and hope.' "

"Ninth-grade English, *The Count of Monte Cristo*," she said quickly.

He laughed. "I hope you'll hurry so I won't have to wait too long."

Now, with more energy that she had felt in days, she continued masking her red-streaked, blotched face.

≡

He put down the book he was reading and stood when she walked into her office, and her first thought was that he looked too young to be her contemporary. He'd said he was two years behind her in school, but he looked ten years younger. Perhaps it was his casual dress that gave him this youthful appearance, because in her usually formal and proper office stood this gangling youth in faded blue jeans, a patch on one knee, a white open-necked shirt, heavy tweed jacket, and running shoes. But the moment she looked at his face, she knew it was one of the sweetest faces she had ever seen. His face was long and angular, his nose large and somewhat hawk-like, but there was a surprising softness to the brown eyes behind rimless spectacles, a special smile that played on his full lips. A lock of his longish hair kept falling on his forehead.

"Do I look familiar?" he asked.

"Yes, yes you do," she said, and then she laughed. "You look like William Butler Yeats."

He reached for her arm. "I don't believe you said that. He's my idol."

She smiled. "Mine, too."

"Then please, Ms. Corcoran, let me tell you what I want."

"Mr. . . . what is your name?"

"I'm so sorry. Terence Bell. Terry, really. Please call me Terry."

"All right, Terry, but won't you sit down?"

"Ms. Corcoran—"

"Since you seem to know me from high school, don't you think it would be proper to call me Bronwyn?"

"I never did in school. You were an older girl, and kids like me didn't talk to smart girls who were older. But, oh, I thought you were the smartest girl. In English Mr. Rovere used to read your essays as examples of teenage brilliance. That's what he said, honestly."

"Well, that sounds a bit excessive to me."

Terry Bell shrugged his shoulders. "The first time he read one of your essays I figured you for one of those fat smart girls. You know, the school was full of them. Then when I found out which one you were, I couldn't believe it. You were just a little bit of a thing, not really what I expected. Then over the years everyone heard about you. So I figured that by now you must weigh five hundred pounds and be twelve feet tall."

"I am," she said solemnly and smiled, for even though he was seated he towered over her.

"Bronwyn, I'm tall, but I'm no big chieftain. Hell, I'm not even a little chief, and you'll probably think I'm one nervy guy to come in here like this. I mean, I know you're accustomed to dealing with entrepreneurs in various shades and stripes, captains of industry and heads of state—"

"Terry," she chastised, "this is not a James Bond movie. What's on your mind? I don't have a lot of time."

He sat folding and unfolding his hands for a full minute. "I want to open a bookstore at Pumpkin Corners, the shopping mall you're leasing outside Boston. And your people have told me that the return on a special bookshop like mine won't work. I can't make the kind of figures you and your group think I should."

"Why can't you?"

"Because I don't want to run just an ordinary bookshop. Look, you love books. Now, where do you buy your books?"

"Me? I go to the book discounters and get them on sale. I have never paid full price for a book."

His mouth fell open. "You mean that you could pay anything for a book, and you go to discount stores?"

"I don't waste money," she said, but as she said the words she knew that for the first time she felt guilty instead of proud at uttering them.

"I—well, maybe I made a mistake. You see, I thought I remembered a girl who loved books and learning enough to want to see a real bookstore someplace in the world."

"What's a real bookstore, Terry?"

"A place where you can go in and sit down and read a book and maybe not even buy one, but you'd be treated with respect and courtesy because anyone who reads a book deserves that."

"All of us readers deserve good prices, too," she snapped.

"But I don't want to sell just the best-sellers and the dictionaries and cookbooks and Bibles of the world. I'm not against people who do, and I think it would be fine if you had that kind of bookshop at Pumpkin Corners, too. But you see, I want to call my bookshop Willie's, after William Butler Yeats—"

"Oh," she said, and she saw. She saw it before her. She saw the little bookshop with someone reading "The Wild Swans at Coole," and she saw this very young man—her age really—presiding over a dream. "How far apart are we on price?" she asked.

"Far apart? We never got to price. All they said was that my kind of store wasn't suitable. I'm not a moneymaker, Bronwyn, in the sense that I'll make millions for you. I won't make millions for myself either, but I am a kind of nice beacon for a place. I say something about the character of a neighborhood. I've been teaching English at a little college in New England, and I want to supplement my income, have a reason for book buying in England during holidays, going to Paris and the Netherlands and the Far East for art books."

She paused. "And will your wife work in the bookshop?"

"No." He shook his head sadly. "No wife. She left for big bucks, a Wall Street guy, a couple of years ago. Hope that doesn't offend you."

"No, it doesn't," she said coolly. "I earned my money. I didn't have to marry it. I was very rich before I married Harold Ashter, and I can do whatever I want in business. I'm not dependent on him, not for anything."

"Then is he dependent on you? I don't mean to be impudent, but I'm asking because, you see, I am dependent on you. I depend on a yes answer from you to kind of straighten out my life, to give me a little extracurricular fun and cash."

She thought for a moment. Whatever it was that she was doing in life right now was not giving her peace and satisfaction. Maybe she ought to try something, try to help someone who seemed too naïve to help himself. She put out her hand. "You have a deal."

He stood and grasped it. "Are you sure I'll pay my bills?" he asked.

She smiled. "You will if you're from my old neighborhood. Now you'd better be on your way because I have some papers to sign and a very important luncheon to attend."

He leaned over the desk and kissed her lightly on her cheek. And as he walked out the door, she heard him recite:

"When you are old and grey and full of sleep,
And nodding by the fire, take down this book,

And slowly read, and dream of the soft look
Your eyes had once, and of their shadows deep . . ."

Terry walked dreamily from the office, and as he passed the sidewalk telephone, he remembered the call he'd promised to make. He dialed the number at the stone cottage in Maine and, as he did, he could picture his cousin Sean, feet up on the kitchen table, beer can at his side, waiting for the phone to ring.

"Bell and Foley," said the male voice that answered.

"Ah, cousin," Terry chortled, "you are pretending once again that we are a great business, and I am here to report that reason, magic, and dreams have worked once again for the Irish."

"Did she say yes?" Sean asked with concern.

"Does a lady who says, 'You have a deal,' mean what she says?" Terry inquired impishly.

"Ho, you did it, my boy. My business plan and your personality. We're an unbeatable combination." Sean laughed.

"It wasn't all business," Terry admitted. "She's—she's a very nice lady," he added softly.

"Careful, cousin, she's married."

"So was Maud Gonne," he replied wistfully.

"Maud Gonne? Did she go to high school with you, too?" Sean asked.

Terry guffawed. "Maud Gonne was Yeats's true love. Aaaah, my faithful cousin, now I know why you sell computers and I dream of poets."

"Well, get back up here to Maine," Sean instructed enthusiastically, overlooking the reference to his lack of scholarship. "We have a lot of work to do. Terry, we can make a fortune. But make sure you keep your Bronwyn's confidence. This could be our turning point."

16

VIRGINIA PAYNE NORTH ALWAYS FOLLOWED HER OWN ADVICE. She told her girls that when meeting someone for lunch, whether guest or host, it was always an advantage to be the first one at the restaurant table.

So now, three minutes before the appointed arrival time, Virginia sat at her customary banquette in the number-one corner at Sylvan's, the restaurant not of the moment but of the decade. Restaurants would come and go in the 1990s, but Sylvan's would continue because it was owned by a true restaurateur: an Italian who cooked like a Frenchman, was as charming as a Hungarian, as political as a Swiss diplomat, as shrewd as a Japanese banker, and as friendly as an American.

Now Sylvan himself stopped at her table. "How good to see you, Mrs. North," Sylvan said as he bowed and gently kissed the empty air just above her extended hand. "I have two messages for you. Mrs. Ashter called to say that she had to stop at her office and might be a few minutes late, and Mrs. Burrows telephoned to say that she was caught in traffic coming from the airport but would be here as soon as conditions permit."

"Thank you," Virginia said with a quiet smile. "I understand the problems of living in this city. And, of course, it's the week before Easter, and you know how busy everyone gets at this time."

"In the restaurant business it's supposed to be a very slow time, but you know how it is here." He stood erect and spread his hands helplessly.

"It means you are full, of course," she said knowingly.

"Of course." He returned the smile and, bowing to his socially important patron, said, "May I offer you a glass of champagne while you wait?"

She shook her head in quiet refusal. "No, thank you. I still do not drink at noon."

He nodded toward a captain who, on cue, came forward with Virginia's favorite mineral water in a stemmed wineglass. That was one of the reasons Virginia always chose Sylvan's for her luncheons. Her needs were anticipated, her preferences known. Virginia sat back on the embroidered cushions of the banquette. The dining room was full of color and fragrance. Large arrangements of lilies and pots of orchids crowded the corners of the painted walls and were displayed on the long service tables at the front, sides, and rear of the room. They were almost-in-season flowers that gave the diners that effect of luxury that comes when a season is hurried for reasons of beauty rather than economy.

When Virginia looked up, Sienna was standing before her. She was wearing a silk printed dress with matching jacket, but instead of looking springlike and real as the flowers around them, Virginia thought there was something forced and unnatural about Sienna. She could see the tenseness in her usually composed, erect body, and under the violet eyes were dark circles.

Sienna came to Virginia's side of the table, kissed her dutifully—yes, Virginia thought, that was a dutiful kiss and not an affectionate one—and asked, "Virginia, dear, am I late?"

Virginia looked at her friend. Something was troubling her. "No, Sienna, I'm early. But you know my habits, so don't fret."

"I'm sure the others will be here shortly."

"No, they won't. They've both been delayed for the usual kind of boring reasons, but, like good little girls, they called to tell us so we can at least have an aperitif while we wait."

Again the captain appeared. "Champagne, madam? Sylvan wants to toast the holiday with you."

"Thank you, I will," Sienna answered.

"I've never seen you drink at noon," Virginia said.

"I never do." She stopped abruptly and lowered her head.

"Were you going to say something?"

Sienna raised her head slowly. "No."

Virginia reached across the table for Sienna's hand. "I've had the feeling that something is disturbing you. Even when we chatted on the telephone yesterday, I sensed that something was amiss. You and I have—oh, I guess you might call it our own secret way of talking. Suddenly it seems gone. What is it, Sienna? Would you like to tell me? Is there something I've done?"

Sienna sorted through the files of her life. What could she tell Virginia that would give her confidence about the security of their relationship without telling her that what had truly come between them was Gregory Sawyer?

"If we have a few minutes . . ." she said to Virginia.

"We do," Virginia assured her.

"Ten days ago I found out that I can never have a child."

"Oh, my dear, I'm so sorry."

"You don't know what this means to me."

"Perhaps I do."

"I don't want a child so that when the photographers come around, I'll have this precious little one in designer clothes. I think there are women who have babies to cement marriages, but I feel that Peter loves me. And he already has children. He and his son, Gene, have an incredible relationship. They work together, and they have a life that—well, that works without me. I'm the outsider. I don't know if it would be different if I were Gene's mother—"

Virginia met her troubled eyes. "I suppose you look at Anne and Bronwyn—"

"I wouldn't be the kind of mother Anne is. I look at Anne with three children, and all she does is worry about where her next deal is . . ."

"I think that suits her husband."

"And Bronwyn is crazed about Gwyneth. I wouldn't be like that either."

"Few women would be."

"I want a baby so much, something of my own," and now her eyes filled, and she reached for her handbag and a small white lace handkerchief.

Virginia was silent for a moment and then she answered, "Do you really believe a child is yours, that you own a child?"

"Well, maybe not own . . ."

"Did your mother own you?"

"My mother definitely does not own me."

"*Does* not? I thought your mother had died."

"That's what I say sometimes, Virginia. I wish she had."

"I remember meeting your mother, Sienna. Oh, she was known as the beautiful Peppy Craig. It was just before John Kennedy's election, and in a roomful of Republican supporters, Peppy said loudly, 'Wouldn't it be fun to have a sexy president?' " Virginia smiled at the memory. "That was a daring remark in 1960, but if that kind of comment were made now, who would remember it thirty years from today?"

Sienna dried her eyes and drew back in her chair. "My mother was an unforgettable woman—*is* an unforgettable woman. I'm so accustomed to speaking of her in the past. Someday I'll have to face her. I know that, and you're the only person in the world I'd talk to about her, but I'm not ready yet. When I am, I'll come to you."

There were lines now in Virginia's forehead, and the shaped brown crescent brows above Virginia's blue eyes met in sadness. "I think it may be time, then, for me to tell you a story," she said. "My life was not always luncheon at Sylvan's and dinner with the hostess

of the week. You know that, of course, but I don't think you know
how my life really came to be.

"I'm almost seventy years old now, and that shocks me. I don't
feel old until I say the number. I was born in 1923 in West Virginia.
My father was a coal miner, and my family was so poor that we slept
four to a bedroom and took turns sleeping on the floor. Everything
about my life was black. My mother was a fine housekeeper, but the
choking dust covered everything. We didn't have curtains because
if poor Mama hung them in the morning, they were thick with coal
dust by night. I never had anything white, so now you know why
I love pastels, why my house is peach and white. From the time I
was old enough to go to the library and read books, I plotted my
escape. If I took typing, I reasoned, and did well in business courses,
I would be able to get out. That was the goal of my life—get out
and own a white dress. So in 1939 when I was graduated from high
school, I left West Virginia and went to the nearest big city, Pittsburgh. In those days Pittsburgh was as coal-black as West Virginia,
but to me it was the big city, the Big Time. I got a job at Kaufman's
Department Store in the credit department, and with the draft and
the shortage of good help, I advanced quickly.

"But the draft meant that there were very few men around. I
was in Pittsburgh for two years before Pearl Harbor, and then when
the war came, I wanted to be a part of everything that was happening. I volunteered to roll bandages, and I knitted for the Red Cross.
But I wanted to do something more—well, dear, I was nineteen
years old, and my youth was going off to war. So I volunteered for
the USO. Each week I went to a little basement canteen and met
soldiers. In 1942 I met a sailor—I'm not sure what a sailor was doing
in Pittsburgh, but there he was. Tall, black-haired, funny, adorable.
I can see him still. I was very naïve, as you can imagine, and when
he told me that it was my patriotic duty to go to bed with him
because he might be killed in two weeks, I agreed. And somewhere
between the glamour of the uniform and the thrill of the bed, I
found the life I thought I wanted. We were married six weeks after
we met. Then he was told he'd have to ship out, and he went to New
York—New Jersey—Connecticut. I never knew exactly where he
was going because it was wartime, and everything was secret. I didn't
tell you his name, did I? It was Bonner Wright. I loved his name.
I loved him. I loved everything about him. I followed him to New

York. It took two days on a coach train sitting on my luggage. You can't imagine the world before the jet plane, can you? I went to New Jersey because that's where the train went, and I got off the train and found a rooming house, and then I got a job at a defense plant. By then, of course, it was called a war plant. I was at work in the secretarial pool when, one day, I fainted. Just like that I fainted. They took me to the plant nurse, and she smiled. I can still see that patronizing smile of that starched woman. 'How far gone are you?' she asked me. I didn't know what she was talking about. Of course, she was telling me I was pregnant. I was frantic. My husband was—well, where was he? On the high seas? Waiting to be shipped? I didn't know. But I had his child. I was happy but frightened. I just wasn't sure how long my money would last, so I did what any war bride would do. I wrote to the U.S. Government to apply for his dependent's allowance and to take care of my medical expenses.

"I was at dinner in the dreary little dining room of the rooming house where I stayed when I got the letter telling me that I was already getting support for my three children. I thought there must be some mistake. So I went to my boss, who was the smartest, sweetest man I'd ever met. I asked him to check it out for me. He did, and it was true. Bonner Wright was married and had three children.

"I miscarried that night, and my boss and his wife were with me the whole time. I swore that I would be good to them and pay them back any way that I could. He said the best thing I could do would be to work for him.

"So I did. In case you haven't figured it out, I'll tell you. My boss was Calvin North, and the woman who was so good to me was his wife. I worked for Calvin and his wife. And as he moved up in the corporate world, so did I. I learned about good restaurants and the best places to vacation. I learned how to order clothes and food and run a house. And when Harriet North had her first heart attack, I took over the full running of their house. She was an invalid for twenty years—my twenty childbearing years. When she died, Calvin and I married. By then it was too late for me to have a child.

"So I did the next best thing. I adopted children. What do I mean? I mean, of course, children like you. Can you imagine how the society women of New York looked down on me? A common working woman invading their territory! So I decided I would make life easier for other common working women like me, women who just happen to marry very rich men. Nowadays, of course, money is the answer. Not that it wasn't always. But generations of wealth tend to make people forget how the money was made. The Vanderbilts aren't as rich today as some of the new money, and the Rockefellers pale in comparison to some of the newer fortunes, but the old families and the old money know something new money doesn't. You see, dear, this generation—your husband and Anne's and Bronwyn's—is concerned with making wealth. The old money is concerned with living with wealth. The quality of life of old money is much—well, much finer. When people are in the money-making mode, they emphasize what is fundamentally grasping and self-serving, and by their emphasis they make it laudable. But it is not laudable. Now, darling, if that's snobbery, so be it. I am a snob. But if I weren't, how could I teach you to be one?"

In the flower-filled restaurant, Sienna looked at the chic, well-coiffed woman opposite her. Virginia was wearing the suit of the season, the trim little restaurant suit that would come in for luncheon today on six other shapely bodies varying in age from early thirties to early eighties. But under Virginia's good haircut and beneath the expensive suit was a story she never knew. "Thank you for telling me this," Sienna said. "I've heard parts of the story but never all of this."

"And you never will again. You see, Sienna, you are my good friend, and the value of friendship is that I knew I could trust you even without telling you this. I knew you would always be both loyal and sympathetic, and so, dear child, you must know that I, too, will be loyal and sympathetic even without knowing all your story."

Sienna began to speak, but Virginia raised her hand to silence her. "Anne just came in, and I can tell from the way she's walking that she's one angry woman. Oh, my darling Seconds, what's happening to all of you?"

17

ANNE, WITHOUT SPEAKING, COMMANDED A ROOM BY HER EXtraordinary presence. Her athlete's body, kept in perfect shape by her daily trainer, was becomingly dressed each day by one of six designers: two French, two Italian, two American. Anne was their belle dame, and each vied for her approval of their collections. It was considered a couturier's triumph of the day to have Mrs. Casey Burrows appear at Sylvan's because she would be photographed, of course, by the paparazzi; the pictures would be seen in daily fashion journals, in newspapers and magazines. And all across America aspiring Annes would hurry to the local discount store in search of today's Anne look-alike dress or suit.

From Virginia Anne had learned not to play the bosom too strongly, to subtly suggest the curves of her body, and from Virginia's own makeup man, Hugo, Anne had learned how to emphasize the cheekbones that were now her trademark. There was a dispassionate coolness Virginia had taught her Seconds, as well. "Never let the world know what's going on underneath the designer clothes," she had warned them.

But Anne, her color high, her body tense, strode into the room without stopping for Sylvan's salutatory kiss of the hand and wan smile. She went directly to Virginia's table, pulled out her own chair with one hand and with the other threw the morning newspaper on the table. "Did either of you see this?" she demanded.

Ignoring her lack of manners, Virginia said softly, "Hello, Anne. I'm so sorry you were delayed."

Now the captain hovered. "Champagne, Mrs. Burrows? It would be Sylvan's pleasure—"

"A martini. Very dry."

Virginia's eyes narrowed. "What's going on?"

"Look at this paper. Look at it. That bitch columnist, Lolly Little. Look what she did. She's trying to ruin my life."

"I wouldn't say that Lolly Little's column could ruin a life," Virginia said dryly.

"It could ruin mine. Obviously you haven't seen the paper." She pushed it toward Sienna, who began scanning it. Anne's martini was served, and she took a large gulp, the kind of swallow that only a nondrinker dares take before lunch.

"Oh," Sienna cried in sympathy. "Oh no."

"Read it, please," Virginia commanded.

Sienna picked up the paper as if it were a dead spider and read in a quiet voice, "Is Casey Burrows, the deal-maker, making private deals with the not-so-ladylike Lady Diandre Devon? His private plane took them to a secret lunch in Bermuda just the other noon, and now he's looking at interesting places to dine. Why not try the Dome dining room, Mr. Burrows? Your wife has turned it into a first-class New York restaurant."

"Oh no," Virginia said sadly.

"How can he do this to me?" Anne raged. "I deliver five million dollars a week before taxes. What other wife does anything like that? I have given him three children. What more does he want?"

"What more do you want?" Virginia asked.

"Me? I want respect," she snapped. "I do not want to be humiliated by a . . . a second-rate woman."

"Respect is earned," Virginia answered. "Calm down, Anne. Compose yourself, and stop drinking that stupid drink."

Anne, chastised, began to speak and then thought better of her words. She remained silent and pushed the drink away from her place.

"You will not keep your husband by acting like a fishwife," Virginia reminded her gently. "Casey is a self-centered man and thinks he invented the deal. He thinks everyone in the world plays a secondary role; only he is the star. You've accommodated that, and you've found a place for yourself. You're very capable, and you've shown all women that even though you have advantages they don't, you haven't simply taken without trying to give to the world. Hold your head up, Anne. No matter what happens with Casey, remember that he's a foolish, vain man. You, however, are a woman of substance. He inherited wealth and made it grow. You began with nothing and attracted a dynamic man, had children, and have been a totally creative woman."

Anne's eyes filled. "Thank you, Virginia."

"Now let's throw away that dirty paper. So many germs in those nasty things. And look, my darlings, here comes Bronwyn."

Sienna squeezed Anne's hand. "We're together no matter what happens," she whispered.

"Bronwyn," Virginia trilled, "you look marvelous."

Indeed Virginia had never seen Bronwyn with her eyes shining so brightly.

Sienna and Anne exchanged a nervous look. What new kind of drug had she found now?

"And that suit, dear, it's just right for you. Ordinarily I don't like trousers on women, but somehow that look is a very good city look."

"Thank you," Bronwyn said. Even under the layers of makeup she felt she was blushing prettily. "I'm very sorry to be late, Virginia, but I had to stop at the office."

"I thought you always worked from home," Anne added in a petulant tone. Ordinarily Bronwyn made her feel guilty for leaving her children while she arranged to do all her work from her dressing room.

"I do, but this involved a leasing that I had to arrange personally," she explained. And then, shrugging her shoulders, she added, "Anne, who would understand better than you?"

The captain arrived at their table. "A glass of champagne as a holiday toast from Sylvan?" he asked Bronwyn.

Again Anne and Sienna exchanged worried glances. With their own emotions running high, they could ill afford Bronwyn's drugs and drinking today.

"No, thank you," Bronwyn said confidently. "I don't need anything."

Virginia gave a little murmur of pleasure. "At least one of us—" She stopped herself in midsentence and waved to the captain. "Let's order luncheon. It's getting late. I've a meeting about housing needs in an hour, and there's something we must discuss."

But it was not until the coffee was served that Virginia broached her subject. Virginia drew her brows together and fingered the handle of her cup. Each of the women was silent. Sienna stared at the flowers on the table, waiting—waiting for what she knew would be a first mention of Gregory Sawyer and the school. Anne, chastened by Virginia's words to her, still reflected on her hurt; finally Casey had made his indiscretions public. Only Bronwyn's thoughts were flowerings of the newly rooted illusions Terry had planted in her daydreams.

Finally Virginia, convinced they were ready to acknowledge that long-ago part of their lives, began. "Isn't it interesting that, like you, I met Gregory Sawyer at a time when I needed him? I know that all of you met because Gregory had that school back in the sixties. He was obviously a very strong influence in your lives. You were—please forgive me for saying this—but you were three rather unremarkable young girls. Evidently that early experience began to shape your lives and caused you to go on and take giant steps. I have become—well, let's say I've become rather attached to Gregory, so I've agreed to help him re-create the Peabody School. I've done some investigating. The school isn't really there; I guess it was never much more than a kind of glorified barracks, but the site is available. I want to raise money, build a new school, and put Gregory where he belongs—in the forefront of American education, a force for youngsters who have trouble coping, running a place where children who"—and now she looked directly at Sienna—"can find the acceptance they don't find at home. Well, what do you say, are you with me?"

Bronwyn was the first to speak. "Are you sure that Gregory is qualified?"

"That's a strange question for you to ask." Virginia laughed. "You're the best examples of his fine work."

"Of course we are," Sienna added lamely. "But, well, it has been a long time, and styles in education change, just as they do in everything else. He's come out of the blue, so to speak. Are you sure he's the best one? I guess that's what we're all asking."

"I have no children," Virginia said, looking once again at Sienna, "and this is my way of contributing. Besides, darlings, you know we can always hire the proper people. The hardest thing is to attract the right people to the project, get some of the right money, and I do think Gregory has extraordinary presence."

Sienna knew she could argue the point no longer. Virginia was telling them in her convoluted way that Gregory would be a strong fund-raiser. Sienna sighed. Only the reappearance of her mother could cause her more concern. She looked at Anne silently, desperately. What were they to say next?

Anne, overcome by her husband's public philandering, now found Gregory playing a secondary role, the building of his school just another necessary exercise in her exercise-filled life. "What do you want us to do?"

Bronwyn, full of a pleasure she could not define, felt unexpectedly strong. "I suppose we can do whatever you want, Virginia."

So, the Seconds would come through after all. Virginia smiled and lifted her coffee cup in a small toast to her group. She had known it always, that bread cast upon the waters would come back a thousandfold in ways that would nourish all their lives. "This is what we're going to do," she said. "We're too late to get on the fall agenda with a big charity event. All the good dates have been taken for two years. So Gregory and I decided that we'd have a sports weekend in

New Hampshire. We'll go up to the original site of the school, invite just one hundred New York people, fly them up to New Hampshire, and put them up at motels in the area. We'll have tennis, hiking, canoeing, fishing, croquet, and all kinds of outdoor fun. We'll go up on Saturday, have our fun and games all day, then have a big barbecue at night. I thought that you, Anne, might get one of your good chefs to come up and do it. And then on Sunday we'll have the groundbreaking."

"But," Sienna asked softly, "is the facility capable of handling this? I mean, I don't know about things like canoeing and fishing—"

"Oh, you must remember," Virginia said in surprise. "Gregory said all of you girls would know that the Peabody School has a marvelous pond."

18

DUCKING THE EVER-PRESENT PHOTOGRAPHERS OUTSIDE SYLvan's, Sienna grasped Anne's arm. "Tell your driver to go on without you, and come in my car," she whispered.

Anne nodded, and the two settled in the back of Sienna's long black limousine.

"What are we going to do?" Sienna asked softly.

"About which one?" Anne asked dejectedly. "Casey or Gregory? Can you believe my whole world is falling apart?"

Sienna, startled, looked at her friend. Was she embroiled only in her own narrow life with Casey? "Anne, we'll talk about Casey later." Now Sienna closed the automatic window between the two women and the driver in the front seat. "I'm talking about Gregory and going up to the Peabody School. My God, I never thought I'd be saying those words."

"Of course 1961 was all an accident."

"But Gregory is going to hold it over us. He's using it, and he's using us, and we can't say a word."

"Maybe the statute of limitations—" Anne volunteered.

"I'm going to get a lawyer," Sienna said. "I've been thinking about it for a week."

"A lawyer? Whatever for?"

"To find out if there's anything legally that can happen to us."

"Who are you going to use?" Anne asked. "I'd want my name kept out of this."

"Anne, when are you going to remember I'm not in this alone? If I'm guilty of anything, so are you. So is Bronwyn."

Anne pounded her fist in frustration on the car seat. "Well, where the devil has he been all these years? That's what I'm trying to find out. Look, just between you and me, I've gone to somebody who'll—well, he'll keep quiet."

"You mean you told?" Sienna heard her voice rise in panic and lunged toward Anne.

"No, no," Anne said, putting a restraining hand on Sienna. "I didn't tell. I asked. I asked—oh look, there's a kind of creepy guy who works for Casey, does his dirty stuff, and I asked him to check out Gregory. So hold off on talking to a lawyer. I'm trying to get something on Gregory, and if I can, then we'll all be okay."

"Meanwhile, how can we help Virginia? How can we get her to stop this whole charity before it starts?" Sienna asked. "Look, you and I both know that Gregory is nothing but a man out for her money. Why doesn't she see it? He could ruin all four of us."

Anne sat back against the expensive upholstery of the car. "Well, let's ask ourselves. What's the worst thing he can do?"

"If he tells Virginia, I think our lives as we know them are over. He's romanced Virginia, and that's what gives him the advantage over us. Can you believe it? At her age sex has become so damned important."

"It's not sex, Sienna. Look at all of us. Are we married for sex? I've had a lot better sex than I give or get with Casey. And I can't believe that Harold Ashter takes that cigar out of his mouth long enough to make love. As for you, tell me the truth, is Peter your best?"

Sienna smoothed the silk print of her skirt and thought for a moment. "Yes. I wouldn't have said that if you hadn't made me think just then. But he's my best lover because he's the only person in my whole life who ever truly loved me. We both had rotten lives before we met. He was married to a woman who thought equality meant her rights. I had a mother who was beautiful and used sex as her weapon to fight all life's battles. When I was a child, she was having one affair after another, paid no attention to me at all. Then, as I was trying to find my own sexuality, she ran off with our estate manager. My father didn't even look up from his practice long enough to protest. So I did all the family protesting. After that terrible summer, the summer we met, the summer we never talked about, I ran away four times. The last time I ran away was to go to California, and that's when I ended up in those porno movies. Peter came along and married me anyway. Some of my past has been publicized, and we managed to launder it a bit and survive, but, between us, I've been in bed with more men than you can count. Now I'm one of the real ladies of New York, and those sordid affairs and embarrassing movies don't worry me anymore. But the accident isn't just fun and games. It's a human life, and just publicizing that could absolutely ruin Peter's chances. Can you imagine how I'd feel? He gave me my life, and I'd be taking his away."

Now it was Anne's turn to be silent. Finally she turned to her friend, put her hand on hers, and said in a voice cracking with emotion, "There's no way out unless I tell Virginia about Gregory. You know the part I mean."

"But how can you?"

She withdrew her hand, and her long body seemed devoid of energy. "You're right. I can't. There's no way out, Sienna. We'll all have to play along with Virginia, give her her dream, even go to New Hampshire in the fall."

"But what about Bronwyn? Can she do it?"

Anne shook her head. "Who knows? By the way, what got into her today? She was either so high on something or so totally relaxed that she seemed almost like a normal person. And did you notice? She didn't mention precious little Gwyneth once." Anne's body tensed and she looked ready to spring once again. "Please ask your driver to stop here. I almost forgot. Today is Casey's birthday, and no matter what Lolly Little writes, I'm still the wife. I'm going to run into the Dome. We have a new jewelry shop in the lobby; I'll get him some cuff links." She paused. "I guess it will be his two hundred and sixtieth set."

Sienna laughed. "It's not easy to shop for a man like that."

"No," said Anne darkly, "especially when he starts doing his own shopping."

Sienna touched Anne's arm in silent understanding.

Nothing was decided.

Nothing was different.

But each knew, too, that nothing was the same.

"Mrs. Marvell," Sienna's driver said as Anne waved good-bye and ran up the steps of the Dome, "Hedda asked me to give you your morning messages. She said you might want to see them now."

Sienna frowned. That was unlike Hedda.

She unfolded each.

An invitation to a charity party.

A call from the vet. It was time for Puff's shots.

She shook her head in surprise. Why did the competent, judicious Hedda think these calls important?

Then she unfolded the third message.

She read the note and put her hands over her eyes, and the paper fluttered to the floor of the car.

It read, "Your mother is arriving tomorrow morning on the Concorde from Paris."

19

B RONWYN SAT AT HER DRESSING TABLE. AFTER LUNCH HER RITual consisted of face washing, pulling back her hair, and letting her skin breathe until the hour before Harold came home, when, once again, she would cream and coat her face into its smooth one color, untie the ponytail, let her hair fall in its usual fashion, and dress for dinner.

Today she sat at the dressing table, reached for her cleansing milk, and stopped. Why bother?

She opened the small drawer on the left side of her table, the drawer where she kept her secret cache of uppers and downers that guided her emotions through the trials of her life. But she closed the drawer without taking out any of the vials.

Bronwyn sat back and looked at herself in the mirror. She closed her eyes. It had been such a satisfying day, but there was something she wanted to do.

What was it?

Oh yes.

She went to the bookshelf in her bedroom and pulled the

well-thumbed volume of Yeats's poetry from the shelf. Did she remember the poem correctly? He had said, "When you are old and grey and full of sleep . . ." when he left, hadn't he?

She opened the book.

Yes, it was marked.

It had always been one of her favorites.

Then, holding the book in front of her, Bronwyn recited in a loud, clear voice—just as she had so many years ago in an assembly before the school:

> *"How many loved your moments of glad grace,*
> *And loved your beauty with love false or true,*
> *But one man loved the pilgrim soul in you,*
> *And loved the sorrows of your changing face."*

20

VIRGINIA CAME OUT THE DOOR OF THE RESTAURANT, SMILED prettily as she was photographed saying her good-byes, and then, as she saw the sunshine, she told her driver to go on without her. Yes, this was a day to walk. The day was perfect. There was a last-of-winter, promise-of-spring chill in the air. The sun overhead was bright but still cold. The streets were free of the black winter slush that dulled and darkened the look of New York, and even the sidewalks seemed clear of the ever-present plastic garbage bags waiting for the next pickup.

She walked leisurely down Madison Avenue, past the constantly changing storefronts, stores that one day housed an Italian shoe designer and the next a freshly decorated jewelry shop. As she covered the familiar blocks, she tried to sort the unfamiliar mixed signals she was getting from her Seconds. There was something troubling Sienna. Was it the desire for a child or was there more? Perhaps she was jealous of Peter's son and his closeness with his father. Or was it those dreadful parents of hers? Had they scarred her so deeply that even now, even as a respected and leading matron, she felt hatred and insecurity? Virginia wished that she knew so that she might help. Still, she raised a restraining hand, for how deeply could she involve herself in old associations from lives before they'd touched hers? She would ask Gregory. The thought gave her a sharp thrill of pleasure.

She turned east to walk the blocks to East House, but now the chill spring winds made her cough. She hailed a cab and rode home.

So, she couldn't quite travel the distance these days. Still she was glad she had walked part of the way, glad she had seen the hint of the greening to come in the city, the promise of the budding. The beginning was special this year. For she, too, would come to blossom this spring, the first spring in a very long time.

She smiled as she paid the driver and greeted her doorman.

She was still smiling when she walked into her drawing room and saw Gregory waiting for her. "It's more than I'd hoped," she said prettily.

He rose and embraced her.

She blushed and pulled away. "That's more than just a little friendly hello, isn't it?"

"You make me feel a way that I haven't felt for many years," he answered.

"I—I—won't you sit down?"

"Only if you will sit with me."

"Gregory," she protested feebly.

He waved his hand. "I never want to discomfit you, my dear."

"Thank you." He sat in the straight chair opposite her. She sat gingerly at the edge of the peach patterned sofa.

"Now, how did the luncheon go?"

"A little strange, Gregory. Perhaps you can explain, but you see, it wasn't the way I thought it would be. My guess would have been that the girls would have been thrilled to help you and would have wanted to give whatever they could. But there was an invisible rein, something that held each back and kept her from running with the idea. I do think that Bronwyn seemed the most receptive, although Bronwyn seemed the most unlike herself."

"Oh? In what way?"

"She seemed almost normal. Now, I don't mean to sound strange, but Bronwyn always seems so tense and preoccupied, as if she can't bear to give anyone except Gwyneth a moment of herself. Today she seemed cool and collected and almost casual about the idea of the school."

"And Anne?"

"She's so distressed by a tacky little item in today's paper that she scarcely heard anything."

"And Sienna?"

"Willing and able, but not entirely ready."

"Do you want to forget about this, Virginia? I don't want to cause you any pain or hurt your relationship with those wonderful women. After all, when I knew them, they—well, they were scarcely worth knowing. Maybe it's embarrassing for them to realize that I'm back in their lives and that they weren't always—well, as comfortable as they are today. Maybe they really don't want to share their good fortune with others. And if it causes you any pain at all, there are countless foundations I can approach for the money. Besides, there's a Boston group—"

"No, you've just made up my mind, Gregory. These girls must realize that they're very fortunate and have a responsibility to others. Your school will be built if it's the last thing I do."

Gregory moved toward Virginia. He put his arms around her and cradled her body against his.

Now her head began to throb. What was happening to her? Where did all this feeling begin? "Oh, Bonner," she whispered.

Her head was spinning. This was all unreal. "What did I call you?" she asked in a frightened voice.

"You said Bonner."

"I haven't said that name for more than forty years."

"What made you say it now, Virginia?"

"I think because," she said weakly, "I haven't felt like this for forty years."

He lifted her to her feet. "Perhaps this is the moment to explore that feeling further."

Then slowly, but purposefully, he led her to her bedroom.

21

LADY DIANDRE DEVON ROLLED OVER IN THE KING-SIZE BED SO SHE might face Central Park, and then she laughed a small, tinkling laugh.

Casey Burrows rolled over behind her and put his hand on

her bare back. "How do you do that?" he asked.

"Which thing?" she teased.

"The last—you know, that laugh. It's kind of British. It doesn't sound like Anne or her friends."

"Oh, my dearest," she said, rolling back toward him and giving him a look that she knew, from other men and other times, made him hers. It was known on three continents as the Lady's Look. Men talked about it in clubs, pubs, and locker rooms. It was always given when the man was naked. Lady Diandre might or might not be dressed, but the man wore no clothes when she looked at him that way. Lady Diandre knew from long experience that a naked man in front of a woman was infinitely more shy than a woman in similar circumstances before a man. What she did was fix her eyes on the man; she would meet him eye-to-eye, and then just as he was beginning to wonder what his next move would be, she would smile, not the smile of a seductress but rather the smile of an indulgent mother or aunt, a smile that said, "Whatever you do or don't do is quite all right. You're my little boy, and I accept you just as you are. If you're not in the mood, so be it. If you want me, I'm here."

For Casey Burrows it was an indication of an overwhelming kindness he had not seen in a woman since his childhood. Even his mother had never looked at him with that blind permissiveness, that acquiescence. "I want you, Didi," he heard himself mumble.

"Of course," she whispered.

"I mean I want you forever. Don't get out of this bed. Don't leave the Dome. Just stay in this suite forever."

"Won't you let me eat?" she teased.

"Room service," he answered, now realizing that she was playing a game. Didn't she know he didn't play games?

"What about shopping? How can a woman live without shopping?" she murmured.

He got out of bed. "I thought it was too good to be true."

"Casey, I was teasing. I thought that made me sound like Anne, and I thought—well, I thought, oh my goodness, I'll bet Casey is lonesome for Anne by now. You haven't seen her all day."

Casey gave a gruff laugh and came back into the bed. "You did sound like her."

"I'll bet I can sound like her other friends, too."

"How do you know so much?"

"I'm a reader, Casey dear, a very good reader."

"Is that what you do for a living?"

"No. We'll get to that later. Want to see my impersonations?"

"Sure."

She took her mane of red hair and covered her face, and in a Bronx accent pruned to a flat sound, she said, "Please call the magazines. I want to have my white canopy bed photographed. I want the world to see my house. This is not just design, world. This is industrial-strength decorating."

Casey lay on his back and laughed. "You've really got Bronwyn down to a T."

"Now get this one," she said. She got out of bed still wearing her teddy, went to the dresser, and opened the drawer. Then she reached in, pulled out a pair of white gloves, put them on, and said, "Oh, my darling girls, I have so much to teach you. This, girls, is a teddy. Do not let a man take it off you. Do not let your husband take it off you. Do not let a man touch you. That is not what New York society is about. New York society is about attracting homosexuals as escorts and friends. After all, dears, everyone knows that in New York the best men are women."

"Hey," Casey asked, "how do you know what Virginia does?"

"Mon dieu," she said in an exaggerated French accent, "who doesn't know about les girls and the woman who teaches them which fork to use and which hostess to use?"

"You didn't get all this just reading newspapers, did you, Didi?"

"Mmmmm, no. I've been around, Casey."

"I'd like you to be around me."

"I am."

"I mean officially."

His words gave Lady Diandre a thrill of pleasure. It was amazing what you could get men to do without sex. After all, she and Casey had been to bed together, but they'd never made love, not by her definition. She had teased and entertained him, and he had been so delighted—was so delighted—is so delighted that she laughed the signature laugh once again.

He came out of the bed and reached for the body under the silk teddy. "What do you want?" he asked.

"Just what every normal American girl wants—you." Now in one small, liquid movement she thrust her body so that he could not escape.

"You got it, kid," he said hoarsely. "It's all here for you."

22

SIENNA OPENED HER EYES, HEAVY WITH THE UNDREAMED dreams of a restless night. She reached for Peter, but he was not there. She sat up fearfully. What time could it be? How had she missed him? She'd awakened at four o'clock; she'd checked the time and had closed her eyes for a minute. It had been only a minute, hadn't it? She shook her head slowly to clear her thoughts. The past two days had been such a jumble, such a . . . a nightmare beginning with Peppy's arrival.

Peppy had swirled into their house. Yes, *swirled* was the only word. Peppy, the girl mother, looking as if she were just about to go on the dance floor or just about to leave it, had swirled through the door of their Park Avenue triplex, and before she'd put her cheek to her daughter's lips for the faintest of kisses had gasped in mock shock, "Oh, Sienna, how could you. You've had Martha Morgan do the apartment. How awful. You've taken two perfectly simple Russian tables with just the right touch of ormolu and covered them with those silly, drippy little candles. Darling, you've made this entrance hall look like Saturday night in Peoria."

Sienna had inhaled sharply and, ignoring the comment, asked, "How was your trip, Peppy?" Before she could hear the answer, Sienna's face had immediately frozen into the mask she wore whenever Peppy Williams Craig Patterson Deauville Antonini came into her life.

Peppy had then directed the disposal of her luggage (she would take the bedroom next to Sienna and Peter's). Oh, that was Sienna's study? Well, Sienna wouldn't mind if she took it over, would she? Now, now, don't pout, darling; it does those *dreadful* little wrinkly things to your face. But really, you do know that it's so much easier for me to be on the same floor. No. No, thank you. I do not want to sleep on the third floor. No, it isn't that I might be lonely. It's that I've heard those *dreadful* stories about the violence in New York, and I just can't imagine sleeping alone on the third floor. Hedda, your secretary, will stay and sleep in the other guest room so I won't be alone? How darling, how simply darling of you to suggest something like that. But if there's not a man *with* me, it would really be much nicer to feel—and the next was said with a long sigh and a sidelong look at Peter— that there was a real man right next door in case of an emergency. The sort of emergency that might require Peter's immediate presence was never defined, but Peter was made to feel that his mother-in-law, unlike his wife, regarded him as a sort of walking alarm system.

≡

"It's like having an Arab terrorist in our midst," Sienna confessed to Anne when she phoned later.

"But she's so worldly and attractive," Anne answered slowly, deep in thought about her own mother's deficiencies. "Imagine how you'd feel if your mother could barely speak English."

"Nowadays," Sienna reminded her, "that's the key to the best drawing rooms. Who wants you unless you're Eurotrash or a South American with twelve houses and sixteen kids who can be married for their money by terribly social New Yorkers?"

Anne started to speak, to say something about adding the English to that list of rapacious foreigners, but then she stopped, for in her head she could hear Virginia speaking. "If your husband ever strays," she had told them one day, "don't acknowledge it. Don't even tell each other. Once the words are in the air, they have a life of their own, and something once said, even in confidence, can never be taken back. You always have time to tell one another. Don't hurry to share family secrets."

And so Anne, despite the Lolly Little item, had not spoken, although she longed to tell someone more about the unladylike lady in her life.

Sienna paused. Cautiously, nervously, she half whispered, "What about the other thing?"

"No word yet on him," Anne answered in the same tentative tone Sienna had used. You never knew who was listening when you spoke by phone.

"Your person didn't find—"

"I told you. No word yet." Now Anne sounded slightly agitated.

Sienna felt her stomach churn in fear. How could a man disappear for so many years without a trace?

≡

"Anne," Bronwyn said, her voice strong and bright, "I'm calling to invite the children to a little birthday party for Gwyneth tomorrow. It's her third, you know, and I'm having just a few children from her class."

Anne hesitated. Tomorrow was a big day. There was a new menu for the Dome's main dining room, a presentation for a convention—

"Please," Bronwyn pleaded.

But there was something different about Bronwyn's pleading. There was a new flirting sound, a cute little tease instead of the old drugged sound to her voice.

"All right." Anne found herself smiling. Then impetuously she asked, "Bronwyn, why do you sound so different to me?"

"What do you mean?"

"You sound sort of healthy."

"I am healthy."

"Is something going on I should know?"

"Oh, Anne, I'm dying to tell you. It's business, so you'll be interested."

"Sure," Anne said flatly. That's how they all think of me. Why would Anne care if it didn't make money?

"I'm doing the sweetest little shopping center north of Boston."

"I know. Pumpkin Corners."

"And instead of just doing big stores I'm going to offer entrepreneurs an opportunity to have little shops. There's going to be a little cookie shop and a place with homemade candies and a candle dipper and a bookshop—"

"Bookshop," Anne sniffed. "You can have lots of loving hands at home running shops, but when it comes to bookstores, don't offend the giants."

"But this bookshop doesn't compete with the giants, Anne."

"Then why do you want it?"

"Honestly?"

"Honestly."

"Because it's run by a boy who went to school with me, and the bookshop—" Bronwyn went on with Terence Bell's dreams as she planned to bring them to reality.

When she finished, Anne asked softly, "Is it the boy or the bookshop, Bronwyn?"

Bronwyn paused. "Is it that obvious?"

"I think so. But the big question is, Will Harold be able to tell?"

"No," Bronwyn answered. "He's so wrapped up in the Driscoll deal that there are days when he can't remember Gwyneth's name. He keeps calling her Vonna."

"Well, at least that's the name of his own daughter. Imagine if he were calling her a girlfriend's name."

Bronwyn longed to tell Anne more about Terry, but she stopped. Anne's unhappy response reminded her of that nasty item about Casey and the Englishwoman in Lolly Little's column. She and Sienna had both agreed to ask nothing further after their luncheon that day. If Anne wanted to unburden herself, they were all there, but until this moment Anne had acted as if her husband's name had never been linked with that of another woman.

So, instead of continuing, Bronwyn asked softly, "Is there anything you want to talk about with me?"

"Everything," Anne sighed. "Everything beginning with the phony school director who came back into our lives."

"Listen to me, Anne," Bronwyn said ferociously. "I think money is the answer. What if we go to him and offer—"

"Don't," Anne said decisively. "Never even hint at that idea. Once we give money, we're damned forever."

"Money didn't damn us," Bronwyn reminded her.

"Didn't it?" Anne asked bitterly. "Do you think if my husband had never made a deal in his life some little title would be wiggling her everything at him? Look, Bronwyn, if you want to go and make a separate deal, you'd better remember that if anything happens to us—"

"I swear," Bronwyn protested, "no matter what happens, I won't pay anything unless we agree. We're together. You and Sienna and I got into it together, and we'll get out of it together."

"I don't want it to be us against Virginia," Anne said.

"We'll do what we have to," Bronwyn promised. "If money isn't the answer, maybe there are other ways."

The toughness of a veiled threat from the usually passive Bronwyn chilled Anne.

What was happening to the Seconds?

≡

Bronwyn's phone call to Virginia started with a self-conscious little laugh. "Virginia, I know you think I'm overly involved with Gwyneth, but still, it's her third birthday tomorrow. I'm inviting a few mothers with their daughters, and since I feel as if you're my mother, will you come?"

There was an unbearably long silence, and Virginia said lamely, "It's not that I wouldn't love to be there—"

"You won't come?" The unspoken hurt underlined the way Bronwyn spoke the words.

"Oh, my dear, I'm flattered, and I shall certainly send a little remembrance."

"It's you I want, Virginia. You and Sienna and Anne are my family."

"Won't Sienna and Anne be there?"

"Anne's coming with the children, but Sienna is going up to the country with her mother. To be truthful, I'm relieved. Her mother is too much for me."

Virginia laughed. "Well, you can be sure that I'd be there if I found it at all possible—"

"Is it Gregory? Are you really so busy with him that you don't have time for your little Seconds anymore? Are we your Thirds now?"

"That's a cruel thing to say," Virginia admonished. "It doesn't become you."

"I'm sorry, but I guess you can tell how much I really want you with us."

There was a long, uncomfortable pause. "I have a doctor's appointment."

"Oh, Virginia, I'm truly sorry. How terrible of me—"

"Stop, dear. Please don't go from one extreme to another. It's nothing. Just an appointment that was made weeks ago, a difficult appointment with a very busy heart specialist—"

"A heart specialist?"

"Bronwyn," she added hastily, "not to worry, dear. But please forgive me for not being at the party."

"Of course, Virginia. I do love you, and I'm just sorry you won't be there."

"I understand. Now just leave me alone," she snapped.

Virginia, surprised at her brusqueness with Bronwyn, put the phone back and sat quietly for a moment. What was the undercurrent in all their lives at the moment? Had it blown through their friendship with Gregory's arrival? Or was she feeling insecure as she faced the possibility that a doctor, a specialist, might give her news she didn't want to hear?

What frightened her most? Death or life?

Gregory put his teacup on the heavy silver tray. "Virginia dear, I don't mean to eavesdrop, but I could scarcely avoid overhearing that conversation. Do you really have a medical appointment tomorrow?"

"I don't lie," she said flatly.

"Why didn't you tell me?"

"Gregory, the day I tell a man everything is the day I die."

He moved his body comfortably back into the deep armchair and laughed, a low, barely audible rumble. "You know what I love most about you, Mrs. North? Your incredible sense of humor."

23

PUFF IS UNDER THE BED, SO I GUESS THAT MEANS A RAINY DAY," Hedda said, her eyes fixed on Sienna. "If you want to cancel the trip to Bedford, I'm sure your mother and Mr. Marvell will have time to reschedule their day."

Sienna wrapped the violet wool robe tighter around her body. "Do you think I look heavier?"

"Sienna," Hedda pleaded, "you're not listening to me."

"Hedda, reality is getting to me. I want to deal with the metaphysical—no, I mean the physical . . ." Sienna's voice trailed into nothingness.

Hedda looked about the room. The large bedroom with its beautiful moldings and corner fireplace was lacquered in pale violet. Sienna's dressing room, which adjoined the north side of the room, was done in deep violet, and Peter's dressing room on the south side was painted in gray with a violet cast. Wasn't this room every woman's dream? Still it was not making Sienna happy, nor had Sienna seemed contented and relaxed for weeks. Hedda wanted to help her, to relieve the distress. Could she show her the way out of her present diffidence—or was it anger? Hedda could not decide, but she longed to do something for her. "Sienna, you've been so thoughtful and helpful. You got my sister into the chemotherapy program that's keeping her alive, and I know I can't ever repay you. But I'd do anything I could for you. Now I don't mean to bring up old hurts, but I know how sad you've been ever since Dr. Palmer called. I'm just a career woman who's never had a child, but if it means so much to you, should we look for an activity for you that involves—well, is about children?"

Sienna looked at Hedda. "How perceptive you are. We *should* look for a project with kids. But today's problem is my mother. I know she's my mother, and you probably think I should send her flowers and a card on Mother's Day, but you have to admit she's not exactly some sweet little old Whistler's mother."

Hedda smiled. "If I can help—"

"Yes." Suddenly Sienna seemed to have an idea she relished. "Yes, you can. See her so I don't have to. She's asleep in the bedroom next to me right now." Sienna paused. "Sure. Now she's next to me, now that I don't need or want her. You see, Hedda, all the years I wanted her she didn't want me. Now I have the most interesting husband in the family, and she's just divorced her fourth. So now I'm the star to follow. Well, tell my dear mother that we're leaving for the country at noon. Mr. Marvell is going to drive the small car with me, so you can tell"—and now Sienna accented slowly and bitterly the next three words—"my dear mother—"

Hedda looked at the floor in embarrassment. Her boss's obvious pain and lack of control were more than she wanted to see. "You'll take Puff?" Hedda interjected.

Sienna paused to consider her answer. "No, but you just gave me a good idea. Puff gets so cranky in a car in the rain, and I don't want to deal with him and my mother, so why don't you go in the limo, and then you can bring up the luggage and anything else we have to take from the City."

"Like your mother?" Hedda asked.

"Good idea. We'll send her up with you. Very clever of you, Hedda, to know how much baggage I have to take with me."

≡

"Come in," Peppy mumbled.

Hedda strode into the room and stood at the foot of the four-poster bed. "Mrs. Antonini, Mrs. Marvell asked me to tell you that we're going to the country at noon today."

"Noon? God, my daughter does everything backwards. Why so early? Doesn't she know that one goes to the country the night before and wakes up there at noon? You don't leave the City at noon—"

"We're leaving at noon," Hedda announced firmly.

"*We* are?" Peppy sat up in bed and clutched the silk sheet around her body.

"The driver will be in front of the building at noon," she continued as if Peppy had not spoken.

Now Peppy flopped back against the silk-cased pillows. "My daughter lives like a pagan in the midst of God's country. Who would ever believe she's mine?"

"Well, looks would tell anyone she's yours," Hedda answered stolidly. Like Sienna, Peppy was small-boned and dark-haired, but where Sienna's dark hair had the beginnings of gray, Peppy's hair was colored to an even brown-black. Against the perfect white skin, the face pulled taut by the expert knives in South America and Switzerland, Peppy looked at the world with the same large violet eyes as Sienna.

Peppy ran her hand through the long dark hair. "When the hairdresser comes today, tell him I want to be combed before we go," she ordered.

"Mrs. Marvell only has the hairdresser before a party," Hedda said.

"You mean she doesn't know enough to have her hairdresser here every day? She never learned anything about the way to live rich, did she? If she'd just paid more attention to me, I could have shown her so much. I know you're standing there looking at me and thinking that she's just Mrs. Antonini, just a mother from Cleveland, so what can she know? But I've lived rich all over the world."

"So I've heard," Hedda answered dryly.

Peppy waved her hand. "Never mind. So much nonsense. I don't know why I bother to tell you this, but I'll talk to anybody."

Hedda turned her square body and started out of the room.

"Oh, one minute—what's your name?" Peppy called.

"Hedda. Hedda Anderson."

"Hedda, I don't like to criticize my daughter, but evidently she doesn't know that one's maids must wear uniforms. You must get some for yourself immediately. With your kind of solid body, you'd look better in a uniform anyway. I think you ought to go out and get some—a blue, a pink, a white, a gray. And for formal service—"

"I'm not a maid, Mrs. Antonini," Hedda replied.

Peppy laughed. "Then what are you?"

"Mrs. Marvell's secretary."

Peppy stopped laughing. "Since when is my daughter important enough for a secretary? Secretaries are for men with jobs."

"Or for women who organize and run significant lives," Hedda added as she walked from the room. She stopped in the doorway and turned back. "Downstairs at noon. The car and driver will be waiting."

≡

Peter spoke to her in the telephone voice that Sienna knew well. Whenever he called from the office, and his secretary dialed the number, she knew that Peter would come on the line sounding as if he were talking to her and reading his mail or business journals at the same time.

If she ever asked, "What's going on?" or "How are things today, dear?" he would answer, "If I tell you now, what will we talk about later?" Peter always made her feel that she was interrupting his life's necessities with her life's silliness. Despite the fact that he always initiated the call, he made her feel an interloper in his business day, a necessary pause in a life that wasn't geared for pauses.

"Sienna, my pet," he began, and her antennae wiggled nervously. He was being unusually affectionate for an office call. What was going on?

"We'll drive up to the country, and I've asked Gene to join us."

"Gene?" She said the name as if it were a groan.

"Yes, that Gene." He laughed. "You know, the one that's my son, your stepson. Isn't that terrific? He's free this weekend, and I thought it would sort of balance things. We have your mother, and it gives us four for dinner. Don't you like that idea?"

"I like alone better. I think that's the best idea."

"Now, now, don't you want to share all this?"

"But you and Gene will talk about business, and my mother and I will—come on, Peter. Tell me the truth. Are you and Gene working on something this weekend?"

"You figure out everything, don't you? As a matter of fact, we're putting together a proposal. You know, I'm starting the Marvell Fund, and I think there's a way to pull Gene in at the beginning. Besides, if I'm named ambassador—" She heard the catch in his voice as if he thought saying the word would make it his impossible dream. "Well, let's just say if I got *it,* then this would make it easier to put my estate in order, and—"

"Oh, Peter." What if she were the reason he didn't get it? What if an ugly story were to break? Knowing Peter, he'd probably withdraw his name before undergoing any embarrassment with a Senate committee.

"Look, Sienna," he continued briskly, unaware of her thoughts, "it's ten fourteen, and if I'm to get out of here by noon and pick you up, I'd better get cracking now. Oh, by the way, I'll have Gene drive up with us, so you might want your mother to come in our car."

"Yes, dear." What else could she say?

The luggage had gone up to the country in the limousine, and Hedda had supervised the loading of the car before climbing in the back with Puff. Now Sienna stood on Park Avenue under the green canopy of her apartment building and, with the kind of undisputed authority used by a prep-school headmistress, directed the seating arrangement in the small four-door sedan. "Peppy, you and Gene get in the back," Sienna ordered. At least she'd drive up to the country in the wife's seat. She knew she had to speak before Peter suggested that the two women ride in back while he and Gene drove together in front and talked.

Peppy took a scented handkerchief from her tiny shoulder bag and said faintly, "Oh, I guess you never noticed, Sienna, but I can't ride in the backseat of a car."

Sienna's violet eyes narrowed, and she looked into the same eyes, wide and wondering, on her mother's face. "I never noticed you riding in front with a chauffeur, Peppy."

"That's the strange part, darling. I can ride in the back of a car in the City, but on a long drive I get carsick if I sit in the back. I suppose it's the speed of the car or something like that, but put me in the back and I'll just start throwing up. Well, it's not the most pleasant thing to talk about."

"Hey, not to worry." Gene shrugged his shoulders. "You can get sick on my shoulder. Hop in the back of the bus with me, Peppy. We'll hold hands and sing camp songs."

"Best to do that with your stepmother, dear," Peppy said. "I'll ride in front with your father."

At that moment the heavens opened, and the heavy rain began.

≡

Peter turned on the car radio and, hearing the classical music station that Peter always tuned to, Peppy reached for the dial. "Yech," she moaned, "none of that boring music for me. Let's find something that helps you ride in the rain."

Peter said nothing.

If I did that, Sienna thought, he'd just reach over and get the station he wanted. Why doesn't he do that with her? Why is he treating her so well? Sienna pulled herself into a corner of the rear seat; she'd show them. She wouldn't talk. Now they were over the Triboro Bridge, but no one seemed to have noticed that she wasn't talking. Gene, over the sounds of the car radio and the more persistent rain, was telling a funny story about a girl who lost a contact lens, and Peter and Peppy were adding their own bright and brittle remarks. Why couldn't Gene have stayed the sullen son he used to be?

When Gene Marvell's parents were divorced, he'd gone to live with his mother. Judith had never told him that the divorce had been her idea, nor had she told him about her romantic relationship with another woman lawyer. As a young boy, he'd been led to believe that his sister, Sidney, and he were the victims of male chauvinism, his exacting father's desire to rule. It was not until his college years that Gene understood the role his mother had played in his life, and he began to resent her for his estrangement from his father. So, his sophomore year in college he'd called Peter and asked to spend the Christmas holiday with him and his new wife.

It was an awkward meeting. Sienna was almost twenty years Gene's senior, old enough to be his mother but not as old as his mother. Still, Sienna wanted to avoid a catastrophic meeting, for she feared that if Peter and Gene did not have a successful reconciliation, both would assume that she was in some way to blame. With tenderness and patience Sienna made that first visit work. From that time on the father and son found the companionship both had missed, and each looked for times to spend together. After a while Sienna was grateful that she and Peter were already married when Gene rediscovered his father. Would Peter have needed her if he'd had Gene? She thought that Gene would be quite enough to give him that sense of family he enjoyed, and certainly Gene's company was more stimulating than hers to him, for with Gene he could talk about the business he loved. And with her? What could he talk about with her? Her life as an unloved child? Her rebellions? The times she ran away from home, or maybe that last time, the time she went to California and ended up in films—porno films? Well, at least that had been the basis for their meeting. She'd been making films for Raoul Wilde—"those creepy little films" was how she thought about them now. But then they were her weapon, her way of staying out of Cleveland, her way of getting back at the father who never looked at her and the mother who ran from bed to bed. She never thought that she was playing her mother's game, only that she was the family embarrassment, and she wanted to keep the pressure going, keep them anxious and angry. Don't get mad, get even. That had been her credo. And so she had taken off her clothes and put on her mask of diffidence and, with a calculated sexual energy, acted her roles. Raoul wrote his sleazy little film scripts on the backs of envelopes. "Vamp, kid. Do it from memory," he'd laugh, the camera rolling. And, with her body undulating with rhythms she created for herself, she built a mystique as the society sexpot. Those were the days she was living with Zeeno, the makeup man, on the beach, the pre-AIDS days of casual sex and twenty-minute relationships. She and Zeeno played a game: who had the prettiest boyfriend? Peter was a blind date arranged by a California lawyer, an acquaintance who thought Peter had been badly burned by marriage and needed an idea of what sex was really like. "How do you know what sex is like when you're married to a woman who has to initiate it fifty percent of the time? Why don't you meet a woman who'll initiate it a hundred percent? Or no percent? Or who's counting, for God's sake?" Peter wasn't ready for a woman like Sienna. He took her out once and, frightened, went back to New York sure that he would never see her again. When he met her again, she was an agent for Raoul Wilde, by then a mainstream director of television commercials. He thought she looked familiar the night he saw her at a restaurant. On the way back from the ladies' room, she'd stopped at his table and given him her card. "I think we've met before," she said. Their meeting was no accident, but he didn't know that. She had looked for him and had known where he would be that night. She remembered him from their one night together as the only man she'd ever met who seemed old enough to be a wise father to her—her own father died that year—and kind enough to be a loving husband. She was not going to let this one get away. And she didn't. This time he married her, for by now he was ready for a woman who, unlike New York women, didn't give answers before questions were asked and, unlike the very young women he saw, didn't need his money. A sweet woman who wasn't after his money, a sweet woman who gave sex as a part of life and not as a payment for life—yes, that was what he had wanted. And their deal of love and life suited them both. All he really knew about Sienna was that her father had been tough, successful, and cold. And her mother had been tough, successful, and hot. And Sienna hated them both.

Now the rain was letting up. Sienna put her hand on her chin and looked at the trees along the Bronx River Parkway. They were already starting to bud. She wiped a tear from her eye. This was supposed to be her time for budding, too. Instead she was stuck in the backseat of life with a grown-up stepson, and riding in front like the queen of all she surveyed was a mother who was calculating and cruel, so calculating and cruel that she could probably take a sweetie like Peter and—

Sienna sat up. She ought to know better than to daydream when her multimarried mama was so close to the driver's seat.

24

AT SEVEN THIRTY BRONWYN AND HAROLD WERE BREAKFASTING in the giant four-poster in their black-and-white bedroom. The room was lacquered in white, and dominating the fireplace wall was a black marble mantle, which, Bobby Binkly had assured them as he accepted their check, was "from one of the finest palazzos in Rome." But when Bobby, to complete this black-and-white bedroom scherzo, said, "Black sheets, darling," Bronwyn had asked Virginia if she really had to do everything the decorator suggested. Virginia had laughed and said, "Oh, why not? At least the morning paper won't come off on your bedclothes." Then, in a more serious tone, she'd answered softly, "You know, dear, it wasn't easy to get Binkly and Bobbers in the first place—"

Bronwyn had nodded gratefully.

"—and," Virginia had continued, "if you want to get some mileage out of a place like this and create a real setting for your daughter, you just have to make waves."

So Bronwyn awakened each morning on what she called her black waves. This morning the black waves were almost hidden by the two white breakfast trays, one holding Bronwyn's grapefruit and black coffee, the other holding Harold's breakfast of melon, cereal, three eggs, bacon, and rye toast. When Bronwyn tried to suggest to Harold that this might not be the healthiest way to start the day, he'd pushed her recommendations aside. "I was born poor, and someday I'm gonna die. But I'm gonna die rich, so in between I should at least eat rich." Further crowding the bed were ten morning newspapers, two copies of each of the four City papers and daily financial paper, a complete set for each of them.

Now, this morning, the black waves began to roll dangerously as Bronwyn turned to Lolly Little's column. Bronwyn's face flushed, and she could feel the angry red splotches begin to blossom on her cheeks and forehead.

"Harold, how could you?" she croaked and thrust the paper at him.

"Where? What?"

"Here." She punched her fist into the column. "Here. Here,

read what your best pal Lolly Little has to say about you," she answered sarcastically.

Harold took the paper from her eagerly and read aloud, " 'Seventy of the richest and most famous little girls and boys in our town think they're going to a small birthday party today at the home of Gwyneth Ashter. My, my, but they and their mommies (or nannies, depending who's on today) are going to be fooled. Gwyneth's mama, the brilliant real-estate lady Bronwyn Corcoran, and Gwyneth's papa, the brilliant deal-maker Harold Ashter, are turning this party into a fairy tale that—well, I won't be the one to tell what happens at the end. But stay tuned, and we'll see. Oh my, dear readers. It's not even April Fool's Day, and already the townfolk are competing for Fool of the Year Award.' "

Harold threw the paper aside. "How could she do that?" he fumed.

"Because you gave her the item," Bronwyn sniffed.

"Sure I did, but I told that idiot P.R. man not to call you brilliant and me brilliant. I don't want them building you up that way. It sounds like I can't do my deals without you."

"You think that's what's wrong with this kind of item?" Bronwyn snapped.

"So what do you think, Miss Moneybrains?"

Bronwyn leaned back against the black satin pillows and looked at her husband biting into his heavily buttered toast, the grease dribbling down the front of the black silk pajamas that his London tailor had made to match the bedroom.

Bronwyn shook her head dejectedly. "You just don't get it, do you?"

"Get it?" he asked, his mouth stuffed with his breakfast egg. "I get as good as I give."

Now Bronwyn shook her head. Had he really said something so inappropriate, so silly and offensive? And then she remembered. Oh, this was a good one for Terry. Wasn't it just yesterday that she and Terry had played a game on the phone, each thinking of the greatest non sequiturs of their lives? She clapped her hands now at the thought of telling him, and she laughed out loud. It would take Terry a long time to match this one. *I get as good as I give.*

"What's so funny?" Harold demanded.

"Nothing. Nothing at all. I'm just . . . mmmm, just trying to do anything to keep from getting upset on a day when I want everything to be perfect." Then Bronwyn paused, absorbed in her own thoughts. "No, Harold," she said with conviction, "I really am not going to let Lolly Little undo me."

"You're right," he said. "Listen, did you ask Vonna to come to the party?"

"Of course," Bronwyn answered quickly.

"I know you don't like her," Harold said.

Bronwyn thought for a moment. Certainly she could not admit that the sight of bulky Vonna always brought Rosabelle to mind. "It's not about liking her or not liking her. I just don't think a nineteen-year-old adores hanging on the coattails of our life."

But Harold was not listening; he had returned to his newspaper.

Bronwyn pushed the paper down so she could see him. "Harold, I know you give Vonna money and apartments, but let me ask you something. When you're doing all those deals down on Wall Street, can't you find some young man for her, someone she might like?"

He peered at her over his glasses. "Look, you know what her problem is. I know what her problem is. She's fat, and she has a face like her mother's. Why should I introduce her to somebody I do business with? So she can screw up my life and kill deals for me? She's a dumb girl, won't go to school and won't work. All she wants is a house in the suburbs and a country club membership so she has a place to go for regular games. It could be tennis games. It could be bridge games. It could be walking lessons. All I know is it's gotta be regular. For her that's the perfect life. A husband who doesn't get in the way while she goes and does something regular. Listen, I'll be happy to give her the house and the country club. I'll buy her the sports car so she can drive to the shopping center and meet her mother for lunch, but I'm not going to give her somebody who's my lifeblood. It has to be some other kind of guy."

"Harold, just knowing that Vonna is going to be around today is enough to make it a two-Valium day for me. Can't you find her the man?"

"What I have to find is some jerkwater hayseed who doesn't know the color of money. I'd give the dummy a gofer job with me, and then we can all live happily ever after. But you think it's so easy to find her a man? Go ahead. You find her some dummy, and I'll do the rest."

"I don't know dummies," she said dejectedly. "I guess it's harder for us to find dummies than smart guys."

"Hey, wait a minute," Harold said, ignoring the white linen napkin on his tray and wiping his mouth on his pajama sleeve. "You do know a dummy. What about that bookseller you're putting in Pumpkin Corners? You know, the one who needs a haircut, that guy who squints. He was here with you the other day going over his floor plan when I came home. Now, there's a guy who looks like he doesn't know reality from the New York Mets. Couldn't he use a rich wife?"

Bronwyn swallowed slowly. "Yes," she replied softly, "yes, he could use a rich wife. I've been thinking that's what he needs."

"So why not Vonna?"

"She's not his type."

He shrugged. "Well, there you are. I tried. So now *you'd* better look."

25

THE FRONT OF THE ASHTER HOUSE ON FIFTH AVENUE HAD BEEN transformed to resemble a storybook palace. All through the night eight Broadway stagehands had created a faux front of white marble and built a drawbridge over the steps, so that seventy toddlers who had just proudly learned to climb steps were now asked to walk across a moat created by a circulating water system over the stairs.

Inside the house in the foyer two uniformed pages waited to check each child's wraps and introduce the child to Mr. Funnybones and Grizelda, the two most popular characters on children's television. Eff and Gee, as the characters were nicknamed, took the children upstairs, where Princess Gwyneth waited to greet her guests.

Princess Gwyneth stood wordlessly outside her very own ballroom as her guests approached. In her pink party dress with its sixteen-tiered tulle skirt, miniature puffed sleeves, and satin-ribboned waist, she looked like a doll, waxen and untouchable.

Next to Princess Gwyneth stood her mother in a long white

dress, a golden crown on her head, and a wand in her hand.

"Hello, Mrs. Ashter," said the first nanny.

"It's not my mother. It's my fairy godmother," Gwyneth corrected her. "That's what we're playing today."

Standing on the other side of Bronwyn was her father, his hair combed neatly over his bald spot. He wore a business suit. "Ha ha," he said. "You can see I don't believe in fairy stories. I'm dressed like a daddy. I pay the bills."

Bronwyn paid no attention. It really didn't matter what he said. This was the birthday party of a princess, and if the father wanted to be a toad, that was his problem.

"Oh, look," Harold exclaimed. "Anne's here. Wait till she gets a load of this. Her old man can't match this one."

Anne, her daughter Fudge, and Fudge's nanny, Miss Patch, stepped off the elevator and, as they did, they shook their heads in disbelief. Through the reception area outside the ballroom they could see the magic in the next room. The drawing room, normally filled with Binkly & Bobber treasures, had been emptied, the ceiling was lowered, and it had been converted into a children's ballroom with miniature crystal chandeliers and tiny tables with miniature gold chairs, and on each small round table was a doll-size birthday cake with three candles. Oh, Miss Patch thought, wait till they hear about this party at the Nanny School in London. She looked around. Yes. There were lots of nannies here to chat it up. This would make the nanny prices soar. If these Americans wanted to spend this on parties, just think what they'd spend next year on nannies.

Even Anne, a much-decorated veteran in the wars of outrageous spending, was speechless as she stooped low to kiss Bronwyn on both cheeks.

"Oh, Anne, what a friend you are. I really need you here today."

"Congratulations, darling," she said to Bronwyn. She searched for words to describe the opulence. "Well, this is some way to announce that you made it through the Terrible Twos. Seriously, I thought you said there would be just a few children from the class."

"Well, it's what *he* wanted," Bronwyn said, "but the strange thing is that now that it's here and done, I kind of like it, too." Her obvious pleasure and pride were reflected in her eyes. She bent down. "Fudge, dear, how beautiful you look."

Fudge, Anne's three-year-old daughter, and Gwyneth's class-mate at the Episcopal Nursery School, responded to the compliment by lifting her smocked dress over her head and wordlessly displaying her lace underpants.

"Put your dress down," Anne commanded.

"No," said Fudge, her voice smothered in the folds of her dress.

"Now," Anne commanded in a tone that sent grown men to their knees.

"No, I won't, and you can't make me," said the three-year-old.

"You won't believe this, Bronwyn," Anne confessed, "but that's the only sentence this child can say."

"I'd really love to talk to you, but here comes one of Harold's partners. Just a minute."

"Miss Patch," Anne called, and the nanny, as if she were a robot operated by remote control, wheeled into action.

"Yes, Mrs. Burrows?"

Anne looked around. There was a sea of nannies. Obviously this was a mother event, not a place for a baroness of business. "I'm leaving. I'll stop by the nursery to kiss the children good-bye before we go out tonight. Don't worry. I'll leave the car here for you. I'll take a cab and go back to my office."

"Yes, ma'am," Miss Patch said. She liked nothing better than being left alone with the child and the car. Miss Patch bade her employer good-bye and now looked at Fudge, her dress still over her head. "Put your dress down at once, Virginia." Miss Patch refused to call Fudge by anything except the name she was christened.

"No, no, no," Fudge answered.

"This is Miss Patch, and I said to put your dress down."

The child put her dress down, looked up at her nanny, and said, "What do I get for being good?"

Miss Patch answered, "A pat on the head and a smile from your nanny."

"Thank you, Miss Patch," the child answered and curtsied politely.

≡

Standing in a corner was a dark-haired, heavyset young woman.

"Who's she?" Miss Patch asked Phoebe Echo, her best friend nanny.

"Doesn't work for anyone on the Upper East Side, I'll wager."

"Dreary-looking person, isn't she?"

"Can't work very hard. She's got nails out to Tenafly."

"Well, her looks won't raise the price of nannies. They can't be paying her much."

"I hear that Maeve's been raised to five hundred dollars a week."

Miss Patch smiled condescendingly. "I've been getting five hundred for a year. I go to five fifty at Christmas."

"My word!"

"And I'm going to ask for three round trips to London each year instead of two. I do want to get home in the summer, don't you?"

"Yes. It seems a bit tight to go just for Easter and Christmas."

"We do get three weekends off a month, but there's no family to share that time, so it's a bit bumpy, don't you think?"

"Do they ever complain about what they pay you?" Phoebe asked.

"They wouldn't dare," Miss Patch said smartly. "You don't think Mrs. Burrows wants my job, do you?"

The heavyset young woman wandered over to the two nannies. "Do you like the party?" she asked.

"More than the children do," said Phoebe.

"Oh wait, there's a big surprise coming," the dark-haired woman said as she reached in her purse for a cigarette.

"You're not smoking here, are you?" Miss Patch asked. "Not with all these children. Do your people permit it?"

"My people?"

"Yes. Aren't you a nanny?"

The heavyset woman laughed. "My name is Vonna Ashter. I'm the original daughter."

The fairy godmother, better known as Gwyneth's mother, tapped her magic wand, and the noise almost stopped for a moment. Then as the harpist played a glissando, Bronwyn said, "This is magic time, children. Outside two magic pumpkins await. Go downstairs, and get your wraps. Go outside the palace, and get into either of the two pumpkins that awaits, and you will be taken to Magic Land."

"Where's that?" Miss Patch whispered to Vonna Ashter.

"Oh, she took two buses and had them fitted up like pumpkins with white horses, and she's dragging all the rotten little brats down to the family store."

"The family store?" Phoebe questioned.

"Uh-huh. My father just bought Toyz and Joyz for Girlz and Boyz, and he's closing it for two hours. The kids can go in and pick out any toy they want."

"Any toy?" Miss Patch asked. "Surely they put some of the expensive things away like the doll houses and those big animals."

"Oh no," Vonna explained, "that's what they left out. It's the little stuff, the wind-up toys, that they put away. If it costs less than a hundred dollars, my father won't give it away."

Miss Patch gasped. "Even Casey Burrows doesn't do things like this."

"I'd tell my father that," Vonna said, "but it would make him happy. And making that bastard happy isn't my job."

26

THE AIR WAS WET WITH THE PROMISE OF SPRING, AND UNDER-foot the uneven sidewalks trapped Anne's heels as she left the Ashter house.

Bellamy appeared at her elbow to aid her.

"Any news?" she asked.

Bellamy shrugged. "Only what I told you. He got some land up in New Haven—"

"New Hampshire," she corrected brusquely.

"Yeah, that's right. So he got this place for a camp, but he made it a school or something—"

"I know that," she interrupted impatiently. "I knew that before you even investigated him, Bellamy."

"I got a few lines out, ma'am."

"Better if you had a few markers," she countered.

Bellamy ran a finger under his collar. The Missus sure must want this guy a lot. He swallowed hard. The Great Man better not find out about this. Wordlessly Bellamy opened the car door.

"No, I'm not taking the car," she told him crisply. "Stay here and wait for Miss Patch and Fudge."

He nodded without speaking.

"Wait," she demanded. "I'm going to check the office before I go over to the hotel. I'll phone from the car."

Again he nodded and led her to the smart little European car, opened the door, and pulled down her carefully concealed desk and telephone. To ensure their security, the Burrowses, like most rich people throughout the world, chose small, unmarked cars to transport their children. Anne, who felt always the need to be near both a telephone and desk, had had her family car specially equipped with a mobile office.

She dialed the familiar number. "Wilfred," she demanded, her office style returning quickly after her moments of motherhood. "Yes, yes, I want Mr. Bilmont. This is Mrs. Burrows." She paused, and then exploded, "Well, if he's my secretary, why isn't he at my desk?" Another short pause and then an irritated, "I don't see why he has to go to the bathroom when I call." She tapped her foot as she waited for him to come to the telephone. "Yes, yes, Wilfred. No, stop telling me why you weren't there. You weren't, and that's that. Now. Quickly. Are there any messages? I can return calls now. Yes. Give me the list." She listened and ticked her response to each. "You make that call. Tell them no sale." Another answer was, "Price is too high. Get them down two million, and we'll take it." The last two names she doodled on the pad in front of her. "Mrs. North? How strange she should call the office. No, never mind. I'll return that call. And Lolly Little. Yes, I'll call Lolly Little myself. She's too calculating for you, Wilfred. I'll handle that. See you later."

Anne first returned her friend's call. "You won't believe the party I just left, Virginia. Bronwyn has redefined birthdays."

"She did invite me," Virginia said, "but I had—umm, I had other plans."

"I hope that doesn't mean you're annoyed with us," Anne said quickly, a small fear clutching her stomach.

"No, no," Virginia answered. "I'm just resting this afternoon. And stop thinking I'm annoyed if I'm not there. What has gotten into my Seconds lately? You all seem so jumpy. I'm happier than I've been in a long time."

"Of course. I'm sorry," Anne said quickly. "Oh, Virginia," she confessed, "I'm worried because my office told me that there's a call from Lolly Little. Why do you think she wants to talk to me? What do you hear?"

"Not a word more about him and—and anything that might worry you," Virginia reported.

"Then why is Lolly Little calling?"

"Perhaps because Gregory and I went to Bonnie Brickmaster's dinner last night—"

"Don't tell me Gregory is buying a co-op," Anne said darkly.

"No." Virginia laughed. "Just because Bonnie invites people who are in the real-estate market doesn't mean she doesn't also invite—"

"—the most interesting people in New York," Anne finished.

"You must admit she's running the only salon in town."

"Yes," Anne said, "but if you're willing to invite people you've never met to your home so that you can buy and sell them apartments, then I suppose you can run a salon."

"You seem very hard on Mrs. Brickmaster today, Anne. You're a tough businesswoman yourself."

"But I don't call strangers and invite them to my home," Anne repeated.

"Enough of that," Virginia said.

Anne was silenced by the only person who could effectively silence her.

"Now," Virginia continued, "perhaps the reason Lolly Little called is that Gregory was seated next to her, and she told him that she was going to do a story for an English magazine about the American spa bathroom, and he thought it would be very good publicity for you. You know, with your wonderful style and taste, you can bring an unusual perspective to the hotel business. I'm sure you understand even better than I because you're smart about public relations, and I'm really rather a novice."

"It is a good idea," Anne admitted. "We want to get a smart British crowd at the hotel, and that would be perfect. My public-relations firm has been working on some kind of story."

"Good. Then ring her up," Virginia advised. "You make the call, dear. Don't ask an assistant to do it, and don't give it to your public-relations person to do. For some reason professionals seem to offend these writers once they get invited to parties. You know, Lolly would rather think she's your friend."

"My friend," Anne responded sarcastically.

"I promise she won't discuss anything unpleasant because if she does"—now Virginia laughed a shy, girlish laugh totally apart from her usual tone—"I won't let her sit next to Gregory at any more of Bonnie Brickmaster's parties."

Anne leaned back against the golden leather seats. "You're a very shrewd woman, Virginia." Then she hung up and waited a moment before calling Lolly Little. No, Miss Little was out. Would Mrs. Burrows care to leave word? Yes, yes she would, and the word was yes. A vocal, definite yes. Yes, yes, Mrs. Burrows would be willing to be photographed in her sybaritic bathroom at the Dome. Yes, yes, Mrs. Burrows would be willing to be photographed in her three-room bathroom in Southampton. Yes, yes, Mrs. Burrows would be willing to be photographed in her rosewood-and-marble bathroom in London.

After the call, Anne breathed a sigh of relief, opened the car door, and headed on foot for the Dome. She wanted to breathe the spring air. She wanted to think about what her friend Virginia had done for her. Virginia had made Lolly beholden to her. Lolly would not print any more innuendo about Casey and some overweight English lady. Now she and the Seconds really must focus on Virginia and find the way to save her from Gregory, if indeed a woman as strong as Virginia needed saving.

≡

"Jeez." Casey Burrows threw the newspaper across the room to Lady Diandre Devon. "Can you believe that Frenchman has his own private Concorde?"

"But he's the premier of the country," Lady Diandre reminded him.

"Yeah. But what's his net worth? Three francs and a French bread?"

"Did you say French bed, darling?"

Casey laughed and got up from the big armchair where he was sitting. "I never had so much fun with anybody," he said.

"Oops, luv, stay on your side of the room," she cautioned flirtatiously.

"I cross the line whenever I want," he said.

She couldn't believe he'd throw her the opening she wanted. "And I am about to make a small crossing myself."

"What does that mean? You don't like this place? Hey, Didi, don't you think I'm good to you?"

"You're super, darling. I mean you're really super. I think this flat—"

"You mean this apartment."

"Well, it's divine. And I do appreciate your putting it in my name."

"It's only four rooms, but it's got that terrace, so it's worth an easy three mil because you're on Fifth Avenue," he assured her.

"You pay the maintenance, and you're very generous, but I feel a bit old-fashioned, darling."

"What do you mean?"

"I do come from good family, and my father wouldn't approve of my being supported without any visible means of support of my own. Do you know what I mean?"

"You think I'm keeping you?"

"Frankly no. I'm keeping you, Casey. I'm keeping you from going totally bonkers with a pursuit of success that leaves no time for you to perfect your extraordinary sexual prowess."

Casey laughed. "You think I'm good?"

Didi smiled. No matter how rich or powerful they were, they all asked the same question, "Am I good?" Sometimes they asked, "Was it good for you?" which she recognized as just another variation of the same question.

"Yes, you're good. You're very good," she assured him, "and that's why it will be so difficult for me to leave. But I am going to sail on the first crossing the QE2 makes this spring."

"You can't leave."

"Can't? I must."

"Why?"

"I've told you. I need a job."

"But you're a lady."

"And that's why I need a job."

"Didi, don't I give you everything you want?"

"You're wonderful to me, Casey, but I can't live on my back."

"You make me happy. Didi, I don't want another bitch on wheels. One Anne is all I can handle."

"I could never be Anne. She's so much smarter than I, and she can run a business. I can't do that."

"For God's sake, I keep telling you that Anne doesn't run the business. I do. Now tell me what you want."

She pouted prettily. "A job, Casey, so that I can feel useful. Otherwise I'm going back to London."

"Don't go." He was pleading. "I can't get along without you."

"In that case, sit next to me, and let's talk about it," she said softly.

Casey loosened his tie and sat next to her on the sofa facing Central Park. Outside this room was the beginning of spring. Inside himself he could feel a new kind of beginning, a new kind of Casey Burrows coming to life. "I never wanted a woman before," he said. "And even if I wanted a woman, I never thought I wanted one like you. I mean, why would I want a woman who doesn't even talk the way I do?"

She nodded sympathetically.

"Don't leave me," he said. He reached for her awkwardly.

She slipped through his arms, opened the doors to the terrace, and walked outside.

"Come back in here," Casey commanded.

Lady Diandre leaned against the railing and turned back to the room where Casey stood. She was wearing a pale blue caftan, and her copper hair was framed against the blue sky.

"You look like some painting in the museum," Casey said in surprise.

"You are a poet," she said.

He walked out on the terrace, oblivious of the chill in the air. "What will it take to keep you here?" he asked. "You've got this apartment, and I'll give you money. Now what kind of job are you talking about?"

"Maybe public relations. I think I'd be rather good at that sort of thing, and I could certainly help attract the London crowd to the hotel."

"Not a bad idea," Casey mused. "You could handle my P.R. personally. Anne's got too much going, and it's starting to look like she owns the hotel. Don't you ever forget I own everything, and she runs what I let her run."

"I don't ever forget that," Lady Diandre said, her eyes meeting his.

"Do you think you can handle a power guy? You know, do you understand my language?"

"Oh, I've a smashing idea," she said with a burst of spontaneous enthusiasm. "Suppose you teach me a word a day. That way I'll know it all in time. And like everything with us, Casey, we'll move ahead—but not too fast."

He laughed and pressed his body against hers. "Tell me a word you want explained."

"Arbitrage," she said, as if it were a part of his body.

He shrugged his shoulders. "Hell, I don't know how to explain it. I just do it."

"Then it's just like love," Lady Diandre said with great understanding as she took his hand and led him back into the warm apartment.

27

As THE CAR PASSED THROUGH THE IRON-GATED ENTRY AND UP the long drive, Sienna realized once again just how much she loved this house in Bedford. Built in the 1920s, it was, as the real-estate agent had assured them, a classic of the period. "It's only thirteen acres," Sienna explained apologetically to her critical mother as they approached the house, "but when you see it all, I know you'll approve."

How could anyone, even a perfectionist like Peppy, fail to warm to this gracious home with its stucco and slate exterior, its wrought-iron portico forming a walkway from the drive to the great oak door?

Sienna moved anxiously in the seat. "What do you think so far, Peppy?"

"Where's the tennis court?" she asked.

"To the right behind the pool. See that grove of maples? Behind it is the pool house, and then there's the tennis house." Sienna now felt a sense of self, her pride returning as she pointed out the sights of her world, a world anchored on one end by a Park Avenue triplex and on the other by this unfarmlike farm. "The barn is there." She pointed to the left.

"You know I ride?" Peppy asked Peter.

"He knows," Sienna answered. Hadn't Peppy told him that each of the few times that she had spoken to him?

"How good are you, Peppy?" Peter asked, once again ignoring Sienna.

"I've won more ribbons than—"

"—than any woman her age," Sienna finished, "but look how many years you've been riding."

"What is the name of your house?" Peppy asked.

"Peter's Principal," Sienna answered.

Peppy shuddered. "Whose idea was that?"

"Sienna's," Peter said with some embarrassment. "Well, actually it wasn't really Sienna. It was—well, it was a kind of friend."

"It was a man I knew in California who came out here and saw the house and named it. It was my friend Zeeno."

"Zeeno. What an unusual name," Peppy said.

"He was like a mother to me," Sienna said pointedly.

Gene Marvell, seated in back with Sienna, sensed that an unfriendly volley was about to begin. He did not want to revisit his childhood memories with his father and yet another wife who was unable to deal with him. "Dad," Gene interrupted, "instead of staying in the main house, I think I'd like to be in the guest house this weekend."

"Sure," his father said.

"Oh," Sienna said, turning to Gene, "I'd planned to have you in the room next to ours." She saw his surprise, but how could she say that she wanted her mother in the guest house, that she wanted her mother as far from her as possible? "Besides, I'm not sure the guest house is ready. It's so early in the season," she added.

"Hey," Gene assured his stepmother, "no sweat, Sienna. Don't worry if it's not made up. I'll take care of things. Slow down, Dad. I'll get out here and go over to the house. I'm tired of sitting anyway."

Peter stopped the car and then watched Gene walk briskly toward the guest house.

"Your son is a very appealing young man," Peppy said to Peter. "It's really such a joy to see children who grow up to be polite and caring."

"Is that supposed to be another criticism?" Sienna asked.

"Stop that, Sienna," Peter said, turning toward her in the

backseat. "Can't your mother compliment my son without your getting offended?"

Sienna sank into the seat and felt that old, familiar squeeze on her heart, that hurt that only her mother could give. She said nothing. She would just wait for Peter to apologize.

But Peter, intent on pursuing more sweet words from Peppy, added, "He's really a good boy, and he's going to be great in business. One thing about kids today. They're smart. They have a kind of guts I never did. I don't know where they get this confidence."

Now Sienna forgot her self-promised rule not to speak. "Maybe he has the one thing you never had, a rich father," she blurted.

"Well, you had a rich father, and you didn't do a thing with it," Peppy said to her daughter.

Sienna tightened her mouth. Why couldn't she learn to keep quiet when her mother was nearby?

When the car stopped in front of the iron portico, Carson and Kathleen, the couple who managed Peter's Principal, came forward to greet the owners. "Welcome home," Carson said formally and then announced, "The other car with your luggage has already arrived, and Miss Hedda went down to the guest house to make sure everything was set for your mother."

"Mr. Gene is staying in the guest house," Peter informed him, "so Mrs. Antonini will stay in the room next to ours. You'll like it," he said, turning to Peppy. "There's our bedroom, a sitting room, and then another bedroom on the other side. We'll share the sitting room with you. We've never done that before, but then you're no ordinary guest. Now I'm going upstairs to unpack. You girls can inspect the house together." He kissed his mother-in-law on the cheek, and Sienna's eyes filled with tears of rage. Did Peter really think that his kindness to Peppy would result in Peppy's kindness to her? Or was his courtesy to Peppy his way of saying that he wanted equal consideration for Gene? Couldn't he see for himself what she saw?

Peppy was silent until Peter disappeared at the top of the stairway. Then she looked about the entrance hall, turned to Sienna, and shrugged. "Not exactly unexpected, dear. You certainly do give a decorator his way." Then, walking briskly ahead, she strode into the paneled living room, its fireplace glowing with a freshly laid fire and the cozy chintz of the room adding a cheery glow.

Sienna lagged two steps behind. What negative could Peppy possibly find in this, the quintessential country room?

Peppy gasped. "My God, darling, I don't believe it. This is so boring. This is the most boring room I've ever seen. Everything looks as if it had been put in place by a nun or old maid headmistress."

Peter laughed out loud. "Thanks for telling her, Peppy. I think it looks like my last wife did it."

Sienna wheeled around. "I thought you were upstairs."

"I was, but I wanted to hear what Peppy really thought, and I figured that if she thought I went upstairs, I'd hear a little unadulterated Peppy."

Peppy put her arm through Peter's. "I've never met a man like you," she said softly. "No wonder you're a winner. Believe me, after four losers I know a winner when I see one."

Sienna took a sharp breath. Damn you. Damn you, Peppy. But I know something you don't. I know how to come up from the gutter and make life work. Keep going, Peppy, because no matter what you do, I won't let you have my husband. I won't let you have my life.

Sienna forced herself to smile. "What a sense of humor you people have. Isn't it good that I can laugh with you? Now run off, you two. By the by, I didn't have a chance to tell you, Peter, but there's a dinner here tonight to welcome"— she paused before she said the word—"Mother."

"I told you to call me Peppy," her mother said quickly.

"I always call things by their rightful names," she said softly. "My mother made me do it."

"Would you like to ride?" Peter asked Peppy.

"Yes," she said brightly, "in your car. Let's go to town, Peter. I want to do a little looking around."

She was wearing jeans and a sweatshirt, her hair piled on top of her head, and she was bent over the tulips in the greenhouse when they left, so they never even noticed her as Peter, behind the wheel of the two-seater English car he loved, sped down the drive with Peppy at his side.

Sienna rubbed her eyes with the sleeve of her sweatshirt and turned toward the imposing house. Was everybody conspiring to

take it all away from her? Could she—should she—just sit by and
watch while Gregory threatened her on one side and Peppy on the
other?

No! She cut a stem ferociously.

No. Despite Anne's assurance that she was investigating on her
own for the Seconds, Sienna knew that Anne was more worried
about Casey's present than Gregory's past. Better slow down and
think this through.

Snip. Put a tulip in the basket.

Cut. Add the green.

Snap. Get Hedda.

Yes, of course.

She straightened her body, shook the kinks from her legs, and
walked quickly into the garden room.

Carson was standing there. "Madam," he inquired, "would you
like to have me take some of these baskets down from the wall for
you?"

"No, thank you. Just ask Miss Anderson to come by, please."
Could he tell that she trusted no one in the house except Hedda?

≡

"Pretty tulips," Hedda said as she fingered the pale pink and
deep rose cuttings.

"Yes, aren't they?" Sienna said, slowly arranging them in the
baskets. Standing back and admiring her handiwork, Sienna murmured, "Confidential mission, Hedda."

"Yes, the colors are lovely," Hedda said loudly. Soft-voiced she
answered, "Whatever you want."

"Your old law firm? Still have good connections?"

"Very."

"Find me a young lawyer, and make sure that he's no one who
knows the people I know. Get me somebody you really trust. I want
a check on Gregory Sawyer."

Hedda put her hand to her mouth in surprise, and a moment
later she smiled knowingly. "I knew he was up to something. I
wondered when you'd all catch on."

"I'm not telling you any more than I just did."

"You mean just his name and not what we're looking for? Old
wives? New treasure?"

"I'm not sure what we're looking for until we find it. Meanwhile I just made you vice president in charge of getting the goods on the old boy."

"Good as done," Hedda replied crisply. "Oh, one more thing," she said in a low voice, "your mother and your husband just returned from town."

"And was my mother giggling and clutching my husband?" The disdain was evident in Sienna's voice.

"No, but she was clutching a package."

"You mean he bought her a present?"

"I think so."

Sienna jammed a red tulip into a basket and broke the stem. "Don't be annoyed," Hedda cautioned.

"But nothing stays where I put it."

"No, nothing does," Hedda agreed as she leaned over and gently placed a white tulip in the basket. It looked perfect. "But you have to be careful because it's so easy to substitute things in this world."

"I get the message," she assured Hedda. She took a breath to calm herself. "These baskets are pretty, aren't they?"

"I love what you've done with this room. I think the hanging baskets on the wall give it a real flair. Your flower room looks like a real workroom for a gardener."

"In the summer when the cutting garden is at its best, we'll be able to do some beautiful arrangements." Sienna paused a moment. "After you finish your little arrangement for me."

"Yes, and it will all be so easy and natural, so much prettier than those stiff professional arrangements," Hedda agreed.

"Remember when we always did those single orchids in their pots for every table?"

Hedda nodded. "Now we have to work to keep the weeds out of the garden."

"Those orchids were very costly, about two hundred dollars each, and they lasted a couple of weeks."

"And everybody thought they were so pretty. No one could see what was killing them underneath. Perhaps," Hedda said slowly, "you could try a weedkiller."

"Good idea. We'll put that thought on hold, however. It may be a little drastic for now. And you know that while I'm not exactly a trendsetter, I do tend to prefer my own arrangements.'"

"I don't think you're like everybody," Hedda said loyally.

Sienna shook her head affirmatively. She could see her mother advancing toward the garden room. It was time to stop playing this word game.

"Sure, I am," Sienna said. "I'm just like all the other women up here. Wait and see. I'll be dressed just like everybody else tonight. I'll wear an ankle-length dress or else pants with a loose flowing top. And instead of the emeralds or rubies, I'll do the country thing and wear strands of some kind of craft beads, probably American craft jewelry because it's the craze of the moment, although there have been times when we all wore Mexican jewelry or Egyptian bracelets. And, of course, in my wild, single days I wouldn't be caught dead without jeans and Indian jewelry."

"Sienna, here you are." It was Peppy's shrill voice, and Sienna, hearing it, turned unhappily. Her cheeks burned, her throat went suddenly dry with the increasingly uncomfortable physical feeling her mother caused in her.

"Sienna, darling," Peppy trilled. "Look what Peter bought for me." And from layers of tissue, she brought forth a stoneware pitcher. "Nineteenth century. Not very valuable, of course, but isn't it dear?"

Sienna nodded, unable to speak a word.

"Look at these cunning drawings on the side. It's called 'September Sport,' and it has these sweet lovers on one side—"

Sienna's eyes burned, the resentment now extending from her mother to Peter. How could he?

"And look at the poem on the side," Peppy said.

"I—I can't read it right now," Sienna choked.

"Oh, I'll read it to you," her mother volunteered. "Listen to this. It's adorable.

"May the Mighty and Great
Roll in Splendor and State
I envy them not I declare it,
I eat my own Lamb,
My Chicken and Ham
I shear my own Sheep and I wear it.

> *So you jolly Boys now,*
> *Here's God speed the Plow*
> *Long life and content to the Farmer."*

"It's very pretty," Hedda said quickly, to cover Sienna's obvious distress.

"Just look at it, Sienna," her mother commanded. "Put down those damned tulips, and look at my present."

Hands shaking, Sienna did as she was told. She took the pretty pitcher in her wet hands, reached to brush back the hair falling in her eyes, and as she did the pitcher crashed to the tile floor and broke into a hundred pieces.

28

WHEN MISS AGNES FOLEY DIED IN THE LATE 1980s AND BE-queathed her small stone cottage in Maine to her two nephews, Terence Bell and Sean Foley, the cousins didn't know what to do with this unexpected gift from an aunt they'd seldom seen and scarcely knew. "Let's live in the place because then we can sell it in two years and make a bundle," the pragmatic Sean, a computer salesman, advised. Terry wasn't certain why a lived-in stone cottage in a remote part of Maine would become more valuable with people in it, but once he saw the cottage, he asked no more questions.

It was the house of his dreams. It fit his fantasy life better than that year clerking in a Boston bookstore or the two years as a ski resort waiter or even the summer as a companion for a shriveled old man with a remarkable library of his own.

At first Terry had thought he'd spend his two years of residency reading and writing, perhaps creating his own paradise of personal freedom, but when Sean finally saw the spare house, he'd shaken his head. "Terry," he'd said, "we'd better get jobs, because it's not going to be much fun in this place, and I'm not sure we'll last two years in this dump." Sean had found a job immediately; it involved travel, and that suited him because he certainly didn't want to spend all his days and nights in this hick place. Terry went into the little village and got a job clerking at The Corners, a combination stationery and newspaper and magazine shop. His warm, outgoing ways made him a town favorite, and when the plans for Pumpkin Corners were announced, Sean saw the opportunity of a lifetime for the cousins. "Let's open a bookstore," he announced when he came home after a beery night at the town tavern. Terry said yes immediately, but he had little talent for putting a business plan together, so Sean pulled the numbers, wrote the proposal, and went to see the hired hand who was sent to scout possible local store participation. When Sean came back and told Terence that the answer was no and showed him the prospectus for Pumpkin Corners, Terence Bell—for the first time—read the names of the people involved. It was then that he recognized Bronwyn's name and, with his cousin's urging, went to New York to see her. Personable Terence Bell presented businesslike Sean Foley's plan, and this time the cousins were awarded the lease.

From that moment on Terry spent his days dreaming dreams about his bookshop, about the little reading room he'd have and the alcove where he'd serve wine and cheese. And dear, wonderful Bronwyn communicated her enthusiasm during their daily phone calls. Each time they finished talking, Terry knew that the gods had finally smiled on him; he'd found a landlord who not only read books but loved them. Clouds of joy buoyed Terry. Sean, accustomed to worrying, fretted over his cousin's preoccupation with the details of the shop. He was not sure where Terry thought today and tomorrow meshed, for Terry sometimes spoke about the future store as if it already existed, and so it did—but only in that world of his mind. Sean listened with concern as Terry told Bronwyn about the poetry readings and the authors' parties, and soon he was caught up in the fanciful invention of his life, a mystical, romantic invention that Sean heard Terry expand to embrace this place where they lived. Terry, with the poet's gift for transforming reality into fantasy, was now describing the dull, drab cottage as something between Ann Hathaway's cottage and an eighteenth-century remodeled farmhouse he'd seen in *Architectural Digest.* Does it have a name? she'd asked. Oh yes, he'd answered. It's called Innisfree.

When Terry confessed to Sean that the house was now named, Sean looked puzzled. "Innisfree? After that bit about Maud Gonne, I looked up Yeats, so I know that's from Yeats. But what's Innisfree?" he questioned as he looked out the windows at the rutted roads outside the barren cottage. "Was it a prison where Yeats was put?"

Terry brushed the lock of hair from his forehead, the cut he insisted his barber give him, the better to emulate Yeats's look, and explained in his dreamlike poet's voice, "When Yeats was a teenager in Sligo, he wanted to live in Innisfree just as Thoreau lived at Walden Pond. I want that, too."

"Then you'd better get out of here and move to Walden Pond," the pragmatic Sean advised.

Terry had turned his back in disgust. "I—well, frankly it's too difficult to explain things like that to you," he responded lamely.

"Can you explain things like Innisfree to *her?*" Sean wondered aloud. Sometimes Sean worried that his cousin would not be able to open and run a shop by himself. Sean's own talents were limited to numbers; he wanted to be sure that Bronwyn continued to understand Terry. Who knew when they'd need Terry's sweetness to counter the sourness of overdue rent?

Terry frowned. His cousin had asked a reasonable question, one he'd considered often these past weeks.

Could he explain himself to Bronwyn?

Could he even understand himself?

29

THE CHILDREN WERE DRIVEN BACK TO THE CASTLE IN THE MAGIC pumpkins, and now all the little girls and boys were collecting their wraps and their nannies preparatory to the trip home.

The trip home, of course, was never longer than across the park.

"Thank you, Mrs. Ashter," the girls mumbled as they curtsied. The boys gave a perfunctory head tilt that passed for a bow.

Harold had stayed at the store to see which toys had been most requested. "You can learn a lot from kids," Harold had told his wife in his new role as retailer. "Here's how it works. I'll see what the kids take, and then I'll tell the buyers what to order for next Christmas. That way the whole party is a business expense. Get it?"

Bronwyn got it. Indeed she was getting more than she wanted

these days, more of Harold's advice, more of Harold's opinions, more of Harold's ego, and more of Harold's presence. Funny, but until Terry Bell came into her life, Harold had not seemed to occupy so many of life's corners.

Now, back at the house, Bronwyn could bid the children good-bye and look forward to—what could she look forward to? Who would talk with her now that the party was over? Certainly not Sienna. She was taking her mother to the country. Bronwyn smiled. She could look forward to talking to Terry. More than anything in life—no, no, she promised herself, not more than loving Gwyneth—but next to Gwyneth, close to Gwyneth, was the aura of Terence Bell, her very own poet-philosopher. Never had the world of ideas been more exciting, never had reading seemed more important, never had such stimulation come from life and talk.

"Mommy," Gwyneth asked, tugging at her mother's long dress and breaking the magic of the moment, "can Sparrow stay?"

Sparrow, Gwyneth's best friend, stood holding her hand. Together the two little girls were begging for the party never to end. Sparrow was the daughter of Sherry Thomas. Like Bronwyn, Sherry was a native New Yorker, but, as Sherry was quick to remind Bronwyn, "If you're not born in Manhattan, you're better off born in a cornfield in Iowa." No question about it, the Bronx and Brooklyn had no cachet once you crossed the Triboro Bridge. Now Sherry, like Bronwyn, had crossed the bridge and was intent on making life work on new terms, terms that included the role of mother.

Sparrow was a pudgy little girl whose rosy looks were the promise of a lifelong weight problem. Even now Sherry looked worried each time her daughter reached for yet another slice of bread, another sweet. "Watch it, darling," she'd caution. At one point she whispered to Bronwyn, "Well, at least we don't have to worry if she'll marry rich."

Like Bronwyn, Sherry Thomas had married a man more than twenty years her senior, and as his third wife she had presented him with his third set of children. "Thank God I could still have children," Sherry had admitted to Bronwyn, "because if I couldn't, I could kiss the whole inheritance good-bye. Generosity is not his middle name, and I won't get the big dollars until he dies."

Sherry was one of Bronwyn's "OH" acquaintances.

There were three categories of women Bronwyn knew, aside

from her Seconds, and none of them provided any intellectual stimulation. The typical young mothers, the young career women who had
had their first children in their late twenties and early thirties, the
women who married their contemporaries, were no longer part of
her peer group. First, their young husbands were intimidated by the
older, successful husbands, and the wives simply could not keep up
with the women who married out of their economic and age groups.
So Bronwyn had sought a new circle of friends, the current crop of
young wife-mothers married to older men. She categorized these
new acquaintances: the "OH" women, the "OOH" women, and the
"OYs."

An "OH" was anyone with an Old Husband.

An "OOH" had an Old, Old Husband.

And an "OY" was an Old Young, anyone who had an Old
Husband who thought he was Young.

OHs were definitely the best. They were very grateful to have
what they called a second chance at life.

An OOH was too old to capture the second chance but didn't
know it.

And an OY, complete with suntan and skiing vacations, spent
most of his time nursing a bad back and cranky knees, the result of
his conviction that he didn't look his age and could, therefore, do
everything a thirty-year-old male in his prime could do.

"Mommy, pul-leez," Gwyneth whined.

Bronwyn pulled herself to attention. She had been so absorbed
in her thoughts she hadn't heard her child. More and more this was
happening to her, but not because she was drifting into a Valium-
aided forgetfulness as she had only weeks before. No. Now her
thoughts strayed to that place where she wanted to be herself, at
Innisfree, next to Terry.

She must talk to Terry, and she had not been listening to
Gwyneth but she guessed her question. "Gwyneth, do you want
Sparrow to stay and play?"

"Please, please."

"If her mother says yes," Bronwyn agreed.

"She's all yours," Sherry said, blowing a kiss to her daughter.
"Bronwyn, give her to a nanny to take home."

"Your nanny?"

"Hey, any nanny that will take her can have her. Tell them that she eats table scraps and only has to be walked three times a day."

Bronwyn laughed and blew a kiss back to Sherry. She thought Sherry was amusing, but she never could understand how she could be so cavalier about motherhood. Still, at this moment, Bronwyn was happy to see Gwyneth with a friend; maybe she could have some private phone-call time to herself. She turned to go upstairs.

"Where are you going, Mommy?" Gwyneth asked.

"To my room. I have some calls to make, and I have to take off my queen's dress."

"No," Gwyneth pouted, "stay here and play."

"I can't." Bronwyn looked at her watch. It was five forty-five. Already she was fifteen minutes late for her standing five-thirty call from Terry. He would be calling from the public telephone booth in the building shed at Pumpkin Corners, calling on her private line, the line only she answered. She had to get to her room. That phone must be ringing off the hook by now.

Bronwyn started up the stairway, only to see Rosabelle—no, no, of course it was Vonna—lumbering down the steps. "Oh, Bronwyn," she said, "I was just coming to get you. Terry is calling."

Terry? How could Vonna possibly know when he called? "Which phone did you answer?" Bronwyn demanded.

"I don't know," Vonna said. "I was in your bedroom—"

"You were *where?*"

"Hey, cool it. It's my father's bedroom, you know."

"All right. All right." She rushed up the stairs past Vonna, and Vonna turned and followed her stepmother. Bronwyn hurried into her dressing room and turned to close the door behind her. But Vonna was standing there, standing there like the witch Rosabelle returning to haunt her happiness. Bronwyn, her hand shaking, picked up the telephone. "Mr. Bell," she said formally.

"Bronwyn, who was the person who answered your phone?"

"I'll explain later," she said quickly.

Still Vonna filled the doorway.

"May I call you back later, Mr. Bell, and we'll discuss the rental terms more fully?"

"I love you, Bronwyn," he whispered, "and I don't care who's standing there. I don't care who hears me. I love you. Do you hear me? I love you. And you'll never guess what book I found for our bookshop. It's a copy of the variorum edition of Yeats's poetry, the one with all the revisions. And you'll love what he says about the changes he makes in his poetry. He says, 'It is myself that I remake.' Like us, Bronwyn, like us."

"Yes, Mr. Bell, very good. I'll call later. Thank you." Bronwyn replaced the telephone. Why was Vonna still there?

"Who was that, Bronwyn?"

"Nobody special. A tenant, just a tenant at Pumpkin Corners," she answered.

"Then why did he say to tell you it was Terry? And why did he say it was a personal call? And why did he tell me he had to talk to you because it was something important to you both? None of my business, I know. But, Bronwyn, you're not cheating on my darling daddy, are you?"

30

THE COUNTRY, THAT AREA OF MULTI-ACRED CONNECTICUT AND northern Westchester County, became the second home of the fashionable rich in the mid-1980s. The move began with the squeeze for position in the summer baseball games among the East Hampton/Bridgehampton intelligentsia and the desire to swim in social waters by the renters and owners of the waterfront homes in Southampton. When the horn-rimmed overflow of the outer Hamptons found themselves benched by belongers, and Wall Street's newly minted millionaires were told that they were not welcome to dip their toes in the social waters of Southampton, both groups paddled across Long Island Sound and washed up amid vast acreage that included water views, apple orchards, working farms, and a commute—they snidely reminded the belongers of the Hamptons— that did not require traversing the dreaded Long Island Expressway.

Until that time, the area was, as Virginia explained to the Seconds, "the well-kept secret of fourth-generation Wasps." Now, complete with the affectations of old-family custom and new-rich style, the residents of the twenty-seven-acre estates were restoring houses, rebuilding barns, buying horses, and tending cutting gardens, while planting trees with Latin names outside their homes and desperately seeking family trees with English names for the inside.

The new people entertained one another all summer long; parties began always with cocktails in the gazebo or pagoda (the special addition of the new owner's wife), but the enormous influx of new partygoers in the late eighties caused the social season to begin in mid-March in order to accommodate the calendars of the recent residents.

Sienna's party for her mother was the first of the many parties that would be held at Peter's Principal. Each would have a guest of honor, but should there be no one worthy of honoring, then there would be a party theme. In spring the theme would be Easter, and later parties might be given for each of the summer holidays. There would be the annual clambake with caterers flown in from Nantucket. This was the party that Sienna would book a year in advance because she knew she would be vying with the Southampton crowd for the best of the flying caterers.

The party tonight had been as successful as early-season parties ever were. The guests came on time, and the guests left on time. No one got drunk; no one got rowdy; no one connected for a new affair or ended an old one.

Last to leave were the Cloughs, Marnie and Horace, now in the library with Peppy. "The Cloughs know you want country guests to leave by ten thirty, but they're always the last," Sienna whispered to Peter as he went to the bar to pour another brandy for Horace. "Don't give him too much," she cautioned, "or they'll never go home."

"That's the trouble with first marriages," Peter mumbled. "They stay at your house so they don't have to go back to theirs."

Sienna patted his hand. "I think that's a compliment," she said softly, "but I don't know why." Carrying Horace's brandy, she walked back into the library.

Marnie Clough was laughing loudly, her big teeth gridlocked in a too-small mouth, and now, obviously still enjoying the second wave of amusement over someone's witticism, she announced loudly, "Your mother is a love."

Horace, red-faced and barrel-chested, had lusted and lost after a score of women throughout his fifty-odd years, the list ranging from secretaries in his company to his wife's friends. Now he sat in the wing chair, his feet on the footstool, enjoying the chance to be the only man in the room. His wife's comment turned on his slightly besotted motor. "Damned good-looking woman for a mother; I see where you get your looks," Horace Clough added, playfully poking Sienna in the ribs as she handed him his brandy.

Marnie fingered her empty glass. "Do let me give a party for—"

"You need a drink, Marnie," Sienna interrupted.

"So I do," she said, looking thoughtfully at her empty glass. "You know, I was born two gins below par, and I've only had one tonight."

"My first husband, Sienna's father, used to say that," Peppy added. "I hated it when he said it, but when you say it, I'm charmed."

Sienna felt her anger rising. "My father never said that," she contradicted.

Peppy, wide-eyed, curled her legs under her body in the big chair where she sat, and laughed the little-girl laugh of a child caught with her hand in the cookie jar. "Didn't he? Oh, how stupid of me. It must have been my second husband. Or was it my third?"

Peter, at the doorway, joined her laughter.

"That's one thing about a first marriage," Marnie admitted. "You never have any trouble knowing who said what."

Horace shrugged. "You don't have any trouble because after two years you stop listening."

"I guess you just changed husbands when they stopped listening," Marnie said to Peppy.

"I don't think any man would stop listening to Peppy," Horace said.

Peppy blushed prettily. My God, Sienna thought, how can a woman who's been married four times still work up a blush over a dumb little compliment from a man she'd never look at twice?

Peppy lowered her eyes. "I wish my son-in-law felt that way about me," she said.

Sienna stiffened, but Peter laughed, this time with what Sienna called his "aw, shucks" laugh. "You know I'm your admirer," he said to Peppy.

"And I'm yours," she added quickly. "If I had ever had a husband like you, Peter, I'd still be married."

"Sienna, you're lucky you saw him first," Horace added with a big, booming laugh. "I don't think there's a man in the world who could say no to you, Peppy."

"Thank you, Bill," Peppy trilled.

"His name is Horace," Sienna added dryly.

Again Peppy gave her little-girl laugh. "I'm really terrible with names. I like to name people the names they grow up to look like. You, darling," she said to Horace, "look like a Bill."

"Yes, he does." Marnie laughed. "A hundred-dollar bill."

"Who knows better than you? I'm your bill payer," Horace snapped.

"I've had enough," Peter said as he stood. "I'm tired. I'm going to bed. You can all stay here, but I've had a long day. Gene and I have a golf date early tomorrow morning. I have to go over some numbers." He shook hands with Horace, kissed Marnie lightly on the cheek. "See you upstairs," he said to Sienna and Peppy as he started to leave the room.

"I'll go up with you," Peppy said, unwinding herself quickly.

Peter stopped at her words and turned toward Peppy. Sienna looked closely at Peter. Was he frowning?

"Stay with the guests, Peppy," he said amiably.

"Yes, Peppy," Sienna urged. "You have some new admirers."

"All the more reason to go upstairs now," Peppy said, blowing kisses as she left the room.

"Hey, go ahead." Horace laughed at the two departing figures. "We'll wait while you tuck your mother-in-law in bed."

Marnie saw the stricken look on Sienna's face. "Enough," she said abruptly. "Find my coat, Bill."

"Why are you calling me that?" Horace asked his wife.

"Because you thought it was so cute when Peppy did it."

Marnie stood up as Sienna rose from her chair. She embraced Sienna. "Go upstairs," she counseled. "You'd better get to Peter's rescue. He looks scared."

"I'm not sure he is, but I am," Sienna admitted and gave her friend a squeeze of thanks and understanding. Then she went upstairs without another word, without the usual kiss-kiss farewells, and without saying good night.

"What the hell is this about?" Horace demanded.

"If you have to ask, you'll never understand," his wife answered. "Get your coat, Horace. The party's over."

≡

Sienna went directly to their bedroom, but Peter was not there. Was he in his dressing room? Probably. But she wouldn't follow him there. No. No man wanted to feel followed. Or trapped. Or chained, she reminded herself. No, it was always best to give a man the right to be—to be what? To be a fool about his mother-in-law. Couldn't Peter see what Peppy was about? She went into her dressing room and sat at her dressing table. Mindlessly she began to brush her long dark hair. Maybe Peter would come in. Maybe she and Peter . . . She put the brush down. She would find Peter. Yes, she'd go to Peter. She'd not wait for him to come to her. She walked soundlessly across the bedroom and toward the sitting room between their room and Peppy's. There was Peter's desk and computer, Peter's chair. He'd said he had work to do, and she knew his regular habits. He would go upstairs, undress, put on his robe, go into the sitting room, and work at his desk. Whether he finished or not, he would be in bed by midnight. Yes, she thought. There are advantages to having a man who lives by the clock. The door to the sitting room was ajar, and she knew just what she would do. This was a night when she needed to upset routine. She would go in there, sit in Peter's big chair, and wait for him. She had never done this before, never tried to come between him and his precious schedule. Tonight she was going to change some things. Maybe it was time to remind Peter that she was his wife. Yes, that's what she'd do. She'd tell him he was her center, her anchor. She'd let him know. She was thinking her words, concentrating on her thoughts, when she looked straight ahead and stood transfixed.

She blinked. No, she wasn't imagining this.

She shook her head. She had drunk nothing, so her vision was not clouded by alcohol, but there in the half-light of the room, curled up on Peter's large upholstered armchair, was her mother.

Peter hadn't—Peter couldn't—but had he? Could he? She tried to find her voice, her balance, but before she could walk into the room, before she could say a word, the door to Peter's bathroom opened, and Peter, belting his robe as he came through the door, saw Peppy.

Peter shook his head, as confused as if he had suddenly walked into someone else's life. "Sienna?" he asked.

Peppy lifted her head and stretched her arms. The white silk robe covering her body slipped from her shoulders to the floor, and

Peppy, her body lean and clean from a series of cosmetic surgeries, advanced silently with the predatory movements of a stalking animal toward her son-in-law.

"Peppy." The name was said with such disdain that Peppy, the golden panther, stopped in her tracks.

Peter took a step back and turned on the overhead lights in the room.

In the doorway Sienna backed away. She knew now that Peter, planned and methodical in his actions, was obviously dealing with a plan he had not plotted. "What do you think you're doing like that?" he demanded.

Peppy, determined to try once more, put her hands out to touch Peter. "I thought this was what you wanted," she said without conviction.

"Why?" he demanded. "Why would you think I wanted"— now he paused as surprise came into his voice—"you?"

"Oh, darling." She laughed. "You're so boring and middle class. You don't have to be so dull. After all, Sienna's not the mother of your children, so you're not defending motherhood. I just thought it would be a little family fun."

"For years Sienna wouldn't even let me know you existed," he said. "Now I know why."

"Oh, Peter." Peppy shrugged. "You've simply got to get the sophistication to match your money, or you'll be no match for those Europeans. Why, even the Japanese have their dalliances. Darling, once you've passed twenty million, I'm what you're entitled to have."

"Forget my entitlement," he said sharply. "I've seen a lot of women in my day, Peppy, but I never saw a mother who'd try something like this—"

"Peter, dear, you don't understand. I'm a woman who happens to be a mother. Most of these—these country bumpkins—are mothers who happen to be women."

"I always thought Sienna was jealous of you, and I felt sorry for you." He laughed a self-deprecating, humorless laugh. "But I was wrong. You're jealous of Sienna. I'm sorry for my wife. You're beneath contempt. You're not a mother. You're a monster."

The words rained on Peppy like a language she'd never learned, the language of rejection. She shrugged. "I'm just someone who tries to please the customers. I thought this was what you wanted."

"No, you didn't," he said. "No, you thought this was what *you* wanted. But I don't want you, Peppy. I married Sienna, and I want Sienna. I don't want you."

"Peter, I'm offering you a gourmet dinner, and you want fast food?"

"You disgust me," he said. "Get your clothes on, and get out of this house tonight."

"Whatever you say," she answered, her poise and self-confidence undiminished as she reached for the robe and put it over her shoulders. "But don't tell me you love Sienna, because I can tell that you don't. You're really wondering, Peter. I can tell. Is Peppy the dessert I'm missing in the feast of life? Too bad you'll never know." She smiled. "I guess I'll have to learn not to answer the unspoken call of a hopeless middle-class man with middle-class values."

"Get out," he demanded, pointing to the door. And then he gasped, as he saw for the first time that his wife was standing in the doorway. "Sienna," he said, his voice trembling, "when did you come in here?"

Sienna, in that moment that comes when one's worst fears suddenly give way to one's best hopes, knew that her private, controlled husband would not have wanted her as a witness to the scene. "I just came here," she said.

"Your mother has decided to leave," he announced, "and I'm making sure that someone from our staff will drive her to the airport."

"Yes," Peppy said, "I just came in here to do some exercises to relax before bed, and well—darling, how was I to know that Peter would walk in? It was a lovely party, lovely for a country party. But"—she stretched her arms high and stood on her toes—"I do need a spa, and so I'm going tomorrow."

"No," Peter answered, "you're going tonight. Go and pack, Peppy, and be ready to leave in ten minutes."

Peppy shrugged. Things didn't always go according to plan; she was accustomed to the occasional no in a yes life. "I'll go when I'm ready," she answered.

"Now," Peter repeated, looking through Peppy, past the temptation she offered, and into the promise his wife's eyes offered.

"I guess I'm ready now," Peppy said, turning toward her bedroom.

"That's my robe," Sienna said accusingly, and as she spoke she knew that Peppy had taken her robe because she'd thought she'd take it all, her robe, her house, and her husband.

"And to think," Peppy said, looking over her shoulder, "I thought you were interesting, but you're both so hopelessly—hopelessly suburban."

Sienna walked into the room as Peppy walked out.

"Sienna," Peter said blankly, "I don't know what brought this about. I never said a word to encourage her."

Sienna nodded. Some things were better left unsaid. "Poor baby," she murmured, soothing her bewildered husband. She put her arms around him and held him in that wordless sympathetic bond that, in time of trouble and bewildering circumstances, unites a man and woman better than words.

"I just thought I was being nice," he explained to himself as much as to her.

Sienna drew away and looked at her husband, this man who was aware of every business nuance, who followed international politics and yet was so innocent about the thinking behind maneuvers made in Peppy's world. "Peter dear, you're a truly nice man. How were you to know that being kind to Peppy is like befriending a man-eating tiger? She's okay as long as she isn't hungry."

31

IN THE MONTHS SINCE THE REAPPEARANCE OF GREGORY SAWYER, the luncheon meetings of Virginia with the Seconds had taken on an undercurrent of tension and fear.

Each time they sat at a restaurant table together, the three Seconds would look at one another, the conspiracy of silence silently reaffirmed. They would throw the conversation from topic to topic like a beanbag each was afraid to hold lest the music stop and leave her the loser.

Today at the Victorian Room in Anne's hotel, the Dome, was no exception.

"Did you hear about Kimberly Cates?" Sienna began as the four assembled and ordered their bottled water aperitifs.

"No," Virginia said.

"She stopped buying designer clothes," Sienna said conspiratorially. "She said the prices have become obscene, so she's just buying off the rack. She wears the clothes once, then gives them to her mother and sisters in Belgium, and with the money she saved from her clothing allowance, she bought her father a car."

"If that's true—" Virginia began.

"Sounds like her publicity man dreamed it up," Anne answered.

"If that's true," Virginia repeated, "then she's just the kind of woman I want to work on the school project with us."

Bronwyn knew it was her turn to jump into the conversation to keep the talk from going to Virginia's continuing plan for the school, but thoughts and words would not come to Bronwyn, even though her mind had never been more clear. She was feeling better than she had ever felt in her life. She had stopped taking pills shortly after meeting Terry Bell; the stimulation of the relationship with him gave her all the highs she wanted. Gwyneth, however, with that sixth sense of childhood that understands the unspoken thoughts of those who love her most, felt that she no longer had her mother's full attention, and was becoming more difficult than ever. Just yesterday, at lunch in a restaurant with Sherry Thomas and her daughter Sparrow, Gwyneth had put her feet on the table and kicked over her food. Bronwyn, in a rage she could not control, had spanked her daughter and dragged her screaming from the restaurant. She had been troubled ever since by the tug at her heartstrings. Had she overreacted to a spoiled child's tantrum? Or had her daughter been justified? Had she been ignoring the child? Which came first, her daughter's needs or her own? Who had the right to demand her time and attention, Terry or Gwyneth?

Bronwyn, desperate now for a comment, looked at Anne. "Your face," she said quickly. "Your face looks different. It's not a facelift because you haven't been away." Now the words slowed, and she focused on the part of the body that always interested her. "What makes your skin glow like that?"

Anne ran her fingers over her face. "It's called glazing," she explained.

"It's a perfect summer look for you," Virginia said, and the other Seconds trumpeted their approval.

Encouraged by their compliments, Anne explained, "Hugo invented it." There was no need to explain who Hugo was, nor was there need to add his last name. Indeed every woman seated at every table in the Victorian Room of the Dome could have identified Hugo as the makeup man discovered by Virginia North, but who had achieved fame as the personal consultant to the famous, fashionable Anne Burrows.

"I thought glazing was what you had done to the walls here," Bronwyn said as she looked around the dining room with its richly lacquered dark red walls, pink-clothed tables, and dark green velvet banquettes.

"This room gave Hugo the idea." Anne laughed. "I'm going to start charging Hugo instead of paying him. I give him all his ideas."

Virginia breathed heavily, and Anne, recognizing that as her mentor's sound of disapproval, stopped speaking. "You're the only one who can let our Anne know when she's gone too far," Sienna said, laughing.

"What's that supposed to mean?" Anne snapped.

"Only," Virginia interjected, "that you're reading your publicity once again, Anne. It's really not becoming to watch a woman lead her own band."

"Casey does it," his wife said defensively, "and the media follows him every step of the way."

"In my day," said Virginia, "a lady was a lady and a gentleman a gentleman so long as they stayed out of the newspapers."

"Things have changed," Bronwyn said sadly.

"That's why we're here," Virginia said. "I've asked Gregory to join us because we have to get cracking. There's really no time to lose if we're to get his school up and running this year."

"You mean you want it to open this fall?" Sienna asked. "It's June now. How can we—"

"Of course I don't mean this fall. I mean next fall. But you girls know that it takes a lot of planning to do this properly. First we've got to get plans approved, a building finished, teachers hired. Oh—" Virginia stopped in midsentence. "Here comes Gregory now."

Gregory Sawyer, lean and muscular, his bright blue eyes scanning the room for the right tables to greet, walked toward Virginia and the Seconds. From the corner of his eye he could see Prince Alex Popodroff at one table with Lorna Dudley, the widow currently fighting for the hundred-million-dollar estate of her third husband.

No need to stop there. He'd wait until the estate was settled. He had an already rich widow.

"Virginia, darling." He bent and kissed her cool cheeks. "You look so beautiful," he said admiringly.

And as he said the words, Virginia seemed to glow with a special prettiness. She fingered the pearl choker at her neck and touched her blond curls in a small, feminine gesture.

Gregory looked at the other three, nodded at each, but kissed none of them. He sat at the empty place to Virginia's right. "You've ordered?" he asked.

"Only a drink," Anne said. "What do you want, Gregory? I'll get a captain here immediately." Damn those captains. They saw that she had a new guest at her table. Where were they? Playing backgammon? Taking bribes? Damn them all. Anne reached her right hand above her head, snapped her fingers, and a captain appeared. "Where were you?" she demanded.

"Madam, my apologies, but the prince—"

"You worry about a prince when—"

"When you have these royal ladies?" Gregory finished graciously. "No harm done," he said, smiling, easing Virginia's obvious discomfort at Anne's chiding the help in front of others. He gave his order and turned back to the table.

"You know, a day like this reminds me of our school," Gregory said softly, "a day when sun can turn to rain, and life and friendship can offer the promise of flowering."

"That's almost poetry," Virginia said appreciatively.

"Oh, my dear," he said, kissing the older woman on the cheek, "I don't mean to be maudlin, but this is just the time of year when I would go up to New Hampshire to open the school. You all remember how wonderful it is there. Still cool, but the promise of so much. Ah yes, Virginia dear, this is the beginning of summer, when the air carries the unspoken pledge of love—"

"We remember what it's like," Sienna interrupted.

But Virginia, flushed and happy, turned impetuously to Gregory. "I think that you are the most tender, understanding man I've ever met."

"Knowing you makes me that way," he responded.

Sienna thought she would be sick.

All through luncheon Gregory and Virginia talked of the

school. They would recruit students from the ranks of the well-to-do, those parents whose multiple activities often precluded giving attention to their children.

As they ordered their espressos, Bronwyn realized that this was not just an ordinary little luncheon with the Seconds. Virginia had brought Gregory for a reason; she had something important on her mind. Bronwyn looked at her watch. Terry would be calling her at home in twenty minutes. She had to get to the bottom of the reason for the lunch and then get out of here. Best to face the music now. "You mean you're really going ahead with this?" Bronwyn asked.

Virginia looked at her in surprise. "I don't see how you could possibly wonder. I've talked of nothing else for months, and I have a lot of important people ready to serve with you girls. I need you to spearhead this because you have the real emotion about the Peabody School. This is going—well, this is going to be my legacy."

"Your legacy?" Bronwyn asked, and as she did she knew that there was no way to escape; the last door had been closed. Virginia, at long last, was exacting payment for the years of tutoring and care she had given.

"We owe you whatever you want," Bronwyn said. This was no time to debate; she had to get out of here.

Sienna, smarting still from the pain of her mother's ugly reappearance in her life, was ready to declare her allegiance to the woman she wanted to be her mother. "I agree," she said softly. "I will do anything in the world for you, Virginia."

"I knew I could count on you. Gregory was uncertain, but I was sure. My plan is to have the groundbreaking in September, and we'll do it as a first-day-of-school benefit because—" Her pace increased, and her voice gathered strength as she confided her plan. "Remember the old saying 'Today is the first day of the rest of your life'?" Without waiting for a response, Virginia continued breathlessly, "I want this benefit to be the first day of the rest of our school."

"Isn't that the most touching, brilliant idea you ever heard?" Gregory asked. "The groundbreaking at the school itself, a gala schoolday opening with guests coming from all over the world—"

"Plenty of wonderful publicity," Virginia added, "and the real benefit of having the press there will be that we can solicit funds from the entire country. Isn't it a masterful idea?"

"Yes, it really is, but this doesn't come at a good time for me,"

Anne said as she looked at her friends. Surely they'd let her out. They would understand that her marriage was teetering, that she needed time and attention to secure her own future.

"Summer is never very good for me either," Bronwyn mumbled in one last, desperate attempt to get Virginia to delay the building of the school.

"Service has no season," Virginia said.

"Can we wait until fall?" Sienna asked. Perhaps there was a way to put things off.

"Gregory owns the land," Virginia said, "the original property where all you girls went to school that summer—"

Virginia looked at Gregory, and the three Seconds exchanged glances. Had Virginia bought the land? Did he own it and come to her? They'd never know, but it didn't matter. The web was getting tighter.

Sienna reached for Virginia's hand. Perhaps she could explain that going back to their past meant pain for each of them. How could she tell Virginia that there were memories they could not face, that there were confessions they had never made? How could she explain that they imagined they heard Rosabelle's cries in every thunderstorm? How could she say to Virginia that if Peter knew the real story about the Seconds, he might be forced to give up *his* second, the second career he was trying to build? And, if that were to happen, then what of the trust and love in their marriage? And how would someone as vain as Casey feel about his wife being part of a deadly prank? As for Harold Ashter, he was so crazy that he could kill Bronwyn if he knew. If only they could buy time. If only that attorney were to learn something, find a key. Sienna wanted to make their excuses, beg Virginia's forgiveness, but as she touched the older woman, she felt a wave of sympathy, for Virginia's hand, on this warm June day, was cold. In an instant Sienna said, "We'll help you get the Peabody School functioning as a first-rate school."

"Thank you," Virginia murmured, and then, blushing prettily, she said, her voice clear and firm, "but it's not going to be called the Peabody School."

There was a pause, and Gregory put his arm protectively around Virginia. "I think it's time to tell the girls," he said proudly. "I want to name our new facility the Virginia Payne North School for Exceptional Children."

No one said a word.

"Oh no, Gregory," Virginia said in surprise. "That's not what we agreed."

"But it's perfect," Sienna said.

"No, it isn't," Virginia said. "I'll tell you what I want. But before I do, I must say that more than anything I want to see the school I'm going to help build." She looked directly at Anne and laughed aloud. "Here's a question with an obvious answer. Who at this table has her own plane to take us there?"

Anne took a deep breath; it wouldn't be easy to refuse Virginia.

"Before you answer," Gregory said, "I would like to give each of you a small gift to express my gratitude for your interest and your willingness to help." He reached into a briefcase at his side and took out three small wrapped packages and handed one to each of the Seconds.

"What is it?" Bronwyn asked fearfully.

"I—" Sienna began.

"Open the package before you say a word," Gregory instructed. "All of you open at the same time."

The gold paper fell to the floor, and each woman looked at a small, black leather album. Embossed on the cover were the words SUMMER '61.

"And now open your book," Gregory commanded.

With the precision of the Rockettes, the three turned back the album cover. There on the first page was a picture of four girls who once had been unafraid of rain and lightning, who had never trembled at the sound of thunder.

"A memento of the time that binds us all," Gregory said. "The album is filled with pictures of all of you—and Rosabelle, of course."

"What a surprise," Bronwyn croaked sadly.

"Gregory gave me mine the other day," Virginia said, "and when I saw the album I told Gregory I didn't want to have a school named for me. And now I will tell you just what I want. I feel that the school should be named for those whose lives were made better and brighter by their time there. When Gregory told me that there had been four of you, four darling girls who loved one another, and when he told me the sad story of your best friend Rosabelle—"

"He did *what?*" Anne's voice rose.

"Our best friend?" Sienna choked.

"Yes," Gregory said in funereal tones. "I told Virginia about the terrible loss of Rosabelle, how she died—

"How she died—" Bronwyn echoed in disbelief.

"—because she disobeyed the rules," Gregory said in a part-scolding tone. "I'm sure it's a story you girls have never told anyone—except your husbands, of course."

The three women sat in stony silence.

Boom!

He'd dropped the bomb. So it was to be blackmail, after all. Tell your husbands or I will.

"How sad for you girls," Virginia said, "but still you managed to hold together. Gregory told me how you used to go together each year to New Orleans where her family lives, and you'd visit her gravesite—" Virginia's eyes misted, and she could not continue.

Sienna, Anne, and Bronwyn remained silent.

Lies upon lies.

Their lives were being padded now with stories not only of their creation, the lies they dreamed and lived, but now the fiction of another more evil storyteller. Gregory had woven them all into the fabric of his school, Virginia, the Seconds, and their husbands. How could the truth sound better than his story?

Virginia touched her nose with a lace-edged handkerchief. "Knowing the real story now, you can imagine how much I appreciate your going up to the school. Still, isn't it wonderful to know that you can keep Rosabelle's memory fresh with this perfect effort? And that is why I want to name this the Rosabelle School for Exceptional Children."

Outside there was a rumbling.

"Oh dear," said Virginia. "I think it's going to rain today, after all. And just when I thought it would be such a pretty day. Gregory, we'll have to leave now and take the car."

Bronwyn wanted to leave when Virginia and Gregory prepared to go, but Sienna said bluntly and loudly in front of Virginia, "You can't go now, Bronwyn. I need you."

"But Gwyneth—" Bronwyn began.

"We'll all stay," Anne assured Sienna. She put her hand on

Bronwyn's arm and prevented her from rising. "But first let's all give Virginia a good-bye kiss."

Virginia waved them away. "Oh, darlings, let's get back to basics. I'm getting rather tired of the perfunctory kiss. Who needs it? Isn't it better simply to know we love one another and can count on each other?" And so saying she blew a small kiss in their direction and sailed through the door on Gregory's arm.

"We're pretty disgusting, aren't we?" Sienna asked as soon as Virginia was out of earshot.

"I told you I can't stay," Bronwyn groused.

"Well, you'll both listen to this," Sienna told them. "I have an attorney checking on Gregory."

"I told you not to do that." Anne scowled.

"Look, you can both stay and argue, but I have to leave," Bronwyn said, half rising.

"Sit," Anne commanded as if Bronwyn were her Doberman.

Bronwyn pouted, but she stayed seated.

Anne wheeled toward Sienna. "What was the idea of telling someone about this?"

"I didn't. All I did was ask Hedda to get us some counsel—"

"For God's sake," Anne shrieked, "why not just call Lolly Little and be done with it?"

"Shhhh, shhhh," Bronwyn cautioned. Even the help was trying to listen.

Anne smiled unctuously toward the captain. She did not want to break her own unwritten rule: never argue in front of the little people. You have to be above personal emotions to get business performance.

"All right, Miss Perfect," Sienna said sarcastically as she turned toward Anne, "so if I'm not to do anything, what has your big secret investigation turned up about Gregory?"

"It will," Anne said defensively. "It will. I know it."

"Bull," Sienna answered.

"Oh, stop all this," Bronwyn interrupted. "Let's just pay him off, forget the school, and get him out of our lives."

"That won't work," Anne said. "He's looking for more than money. Look at the life Virginia's showing him. He has a passport to society."

"Just like us," Sienna concluded bitterly. "He's her newest Second."

Bronwyn laughed. "I never thought of it that way. Still, I say give him money. Money talks."

"You'd better not make any separate deals," Anne warned.

Glancing at her watch, Bronwyn said, "All right. All right. Let me go, and I won't. Just let me out of here."

"You'd better show up for the trip to New Hampshire," Sienna said darkly. She was torn between sympathizing with Bronwyn's weakness and agonizing over the possibility of her negotiating a separate peace. "Just don't contact anyone," she added.

"Oh, of course not," Bronwyn said sarcastically. "It's wrong for me, but it's all right for you to hire attorneys behind our backs."

"Someone had to do something."

"I was already doing something," Anne said haughtily.

"But what do you have to show for it?" Sienna asked.

Bronwyn waved her hand as if to push back the arguments. "We're businesswomen. Let's cut to the bottom line. What have you learned, Sienna?"

"That there was no Gregory Sawyer from 1961 until now."

Anne, her eyes big, gasped. "Does that mean—"

Sienna nodded. "Yes, that's what it means. It means we'd better start looking for somebody besides Gregory Sawyer. The young lawyer I hired says it's impossible to hide someone for almost thirty years. There's Social Security and income tax, all kinds of forms and computer printouts on people. But Gregory Sawyer could have disappeared only if he hadn't existed."

"Didn't exist?" Bronwyn asked.

"Wilson Tibbitt, our lawyer, thinks we may have someone who slips in and out of identities the way we change dresses. In other words, my dear friends, he thinks Gregory may be an enigma cloaked in a puzzle. And his advice is for us to follow Gregory wherever he leads us in order to unmask him. At the moment I guess that definitely leads us to New Hampshire. That's my news, and now," she said, turning to Bronwyn, "you may leave."

32

N EW YORK SOCIETY, AS PROOF OF ITS COMMITMENT TO THE world, as tangible evidence of its concerns with more than dressing up and going out to vast public places transformed into one-night fairylands, gave its galas a reason for being. The private ball was gone; in its place the City, in the dying years of the twentieth century, lived it up by dancing for the arts, dining on dollars meant to feed the homeless, and watching shows in order to cure a variety of diseases.

There was an audience for everything, a market for every cause. In a world made socially responsible for people who sold tickets for their pet charities and repaid by buying tickets for a friend's, the Seconds knew that they would have no difficulty attracting the much-moneyed to a reputed nongala school opening. By concentrating on a Spartan party approach and holding their event in a remote place, they knew instinctively that they would make it even more fashionable to be among those attending. The Rosabelle Retreat, as the nongala was called, was going to be subtitled a weekend of return to self, a vacation from the relentless pace of the City, a refreshment of the spirit in the New England woods. There would certainly be no trouble interesting the right columnists in their new cause. No, the difficulty for the Seconds would come when they had to explain to their husbands the reason for committing that most precious commodity, time, to yet another worthy cause.

Out of a common emotion, fear, each of the three women tailor-made a common scenario. The Rosabelle Retreat was a memory of a past that had shaped them, but even more important it was something Virginia wanted, and Virginia had been good to each of them.

But despite the commonality of the cause, each husband responded differently when hearing that the Seconds had to visit New Hampshire in advance of the benefit. Casey was pleased his wife wanted to go away for twenty-four hours; he welcomed her trip as an interruption that would let him see Lady Diandre, no questions asked. Harold Ashter was annoyed because it meant he would have to reschedule a dinner he wanted to host to introduce himself to the present management of Driscoll's. Peter was suspicious because Sienna's reason seemed to be given halfheartedly. He felt she was withholding something. Did she have a lover? Considering her history, anything was possible.

≡

"Mrs. Burrows, there's some turbulence reported ahead, and I can't change altitude," the pilot's voice said clearly over the intercom.

"Fasten your seat belts," Anne warned Sienna and Bronwyn, "it's going to be a bumpy day."

"I knew that from the start," Sienna said.

Bronwyn leaned forward in her seat and reached for Anne's and Sienna's hands. In a small circle now, they looked at each other with the same frightened stare of that other bumpy time and whispered the word that had bound them over the years.

"Together," they promised.

And as they said the word, the years rolled back.

BOOK FOUR

"In bad days we can very vividly recall the good time that is now no more; but . . . in good days we have only a very cold and imperfect memory of the bad."

ARTHUR SCHOPENHAUER

33

I T WAS 1961 AGAIN, AND DESPITE THE LIGHTNING, THE THUNDER, and the intermittent rain, despite the automobile sinking in a pond just in front of them, despite the fact that they knew who was in the back of the car, the three girls sitting on the wet ground clasped hands and half-choked, half-whispered, "Together." Sienna had said it first, then Anne. Now Bronwyn, too, knew what their salvation must be. Together.

Bronwyn squeezed their hands. "Together," she echoed hoarsely. Then, with a brusqueness calculated to mask her own fears, she looked at her two partners and dropped their hands. "Enough," she assured them. "Now let's get going."

The three knew that those few seconds had grounded them in reality and had given them the determination to take the next steps.

"Let's try to get Rosabelle out of the—out of there," Sienna said as she tried to get up from the ground. The blood was still seeping from the head wound sustained when she'd crashed into the steering wheel of the car as it flew through the air. She felt a strange dizziness. Somehow her legs would not hold her any longer. This was no time for her body to betray her. "Damn," she whispered as she fell with a thud even before she could stand.

"Don't faint," Bronwyn commanded, her authority fully returned.

"I won't," Sienna promised.

Bronwyn turned to Anne. "You're the strong swimmer, and you're the biggest one. You have to go back and try to get Rosabelle out of the backseat."

Anne blinked rapidly. Until now she had never been afraid of thunder or lightning or rain. Until now she had liked to put on her boots and slicker and walk down Park Avenue pretending that she was somebody's rich young daughter. But now as she sat trembling on the grass, afraid of what the car held, and even more afraid of what the future held, she hated the rain and the booming thunder; she was afraid of the flashes of lightning. But she knew she had no choice. She rose slowly and walked to the edge of the pond.

The car had stopped sinking, its left rear wheel moored in the silt of the pond. The front right fender was clear of the water. The tilt of the car now made a part of the rear visible. Anne looked at the car, and as she did she began to make decisions, to formulate her plan. She wouldn't be able to stand in the muddy pond—she might sink in quicksand, and even if she didn't, even if that wasn't quicksand, there would be no good foothold on that slimy bottom; it would be best to swim to the car, figure a way to release the front seat, then try to free Rosabelle and bring her back. Anne squared her shoulders. It felt good to think; now it was time to act. How to enter the water?

She was surprised at her own calm, cool judgment as she prepared to dive into the shallow pond. She closed her eyes and tried to pray, but no prayer came. Instead she saw her mother—how strange, the mother who all summer long she'd been trying to forget, to push to the back of memory, came to her now.

Mama was in the front seat of the Masters' station wagon as the chauffeur waited to take Anne to school and Mama on errands, but Anne—although she was six—had never climbed into a rear seat by herself. She didn't know how to get into the car. Mama leaned forward in her seat. "Reach under," she directed, "look behind my seat and find the button, and push. You must push the button before I can move the seat." But Anne knew her mother would know nothing, nothing of cars, nothing of people, nothing of life. She would disgrace her always. "No," Anne responded, holding her body immobile. Just then Westerford the chauffeur came to the car and said to Anne, "Why are you standing there?" He came around to help her. "Oh, I guess your ma doesn't know. Just reach under the seat like this," he said as he leaned over, "and find the button—and there you are, little lady." Then he gave Anne a little nudge. "Foreigners never know this kind of stuff." Anne climbed into the back without looking at her mother, and for the rest of the day she maintained a sullen silence. How could her mother, her dumb mother, know anything about some dumb car?

Now, as Anne hit the water, skimming the surface of the pond and miraculously avoiding the tangle of water weeds, her mother's words played in her head. She knew she would swim to the car and look for the little button that held the car seat upright. In that moment of fear, her subconscious took her back to her mother, and the new Anne Cross knew something the old Svetlana would not have bothered to learn. She learned if she didn't let fear overpower her, if she didn't become paralyzed with "what-ifs," and if she didn't let her thinking processes shut down, she'd win. It would not be prayer that would save her; it would be the ability to concentrate, to remember, and to act. She swam with strong strokes now. She'd win. She knew she'd win. She was a new Anne with old wisdom.

One more stroke and she reached the car.

All right, now.

Fumble with the button.

Push.

That did it.

The seat moved forward.

She reached for the cramped body of Rosabelle, pulled her out, and swam for the shore.

≡

Bronwyn closed her eyes and said a prayer. "Please, God, let Rosabelle live, and I'll never again ask You to make my skin clear." Then she ran to the edge of the pond and helped Anne beach her load.

"There's no pulse," Bronwyn announced as she dropped Rosabelle's lifeless wrist.

"Give her first aid," Sienna advised.

"I forget how," Anne whispered.

"I'll do it," Bronwyn, the druggist's daughter, volunteered. Bronwyn straddled the inert body of Rosabelle and tried to remember. When you breathe into a victim's mouth, do you hold her nose or yours? She pushed her elbows into the ground and tried to adjust to the big body under her.

"Stop," Anne whispered.

Bronwyn looked up at her. "What?"

"Listen. In the woods," Anne croaked, her voice and body shaking violently. "I think—oh my God, someone's there."

Bronwyn rolled off Rosabelle's body, and the three girls stared in silence toward the woods. Then they turned slowly back to one another and slowly regarded the inert body on the ground.

It was not Anne's imagination.

They could all sense it.

In the dark, in the aftermath of the storm, somewhere in the wet woods surrounding the pond someone was watching them.

34

B UT WE CAN'T STOP," SIENNA WHIMPERED.

"Keep trying," Anne urged. "Go on. Do the first aid."

Bronwyn straddled the lifeless body of Rosabelle once more.

"We'll watch for—for him," Anne promised.

Without asking one another, each knew it was a him.

Each knew the him was Dr. Gregory. But if he was there, why didn't he come out? Why didn't he help them?

"We didn't mean it," Sienna whispered to the woods.

But Bronwyn was not listening. "I can't get Rosabelle to breathe!" she cried.

She put her mouth against Rosabelle's once again to try to force air into her lungs, and from the depths of her longing to bring the girl to life, from the fears propelling her beyond her own endurance, she heard his voice, his voice sounding strange and faraway: "What kind of sex games are you little girls playing in the woods?"

Sienna screamed.

Anne sat open-mouthed.

Bronwyn looked up. Looming over her and Rosabelle was the smirking face of Dr. Gregory.

"We didn't mean it," Anne said. How many times had she said that? "We just thought we'd take your car and see if witches could escape—"

"Stop." Gregory was irritated by this meaningless explanation. He already knew that this was no ordinary little summer-school prank.

He pushed Bronwyn away and checked Rosabelle's pulse and heart for himself. The child was dead. Damn these girls. These girls had gambled with life and lost. But he was a loser, too. He could castigate them, but that would do no good.

When he'd first discovered that his car was missing, he'd thought the girls were on to his secrets; he'd assumed that they'd looked in the back, found those women's clothes, and would confront him about his questionable sexual practices. So the moment he guessed they'd gone down to the pond, he suspected them of those motives that would have been his. And when he found Bronwyn and Rosabelle in what he assumed to be a compromising position, he attacked where he was most vulnerable. But as soon as he realized that their predicament was more dangerous than his, Dr. Gregory knew he would become their protector. And by so doing, they would become his protectors. He saw it all quickly and clearly. You couldn't be a fool and run this school. A silly man couldn't convince all those parents that he was a graduate psychologist with a deep interest in young boys and girls with problems. No, it took a man with a silver tongue and a golden promise to persuade those mothers and fathers and guardians that he was there to protect their children, not exploit them. No, he was not interested in the children's sexuality or their parents' money. His interest was only directed to the children's welfare. Gregory took a deep breath.

He had stood in the woods and watched them for ten minutes, long enough to know the real story, long enough to shape a real alibi. "Who brought her out of the car?" he asked.

"I did," Anne said quickly.

"And she was behind the wheel," he assumed authoritatively.

Before the others could answer, Anne said briskly, "I think so." Listen, listen to this man. Don't make the same mistake you once made with your mother. Listen, he may be showing you the way out of this night.

Now Sienna began to sob loudly. They hadn't meant to have Rosabelle die. They had just wanted to scare her. Sienna tried to talk, but only screams came from her throat.

A slight tremor passed over Gregory's face. He didn't want to do it, but he had to. He lifted his hand and slapped Sienna's face.

The others were as stunned as Sienna.

"I'm sorry," Gregory said apologetically, "but I did that because I had to. We don't have time for girlie hysterics. I have to call the sheriff. We have to have an inquest."

Bronwyn clutched at her face and could feel herself tearing the skin. God, oh God! she screamed silently, take out my guilt.

"It was an accident," Sienna tried to explain.

"Yes, I'm sure it was," Gregory said quietly, "but why did you take my car?"

"Rosabelle said—" Sienna began.

"—she was a witch," Anne continued.

"I don't think the sheriff will approve of your story," Gregory Sawyer said.

Anne nodded hypnotically, but the others remained motionless.

Gregory turned to Anne. "I suppose Rosabelle took my car keys, got into the car, and the car went into the pond, and she didn't know what she was doing." Gregory's voice was pitched low, his words coming like small signposts along the road back to life and sanity.

Anne listened and understood the words Dr. Gregory didn't say even more than she understood the spoken words. He was acting as their teacher, their counselor, explaining that they must tell a story grownups can believe. He was showing them the way to the rest of their lives.

Anne knew what she had to do. She picked up the thread of the story from Gregory. Isn't this what they played at night, the game where one bunkmate started a story, another continued it? Yes, this was just another story about bunkmates. Anne was growing up very fast this night. She was learning what it took to get on in the world. You had to think, stay sharp. Anne could do it. "Rosabelle didn't mean to take the car; she was sleepwalking. It all happened in her sleep. We girls were asleep. But when you woke up during the night—" She turned to look at Sienna and Bronwyn, but Sienna with her head injury didn't look as if she would be able to go on with the story. "So you, Bronwyn . . . yes, you're the one. You woke up to go outside to go to the bathroom, and when you did, you heard Dr. Gregory's car. You wondered why he'd be going away in the middle of the night, and then you saw the car go wildly into the pond. You ran back and woke us, and that's when the three of us came down here."

Now Bronwyn understood. She picked the next story thread. "We tried to get Rosabelle out of the car, but she was stuck behind the wheel—"

"No," Anne contradicted, a new coolness evident. "You're so upset trying to get her to breathe. Remember? I did get her out of the car. I am a strong swimmer, and I got her out of the car, and we tried artificial respiration. When that didn't work, we ran to get you."

Sienna nodded numbly. She'd better think fast, too. "The reason Bronwyn didn't run for you when she saw the car go into the pond is that she thought you were driving, and then I—we—" Sienna's jaw dropped. She tried to talk, but she couldn't form the words.

Bronwyn, her burgeoning storytelling talents overcoming her fear, rushed into the breach. "I went to get the others in order to rescue you, Dr. Gregory. I called to everyone and told them to get robes or jeans and come running to the pond. I figured it would take all of us to rescue you, Dr. Gregory. Only when we got to the pond we looked and suddenly realized that Rosabelle wasn't with us."

It was Anne's turn once more. Cool and collected, she polished the story like a small gem. "But we still had no idea she was in the car, so when I went into the water I was thinking I'd be rescuing *you*. When I got to the car, I was shocked to find Rosabelle. We didn't even know she was out of bed."

Gregory looked at her and nodded his approval. This was a girl who could go far. She took good care of herself. She had shown the others how to do it. Good. They all had their story together. They had created it, so they would believe it, and so would those who heard it. Better for all of them.

"I'll call the sheriff now," Gregory said. "We all know the story. Make sure you remember it tomorrow for Parents' Visiting Day. I'll handle Rosabelle's parents. You girls make sure you handle your own families."

"My mother won't be here," Sienna said.

"Why?" Gregory asked.

"She has a boyfriend. She thinks I don't know, but she's with him. I know about it, but my father doesn't. And my father won't come because he doesn't ever come to anything. He's always got a trial or a meeting or something."

"My parents aren't coming either," Bronwyn said.

When her admission was greeted by silence, she went on to explain, "It's . . . ummm . . . my dad . . . uh . . . my dad can't leave his business." They didn't have to know that her parents couldn't afford to come up here.

Anne shook her head. "My mother is in Europe for the summer." She didn't add that her mother was there as a personal maid.

Gregory smiled. He could deal with this. He could deal with

this just fine. Three girls with no one who really gave a damn about any of them. Only one little detail to clear up. How much did the girls think they knew about him? "By the way," he said. He'd begun walking toward his cabin but stopped and turned around now. "What did you girls do with the clothes for the school play that were in the back of my car?"

Bronwyn paused. So they weren't some weird sex joke after all.

"We put them under the tree," Bronwyn told him easily. It would be years before she would question his words.

"Thanks." Dr. Gregory smiled. He'd pick them up on the way back, throw them in a closet, and burn them in a few days. And by next week this would all be forgotten.

35

BRONWYN WAS THINKING ABOUT GREGORY WHEN THE STORM hit. The plane was bounced by the winds with such force that cups flew, coffee spilled, and all she could swallow was the dark taste of tension. Lucky Virginia. She had a cold, and only this morning she'd canceled.

"Tighten your seat belts," Anne directed in her low, tough voice. Bronwyn already felt that she was upholstered into the large chair.

"I should have known," Sienna muttered. "We let that man back in our life, and no good can come of it." Now her voice grew louder and shriller. "Why are we going to this stupid camp?" She heard herself ask the question, but the winds—up here and down there—had unnerved her, and so she kept talking, asking the questions although she knew the answers. "Why? Why can't we stand up and say we had an accident almost thirty years ago and stop letting this haunt us?"

Anne laughed, but there was no humor in the sound. "Tell her, Bronwyn."

For the moment Bronwyn's fears of flying were canceled, and she was caught in the passion of her reasoning. "If I had told the truth, do you think I'd ever have been able to get a college scholarship? If I'd told about the—the accident—do you think any bank would have given me credit and let me build my business? And, okay, now I'm rich, and I've got my own money. But if I told that"—now Bronwyn paused and strained for great gulps of air—"that psychopathic husband of mine, he would think I'm the one who's crazy and take Gwyneth from me." The unbearable tension she felt was in her voice, and her voice broke. "I'd die. I'd die if anything or anybody took Gwyneth from me."

"As for me," Anne explained, "I meant to tell people about fifty times. I was going to tell my mother when I came back that summer, but each time I tried, she was busy explaining why she was proud of me. You remember I was a good swimmer? Well, I wanted to make the Olympic team. Wouldn't that be a cute story? 'Girl swimmer drowns schoolmate.' Then, from the day I flew to New Hampshire to go to the Peabody School and saw my first stewardess, I decided that's what I wanted to be. Wouldn't they have eaten that story up at the airlines? And Casey with his love of publicity—come on, isn't that his kind of story, too? No, the longer we go on forgetting, the harder it is to remember."

"Hey, forget I asked," Sienna said. "It's just that Gregory is so smug that it makes me furious that he acts as if he's our protector when all the time we're also protecting him—that weird sexual side of him—and we're letting Virginia believe in a man we know is a phony. Don't we have some responsibility to Virginia?"

"Sure we do," Bronwyn said. "We have to be responsible for letting her live her fantasy just the way we're all living ours. Don't you live a fantasy, Sienna?"

Sienna lowered her head. "I did tell someone once. When I was living in California, I told Zeeno. I've told you about him before. You know, the gay man who was really good to me and let me live with him and sort of mothered me. I know that sounds weird, but that's how it was. Well, I was in one of my periods when I was blaming my mother for the way my life was turning out. I thought my mother was responsible for everything. I thought the Vietnam War was my mother's fault. Anyway, I told Zeeno the story and explained that the accident was really my acting out my anger toward my mother, and he held my hand and said to me, 'Pretend you didn't tell me. And don't ever tell that story to anyone again because it makes you sound like a cold-blooded murderess.' Each time I'm tempted to tell all and cleanse my own soul, I remember that. I've wanted to tell Peter a lot of times, but now? The timing couldn't be worse. So, like both of you, I need to keep quiet just now."

"The conspiracy of silence," Bronwyn said softly.

"And we're in it together," Anne said.

"Together," the three repeated in unison.

36

B RONWYN GAVE A SMALL PRAYER OF THANKSGIVING WHEN THE plane finally bounced to a rocky landing. No one said a word, but Bronwyn was sure the others were as relieved as she to be on the ground.

"I'd rather fly through that storm one more time than have to come to the Peabody School," Sienna said in a low voice.

Anne smiled. "I'm the tough one. The storm didn't scare me, and this place doesn't either." She paused and smiled slyly. "I'm not only tough; I'm a liar."

"Look," said Sienna as they climbed into the waiting limousine, "let's pretend it didn't happen. Here we are, three friends who've escaped from everything that ties us to reality. Why don't we just have room service in the motel, have a kind of pajama party, go out and look at the site tomorrow, and then get back home? It's raining and ugly now, so why go to look at this? And why have another nightmare? I say we ought to order a couple of bottles of champagne and some chicken sandwiches or pizza, something really stupid, and let's—"

"Let's," Anne agreed.

Bronwyn's hands moved deliberately to her face.

"Come on, Bronwyn," Sienna urged.

She spoke so softly they had to strain to hear her. "If I thought we were just going to have dinner by ourselves, I would have stayed home with Gwyneth."

"Bronwyn, kill the guilt trip. You're not the first mother in the world," Anne snapped. "I have a child, too."

"You have children," Sienna reminded her tartly, as if to underscore her own childlessness.

"Let's just have some real fun together," Anne urged. "We're the only people in the world we can trust. We're the only ones who know the worst thing about each other."

They paused and looked at one another. They never had to say it, but each knew their secret was known by at least two other people. Still there was no reason to end the charade.

"You're right," Sienna said. "We're the only ones who know everything about each other, so let's have a wild fling tonight and let tomorrow take care of itself."

≡

When the door to their three-bedroom suite was opened, Anne gasped. "My God," she said, "this motel is worse than being poor."

Sienna laughed. "Oh, I'm so glad we have the world's number-one hotel rater with us. Look, Madam," she said, running to the bathroom and pulling a towel from a rack, "our motel has everything you big-city ladies could possibly want. The towels are as thick as sheets, and the sheets are as coarse as towels."

Even Bronwyn joined the play as she ran her finger along the plastic dresser top. "Don't forget our careful housekeeping. This place was dusted in 1982, and the money we saved on maids has been put into this beautiful antique furniture."

But Bronwyn could not maintain a playful attitude. A moment later she said in a serious tone, "Tell me something. Why isn't Gregory on this trip? If we're here to look at this place to try to plan the benefit, why didn't he come with us?"

"He didn't want to be in our way. I think Virginia wanted us to have freedom to plan whatever we thought would be best," Sienna said.

"I don't believe that." Anne cocked her head, and her eyes narrowed. "He's shrewder than that. We'll just have to wait and see. But come on," she urged her friends, "let's not get nervous. Relax, Bronwyn."

So Bronwyn, regretting her introduction of the name that always recalled the worst moments of their life, went back to the playful fun of a few minutes before. "All right then, another serious question. This is the worst-looking furniture I've ever seen, but in thirty years when it's old, my daughter will buy it in some antiques shop for twenty times its original price. Why?"

"Because some interior designer with more designs on her money than her interior will tell her that it's collectible," Sienna said. "And we're all too scared and too rich to think we can decide things like furniture and dishes and linen. It's always been that way. The more money you spend, the less you trust your own judgment."

"After a while, though, you don't even notice all the wonderful things you have. You just take everything for granted. In the place where I grew up on Park Avenue," Anne remembered, "they had incredible Sèvres and so much beautiful china that I thought everybody had that. But you know what? It was so valuable I wasn't even allowed to dry the dishes. Oh, I used to wish I was old enough to dry just one plate. Can you believe it? The thing I wanted most in the world when I was a little kid was to be able to be grown up enough to dry a real china plate."

"Did you ever think you'd be this rich?" Bronwyn asked.

"Not in the beginning," Anne said, "but later I thought so. No, later I knew so. I knew I was going to be so rich that my mother would never have to work again." Her eyes filled. "So much for dreams. Right?"

"How long has it been now since your mother died?" Sienna asked.

"Twelve years and three months and two days."

Sienna shook her head sadly. "Life is strange. You loved your mother and lost her. I lost my mother before I had a chance to love her. I wish I could have loved my mother. I wish I could love her now, but my mother's one of those women who never should have been a mother. She's really smart. I know that, and I know she's frightened now because a woman who's been a great beauty always has trouble with aging. For the first time she thinks I'm better than she is, but I think that maybe if I am better it's because I have something inside, not because of my outside."

"Do you think you'll be a good mother because you know what a bad mother is?" Bronwyn asked tentatively.

"I'm never going to be a mother," Sienna said, her heart suddenly becoming a full, unhappy place. "I just found out, and I'm having trouble with it. Peter doesn't give a damn. He's got grown kids, so why does he need another child? But I need a family. I don't have anybody."

The two mothers stayed silent in unspoken sympathy. Finally Anne said firmly, "You have us."

"Not if I ever told Peter our story. You know that, too. You couldn't afford to be my friends because you'd always be afraid of me."

There was silence.

"Let's order that champagne and some sandwiches, and let's get into our robes. I'm going to need a little fortification before I face daylight and that school again," Sienna said, looking at the two.

Anne laughed. "You don't really think this place is going to have champagne, do you? I'll call the pilot, and they'll send some from the wine cellar on the plane. And you can forget the chicken sandwiches; I'm ordering caviar with the champagne."

"It's just like summer camp," Sienna said with an artificial smile.

Only Bronwyn sat unmoved by the forced gaiety. Instead, quietly and purposefully her hands went to her face, and she shook her head sadly. Just as she suspected, there were new swellings under the skin, and it had all happened in the fifteen minutes since they'd arrived at the motel. She'd have to go into her own room and find something to take, something to calm her for the next twenty-four hours. Champagne wasn't the answer. No, her answer lay at the bottom of her overnight bag in a bottle labeled aspirin. She smiled at the thought of what really awaited her in that bottle.

Ah yes, one of the good things about money was that it did get you prescriptions for a lot more things than a teenager could steal from her daddy's drugstore.

37

ANNE WAS CONSCIOUS OF THE DULL CHAMPAGNE ACHE IN HER head before she was conscious of her own wakefulness. It was 3 A.M., and still the storm raged outside. She pulled the covers over her, but that did not seem to quiet the storm inside her. Finally she sat up and turned on the light. Whenever reality impinged on her subconscious, Anne reached for that one soporific that would bring her not only sleep but sweet dreams. She reached for her notebook and began to outline her plans for the hotel in London. By 5 A.M. she was ready to sleep once more, and even as she drifted toward her new dreams, she knew she would be all right and ready for the day when the call came at 7 A.M.

Sienna awoke fully aware of her surroundings. She knew she was in a cheap but respectable dump on the edge of the dark part of her life. Her mouth was dry; that was the result of the champagne and caviar. She wanted to brush her teeth, and she wanted a glass of water. But more than anything she wanted to be out of this place and out of her past.

In a kind of golden haze, Bronwyn fought her way to morning. She opened her eyes when her tiny jeweled alarm clock rang at seven, and she made out the indistinct shapes of the ugly furniture. She had seen this furniture before, but where? Where was she? "Gwyneth!" she called. "Gwyneth!" she repeated, but there was no answer. Instead she saw Rosabelle's head floating above her. But where was the rest of Rosabelle? How did she get here without a body? Bronwyn laughed loudly. She'd never seen anything so funny, but Rosabelle wouldn't laugh. Instead Rosabelle kept repeating, "No, no, no," and then came the word "Don't." "Oh, shut up!" Bronwyn screamed. But Rosabelle wouldn't shut up. Instead she was starting in once again. "No, no, no," Rosabelle kept saying. "I told you to stop!" Bronwyn shouted. "Shut up, shut up!" Bronwyn repeated again and again. And then Rosabelle put her arms around Bronwyn, and Bronwyn felt her whole body melt away like Rosabelle's. She was melting away in sobs. Soon there would be nothing of her to hold.

Then, just as she was about to wash away, just as all of her was being spirited to a strange new place by Rosabelle, Bronwyn heard more voices.

"Bronwyn, we're here. We're here," Sienna repeated. "Anne and Sienna, we're with you. I think you're having a bad dream. We're here. Don't be frightened. We're together. Remember? We're together."

Bronwyn parachuted gently into a bed, but where was the bed? And what were her friends doing here? "How did you get here?" she asked, her voice barely above a whisper.

"Hush, hush," Sienna crooned as she rocked her gently in the bed.

"Are you well enough to go with us?" Anne asked.

Where were her friends going? Bronwyn didn't want them to

leave her. "Oh yes," she answered. Her voice surprised her. It came from some great distance from this room.

"Then get dressed," Sienna urged, "but first drink a little coffee. I guess you went overboard on the champagne last night."

"I guess." Bronwyn nodded. She wished they would leave; she wanted to see if her feet could reach the floor.

Almost as if she were reading her mind, Anne said, "We'll meet you in the lobby. Get dressed. I'll send some coffee to you right away."

Bronwyn lifted her arm as if to reach for a cup. "Coffee," she agreed. "Coffee. That'll do it."

≡

Sienna and Anne carefully refrained from mentioning either the heavy rain—how like the night they would never forget—or their concerns about Bronwyn as they waited in the lobby. Instead Anne concentrated on their benefit for the school. "How can we possibly bring people up here to stay overnight?" she asked Sienna. "Can you imagine Virginia staying here?"

"I can imagine Virginia staying here, but I can't imagine some of those other women. Come on, how can you take an eighty-six-year-old woman like Evangeline DuBarry and bring her up here? And if Virginia doesn't have Evangeline's blessings on this project, you know she'll think it's a failure."

"I really don't want to fail Virginia, and I know you don't, but how can we possibly do this?"

"What if we did the entire dedication in one day?" Anne asked. "I'll fly everyone up here, and we'll do one big, festive day."

"I'm not sure Virginia is strong enough for that."

"Then we'll bring Virginia up the night before or let her stay an extra night, but honestly, Sienna, there's no way that these women can stay in a motel as bad as the one we're in."

"Maybe. Meanwhile—oh, there's Bronwyn. We can go out and look at the site now."

≡

Bronwyn, fortified by coffee, a few pills to awaken her, and the sense of her friends with her, seemed totally in control of herself. "I have the plans with me," she said, patting her briefcase as they drove toward the proposed site of the new school.

"It was smart of Gregory to be able to blackmail women with our knowledge and money, wasn't it?" Anne asked.

"No," Sienna answered, "it was dumb of us to be those women. We're stooges and tools, and we don't know how to be anything else."

"I've looked at these plans," Bronwyn said, "and I haven't said anything to all of you, but the costs look high to me. I wish you'd run them past your people, Anne. The land cost, of course, is something we don't know anything about, but I have the feeling that he really fleeced Virginia on that."

Anne shrugged. "There's no ceiling on blackmail, is there?"

"Or on guilt," Anne answered.

Bronwyn put her fingers over Anne's mouth. "Never say anything unless we're outside and can be sure we're not being taped."

Sienna's violet eyes widened and she sank back against the leather seats, silent and disturbed.

Anne shook her head sadly. "I wish I were home."

Bronwyn, once again in control of her talents, opened the glass partition between the passengers and driver. "The property we want to see is to the left of that road ahead," she directed. "I'm keeping the glass opened," she continued, nodding at her friends to inform them of the need for discretion in their remarks.

The car turned onto an unpaved road, and all three tried to gaze blankly from the rain- and mud-spattered windows.

No one said a word, and they did not dare to look at one another, but each knew how the others felt.

The pond, the dreaded, nightmarish pond, lay before them.

38

THE DRIVER, ACCUSTOMED TO THE FOIBLES OF THE RICH, CURSED under his breath. Some road these ladies had picked. The relentless rain muddied the road and pounded the windshield with its steady beat. He'd almost missed the turn even though he'd switched on the headlights, but the foggy yellow light on the muddy road gave little help. This was the kind of bleak day when early morning confuses itself with twilight and creates a murky darkness before daylight.

But, after careful navigation of the boatlike car, he managed to pull onto a grassy embankment. He got out of the car and came around to open the door for his passengers, then he raised three umbrellas and handed one to each of the women as they stepped from the limousine.

As they left the car, each felt a sudden rush of cold air, air colder than the day itself, air made cold by memory and the threat of yet another moral dilemma. Anne took deep breaths; always the swimmer, she was reaching now for the extra air, the push she needed to cross the line a winner. She was aware, however, that there was nothing for her to win. The best she could ask for was a delay of decision in every part of her life, delay in a decision about Casey and his English lady, delay in a decision about going ahead with the school. Life was on hold.

Sienna trembled in the cold. All her life she had sought the warm hearth, the dream of a family that had never been hers. She was so close to having it all with Peter. If only she could hold him, keep him for another year. Now she had another challenge. Could she keep him from knowing the real truth about this part of her past? If only she could get pregnant . . . maybe he'd adopt a baby . . . maybe no one would ever know about Gregory . . . maybe he would disappear . . . maybe . . .

Bronwyn shuddered at the thought of yet another risk in her life. That's all she had ever known. When she was young, she'd decided to risk it all on acceptance, and so she hadn't told these girls about her ordinary, middle-class family. Later she'd risked her health for grades, working two jobs and seesawing between uppers and downers to stay awake for classes and sleep after homework. She'd risked her business reputation for marriage to a maverick, her life for a child, and now she was risking both for a man who read poetry and could see beyond her scarred face into her tormented soul. No wonder the soul was tormented. No wonder. No wonder. She looked at the rain on the pond, and for a moment— just for a moment—she thought she saw the car, the long gray limousine that brought them here; she thought she saw it slide over the bank and slip into the black water. But no, nothing so easy, nothing so final as that. All she'd felt was the movement of the two bodies on either side of her.

"Why did you pick this spot to start, Bronwyn?" Anne asked.

"I was just following the plan," she answered. "He wants to

make the pond a centerpoint and build the school on that hill overlooking it."

"That's madness," Anne said. "The school should go a mile the other way. This makes no sense."

"Maybe it does to Gregory," Sienna answered. "Maybe he just wants to bring us up here and scare us and—"

Bronwyn put her umbrella down. Let the cold rain fall on her face. Let the cold rain cleanse her soul.

"Bronwyn, what are you doing?" Anne asked. "You're shaking. You're going to catch—"

"No," she interrupted. "I won't catch anything. I'm shaking for all the reasons you are, too. Maybe if we'd been more worried then, maybe if we'd been scared then, we wouldn't be shaking now."

"I'm not shaking," Anne said loudly. "There are no ghosts except those we make."

Bronwyn dutifully raised her umbrella to shelter her body from the rain, and the three stood in sodden silence. In the eerie nightlike day the trees formed spiky sentinels around the pond.

Suddenly Sienna moaned, a low, long, plaintive moan.

"What is it?" Anne asked.

"It's him," she choked. "He's watching us. He's behind the tree, the same tree. I don't have to see him. I can feel him. I feel those eyes. Gregory has come for us."

In petrified silence, the three women stared at òne another.

Without saying a word each knew that finally time had run out.

BOOK FIVE

"Ah, la, la and again la, la! We are an untold number of women tormented with anxiety about tomorrow."

COLETTE

39

I N THAT MOMENT ALL LIFE SEEMED TO SHUT DOWN.
The women held tight to their umbrellas, afraid to move,
afraid to speak. They were certain that everywhere else the sun was
shining, everywhere but here, where unleashed memory ran wild in
their bodies.

Finally Anne spoke from that place that was the core of her,
and it seemed that Gregory's presence did not touch her. Her voice
was firm, low, and controlled. "We are going back to New York,"
she announced. And after a pause, she added, "Now." There was a
singular detachment in her instructions, that detachment she had
first learned on this very spot when she cleared her head and created
their alibi. It was a detachment reinforced by the unemotional
coping that a New York woman learns each day from her own life.
She learns it from the reasons she triple-locks the doors of her
apartment and from the agitated, mentally disturbed who beg on the
streets. She learns it from those huddled in doorways because they
have no other place to sleep, and she learns it from kids with blaring
radios on their shoulders and a penchant for grabbing gold chains
and handbags. Now that instinctive awareness to danger, that subconscious ability to come to one's own defense, gave her strength for
this special day. She would cope with this, too, and so would Sienna
and Bronwyn. She would show them how. Both of her friends looked
as if they had seen a ghost. Maybe they had. But hadn't she said just
a minute ago that there are no ghosts except those we make?

≡

Anne had taken charge at that moment, and she knew that she
would not relinquish the role so long as Gregory remained a threat
to their lives.

Seat belts buckled, they were sipping hot tea and waiting for
takeoff. "It won't be as rough going back," Anne promised.

"It never is," Sienna answered.

"Wrong," Bronwyn contradicted. "We just went back, and we
proved how rough it is."

"Listen to me," Anne insisted. "We can't go on—"

The pilot's voice came over the intercom. "Prepare for takeoff, ladies. We've been cleared into LaGuardia. There will be a few bumps until we reach our cruising altitude, and then we'll turn off the seat belt sign. It's sunny, a few high clouds in New York."

"You see," Anne continued, "it will all get better. Now let's talk about ourselves."

The throb of the engines did not bother Bronwyn. Her usual fear of planes was replaced by her relief in escaping the school.

Sienna barely heard Anne; she was watching the ground disappear beneath them. She would never come back here. Never. Not even for the groundbreaking of the school.

"Listen to me carefully, both of you," Anne insisted. "We can't go on like this. We have to stop letting Gregory control our lives. I've thought about it for the last hour, and I think I know what we have to do."

"What?" Sienna asked. "Do we have to kill him, too?"

Bronwyn laughed bitterly. "Why not? I'm for that."

Anne shook her head. "It's too easy for him and too hard for us. What I want to do is just hard for us. We know he's not going to report us to the police because if he does, then we implicate him. The only real threat he is to us is with Virginia and our husbands. I realize now that if our husbands never know the truth, then Gregory will hound us all our lives. I propose that we go back home and tell our husbands what happened."

"Ridiculous," Bronwyn snapped. "Besides, how do we do it? Do we invite them to come together in one room and say, 'You'll never guess what we did'?"

"Of course not," Anne said. "We each tell our own husband, but we have to agree to do it the same day because—"

"—because it's like a suicide pact," Sienna said slowly. "We are all going to kill ourselves together."

"What if one of us doesn't tell?" Bronwyn asked.

"We will all do the same thing," Anne said confidently, but inside she was trembling with fear that she had gone too far.

The shadows lengthened inside the cabin, and no one spoke.

Sienna stood and walked to the bar. She poured her tea into the sink and opened a bottle of vodka. "Where's the tomato juice?" she asked.

Anne pointed to the cabinet below the bar.

Sienna took out three glasses and made three Bloody Marys.

"I don't feel like drinking," Anne said.

"From now on," Sienna said as she lifted her glass, "we all do the same thing at the same time."

"That's silly," Bronwyn said. "If Anne doesn't want—"

"She'll drink," Sienna said, toughness now in her tone, too.

"Are we doing this today?" Bronwyn asked Anne.

"No," Anne answered without thinking. This was a question she hadn't anticipated, but her answer had been instinctive. Of course not today. How could she tell before she took care of things? Before she pulled together the London package?

Sienna felt the bitterness welling within her. Maybe today would be right. Go back and tell Peter now, and then let him leave her before he received his ambassador's appointment. Or maybe she should say she was leaving him and give no reason. Would he stop her? Would he hate her? If only she could turn to Virginia for advice—well, she couldn't. Somehow she'd have to reach for the courage. But did it have to be today?

Bronwyn, who'd spent most of her life avoiding reality, now had a new sense of the real world. It was a fragile place, wasn't it? One little conversation, and it could all end. And then where would she be? Harold would be angry at her for telling, for upsetting his world. He'd see this all as some kind of plot against him. She knew his madness well, and his response would be to hurt her because she would have hurt him. There was only one way to hurt her, and the way was Gwyneth. He'd take her baby just to prevent Bronwyn from having her. But if she were to secure Gwyneth's future and hers . . . Yes, it would take a little time, but she could do it. Terry . . . she could count on Terry. Didn't he love her? Didn't he whisper, "Let me count the ways . . ."? He'd been wanting her to come to his place near Pumpkin Corners for a weekend. She'd do it. She'd tell him that she needed him and wanted him now, and he would be there for her. Maybe she wouldn't have as much money. So what? She'd have love, and who ever said any woman had it all? She could go away for two days. Of course she could. She had a precedent now. She'd gone to the school, and Harold had seen that she'd leave Gwyneth for twenty-four hours. She'd do it again. But this time it would be for forty-eight hours. Plan it, do it, live with it. Terry had been telling her he was ready; now she was.

The three, lockstepped in silence and trapped by their separate thoughts, did not speak.

Only when they looked up did each remember that the others had problems as individual, as perplexing, and as deep as hers.

"It can't be soon, can it?" Bronwyn asked.

Anne shook her head. "I'll need a month."

"Can we make it two?" Sienna asked.

"We are like outlaws going back to face the music." Anne smiled. "So let's make it three months. September fifteenth."

"The groundbreaking will take place in September," Sienna reminded her.

"So much the better," Anne said. "Full circle. We'll come full circle on that day."

"Together," Sienna assured her.

"Together," the others echoed.

■

Virginia was propped against the pale peach pillows of her bed, and she reached a thin, veined hand to answer her telephone.

"Dearest," came the now-familiar voice, "I'm so sorry you had a cold and couldn't go with the girls, but I'll tell you a little secret."

"What is it, Gregory?"

"Let's save it for the next time we see each another."

"Soon, then," she whispered.

"Sooner than you think," he promised.

40

WHEN, IN THE LATE 1980s, MANY PEOPLE OF WEALTH AND influence made fashion their most noble and sought-after concept of life, many people of small wealth and even lesser influence spent their time studying fashion, disseminating information about fashion, and—in the buzzword of the time—*marketing* fashion. Fashion was, for the moment, the identifying mark of the woman who was both rich and aware. It was a peculiarly New York trademark, employed not only by women whose primary residence was bounded by expensive real estate that stretched from Central Park South north to 90th Street and ran from Central Park West to the East River, but also women everywhere who felt as if they lived there. Indeed these were women who would have been bounded by that residential geography if only God, their husbands, companies, or lovers had decreed that they live in New York.

"The fashionables," as some of the smart magazines called these women, made much and gave much of themselves to a variety of worthy, semiworthy, and utterly phony charities. No outsider was ever totally certain which charity was real and which was masquerading as a righteous cause.

But regardless of the worthiness of the cause, the result of the charity chase was a long season of balls, openings, and dinners, all of which required a series of new gowns for the fashionables. The charity mania spawned its own cottage industry: the ball gown.

The queen of the ball gown, the designer of the most-wanted grown-up prom dresses of the decade, was a former princess, Shotsie von Thrum.

There were certain detractors who claimed that it was the superior press relations, not superior design, that really made Shotsie. The fashion press touted her as a sizzler with too-cute-for-words headlines such as "Hotsy Shotsie!" "Yum-Yum Thrum Thrum," and "Von-derful Shotsie." But the ladies who launch the galas knew why they bought Shotsie's dresses: no one but Shotsie understood how to keep an aging body looking forever young. Shotsie was the queen of darts, those sophisticated tucks that added wanted curves to bony bodies and subtracted inches from tubby tummies.

As eagerly awaited as the publication of the Social Register was the fall showing of Shotsie's gowns. Any woman who received the engraved card inviting her to the showing attended. It was not a command performance, but it was a statement, a pronouncement that this was a woman who mattered in the whole social structure of New York.

Attendance at Shotsie's showings changed over the years. In the 1970s the audience was made up of well-to-do wives, widows, divorcees, assorted half-titled royalty, and an occasional kept woman. By the end of the 1980s, however, there were many women in the audience who were capable of buying their own clothes—and did.

Included among the latter were the queen of the advertising business, several network newscasters, all the major magazine editors and fashion writers, as well as a passel of stockbrokers, lawyers, real-estate operators, and entrepreneurs.

To do homage to the designer, the regulars, the women who wore her clothes day and night, sat in the first row to be photographed in last season's choice hits from the collection. Few of the readers of the newspapers realized that many of the clothes were given to the socially important, and still other celebrities paid wholesale or less than wholesale prices by buying directly from the design showroom.

In fashion, as in every part of New York life, the visibly rich paid far less to live their well-reported lives than did the invisible middle class.

By the turn of the decade Shotsie had the press so firmly on her side that she dismissed her long-time public-relations firm and gave the job of fielding the paparazzi and coddling the columnists to her assistant, Jamie.

In addition to supervising press relations, Jamie selected the music, the décor, and the site for each showing. Where to hold the showing was always as important as the guest list itself. This year the place to show one's clothes was the Petite Ballroom at the Dome. Each designer made his or her own arrangements with Anne's office, and everyone agreed that the Dome, under Anne's direction, did the best job with the audience, the designers, and the world at large.

Jamie surveyed the room as Michael Morovy began playing the piano. None of the "Pretty Girl Is Like a Melody" stuff, of course, and no rock, for by now rock had run its course. No, Jamie had given Shotsie just the touch he knew she wanted. He'd hired Michael Morovy, the current star of the party circuit, and asked him to write and play a special song for Shotsie's showing. It wasn't to be a parody—that was truly tacky. No, the idea now was to write original music and lyrics using the names of the clients, the names of the charities, and just names. The song for Shotsie ended with a wonderful quatrain. It wasn't a really bitchy ending unless, of course, you knew that Shotsie really hated Buffy Benedict, the social butterfly who flitted through the design world. Shotsie and Buffy were kissy-kissy for photographers at balls, but

Shotsie knew that Buffy wanted her clients, and Buffy knew that even though she didn't have to earn a living making clothes—after all, her husband was the biggest deal in the big-deal world of Wall Street—she had to act as if she did.

Jamie stood on his tiptoes and put his hand over his mouth. Ah, the ending to the song was coming now. Jamie peered to watch the back row. The real test would be to see if Virginia Payne North laughed. If she did, the rest of the room would. Michael lifted his hands from the keys for an instant and then went into the big finish:

No need to Buff your reputation,

Virginia roared. She got it. By God, the woman got it. Jamie breathed a sigh of relief. And when Virginia roared, so did the rest of the audience. Virginia leaned forward and strained to hear the last lines:

Be your own sensation,
Watch the smartest ladies come
To Shotsie von Thrum
It's the act of creation.

It didn't really matter whether they all heard those lines. Tomorrow the fashion press would allude to witty Shotsie, and the wit would somehow extend to include all of her new designs.

From their private perch in the back where the Seconds were seated with Virginia on the traditional little gold chairs, Anne turned to Virginia. "Clever of her to hire Michael, wasn't it?" Anne asked.

"She knows her audience," Virginia agreed, "and I always admire a woman who knows what to do. By the by, darling, see that woman in the front row?"

"I hope you understand, then, why I put us in the last row," Anne said.

"To avoid that caricature," Bronwyn whispered.

"Who is she?" Sienna asked, masking her laughter. Why would Anne put a woman like that up front? She had preternaturally black hair banded by a wide diamond hairband. She was wearing a Paris suit—the shortest suit in the room—revealing her long, shapely legs. Her hands were so heavy with rings she could scarcely raise the clawed, lacquered fingers to wave to Virginia.

"Is she waving to you?" Sienna asked with disgust.

"Of course, dear. She's Juliet Caesar," Virginia said evenly.

"So that's Juliet," Sienna gasped. "She New York's newest widow-to-be."

"Just because Pontius Caesar is considerably older than his wife is no reason for snide remarks," Virginia said, looking straight at Sienna.

"But Peter doesn't seem older, and besides, Old Pontius must be eighty," Sienna protested.

"I wasn't addressing you, dear," Virginia said softly. Turning to Anne, she said, "I think you're wise to put her in the front row. She'll think it's the best place to be, and she'll buy. She can make the whole day a success for Shotsie."

"I get it," Bronwyn said slowly. "We're at the back because if Virginia sits here, that makes this the place to sit."

"And as for Juliet," Virginia began, "she needs help."

The three Seconds exchanged glances. What were they supposed to do? Open a charm school for her?

"She is a Second," Virginia added pointedly. "She doesn't yet know her way, and I'm going to introduce her to all of you."

"Oh no," Bronwyn said involuntarily.

"I think that's what I've heard some of my so-called friends say about you three over the years—'Oh no.' Let me ask you something, my proud beauties. Did you ever try saying, 'Oh yes'?"

"Of course we'll help," Sienna said with forced brightness. "Besides, I just said yes to something else I never thought I'd agree to do. I said yes to my stepdaughter, and I'm going to help with her wedding. So look at all these clothes. If you can believe it, I'm looking for bridesmaids' dresses. For Sidney."

"Sidney?" Anne asked.

"Remember? That's Peter's daughter. The one who doesn't much like me."

"I'd forgotten about her," Bronwyn said.

"Peter hasn't," Sienna said. "Sidney wants to have a big, fancy wedding and she wants to wear a big, fancy gown. Her feminist mother thinks that brides and razzle-dazzle weddings are something out of a Barbara Cartland novel, and so she won't have anything to do with the wedding—"

"Who's the groom?" Anne asked.

"A Wall Street type," Sienna answered.

"What does that mean?" Virginia wondered.

"It means that he has a very tiny job in Peter's office. You know, Peter doesn't really ask me to do much, and this is something he wants. I suppose this isn't the time to bring this up, but, Virginia, I can't get involved in the Rosabelle Retreat for two months. I've got to do the wedding. There's really no one else."

Virginia looked at Sienna. "Well, you didn't seem to have that wedding on your mind when you went up to New Hampshire two days ago."

"I didn't know two days ago," Sienna said quickly. "When I came back that night, Peter told me. Yesterday I met with Sidney, and now I've agreed to help."

"You girls had a rather giggly time on your trip, I gather," Virginia added mysteriously.

"Giggly?" Anne asked. "We had a terrible plane trip."

"It was so scary," Bronwyn admitted.

"Is that why you had the party with champagne and caviar in your hotel suite?" Virginia asked, a small note of triumph in her voice. It was fun to let the girls know she knew something they thought was secret.

Sienna felt the hair on the back of her neck stiffen. She felt her body grow cold with fear. She had not told Virginia about the party. She looked at Anne. Anne was pale under her golden make-up. Next she looked at Bronwyn. Bronwyn's hands were on her face, exploring the blotches she knew were growing under the delicate skin.

The three looked quietly at one another.

"Oh, darlings, don't look so stricken," Virginia cautioned. "It was Gregory who told me, and he wasn't being a tattletale. He just thought it was adorable that you played together."

Behind them the trio was playing. The models had started dancing down the runway.

But the Seconds felt no joy.

It hadn't been their imagination. It hadn't been a ghost they'd invented.

No, it had been true.

Gregory had followed them. Gregory was letting them know, through Virginia, that they would never be free of him.

≡

As the showing ended Bronwyn whispered to Anne, "We don't have much time. Things are only going to get worse with Gregory. I know we can't wait. We do have to tell our husbands. Look, if you'll both do it, I'll tell in one month."

Anne nodded. "All right. I know you're right. I'll tell in a month, too." She turned to Sienna. "Can you finish with Sidney in one month?"

Sienna felt her heart turn as she nodded in agreement.

The date was set.

The die was cast.

She had one month to live the rest of her marriage, one month before Peter knew what the other husbands would know, that each had married a woman with a deadly secret.

41

IT WAS A PERFECT NEW YORK DAY. THE SUN WAS SHINING THROUGH the trees in Central Park, and the city overflowed with a kind of positive energy that made taxi riders want to walk and lazy people consider jogging.

There was promise in the clean, cool air, and as Sienna sat at a window table at Punch, the smart little restaurant in the heart of the Park, she was pleased that Hedda had selected this place for her luncheon today with Sidney. How smart of Hedda, the perfect secretary, to give them the feeling of outdoors and perhaps add openness to their stiff, formal relationship. Sienna was anticipating the luncheon now with pleasure instead of dread. Perhaps in sunshine she could come to a more amicable way of dealing with Sidney; certainly this girl was not an easy child. Child? Sienna half-smiled. There was only twelve years' difference in their ages; sisters would be more appropriate roles for them than stepmother and stepdaughter.

Sienna drew herself tall and swept her dark hair back. She

played at the folds of the expensive challis scarf that she wore over the black cashmere sweater. She had dressed down today; deliberately she had passed over the pretty little city suits in her closets and settled instead for a well-tailored black skirt and sweater. Then, in another deliberate ploy at simplicity, she'd chosen to wear a scarf rather than the freshwater pearls or the heavy gold choker with the Roman coin. Sidney must be the star, she kept repeating to herself. Now, to give her the courage to plant herself firmly in the reality of the moment, she closed her eyes and whispered his name. "Peter," she murmured. "Peter." It was her mantra, her center.

But before she could repeat the name a third time, Sidney's voice came loud and clear. "Wake up, Sienna, your prayers won't be answered. I showed up."

Sienna opened her eyes and laughed at the supposed joke. She stood and kissed her stepdaughter on the cheek.

"It's okay, Sienna. You don't have to kiss me today. Daddy's not watching."

Sienna sighed. Give me a break, she said silently. Aloud she assured her stepdaughter, "I didn't kiss you for him. I kissed you for me. Besides," she added, "brides have to get used to being kissed. It's all part of the act."

"Let's cut all the playacting," Sidney insisted brusquely. She threw her heavy shoulder bag on the floor next to the table and sat down.

Sidney was a pale version of her father. Where Peter had almost black hair and black eyes, Sidney had mousy brown hair and pale brown-green eyes. The shape of Peter's square jaw was repeated on Sidney, but while it gave Peter his strong, authoritarian look, it provided Sidney with a feature too powerful for her small face. Her downcast mouth gave her a perpetual sullen look.

Sienna folded her hands on the table; she was determined not to let the bitterness of this young woman drown her intentions to satisfy Peter. "Stop this, Sidney," she said softly.

Sidney thrust her head forward. "What did you say to me?"

"I told you to stop this foolish behavior." Sienna paused to let the words sink into Sidney's consciousness, and then buoyed by her overwhelming desire to do Peter's bidding, she continued. "When your father asked me to plan your wedding with you, it was because your mother decided not to help you."

"My mother hates weddings."

"A wedding is a responsibility, and it's not something I'd choose to do, Sidney. But let's get something straight right now. I'm doing this because I love your father—"

Sidney laughed a dark, humorless laugh.

"I do love him."

"Love isn't exactly plentiful in this family, not as plentiful as money."

"I think your father has given you both."

"You, maybe. Not me."

Sienna sat back and made the letter *T* with her two forefingers. "Time out," she said. "Let's order. I'm prepared to spend the afternoon. I want to know, Sidney, what this is all about. Why don't you give your father a chance?"

Sidney sniffed and looked at the menu. After a few minutes, she put the menu down and, with her lids still lowered, said, "We can eat later. I'd rather talk first."

Sienna motioned the captain away, looked out at the park that only minutes ago had made the day seem so inviting, and now fearful of what her own frankness might prompt, answered, "I'll listen."

Sidney opened her eyes and looked squarely at Sienna. It was, Sienna thought, the first time she had ever looked directly into her stepdaughter's eyes. "Let's talk history, Sienna. Family history," Sidney began. "You know a lot of stories about my mother, I'm sure. She's been written about and talked about, and everybody seems to think she's some kind of bra-burning nut. Maybe in her day she was. But she did some good things for us. I think she made Gene understand something about women, and when he gets married, he'll probably be a better husband and father than Daddy. My mother's an angry, bitter woman, and I'm her angry, bitter daughter."

Sienna began to speak, but Sidney silenced her with a wave of her hand. "Don't talk yet. This is still my story. I'm not mad at my father for the same reasons my mother is, although maybe I am. Maybe my father just never paid any attention to her, and she decided a woman lover would be better than a man. But I'll tell you straight out what's bugging me. I'm mad at my father because he never noticed me. My mother noticed us too much, and she made us into little sexless symbols of the way she thought the world should be, but my father never paid any attention to me. He related to Gene the day he was born. A father with a son. That was great for a man of my father's generation. There was someone to throw a football with him, someone to take to the office, someone he could put in the business. But a daughter? What could my father do with a daughter? I was never the smartest one in my school. I wasn't the prettiest, and that's what really got to my father. It was okay if I wasn't an all-A student; after all, I was only a girl. But not pretty? Come on. How could I land a husband if I wasn't pretty? And then when he married you, this sexy young torpedo, how could I compete? Well, he's been right. I'm not beautiful. How can I be? I look like him. And next week I'm going to be thirty years old, and he's been convinced for years that I'll never get married. If a girl isn't grabbed from the stag line by the time she's twenty-two, my father thinks she's never going to hook a man. Now he's excited because I'm going to be married, and I'm going to have a big wedding. But I'm going to have a big wedding because I want to show him that I *can* get married, and I can get a family that thinks I'm okay, and I want him to understand that."

"May I say something now?" Sienna asked.

Sidney nodded.

"Do I understand that you don't really want this big, fancy wedding, that you're doing it to make some kind of statement to your father?"

"I want him to spend a lot of money on me and realize it's my wedding and me that's being celebrated, and for once it's not about him."

"That can't happen, Sidney. It won't be your wedding if it's a big wedding. It can't be, because you'll be getting married as your father's daughter. If you really want to make a statement, then I think it should be your statement. You should have exactly the kind of wedding you and your groom want. Incidentally, you haven't said a word about him yet."

"Alvin Horn is a nice man who's two years younger than I, and if he didn't work for Daddy and didn't want to get ahead, he probably wouldn't marry me."

"Do you love him, Sidney?"

"Love? What is love? Love is probably the dumbest reason to get married, because nobody can define love. And don't tell me how you love Daddy. He married you so fast that he must wonder every day if he didn't make a mistake."

Sienna waited a moment. What an ugly thing for Sidney to say. How angry she must be to say something so spiteful. Sienna waited for the words to come to her. How could she hurl an equally vindictive answer? As she sat the idea came to her—was it from the pretty park outside the window? All she knew was that from some place within herself she found herself smiling sweetly and saying words not prompted by any thought she'd ever had. "Interesting that you should say that, because, frankly, I've been wondering for some time if I didn't make a mistake. I could have married Bingham Burke, the corporate raider you read about all the time, and I know he's a lot richer than Peter. So, you're right. Did I marry Peter too fast? Did I really check all my options?"

A slow smile played on Sidney's thin lips. Finally she could contain her amusement no longer and laughed, a real laugh. "You got me, Sienna. You really got me."

It had worked! Sienna could scarcely believe her luck. All right. Now she'd really say what she believed. "I'm not going to let you play this poor-little-rich-girl game with me, Sidney. If you want Alvin, that's okay with me, and I'll work to give you any kind of wedding you want. And if you don't want him, I'll defend your right to stay single."

For the first time there was a softness and a sweet, caring look in Sidney's eyes. "I do love Alvin," she said, and in a rush of overwhelming emotion, her eyes filled, and her voice trembled as she whispered, "I've been afraid to let anyone know. I'm so afraid everyone's going to think I'm a fool. He's so good looking and younger than I, and he works for Daddy, and nobody will ever believe I'm good enough—"

Sienna reached across the table and put her hand gently to Sidney's face. "It doesn't matter what anyone thinks, dear. It's your life. You must believe you're good enough, and if you love him—"

"I do. I do," she repeated, the second time with conviction.

Sienna's small body straightened. "In that case, Ms. Sidney Marvell, you are going to have the best damned wedding New York has ever seen."

"What do you mean?" Sidney asked.

"We're going to have a lovely, loving wedding, and we'll do it at home in Bedford."

"At home in Bedford," Sidney echoed.

Sienna looked at Sidney.

How differently she saw her now.

How powerful love was when you used it in your life.

If she had not loved Peter so much, she never would have listened to Sidney, and if Sidney had not loved Alvin so much, she never could have touched Sienna.

Suddenly Sienna wanted to plan this wedding.

"It should be a dress that Shotsie makes for you, tight bodice, romantic chiffon, I think," Sienna said.

"Won't I look ridiculous?"

"Why?"

"I'm not little and adorable like you. I'm sort of a big, hulking girl."

Sienna shook her head. "Not on your wedding day. You're going to lose ten pounds between now and then, and you're going to be one stately, beautiful bride. Oh, don't you see? You think I'm little and look good, and I always wished I was your height."

Sidney laughed again. "I think I'm ready to order. Suddenly I feel ravenous."

Sienna picked up her menu and shrugged. "We can always start the diet tomorrow."

Sidney dropped the menu to the table. "For the first time I don't mind thinking about tomorrow. Thank you, Sienna. I guess I can see why Daddy married you."

"This family really is a mixed bag." Sienna laughed, but as she laughed she was struck with the thought that for the first time she thought of Peter and his child as *family*. What a new sensation this was.

"A mixed-up mixed bag," Sidney added.

Sienna took a breath and said words she could scarcely believe. "Well, I have an idea we're going to make our mixed bag into a well-mixed blessing."

42

I N THE 1930s, WHEN NEW YORK WAS RECOVERING FROM THE DE-pression, the speakeasy, and the Roaring Twenties, there was a new kind of romantic place where people met to dine, dance, look down on the world, and assure themselves that happy days were here again.

The room, atop a landmark skyscraper, was aspirational, inspirational, and a marked success. Indeed, its very name, the Bellisima Room, became a synonym for thirties rich and right. Its black-and-silver Deco style was widely imitated in lesser places, but by the 1940s the look and attitude were judged passé, and the room metamorphosed from its distinctive style to the well-leathered look of an English gentlemen's club—or at least what an American decorator thought Americans believed to be an English gentleman's club. In the 1950s the Bellisima Room—its name never changed because its owners remained the same—existed as a quasimodern supper club for midwestern businessmen, and in the 1960s the running of the room was turned over to a burgeoning food conglomerate who promptly made it office space. By 1970 the room and the economy had recovered sufficiently to let the room open as a public dining room with the food choice somewhere between birdseed and dog food. In the go-go 1980s the room was stripped down to its origins and was once again a chic New York supper club decorated, of course, in black-and-silver Deco style. And that, of course, was when it was sold to the Japanese, who pledged never to change one thing in their American icon. They promised to keep it the kind of room where a gentleman took a lady, and so it was the perfect room for Gregory Sawyer to choose to dine in with Virginia Payne North. Strangely, it hadn't been a calculated decision. He'd called Virginia around six o'clock, and he'd thought she sounded strangely alone. Impulsively he'd asked her for dinner, and immediately she'd agreed. It had taken only a few phone calls to get the window table looking north past Central Park.

"How pretty it still is," Virginia said as she raised her glass of champagne to proffer a symbolic toast. "Calvin loved this room. He said it made princes of us all."

"Calvin must have been very special," Gregory said.

"He was life, and if you think life is special—and I do think so—then you're right, of course. There never was a man quite like Calvin. He was educated not only in business but in the arts. He was truly a cultured man."

"Was he always rich?"

Virginia smiled. "You always get to the heart of the matter."

"No," said Gregory calmly, "I always look for the heart of you. Don't you think that money made Calvin the cultured man he was?"

"As opposed to you, who have achieved culture without cash?" she asked.

Gregory ignored her question, choosing instead to study the menu intently. In their previous conversations, Virginia had been the one who led the discussions. He usually played with words and kept the talk gossipy, amusing, and above reproach. But there was a difference in Virginia tonight, and he could not quite identify it. He'd invited her here because he'd sensed that somehow he was losing ground; it was all so subtle, actually nothing that he could identify. It had begun just during the past few days, really since the Seconds had come back from the school. What was causing Virginia to be different? He knew the Seconds wouldn't reveal anything. Even now Virginia's answer to him was not a typical Virginia response, but he would not lose his cool. All his life he had played his hand well. Now he was in the biggest game of all, and he would stay calm.

"Virginia, some people don't have to be rich to learn to live well." His voice did not hint at the concern he felt.

"Of course not," she said, and her hand swept the table as if she were brushing aside the remarks she'd made just a few minutes ago. "Now look, Calvin—"

He leaned forward. "I wish I were Calvin. I'm Gregory, dear, but I want to give you the sort of kindness Calvin would if he were here."

Virginia flushed. Why did she call this new man the names of old loves? Perhaps that similarity with men she'd once loved was the magnetic force that had attracted her to Gregory from the moment she'd met him at the New York Coalition. Their meeting had been one of those accidents of New York social life. They'd been there to do good; they wound up having something good happen to them both. Now for so many months he'd been her confidant, her pal, her best friend. He had been in her bedroom with her many times, yet each time they had stopped just short of physical lovemaking, and that suited her. He seemed to know just how far her emotional strength could carry her, and while Virginia enjoyed the sense of warmth and devotion she felt from his arms around her and his lips on hers, she wanted neither the consummation of his ardor nor did she want a man to spend a night in her bed.

She decided to answer his question.

"Maybe I called you Calvin because there's something you do that is so like him. You keep me from pontificating. I get off on a subject every so often and think I know everything, and then with just one sly remark, Calvin would remind me that I'm human."

Gregory shook off his anxiety of minutes ago with a small shrug. "We all are."

"Well then, please forgive my rudeness—"

"Nonsense. There was no rudeness, only concern." Then, in an effort to relax his companion and let her talk in comfort about Calvin, Gregory said, "I'm grateful to Calvin. He gave you so much freedom to live and express yourself that you make life wonderful for everyone around you."

Virginia took a sip of the champagne. She felt a bubbly party glow where only minutes ago there had been a shadowy feeling of foreboding. How strangely alcohol affected her. She leaned across the table, and she laughed a small, tinkling, intimate laugh.

Gregory looked at her with charmed amusement. He was seeing for the first time a little-girl part of her coming to life. This was the way she must have been with Calvin. It was fetching, and he felt a new tenderness at this innocent charm in a sophisticated woman.

"I don't really make life wonderful for me," she confided. "I've never said this before, but somehow I'm finding myself in a strange, new place tonight. Or maybe it's a strange old place. Anyway, I do my best for a lot of people in my life. I love our darling Seconds. They are all very dear, and I know they've had and still have troubles in their lives, but they try. Oh, my dear, how they try to make things work. But at the end of the day they do go home to husbands and lives. I go home to a staff."

Gregory wisely stayed silent.

Virginia's body started to sway slightly. She could hear the music of the orchestra, and couples were dancing around them, but Gregory did not want to interrupt her. He wanted her to keep talking.

She took another sip of the champagne and continued. "There are only a few people who will call me spontaneously and ask, 'What are you doing tonight?' No, I take that back. There's only one person in my life who will call me at six o'clock and say, 'If you're not doing anything tonight, Virginia, how about going to the Bellisima Room with me?' You're the only one, as you can see. How wonderful of you to have called me tonight. This is the anniversary of Calvin's death. Nobody knows things like that anymore. At first we widows mark the day. Then it becomes a week. And after the weeks become too numerous, we change the anniversaries to months. Once we are widowed a year, everyone expects us to pick ourselves up and be fully recovered. But that isn't what true widowhood is about. Oh, I know there are widows who are freer than ever, but I'm not one of them. I am not a merry widow, my dear. I am a married widow."

Gregory nodded an understanding he did not feel.

Virginia paused. "Am I being too melancholy for you, dear?"

He shook his head. "I love listening to you, and when you feel you want to stop, just stop talking. Meanwhile I am deeply touched by your thoughts."

"You know, you're very sympathetic, very understanding, and that's why I'm attracted to you as a friend. Everyone assumes that women with money and high visibility are busy every minute. Of course we're not. I remember a story that an actress friend of mine told me. It was about one of those very popular movie queens of the 1940s or 1950s. I'm not sure which one, but the name doesn't matter. The whole thing is that anyone who needed a date could always call one of those big stars because everyone else was too intimidated to ask them at the last minute. Oh, the big stars get invited to the big parties. But life just isn't one big, long party. Sometimes the nicest part of life is dinner at the Bellisima and dancing with one man who makes you feel like a woman again."

Her words were like a comforting arm around his shoulders. He stood. "Shall we have this dance for Calvin?"

She rose and walked gracefully to the dance floor. The music was an old standard. The man holding her was like an old standard, too. It all felt very good. There were times when life stopped only to go on.

"How sad that Calvin died when he did," Gregory said.

Virginia pulled herself away slightly and looked at her partner. "He is gone, but he didn't die. The truth is that I don't try to keep him alive. But Calvin, my Calvin refuses to die. He is in the music and the moment. He is there in a new ballet and in the beggar on the street who always knew he was an easy touch. I'm not a Queen

Victoria kind of widow. I don't put his clothes on a dummy opposite me at dinner. But I come to a room like the Bellisima, and I dance to music he loved, and he's right here, too."

They moved silently to the music, and each felt the harmony of the moment.

But the moment passed.

And Virginia felt, not for the first time, an increasing uneasiness.

Was Calvin trying to tell her something?

43

DIANDRE DEVON SQUINTED, STOOD SIDEWISE, AND LOOKED AT her naked, freshly bathed self in the mirror. Not bad, old girl, she assured herself. A bit plump by American standards, but this not-so-svelte body had grown fat and happy on the pleasures of the flesh: good food, good wine, good love. She smiled to herself and rubbed briskly, her dimpled thighs now glowing with a pinkness American husbands found so fetching. These American wives with their pills and diets and incessant chatter about their bodies all seemed to have their eyes on the race instead of the finish line. Instead of lusting in hot pursuit of sexual pleasures, the New York ladies seemed to be competing in one giant marathon of thinness, each running off to her favorite gym and then prolonging the pain by panting and sweating at home with a personal trainer. Goodness, she sighed audibly, those ladies spent so much time worrying about their weight that they never have time to enjoy their sleek, slim bodies. Poor things! She shook her head. Thank goodness she'd had a mum who'd believed good bones and good manners would get a girl farther than that incessant calorie counting.

Certainly the good bones and good manners were working for Didi these days and nights. Lady Diandre Devon had moved from her suite at the Wingate ("I don't want my wife checking your bills," Casey had said brusquely) to a penthouse in a condo overlooking the East River. After a month there Lady Diandre had mentioned casually that she knew about an absolutely marvelous penthouse coming on the market on Fifth Avenue. "One good thing

about my being English and Mummy's and Daddy's connections is
that I can waltz into any good co-op in the city," she'd said in her
deliberate offhand manner. Casey got the message immediately. He
understood even without her saying so, precisely what she meant to
communicate: he, Casey, couldn't get into old-line, old-family,
super-Wasp buildings in this city he pretended to own, but he could
get around those snooty co-op boards by having her buy the apartment, appear before the title-happy board members, and charm
them with her accent and connections. Why not? Why not have
Casey own an apartment in a building no one thought would have
him? Of course, she reminded him sweetly at the closing, the apartment has to be in my name only. He hadn't thought about that. But
why not? It was a way to keep her around.

Her public-relations job with Casey was an easy one, for Casey
had proven to be an easy story to sell everywhere in the world. He
had the kind of good looks that made for photo opportunities, and
Casey reveled in each; he was the new corporate Superman for the
TV newsmen and magazine photographers, and he was always available for interviews and photo sessions; his identifiable, caricatured
features now became familiar to the readers of the tabloids and the
personality magazines. His office walls were lined with photographic
evidence of his newfound fame: Casey with the president, Casey
with the governor, Casey with the mayor, Casey with Miss America,
Casey with the poster child. The pictures had grown from the walls
of his office to the boardroom to the hallways until there were now
dozens of pictures of Casey, always the same Casey, the black fore-
lock pulled down and partly hiding his customary insolent stare at
the world, the thick-lipped pout, the defiant stance. No matter who
was in the picture with him, the camera always caught that same
Casey. One day, teasing him lightly, Diandre had said, "I think
you've been photographed with everyone but God and the pope."
Casey had wheeled instantly. "The pope? Can you do it? We'll need
it for the Catholic vote."

Diandre hadn't answered, but that was the day she knew that
his ambitions had no bounds. He wanted to be president. She rather
fancied that idea herself. It would be great fun for a nice English
girl to be America's first lady.

≡

When the doorman called to announce Mr. Burrows, Diandre moved from the cloud of bath powder she'd created, sprayed Casey's favorite scent in a few perfect places, threw her new sable coat over her naked body, and went to the door.

"Aaah, a gentleman caller," she said bewitchingly as she opened the door and hugged the coat close to her body.

"Hi, hi," Casey said. The corners of his mouth, turned down as usual, seemed more bitter today.

She put her arms around him. "I have something for you."

"What?" he asked, his interest now piqued.

"Me."

"That can wait," he said.

"Maybe for you, but not for me," she said as she opened her coat.

"You win," he said. "We'll talk later." He put his arms around her, and the fur fell to the floor. But Casey didn't notice as his hand-made English shoes left footprints in the sable on the way to the bedroom.

≡

Diandre rolled on her back and looked up at the rococo angels on the ceiling. "Ah, Casey," she sighed, "I wonder what the poor people are doing this afternoon."

"You have a great sense of humor, Didi."

"But you must admit I'm funnier when we're undressed."

"Not funnier, more fun," he said in a rare attempt to amuse her.

"My darling, I do think I detect the beginning of a sense of humor."

He looked queerly at her, and she knew the teasing was not appreciated. "Forgive me, Casey. I'll say anything after sex."

Casey, his steely eyes on the far wall, did not hear her. He sat up on one elbow. "Let's talk business."

"What else is there?" she asked archly. The minute she said the words she regretted them. She was getting so—so American. She'd have to stop this fast, cute-answer kind of thing. He already had a wife who did it better than she.

"Give me the lowdown on the London deal, Didi. She's not going to get too much press, is she?"

Lady Diandre inhaled slowly. That wife was always on his mind. "I've got Anne booked for a press conference tomorrow morning. She'll announce the decorating—or redecorating—of the old hotel, but she won't break the news of your building the new hotel. The hotel in Knightsbridge will be yours to announce next week. She's on her way to London now, I reckon, and she'll return in a day or two. When she's safely back, you go and get the big, splashy press. I've got Sky Channel and all the international press set for you, but not for her. She's got the stock stuff, women's news service, and a couple of dotty home service shows."

"Good." He nodded. Casey swung his legs over the side of the bed and sat up, pulling on his socks. "Look, Anne's not a bad kid or anything, but she likes to grab headlines. You know, she was poor, didn't have a dime. She doesn't have your kind of class. She thinks you have to go out and beat up on somebody to get what you want."

"She's tough. But poor Anne, she thinks that's the only way to play."

"Still, you've got to push the magazines. Maybe you ought to try a little of her toughness, Didi, especially with the print media. I don't like what they're saying this week."

"But, darling, weren't you just where you wanted to be in the listing of *Bumper Magazine*'s four hundred richest Americans?"

"Hell no. I made the list, but they underestimated me by two billion dollars. Jesus, two billion. My kid Fudge can count better than that."

"I'm sure she can, Casey. But if you didn't like the *Bumper*'s list, I'm sure you liked the mayor's list of the twenty most important New Yorkers. You were number four."

"But I was beaten out by two old ladies with those ridiculous puny family fortunes and an ex-ambassador."

"You were the only businessman in the top five."

"But then they described me as 'controversial.' What's controversial about seven billion dollars?"

"I don't think they were talking about money," Diandre assured him.

He said nothing and glumly looked at the sock on his foot.

Didi kept her eyes on him. He was such a little boy. But then, weren't they all? She'd have to find something to remind him he was still her prince. She giggled softly. "I was just remembering the time you kicked the reporter who wrote about your Park Avenue building and said, 'The only valid thing is its vulgarity.' "

"I kicked his leg. I should have kicked higher," Casey recalled morosely.

"Why, luv? You're no Rockette." Diandre rolled across the bed and pulled him back down beside her. One of her rules was never to let a man leave her bed unhappy. "Let me make you smile," she said.

He pushed her away. "Naw, not that way again."

Diandre released him and nodded. It was with her first lover that she'd learned the greater the ego, the less the libido. She'd thought once of having "Great egos make little libidos" embroidered on a pillow and sold in those fancy Madison Avenue boutiques, the shops where ladies who lived on their backs went to put up their front.

She was aware that sex wasn't an answer—or even a question— at this moment. Her only real problem was how to keep this man's vacillating ego up.

She tried another ploy. "The mayor's dinner should be a dilly tonight because you're definitely going to be the most important person there," she half-whispered seductively.

Now his camera-ready smile returned. "You think so?"

"I'm sure. I'm very sure."

"What do I say when they ask where Anne is?"

"Oh, darling, just say she's at home with the children."

Casey laughed. "At home with the children. Doesn't sound like Anne to me."

Diandre laughed with him. She didn't mention that it didn't sound like Casey either.

44

ANNE GLANCED NERVOUSLY AT HER WATCH. SHE HADN'T IN-tended to be a part of Virginia's luncheon group today, but really there had been no choice. "Of course you'll come, darling," Virginia had said in that offhand, casual tone that served as a command to the Seconds.

"I'm leaving on the morning Concorde. I won't be in town,"

Anne explained. "I want to get to London refreshed and relaxed because I have a lot of interviews, people to see—"

"I want you there," Virginia now said, but this time her tone was a shade softer. "This one is for me, Anne, and you're the only one of the Seconds with enough clout to get the women I need for the seed group." Then Virginia paused. "You know, my dear, I always say that in New York charity begins at home. No charity can get its first dollar until there is a core group to raise that money, and the only way to get the group started is with a luncheon at home. So you see, I not only want you, I need you."

As if the words were not convincing enough, Virginia had couched her thoughts in that supersoft tone that moved millions every year, the famous Virginia plea that raised hard cash and moved hard hearts throughout New York. Thanks to Virginia's imprimatur, millions of people became aware of charities and diseases they might otherwise have ignored, and millions of dollars flowed into charity's channels.

In the end Anne came because she couldn't say no to Virginia; in her soft-spoken, underplayed authority lay Virginia's real strength and service to her city. From the mayor on down, no one had ever really learned a way to say no to Virginia Payne North. Virginia knew almost instinctively from her many years as the executive assistant to Calvin Forbes North how to play power against power, how to apply the pressures of business to charity. If you wanted a donation, you put someone in charge who was in a business position to grant favors. Never mind who worked hard. Never mind who came to the meetings. All that mattered were the pressure points.

And that was why, instead of flying over the Atlantic at that moment as she had told her husband she would, Anne sat at luncheon in Virginia's pale peach dining room with Tess Waters, Bonnie Brickmaster, and Juliet Caesar, listening to Gregory Sawyer, his blue eyes growing misty, as he spoke with love of the Rosabelle School. "It was my desire and the wish of Anne and her dear friends to name the school for Virginia, but in her modesty Virginia simply wouldn't hear of it. The school, therefore, will be called"—now Gregory's voice cracked emotionally—"the Rosabelle School."

Anne was glad she hadn't eaten more than a roll; Gregory's unctuous style was making her feel more nauseated than would a bumpy plane ride.

Bonnie Brickmaster, the woman who sold the co-ops and townhouses to the rich and famous and then stayed in their lives as a kind of fairy godmother to entertain them and become their friend, sighed deeply. "Virginia, this is just the kind of commitment and dedication we've learned to expect from you. What would New York be without you?"

Did these women think she could be flattered with that kind of talk? Virginia faced her directly and said briskly, "Without me I guess New York would be just another dirty city with the homeless on the streets, the rich in the apartments you sell them and Tess here decorates. What I'm saying, Bonnie, if you'll forgive me, is that despite your kind words about my participation, we're still a dirty city with the homeless on the streets and the rich looking down from safe havens like this one. But if you women will agree to help with the Rosabelle School, maybe we can save a few lives. Maybe we can make a difference, and the thing I like best is that we can see those we help. It's not that same faceless medical research—not that I don't give millions a year to medicine; I do and I'll continue to do that—but every once in a while I like to remember that somewhere there are names and faces to be helped. The Rosabelle School will make that possible."

Juliet Caesar wiped a tear from her eyes. "What do you want me to do?"

Virginia looked at her for a moment and put an arm around her. Of the women in the room, probably Juliet was the only one besides Virginia who'd ever lived in real poverty. Only a year earlier Juliet Caesar (under her given name Hester) was stripping for a living in Las Vegas; now she was the recent fourth wife of Pontius "Shopping Centers" Caesar, a seventy-five-year-old mega-merger genius who'd made his first real millions building some of America's ugliest and most successful shopping centers. Virginia knew that Old Shopping Centers was eager to make Young Wife the toast of New York, but Virginia knew she'd never do it flaunting those daytime diamonds and *wow baby* hemlines. Her own Seconds, now established and centered in their own lives, had made Virginia think it was time to take on a new project. So after Shotsie's fashion show Virginia had called Juliet. She'd convinced her not to flaunt her gems by day; instead Juliet was now banded and bonded in gold. Virginia introduced her to Bonnie, who, of course, sold her the new apartment; Tess was decorating it. Those two pros wouldn't let Juliet fail. They couldn't afford to. "Juliet," Virginia said in her well-known super-soft tone, "you have a truly good heart; I want you to be the chairman of the fund-raiser for the Rosabelle School."

"Oh, thank you, Vir—Mrs. North," she said. Being part of a hot charity was even better than having a baby for holding Daddy Warbucks in place. He'd be damned impressed. Three wives, and he'd never even been invited to Virginia Payne North's apartment.

"Call me Virginia," the hostess said firmly.

Juliet sighed in relief. Boy oh boy, was it ever fun being rich.

Gregory leaned back, a wave of satisfaction warming his lean body. Virginia was in his hip pocket; no matter what anyone thought, charm was still the key to life at the top.

"Thank you, Gregory," he heard Virginia say, and the words brought him back to the luncheon table.

He stood and nodded. He knew Virginia's words of dismissal, and he knew the tone if not the words. Damn. Just when he'd hoped he could stay a while and get to know these women better. Especially Juliet. She was ripe for his kind of man. She needed someone to teach her the ropes, and Virginia wasn't really strong enough to take on another pupil. Oh well, he'd call Juliet; certainly Virginia had given him reason, and perhaps one night when her aging prince wasn't able to attend a royal ball, he'd escort her. How nice of Virginia to give him this one. He smiled and thanked each of the ladies, shook their hands, kissed Virginia and Anne, and left the room.

Anne knew this was her signal to leave, too, but as she was ready to say good-bye, Virginia turned to the women and said in an almost conspiratorial tone, "Now tell me what's going on in the City. I haven't been out in weeks—"

As she spoke, Anne realized that she had been so involved in her own life that she'd scarcely realized that indeed Virginia had remained at home these past weeks. Anne felt a flood of guilt, and instead of preparing to leave, she settled in her chair and asked for another cup of coffee. She would not break up this luncheon that Virginia still wanted to enjoy.

The women sat in silence for a moment, each thinking what news she might bring Virginia.

Juliet Caesar was the first to speak. "Albert Baxter died, and we went to pay our respects," she announced.

Anne shuddered. The Seconds had never been that dumb. This woman was in desperate need of coaching. Bonnie and Tess had their work cut out for them.

Virginia, ever the perfect lady, smiled at Juliet. "Well, that's not quite the news I'm seeking. I like to know what's happening that the newspapers don't report. You know, I love the stories about the ways all of you beard the social lions in this town. Frankly, don't you think it's kind of wonderful the way we outsiders show the insiders how to live? If it weren't for Bonnie and Tess, the sort of Bonnie and Clyde of New York life, all those wary Wasps would still be sitting on their grandmothers' threadbare chairs in old apartments. But thanks to us, the upholsterers all got rich, and the decorators made a killing. And plenty of old-line families got their hands on a few new millions selling the family homestead. Frankly, Juliet dear, a marriage like yours is very good for everybody. It just keeps all the money in circulation."

Juliet smiled. Was this old lady for real?

Tess wiggled comfortably in her chair. She'd been waiting to tell her latest piece of news. What better place to drop it than here? "Have you heard about Montana Richardson?" she asked quietly.

"What?" Virginia inquired, a girlish excitement coming into her voice.

"She and Tex McDonald are seeing each other."

"What about Rose McDonald?" Anne asked with the concern of a wife whose husband's philandering was as well-known as Tex's.

"Oh, darling, Rose is so involved with the downtown art scene that she probably doesn't even know that Tex hasn't been home for two years."

"I guess Montana is a new taste for Tex," Virginia commented.

"Montana is fabulous," Tess reported with the enthusiasm of a decorator who knows a client is on the horizon. "She's got that European charm. Nobody knows how to hold a man better than a European woman. And Montana is funny and good-looking."

Anne said nothing; she wondered if this was what people said about Diandre, too. A European woman—

"There's the funniest scene in town with Montana," Bonnie added enthusiastically. "She left her husband, T.J., and guess who's consoling T.J.?"

"A downtown artist?" Virginia guessed.

"No, no," Bonnie said. "It's better than that." Now she paused to let the full effect sink in. "T.J. is being comforted by Alan Packer, who was Montana's lover. Isn't that wonderful? The two jilted men are going everywhere together sobbing over their loss."

Juliet blinked. So this is what rich was like. God, she'd heard better stories backstage. "This reminds me of a girl I used to work with, name of Rocky Rippo."

A hush fell over the room.

"Rocky had this boyfriend Chester from before she was married. Chester was a big-bucks guy. They said he had mob connections, but I never saw them, and you know what I don't see, I don't say. That's a line I always use, 'What I don't see, I don't say.' So Chester bought her stuff like, I mean, like you wouldn't believe. Real stuff. The big-ticket items. Some people think it was hot, but like I say, what I don't see, I don't say. So Chester was taking her out for like, years, and he never said any of the *m* words—you know, *marriage, motherhood*—the *m* words. Get it? Well, so she figures this is leading fast to Nowheresville, and pretty soon she finds out he never talks about the future because this creep has a wife. So pretty soon Rocky meets a guy in the club, and he's there on one of those conventions. He's a big shot in some company, and before you know what's really happening, he decides to marry her. Oh my God, did we have parties for days. It was something. So there they are married and everything. To tell the truth, he didn't marry her until she had one in the oven, but then he did the right thing. So they get married, and she sort of settles down, and then one day she goes to some convention with her husband in New York, and who's there? You guessed it. Chester. Jeez. She can hardly believe it, and neither can he. So pretty soon they start foolin' around, and before you know it, she skips out on her husband and takes the kids. Well, the husband is real broken up, but she sets up housekeeping on her own, and before anybody really knows what's flying, Chester is out of his house and in an apartment near her. So, next thing you know he's spending more and more time at her house, and pretty soon the kids are calling him Uncle Chester, and he's telling his wife that this is his real love, and it's good-bye, Tootsie. The wife is a tough fighter, and even though she's had this creep for forty years, she acts like she wants him another forty. So she hollers and sets up a big stink and calls him. You know, that's the unwritten rule. You never call the husband, but this wife calls the husband, and they both yell so loud you can hear them over the sound of the slot machines. Then we learn that she wants him because this Chester guy is now worth big bucks. But pretty soon he gets tired of Rocky and the kids because, let's face it, this is one old guy—not as old as my husband, of course—but so old that he can't handle little kids, and she's got little kids. Also she thinks maybe she's pregnant, and she doesn't know if it's Chester's or not. But Rocky is a lady. She doesn't breathe a word to Chester. He goes back to the rotten wife, and after a couple of weeks he can't stand the old lady's bitching so he comes back to Rocky. Now she knows she's pregnant, but she doesn't want to get an abortion because she really likes kids, so she says to Chester that she's gotta get married. And Chester say, 'Listen, honey, you're the best lay I ever had, but I'm not sure it's worth seven million dollars.' "

Now Juliet took a deep breath. At last she was one of the girls.

Anne sat dumbfounded. This was the difference between a poor family and the rest of the world. Anne had been poor, but she had been raised by a mother with standards and values that had been imparted in many ways to her. This—this woman might have come to them in New York from Mars or Jupiter. This was another world, another culture. There was nothing she could say, nothing she wanted to say.

Bonnie leaned over and patted Juliet's hand. "That's quite a story, dear, but there are some stories that are so sad they shouldn't be told."

"I guess you're right," Juliet said.

Virginia looked at Juliet and sighed. She'd never had one this rough, this unknowing. One of the reasons she'd always enjoyed her Seconds was that they had become successful with ease. They had no background, so each was able to invent herself. In a way each of them came from nowhere—although Sienna did have a well-connected family in Cleveland, still it was Cleveland and not New York, so she wasn't truly known—but the Seconds were never embarrassed or afraid to invent themselves. This poor child didn't need inventing; she needed to be melted down and recast. Well, Bonnie and Tess would try. They'd smell the money and rush to the race. But this was a job for the Seconds.

Virginia knew she was right when Tess turned sweetly, and as if nothing had been said, purred, "Oh, guess who I saw just before I came here." And then without waiting for the guessing to begin, she rushed to tell her story. "I stopped in at Von Hoffens to get my diamond-and-ruby earrings eased—I can hardly wear them, they pinch me so badly—and there was Rebecca Houseman, that woman who lives with Henry Wimple. Well, there she was with absolutely the biggest diamond this side of the Ritz. I just blinked and blinked. 'What's it for?' I asked, and she just laughed and said, 'Oh, that was for dessert.'"

Bonnie looked at her watch. "I'd like this dessert to go on for days, but I've got an appointment to show the Killington apartment to the Japanese."

"Darling, they'll never get in that building," Tess said with authority.

"You're right," Bonnie said, "but if I don't show them that apartment, someone else will. What this does is establish my taste level so that they know that anything I show them will be class with a capital c."

Tess rose to leave, too. "When's the first meeting of the Rosabelle School, Juliet?" she asked.

Juliet rose and flushed slightly. "Ask Virginia."

"It will be decided, and you'll be there, dear," Virginia said to Juliet.

Now Anne stood and went to kiss Virginia. "Don't leave just yet, Anne," Virginia said. It was the super-soft tone. Anne stood riveted.

The others said their brief good-byes, and since Virginia had dismissed her with the real-estate tycoon and the interior designer, Juliet left, too.

"Come help me into the library," Virginia said to Anne. Anne pulled out Virginia's chair and was surprised at how weak her friend seemed. At the table she had seemed so commanding; now she was dependent.

Seated at her desk, Virginia turned to Anne. "You have a lot of questions about this whole venture, don't you, dear?"

"Venture?"

"Don't play games, Miss Smart Girl. I'm talking about the Rosabelle School."

"I think you answered some of my questions at lunch."

"Yes, it's true. I want to give something more personal than research dollars to scientists. I also want to continue to affect lives as I think I did with you girls."

"You certainly have helped us."

"I want to help you once more, Anne."

Anne felt her hands grow cold. "What do you want to tell me?"

"Nothing that you don't already know. But I want to remind you of something. I'm older than you, and I have plenty of money. No matter what happens, I guess you'll have money, too, Anne. But you have something that I don't. You have children. You have a real legacy. You won't have to go out and look for someplace to leave a human trace, an evidence of your life. It's there in your home. All I want to say to you, Anne, is that I hope you won't get so involved in money and position and this sometimes difficult and embarrassing life that you forget those in your life who really need you. This woman, this Juliet, is one of New York's neediest cases. She has the potential to be a great asset to the charities in the City, and with the needs we have and the curtailed budgets, that could be a god-send. So don't look down your nose. Help her. And help yourself, too. Now come and give me a kiss good-bye, darling, and don't forget that for you, New York will let you give much more than a big party."

45

BEING A MAN WAS NOT EASY WHEN YOU WERE A MEMBER OF THE No Generation. That was what Peter Marvell called his contemporaries, the No Generation, that group made up of those males who were a part of no generation characterized by a major event of the twentieth century. These were the men born after the depths of the Depression, too young for the Good War and too old for the Good Times.

The Good War began with Pearl Harbor, a time when boys Peter's age were learning how to spell three-syllable words while their older brothers and uncles and cousins were learning how to pronounce the names of three-syllable islands, places where some would fight and some would die. No, they would miss the adventure of the Good War.

The Good Times would start with Haight-Ashbury, but there would be no Beat Generation philosophers or even hippies among Peter and his pals, for by the time the generation of flower children went on the road, Peter and his friends were deep into the conventional 1950s number. They'd graduated from good schools, found good jobs, married good girls, and started raising good kids.

As the 1970s approached and these young men were ready at last to raise a little hell of their own, they found that the women they'd married had decided to assert themselves. Dumbfounded and dejected, the men now learned that women were equal, and damned if guys hadn't missed the Good Times.

It was a topsy-turvy world, and Peter adjusted slowly to the revolutions and the plethora of changed rules under which men were supposed to be tender instead of tough, and women were to be tough instead of tender.

By 1990 the world had changed once more. Money was the name of the game, and for the first time Peter seemed to be playing the right game at the right time. Indeed, all things considered, Peter thought he was doing better than most men, regardless of age.

As he looked about him, he saw the fragmented results of the revolutions. Men who had been on time for a few of the generational changes were now completely bewildered by women and annoyed, annoyed at uppity women. How dare they force their way into clubs where they weren't wanted, into jobs where they weren't needed, and ignore the place where they were necessary—at a man's side, to support and sustain him against the slings and arrows of a sloppy world.

The men Peter's age had now graduated to a truculent truce as they reached down to lend a somewhat reluctant hand to the women on their way up.

But those men young enough to be Peter's son—and most particularly, his own son, Gene—made no secret of their resentment toward the females of the corporate world. "Listen," Gene would grumble to his father, "every girl I ever met could beat me out of a place in law school or medical school. These women are so damned aggressive that they've even taken over the business schools."

Peter suppressed his urge to ask Gene what his feminist mother thought of her angry son, but the reason he never asked was that he was not certain of the source of Gene's anger. And Peter didn't really want to know if Gene's anger had to do with real or imagined career disappointments, real or imagined romantic failures, or real or imagined parental lapses. Then, too, Peter did not discount Gene's ability to play his own political games. Was his son simply saying what he thought his father wanted to hear? Was this just another put-down of his mother, after all?

What made Peter's world truly topsy-turvy was that he'd reversed the contemporary wife roles in his marriages. His wives had been out of sync with history, for his first wife had the independence of today's second wives, and his second wife had the homing instincts of a first wife.

In the world of new women and old women, Sienna played an old-fashioned role. It was almost as if she had done every bad thing a young girl could do and now wanted to do every good thing an older woman could do. Certainly Virginia was a calming influence in the lives of all the once-wild Seconds.

Peter had no illusions about the backgrounds of the Seconds. Abused by life, they had fought and slept their way to the place where they found themselves now—on the letterheads of all the best charities, where they hoped their dollars would expunge their sins.

≡

Peter reached down to tie his running shoes.

Well, proof of his husbandhood was this gesture.

"Darling," Sienna had said in her doll-wife voice as he was leaving their bedroom to go to work this morning, "I almost forgot to tell you something."

"Yes?"

"The Dome has a track."

"The Dome has a track?" He'd stopped at the door of the room, retraced his steps to her bedside, and repeated her statement in order to have time to think of what she'd said, for even though he was still in their bedroom, his mind had already traveled to his office.

"Anne put in a health club, and she has a one-mile track."

He had smiled indulgently and rolled her words over in his mind. Sometimes he was not aware of what she said because of the way she often spoke, in a voice that had the freshness and wonder of a little girl's. That naïveté was in her tone this morning, and despite his desire to go to the office, he had an even greater desire to tease that girlie-girl side of Sienna. "A one-mile track? I think not, Sienna."

"No? Well, I guess I heard wrong," she'd admitted, her eyes wide. "Maybe I made a mistake."

"It's probably a quarter-mile track," he'd said, patting her cheek.

"Good." She'd smiled. "Then it will be easier for you to run tonight."

"Oh no, now you lost me," he'd said as he backed away from the bed. "Now you're playing games. If you want something, tell me. But don't do this TV-wifey nitwit-show stuff with me."

"All right," she'd answered, quickly erasing the coyness and resuming her normal voice. "Anne has added a three-million-dollar health club to the Dome. It will be a members-only kind of club, and of course they'd like you to join. They don't even want you to pay, but I said I knew you'd have to see it for yourself. So I told Anne you'd go over to the health club tonight, and Bronwyn said she'd send Harold, and Anne is going to have Casey there, and we thought it would be really nice if the three of you worked out together in the gym, maybe had a drink and then—"

"Sienna, you know I'm not going to be at home for dinner tonight. I told you that last night, and, darling, the men I'm going to see are about to make me richer than I ever thought I could be."

"You mean you won't go to the Dome?"

Peter paused. Ever since that night that Sienna's mother had left their house, Peter had sensed something different in his wife. Was it his fault that Peppy had come on to him as she had? Sienna just seemed so—so preoccupied these days—but damn it, so was he. Preoccupied with creating the Fund. Preoccupied with this ambassador thing. *What interests you, Mr. Marvell? Of course, it's not really your choice, Mr. Marvell.* These guys could make you crazy, acting as if it weren't your big bucks that made you eligible in the first place. Big bucks for the presidential campaign. Big bucks to keep an embassy running. Who could do it all on government money? Was Sienna afraid of being an ambassador's wife? No, she could do it with the back of her hand. Look how she ran these houses. Look what she was doing for Sidney, turning that thorn in his life into a rose. And all Sienna was asking in return was one evening with those silly men.

Somehow he sensed that by agreeing to go to the Dome he could give inordinate pleasure to Sienna. He softened his voice and assumed an unaccustomed gentleness for early-morning-on-the-way-to-office time. "Sienna, are you trying to tell me that it's important to you that I go? Does it affect your friendship with Anne?"

Sienna felt a comfortable wave of pleasure; she'd just had an unexpected view of her husband's sensitivity to her needs. "Yes, it's important to Anne, so I guess that makes it important to me. This is some sort of a dry run, and Anne'd like our husbands to see what they think of the facility. And it would be kind of nice if the husbands—" Now her voice trailed.

Peter nodded. "If I read you right, you want me to go to this gym, but underneath it all, you want me to be friendly with the husbands of your best friends. The former is not difficult; the latter is impossible."

"Oh, Peter, you're the one husband I'd thought would do it."

Now he laughed. What would Wall Street think of tough Peter Marvell, who said no colder and faster than anyone on the Street now saying yes to a deal that didn't net him a dime? "All right, love. Here's what I'll do for you. When I leave the office, I'll work out at the Dome instead of the club, shower and dress, have a drink with Casey and Harold, and go on to my dinner."

"Thank you, dear," she whispered softly as she got out of bed and reached for his arm.

"I'm already seven minutes late," he protested, the frown lines appearing now between his eyes. Enough was enough.

"I just wanted to thank you," she said as she stood on tiptoes and kissed his cheek.

Peter felt the frown ease from his face and the tension from his body. She really was sweet. He bent over and kissed her with a new enthusiasm, for somewhere in his body an old guilt had been put to rest, but damned if he could even remember the reason he'd felt guilty in the first place.

Everyone had said that it was impossible to build a health club in the Dome; there simply wasn't enough room. You'd have to give up too many rentable rooms; you'd lose revenue. But Casey had laughed. He knew what he wanted. He wanted the one place in New

York that would be a clublike club without clublike rules. All the money players could get in here, and money would be the key to the sense of belonging.

So Casey had gutted the old rooms and built the new club with spectacular city and park views. He'd raised the room rates, upped the service fees, charged more in the dining rooms, and knew that, in the long run, he'd win.

The club living room was paneled in oak from an English castle, and the locker rooms for men—instead of being gymlike and utilitarian—were almost baronial.

Even Peter, blasé as he was about such things as comfort and ostentatious décor, was taken aback. The locker room's heavy carved walls were hung with—were they the real stuff or just good imitations?—Old Masters. The floors were not tiled; they were covered wall-to-wall with soft, plush, dark red wool carpet. Instead of individual lockers, there were individual dressing rooms, and in place of an attendant was an English valet to attend to each gentleman's needs.

It was the valet who escorted Peter around the club when he arrived. "You're a touch early," the valet informed him in a clipped accent, "but I'm certain Mr. Burrows wouldn't want to keep you waiting."

Peter smiled. That had been his plan. Arrive early, and with a little luck he might even miss Mine Host.

Peter went into his dressing room and put on his gym clothes quickly. He walked from the room, and there was his valet. Still he was in luck.

No sign of those other husbands. Well, that was all right with him. He'd done his job. He'd shown up. Peter looked around the locker room. Maybe if he moved fast, he could miss Casey and Harold. Not exactly two of anybody's favorites. Casey with that overweening ego, and Harold with that underlying madness.

Oops. He felt the tightness in his legs. Better warm up those muscles before taking a little run. He put his arms out toward the carved wall, reached for a smooth place, and started his stretches. It was just then that he saw Casey, already in running shorts, coming toward him. Peter groaned. So he wasn't going to get out free after all.

Peter had his own style of running. He called it the Prima Donna Method. It allowed for no outside influences. What Peter liked was to go to the Athletic Club each night, head directly for the track, and run alone. In the quiet of that run, he sorted out his life. It was while running on that track that he'd made the biggest decisions of his life. It was both his personal and professional lives that he put under the microscope each day. It was his way of dealing with the pressures of being a No Generation Man on the verge of the twenty-first century. It was while on the track he'd decided his marriage to Judith must end. On the track he'd first thought of and later put together the plan that resulted in the first big merger of Wall Street firms. And it was on the track that he'd decided to marry Sienna. Running wasn't just exercise; it was therapy. No, it was more than therapy. It was a way of life. Peter didn't like disruptions in his carefully constructed life.

He was uncomfortable in this locker room in the Dome, for he was about to make a change in his daily pattern. And then, as if it wasn't bad enough running in a new place, Casey had shown up.

"Hey, Peter." Casey gave Peter a punch on the arm. Peter breathed deeply. He did not like being touched. "How do you like my place." Casey asked the question as a statement, for he was sure of the answer.

Casey's pride was so evident that Peter had a great desire to bring the owner down to earth. "Do the showers work?" Peter asked with a small smile.

An anxious look came into Casey's eyes. "Oh my God, don't tell me—"

"Not telling. Just asking," Peter said. He wondered why he was deliberately baiting Casey. This was not the way he usually treated people. But the bastard was so smug about this place.

Casey paused. "You're not kidding me, are you?"

"Maybe I am," Peter said. Now he punched Casey's arm. Hey, two could play the old punch-in-the arm game.

"Yeah, yeah," Casey said, but as he spoke he looked at Peter suspiciously. Hard to believe this guy was some kind of merger genius.

"I'm going to try your track," Peter said.

"Aw, don't go on the track. If you run on a track, you might as well go to the park. You ought to see the equipment we have here.

We got the latest machines, two trainers from European spas—"

"I'm going to try your track," Peter repeated.

"I'll go with you," Casey said.

Peter shrugged. Just what he didn't want, someone to tag along. Well, in for a dime, in for a dollar. As long as he was here, he'd let Casey run with him. "Better stretch your hamstrings," Peter advised. "You don't want to end up with sore muscles."

"Don't worry about me," Casey said. "I get a lot of exercise all day long."

Peter decided not to explore that statement; he'd heard all the gossip about Casey and the English lady.

Peter started his run slowly; he'd pick up speed later and leave Casey behind. "Hey," Casey puffed, "slow down, and we can talk."

Peter eyed his running companion. What did this lazy bum want? A walkathon?

Still, he'd told Sienna he'd come. Now Peter searched his mind for a topic of conversation. "Market closed up today."

"Wait until tomorrow," Casey snorted. "I'm making a play that'll make all you downtown guys crazy."

"You going for the cola business?" Peter asked.

"Bigger," Casey answered.

"Good luck," Peter said in as gracious a tone as he could muster.

"I'd give you a tip if I could," Casey acknowledged.

Peter said nothing. This dummy didn't realize that by saying he was going after another company he'd already violated the ethics of the business.

"Want to buy a baseball team?" Casey asked.

"No," Peter said. Then, lest he seem too abrupt, he added, "I'm not a sports nut."

"Who is?" Casey asked. "Outside of screwing women, I can't think of one good physical activity."

A real charmer, Peter thought, but if he's offering, I'd better let him know the answer is no. One Peppy episode had taught him the dangers of playing with words. "Other women isn't one of my interests. I have enough at home."

"You have enough at home? Sienna's a little girl. I've got a big one, Anne, and that's not enough. A man's gotta have a lot of challenge. Business is good. I like to keep score; I like business, but you gotta get your mind off things. That's what women are good for, and besides—what the hell. It's another way of keeping score."

Peter said nothing.

"I know a woman you'd like a lot," Casey offered. "Different from Sienna. Tall, great body. I'll introduce you. Listen, why should the girls have all the fun? Our wives go out and buy clothes to impress each other. With us guys, it's women. You know, that's something most women don't understand. That's what's so fantastic about Didi—"

"Didi?"

"Woman I'm seeing now. English broad. Maybe you remember her. She was at Virginia's the night we all had dinner there."

"So the tabloids have the right story?" Peter asked.

"Not the good stuff," Casey confided. "She's a very smart dame. Englishwomen have a lot of class. Fact of the matter is, Peter, she has this friend you'd really go for."

"I just told you I don't go for other women," Peter reminded him.

"Ha," Casey retorted. "What are you so high and mighty about? Sienna was nothing but a little Hollywood tramp. Everybody knew that. Somebody offered her to me before you. Just because you think you're going to be ambassador in some godforsaken country—"

Peter did not quicken his pace, but he knew he wanted to leave Casey far behind. He wanted to burn up the track. He wanted to put a blowtorch to this creep. What was he trying to prove? Which wife was better? Or that all women wanted him? And did it matter what he was trying to say? Peter knew that men played all kinds of games. God knows that Peter himself played plenty of games and put his business at risk each day, but he wasn't going to put his marriage on the gaming table for any Casey Burrows call girl. For the first time Peter saw how ugly and distasteful it was when a successful man tried to turn everything in his life into a toy, competing at every level, finding nothing too distasteful to discuss, nothing too sacred to explore. Everything had to be shaped into another way of saying, "Mine is bigger and better than yours—nyah, nyah, nyah."

Peter slowed his speed. How much was he willing to pay for an ambassadorship? Would he be willing to give up his marriage as he

knew it now? Is this what was making Sienna so touchy? What kinds
of worms would come crawling out from under the rocks before he
was approved by the Senate—*if* he could even be approved by the
Senate?

He had to get out of here. "Owwww, I just pulled a hamstring."
Peter gasped in mock pain. "I've got to get off the track, Casey. I
think I'll take a good hot shower and leave."

"Why leave? Harold's coming," Casey offered.

Peter shuddered. That was all he needed. "Give him my re-
gards," Peter said.

"Well, you know Harold. He's so crazy he probably won't even
show."

"Right," Peter agreed as he ran off the track, "Harold's really
the crazy one."

"Hey!" Casey shouted. "You're running; I thought you said you
pulled a muscle."

"I did," Peter said as he remembered to limp, "but I feel a lot
better now."

A few minutes later, with the hot, stinging spray of the shower
on his body, Peter wondered about the men of the No Generation.
Maybe there was a name for these men, after all. Maybe they'd all
be remembered by their most famous financial ploy. It would serve
us right, he thought in a sudden moment of self-incrimination, if the
history books of the twenty-first century labeled us—the Junk Bond
Generation.

46

"MRS. BURROWS, WE HAVE A PROBLEM."
Anne looked up as she entered her penthouse.

The speaker was Miss Patch.

Of course it had to be Miss Patch. Who but the nanny in a rich
woman's home felt privileged enough to use the editorial "we"?

"What's wrong, Miss Patch?"

"It's Cissy."

"Five isn't an easy age, Miss Patch. What is it now?"

"She's crying for you."

"For me?"

"She wants you to hold her."

Anne shrugged. "She's too big for that."

"That's what I told her."

"And?"

"She's in the midst of a tantrum. She's thrown her Bootsie Wootsie doll in the loo, and there's a flood in the children's bathroom. The water has come down into the dining room."

"The hand-painted antique wallpaper from Paris?"

"Ruined, I think."

Anne rolled her eyes heavenward. Darling Virginia with all her prating about human legacy had never had to face the consequences of children's actions. "Just call the maintenance department here at the Dome, and they'll send someone up. Then have my office call—never mind. Just call maintenance. I'm going to see Cissy."

Miss Patch pursed her thin lips. "I wouldn't do that, Mrs. Burrows."

"Why?"

"The child should be punished. You're what she wants, so you're precisely what she shouldn't get."

"Is that your philosophy of child raising, Miss Patch?"

Miss Patch raised her head, and her chin quivered slightly. She was not accustomed to criticism from her part-time mothers. "I have raised some of the wealthiest children—"

"And money, of course, is all a child needs to be happy?" Anne asked quietly.

"Not *all,*" Miss Patch admitted.

Anne looked at Miss Patch and saw her as if they were meeting for the first time. Miss Patch was part of that long line of women born to service, a breed that was rapidly dying out. What was she doing in Anne's home except what Anne had given her to do—and that was to act as the replacement mother, the mother-in-house while Anne operated as the mother-in-fact and the mother-in-office. Suddenly Anne felt weary, embarrassed by her tone and words. "I'm being harsh, Miss Patch, and I've no right. You deal with the children every day, but I do want to see Cissy now. Maybe what we should be is a better team."

Miss Patch looked in wordless surprise at Anne. This was the first time she had ever seen Mrs. Burrows with her defenses down, her mouth not drawn in that thin, cold line of ruthless judgment.

Anne, her shoulders hunched, crossed the gallery filled with the paintings her art consultant had collected, climbed the stairs her architect had designed, and walked into the nursery her decorator had furnished. Huddled in the corner was the daughter her nanny had scolded. "Cissy," Anne whispered. "Cissy, Mommy's here for you."

Cissy lifted her tearstained face. Her long blond hair was pulled up in a ponytail, and wisps curled about her damp forehead. Anne reached for her, and Cissy pulled back, curling her body into a small ball. "Come to Mommy. I'm here for you," Anne repeated.

Cissy shook her head and began to cry loudly.

"Why won't you come to Mommy?" Anne asked, still afraid to touch her child.

"B-b-b-because," Cissy sobbed, "my tooth is loose, and Miss Patch wants me to spit it out, and I won't. You went away. I wanted you to take it, and you didn't. You didn't come home. I hate you."

Anne pulled back and looked at her firstborn crouched in a corner, a child angry with her mother, angry with her nanny, and angry because she had to face a world without the two people she needed—and disliked—the most. For a moment Anne saw herself, an original of the unhappy child who now looked up at her. Yet for all Anne's childhood anxiety, Anne's mother had never failed to be there when she was needed. Anne rose slowly and walked into her dressing room. It was time to pack to go to London. She rang for her maid. "Just throw a few things from the black wardrobe in a small bag," she instructed. "I'll be away overnight."

Wordlessly the maid who'd heard the battle between child and nanny followed instructions. As she packed for Anne in the executive way Anne had taught (all clothes in only one color so that only one kind of accessory was required), she saw Anne walk into her bathroom. But what she did not see was Anne as she opened the door to her linen closet and pulled out a white box from under the neatly lined shelves of towels. Anne's hands trembled as she unfolded the sheets of tissue, and there at the bottom of the box lay a pink angora sweater.

Pink angora!

How she'd hated it. She'd put it away the moment her mother gave it to her. She'd never worn anything so disgusting. Pink angora!

And to make things worse, her mother had made it. Made a sweater! In a world where other girls wore fabulous black cashmeres that their mothers brought back from Scotland, her mother had expected her to wear a pink angora sweater that she had knitted.

Anne looked at the sweater and touched it.

She'd never even opened the box since that Christmas day twenty-five years ago when her mother had proudly given her this evidence of her love. Anne ran her fingers over the fluffy wool. How much of her mother had gone into this, and how little had she appreciated or understood what it meant, this gift of love? No, all she had thought when her mother gave it to her was, "Why are we so poor? Why can't I get a black cashmere sweater like the other girls? Why can't I be rich?" The pink angora sweater had suddenly been what her second-class life was all about, and as her mother had asked in her halting English, "Like it? You like it?" Anne had swallowed hard. "Sure, sure," she'd said, and under her breath she had whispered those dreaded words, "I hate you." Had her mother heard? Anne never knew.

At that moment she had hated her mother. She'd hated the poverty, the sham, the pretense of a Park Avenue life that wasn't a Park Avenue life. She'd hated her mother for being a maid, and most of all, she'd hated herself for hating it all. Now it was all coming full circle, wasn't it? Her own firstborn had turned to her and said, "I hate you." Anne put her head down in the pink fuzz and wept. It was too late, too late to say, "Mama, I love you. I don't hate you." But it wasn't too late for Cissy or Fudge or Casey Junior.

≡

When the plane lifted off, Anne saw the glittering necklace of New York bridges, and there—there off to the side—was the Statue of Liberty. That was really what her mother's life had been about, wasn't it?

She stirred in her seat. The seat belt sign was still on, but this was worth seeing. Anne tiptoed to the bedroom at the back of the plane. "Cissy," she whispered to the little girl in pajamas asleep in a small bed, "Mommy wants to show you something pretty."

"Let her sleep," Miss Patch warned.

Anne shook her head. "She won't remember sleeping, but she'll always remember her first trip to London when her mommy woke her up to show her the Statue of Liberty."

"You'll spoil her, Mrs. Burrows," Miss Patch warned. "That child will be off her schedule."

"Maybe that's what she needs, Miss Patch. Maybe that's what we all need. Maybe it's the schedule that's been killing us all."

Anne lifted her daughter and put her soft cheek against her child's.

"Are you the toof fairy?" Cissy whispered from her sleep.

Anne laughed. "Yes, my darling daughter, yes, I am the toof fairy, and I'm here to take all three of you on a magical trip to a new land, and then we're going to come back to our own house together."

" 'gether," Cissy repeated, and she sighed a small, satisfied sigh of childhood as she snuggled her head against her mother's soft, warm, pink angora sweater.

47

FOR BRONWYN THE COUNTDOWN HAD BEGUN THE MOMENT THE Seconds agreed to tell their husbands about the accident. It was not the moment of truth that she dreaded; she knew she would be able to tell her story well. What she feared was her irascible husband's reaction. She could still remember the night he'd learned that, after six weeks of negotiating, he wasn't going to win the takeover battle for the Bibliocrest Publishing Company, and he'd stormed from their bedroom in the Southampton house, gathered all the books in their two-thousand-volume library, piled them in the cabana, taken his hunting rifle, and fired at them. He'd started shooting wildly and knocked out four windows before the estate manager was able to subdue him. He didn't care that in his anger he'd ruined first editions of Blake, Dickens, and the twentieth-century poets his wife had collected all her life. He didn't care that he'd frightened the help—two maids left the grounds that night. He cared only that he didn't get what he wanted.

So, while Bronwyn did not relish a scene with Harold Ashter, she knew that she would have to build her strength in order to face him with a revelation that could destroy her life. The Seconds could not be counted on as her main support just now. Wasn't each of them facing her own crisis of truth-telling?

Intuitively she had sensed that her redemption lay in the pure loves of her life, that mother's share for Gwyneth and this first true romantic love, the love for Terence Bell. Terry was every romantic fantasy come to life. He'd sent her the poems of Robert Browning and tried to turn her into his Elizabeth Barrett. He'd sent her lines from Yeats and the love poems of Robert Graves. When she'd tried to respond with lines of her own, he'd cautioned her that only one in twenty really understands poetry and only one in a generation is a true poet. So, rebuffed as a poet, but accepted as a reader, she'd confined herself to picking and choosing the words of others, and her letters to Terry went from weekly missives to twice weekly and finally to daily communications—not always a letter, sometimes simply a clipping, a page torn from a magazine, a poem photocopied from a book. And, like Bronwyn, Terry picked up the pace and wrote to her daily, too. The telephone calls were reduced and were marked by their terseness: "How are the plans coming for the shop?" "Will Pumpkin Corners open on time?" It was almost as if Bronwyn and Terry had two identities. In the written part of their life, they were conducting the idyllic romantic relationship of both their lives; in the spoken part, they were two business people sorting out the nitty-gritty of leases and plumbing contracts.

It was in a letter that Terry had first urged her to spend a day with him—so that meant he wanted to test their love. But it was a telephone call that convinced her to spend the two days, for when he said by telephone that he wanted to see her, she knew that it would be a reason attributable to business. She didn't need to have a business reason to leave Harold for two days, but in her heart she needed a business reason to leave Gwyneth. In the end she decided to go, but only after Sherry Thomas agreed to have Gwyneth stay at her house and assured her that Sparrow would love having her best friend with her.

So, three weeks after the trip with the Seconds and just a week before they were to tell their husbands, Bronwyn faced her husband across the dinner table. "I have to go up to Pumpkin Corners tomorrow," she said as she stirred and restirred her black coffee.

"Tomorrow?" he barked. "You can't go tomorrow."

She felt her heart beat wildly in her chest, another sign of his power over her. "Why?"

His toughness seemed to melt perceptibly, replaced now by conscious pride. "I'm going to have my first meeting with the executive group of Driscoll's, and I want my bride at my side."

Grown men using the word *bride* to refer to their wives always made Bronwyn cringe. "Your bride?"

"Yep." Harold dug into his second piece of lemon pie.

Again Bronwyn shuddered. How could a man as overweight as Harold eat like that? Young men died of heart attacks—why? She shook her head; she had to stop wishing him dead. God would surely punish her and take Gwyneth. She closed her eyes. Please, God, I didn't mean that, she implored silently.

"Yep, you and Hal and Vonna and Gwynnie."

She hated it when he called Gwyneth by that made-up nickname.

"I want all the kids there. I think it shows that management group something."

"What?"

"Well, Hal is like me; he's going to run things, and they better get used to seeing him around. Vonna's a fat woman, and I'll show them I've got this family all sizes. A daughter like Vonna and a bitsy baby like Gwynnie, and I've got this wife who's friends with all the rich bitches of New York and can bring them into the store. They're gonna love me."

"I'll bet," Bronwyn said with some bitterness.

"So you can't go to Pumpkin Corners tomorrow," he announced.

"What time is the meeting?"

"Eight o'clock."

"In the morning?"

"Naw. Night. I wanna keep 'em after hours, show 'em who's boss."

"Oh, that will certainly show them, Harold. You'll win all kinds of popularity contests for that."

"I don't wanna be popular. I just wanna be rich."

"I guess you've succeeded, but if you're doing this at eight at night, then you can't have Gwyneth there. That child can't stay up that late, particularly if she's in front of a lot of people. She'll be cranky, I promise you."

"Okay. Seven o'clock."

Bronwyn started to protest, but she knew that if she did, Harold was capable of striking back in some strange way. There was no logic to Harold's actions, and just as she had learned long ago that only smart people can be trusted in business, so she had learned that only emotionally stable people can be trusted in a private life. It was odd, but Virginia and the Seconds were to be trusted in both areas. Despite their oddities, they were smart in business *and* emotionally sound. And, as long as she had her pals, the pills, she was sound, too. She sighed. She'd go upstairs and get a little something and then change her plans. Her forty-eight hours with Terry would be reduced to twenty-four. She'd call him later, after that small dose of confidence. If only she had planes of her own the way Anne did. She could always charter one, of course, but if she did—no, it would make Terry nervous. She'd be flaunting her wealth and power, and that would make the romance uneven. She knew only too well how difficult it was when one partner had a lot more money than the other. She was already richer than anyone in her book lover's life, and to use her wealth in combination with Harold's would distance Terry just at the moment she wanted and needed him closer than ever.

48

THROUGHOUT THE 1980s, SOCIETY LADIES BY THE DOZENS TRANS-formed themselves into entrepreneurial executives. They founded a variety of service companies, coproduced Broadway shows, and opened brokerages and real-estate firms. The nouveau workers with the highest profiles, however, were the society darlings who went to work as dress designers and owners of cosmetics companies. Although the activities of these ladies who made fashion were accorded major press coverage, the ladies who bought fashion, perhaps in a combination of stillborn jealousy and unborn confidence, continued to patronize the Old Favorites.

The Old Favorites were best-known to the readers of the fashion publications as the TOFFs, the almost acronym given them by the columnists. King of the TOFFs was Constani, whose atelier on the Upper East Side was frequented by first ladies, sometime ladies and women who were moneyed but definitely not ladies.

From the moment Sidney Marvell decided to let Sienna plan

her wedding for her, it was agreed that Shotsie von Thrum would design the wedding dress and bridesmaids' gowns, but the wardrobe for the bride-to-be would be the responsibility of Constani. It was also known, almost without discussion, that the wedding would be catered by Incredible Foods; the flowers would be under the green thumb of Kingston Carlyle, one of the three power flower designers in New York City; the wedding cake would be made by Maude Bienbaum, the foremost cake baker; the couple would buy a co-op from Bonnie Brickmaster, and before moving in, they would live in the Dome while Ned Beekman, the society renovator, contempo-rized the kitchen and bathrooms in the couple's apartment and restored the original Old World (pre–World War I) elegance to the public rooms.

"Must we do it all?" Sidney had asked.

"Of course, dear," Sienna had assured her. "It's the rich girl's rite of passage."

"I'm not sure I like it."

"You will. Trust me," Sienna promised.

And over the weeks Sidney had learned to trust Sienna and to find that her stepmother was right. It was *fun* to do these things, particularly when one had a stepmother as well organized as Sienna. All details of the small wedding were entrusted to Hedda, and Sidney found herself calling her father's home to speak to Sienna and Hedda at all hours of the day and night.

Peter, precise as ever, found the calls a surprise. "Why doesn't she call on weekends?" he asked one Wednesday night when Sidney's call came after they had retired at eleven.

"Because we have a lot to discuss," Sienna explained. Her reading light was still on, and she was paging through the morning paper that only at this hour had she found time to read.

Peter, his attempt to sleep now interrupted, turned and faced his wife and complained, "Why doesn't she call her mother?"

Sienna sighed. "I really didn't want to bother you with this, but she did try to get Judith to become involved in the wedding. Judith told her that if she thought marriage was going to make her happy, then she couldn't help her. She told her that marriage was a prison and a way for a woman to be a slave all her life. She told Sidney to live with Alvin but not to marry him."

Peter sat up. "She did *what?*"

"I just told you, darling."

He shook his head in utter disbelief. "I knew the woman was mad, but why would she try to take her own daughter down to her level of unhappiness?"

"I don't think having a child makes a woman a mother. I don't think Judith is capable of being a mother."

"How would you know?"

"This whole experience with Sidney is—oh, look, I know that biologically I'm not her mother, but I love her enough to mother her. Do you understand?"

"What brought this about?"

"Maybe because I sensed that she needed me and had no place to turn, and maybe I've seen me at times in my life with no place to turn, and maybe because you've been my safe harbor and I trust you with me—well, maybe I wanted to do something to help cement us, all of us, you and me and Sidney and Gene and now Alvin, into a family."

"I never expected this kind of—"

"—of love?" she asked.

Peter cupped his hands around Sienna's face and looked into her eyes.

Sienna felt as if her heart would overflow with an enormous love that was born of a sense of family, a love she had never before felt and thought she could not have until she gave birth to her own child.

"What amazes me most," Peter confessed, "is that I didn't think you two had a chance even to like one another."

Sienna's pulse quickened; for the first time in years Peter was not worried about his schedule, not ending a conversation in order to get his sleep when he wanted it. She was free to say the things she felt. She spoke slowly and from her heart. "I'm learning that the things that start with love work a lot better for me than the things that start with hate."

Peter, confused by her words, asked, "Did you hate Sidney?"

She sighed deeply and moved to her side of the bed and felt him turn now, his back toward her. "No, not Sidney. Not Gene and not you. Not even Judith. It's heavy, but listen to me for a minute. I really dislike my mother, and that relationship poisons all my life. But I really love you, and if I take that love and use it for the people *you* love, it works for me."

Peter did not speak.

"Did you go to sleep, or do you think I'm being ridiculous? Don't you believe me?"

He lay still another moment, her words still echoing. Was any ambassadorship going to give him this sense of completeness? Then Peter turned toward Sienna. "I've never loved you more than I do at this moment, and even though I have an early breakfast tomorrow—"

Sienna slid farther under the duvet and whispered, "Come here, and I promise that if the phone rings once more, I won't answer. Sometimes our side of the family comes first."

≡

"Sienna, do you mind that I call at all those crazy hours?" Sidney asked.

"No, but it does surprise your father."

The two women were at Constani's, whose atelier occupied a floor-through in an Upper East Side townhouse. Sidney stood in the tiny dressing room just off the showroom and Sienna, outside the curtained area, was waiting to button, zip, and comment. Even though they were separated by a drapery, the two chatted as intimately as if they were in the same room, for the only person within earshot was Clementine, best-known as the keeper of Constani's books, appointments, and travels, and keeper of the secrets of New York's best undressed women. Clementine was a part of that brigade of women who worked in fashion but never wore it. For Clementine, the extent of her personal fashion statement was a plain black dress with plain black shoes, a slash of lip pomade—no color—and small pearl earrings. Clementine, who never whispered a word about any of the ladies, nonetheless steered purchases so that best friends and intimate enemies knew when they were buying the same clothes. "The wedding dress is Constani's favorite," Clementine assured them as she walked past.

"I love the neckline for Sidney," Sienna said.

"Well, with her new figure," Clementine assured them in a voice loud enough to be certain to be heard behind the curtain, "she'll be spectacular."

"I can thank Sienna for pushing me into this new body," Sidney called out. "She sent me to the gym and the nutritionist—"

"Hush," Sienna cautioned, "do you want the world to know our secrets?"

Sidney came out of the curtained area wearing a pale green linen dress. "How beautiful that looks," Clementine said. "Suzette Shaughnessy ordered it in pink, but I think the green is more sophisticated."

"More sophisticated than Suzette? That's something," Sienna admitted.

"I'm going to make some calls for Constani; he forgot to book a hotel in Milan for the showings. You can get along without me, can't you?"

"Yes, but first give us the suit and the two long dresses to try." Clementine brought the clothes to them.

"Am I supposed to be mad or glad that the great Suzette is wearing my dress?" Sidney asked.

"Darling, if this dress gets you everything it got her, you'll be fine."

"Alvin isn't any Sean Shaughnessy."

"I scarcely think Sean Shaughnessy is what you'd want. He's as old as your father, and she's more your age than even mine."

Sidney sat down. "Oh, good, she's brought us some coffee. Let's relax for a minute. God, Sienna, I'm not sure this is all for me. I mean, I feel like an actress, not at all like me."

"Most brides do."

"I have to keep reminding you that I'm not like most of the brides you know. Do you think I could ever do what Suzette did? I couldn't marry some rich man and leave him for one who's richer and then another who's even richer—"

"Let's begin by saying that you don't have to. After all, Suzette was born in some town in Kansas, and she didn't even have a row of corn to call her own. She took herself to Chicago, slimmed down, and took up with a heavy-duty meatpacker. The fellow was divorced and playing around with a lot of young girls; he had no intention of getting married. But Suzette had a plan. She got pregnant and told him she was going to have the baby. No, said the boyfriend. I don't need more kids. Okay, said Suzette. Then I'll get an abortion, but I'll get it only if you marry me. You marry me, and you set me up for two years, and together we'll find me a rich husband, and then I'll leave you, and we'll always be good friends. Great, said the meatpacker. And so they were married. Then Suzette, at a luncheon, listened while two ladies complained about their husbands. One of the ladies, however, said that even though her husband was as boring as TV on a bad night, he did provide the money for the ski instructors and tennis instructors who occupied her bed and body both summer and winter. So Suzette, ever the entrepreneur, gave a dinner party and invited the errant lady with husband. She put herself next to the husband, twinkled brightly all through dinner, and wound up as his girlfriend. Meatpacker husband got his kicks introducing her to men and watching her take over. Errant lady's husband said he couldn't ever leave wifey for Suzette because she'd been so faithful and good for twenty years, and Suzette, blinking brightly through her heavy mascara, informed him that wifey had been bed-hopping. He was so angry he immediately divorced her, married Suzette—who by then had gotten rid of meatpacker. When Suzette met Sean, she turned to Husband Number Two and whispered bye-bye. So Suzette, at your age, is with Husband Number Three, who bought her a watch company because he feels that this is her time—corny, but that's love in the big city—and now she is practically the toast of the world."

"What are you telling me?"

"That you're right, and I agree that you could never do what Suzette did. But you have to understand that in the dog-eat-dog world that Suzette was in, she did what women today do. She improved her status through serial marriage, and then just for good measure she took a little company for her own. In the old days women used to get only money from men. Now they figure ways to get money and a business for themselves so that even if the men and the marriages fall apart, they'll have an identity. Now, in addition to rich men, they want a career."

"But I can't be like that."

"You were raised differently. You had a mother who'd have hated Suzette and all she stood for, and you have a father—"

"I have a father who didn't stand for much. I don't think most men do, Sienna."

"That's not really fair. Your father has withdrawn from a lot of the world because he found his only real security and identity in business, but maybe that's changing."

"I'm not sure."

"Nor am I."

"Then why did you sound so confident?"

"Because I want to be, but underneath I'm absolutely jelly."

"What are you so nervous about?"

"It—umm, well it—" She wanted to say the words, break the spell, and tell the secret. But nothing except those stumbling, halting sounds came from her mouth. Now even the coffee cup in her hand was clattering against the saucer.

Sidney reached over, took the cup and saucer and put them on the floor. "What's bothering you? You can trust me. After all the things I've told you—"

Sienna waved her hand as if to stop the flow of words. "I trust you. I do. It's just—"

"Just what?"

"I can only tell your father, and I'm afraid."

"But you keep telling me he's okay even if he only thinks about business."

Sienna breathed deeply. "That's why I'm afraid to tell him. What I tell him can affect his business life."

"Did you steal something?"

"No, but it's not a good story."

"Let me ask you something, Sienna."

"Yes."

"If my father did what you did and came to tell you, how would you feel?"

"It wouldn't make any difference, of course."

"Then why do you think he's less a person than you?"

"You're right," Sienna whispered. "You're right."

"And no matter what my father says or does," Sidney promised, her hand covering Sienna's, "you have me on your side."

Sienna leaned forward in the little gold chair and picked the coffee up from the floor. It was cold, but she suddenly felt warmed and comfortable. So this was how being loved in a family made you feel.

She smiled. Her family was behind her. Right or wrong, she had a support system.

"My, oh my," Clementine clucked as she walked back into the showroom, "you two are gabbing so much you haven't even noticed that it's raining outside. There's thunder and lightning. Is your car here, Sienna?"

Sienna looked outside and saw the rain pelting the long windows. The lightning flashed, and she could hear the distant thunder, but for the first time in years she felt no fear. "Oh, let it rain," she said. "Sidney and I can handle any kind of weather."

49

BRONWYN ROLLED OVER ON HER BACK AND LOOKED UP AT THE cracked, peeling ceiling. Who would ever believe that she, a girl who had dreamed of getting out of the Bronx, out of the middle-class vulgarity of her childhood, would end up making more money than she ever dreamed, know more celebrities than she ever expected—but not find happiness until she went to a second-rate motel with the only first-rate man her life had produced?

"Terry," she whispered, half-expecting to find herself still in a drugged dream.

"Yes, darling," he answered, and she felt his hands move easily over her naked body.

So she hadn't dreamed it after all. Bronwyn sat up in bed, the sheet wrapped closely around her. "What time is it, Terry?"

"Is it still dark?" he mumbled.

"I don't know. The blinds are closed."

"Those blinds are so thin that if it were light, you'd know," he answered.

An old fear with a new theme chilled her. If he knew so much about the thin blinds, if he knew this cheapo motel so intimately, then didn't that mean that he'd been here before, loved here before?

"On second thought, maybe they're lined with that black stuff so we wouldn't know," he said, as if he were reading her mind, answering the question she was afraid to ask.

"You mean you're not the local guide to motels?" she asked lightly.

He laughed. "We all come with some baggage at this time of life, Bronwyn. As for me, at this moment, I can but quote Thomas Hood: " 'O bed! O bed! delicious bed!' "

She slid down and murmured, "Delicious bed."

He held her tight. "Did you ever dream this would happen?"

"Not to me. Not anymore."

"Why? Why not anymore?"

"I thought I was too old."

"You're a whisper older than I, and I find myself young enough for new friendships and old enough for new love."

She frowned. "I never heard that. Who wrote it?"

"I did. Just now."

She giggled. When was the last time Bronwyn with the serious eyes had giggled?

"You think everything I say is quoted from your poets?"

"Yes."

He whispered in her ear, "Yes is a pleasant country."

"e.e. cummings," she answered quickly.

"Do you remember how that poem ends?"

She closed her eyes to search her memory.

"Let me tell you, Bronwyn dear. Let me say two lines and let them stand for us."

Her eyes filled. She did not have to feel her face to know that there were no bumps, no ugly reminders of a distressing marriage and a life that made her question all her choices all the time.

> "*. . . love is a deeper season*
> *than reason*
> *My sweet one*
> *and April's where we're.*"

She heard him say the words, and she felt her body melt once more into his. So this is what it was like to love for no reason but love, to consider no season but love. This is what the poets had been telling her; this was the ultimate consequence of the books she had read, the poets she had worshiped. It had all been for this, this moment to lie beside the perfect man and with him translate the written word into the act of life and the remembered rhymes into the rhythm of love.

≡

"I was right." He laughed.

"About what?"

"The light does come through the shades; they are cheap and

shabby. Everything about this place is discounted, Bronwyn. Even
our time is cut rate. You promised me two days and gave me one."

"I'm lucky it was one."

"Why?"

"It's a long story and a boring one."

"I love long stories, and nothing bores me."

"This would."

"Try me. Besides, how can I know you better if you don't tell
me your stories, if you don't tell me about being a little girl, if you
don't tell me about growing up rich—"

"Rich?" She laughed, and then she stopped.

"Why did you laugh like that?"

"I guess rich is a funny word. I'm very rich. I was just thinking
about it maybe a couple of hours ago, and I was thinking that even
though I've got big houses and lots of money, I'm happier in this
little motel than with—"

"—than with him," Terry finished. "That's what you want to
say, isn't it? You want to say he doesn't make you happy."

"He's, well, he's sort of strange. Terry, he's not strange, he's
mad. I'm not going to keep lying and playing games. He's an out-
and-out nut. A crazy person. A madman. A manic-depressive."

"Is he on lithium?"

Her eyes narrowed. "How do you know about drugs?"

"I read a lot. I never really did drugs. It wasn't the sin of choice
when I went to school. Alcohol was the way to get where you wanted
to go. It was cheaper, easier to buy. But tell me about Harold Ashter.
He's nothing but a figure in the financial pages to me."

"That's what he is to Gwyneth, too," she said.

"What does he do that's so crazy? He sounds pretty interesting
to me."

"What does he do?" Bronwyn's voice hardened. "Let me tell
you why I was reduced—marked down—to one day with you instead
of two. In some ways we have to go back to the beginning, I mean
the beginning of Harold. He made his big money in the liquid
plastics business, and while he liked the dollars, he didn't like it when
he and his first wife went to parties, and no one knew who he was.
There he was in a city with men who advised the mayor and saved
the city from bankruptcy, men who ran networks and magazines,
men who bought airlines and railroads and cosmetics companies,

men he knew were sometimes less smart and shrewd than he, but, by God, everybody knew what these men did. No one knew what Harold did. I think part of the reason he left his first wife was that she wasn't ever in the newspapers."

"Were you?"

"Oh, I wasn't any Suzette Shaughnessy."

Terry's eyes grew big. "You mean you actually know Suzette Shaughnessy?"

"Everyone in New York does. If you go to a charity ball or sit on a committee or walk your dog, you know Suzette. She has her master's in social climbing. I mean, she's way up there."

"I want to hear her story and your story and Harold's. I have an idea," Terry said. "Let's stay in bed all day. I'd thought we'd go to Pumpkin Corners and look at the store, but let's not. Let's just stay in bed until you have to go. You tell me stories, and in between we'll make love and—"

"Yes," Bronwyn agreed. "We'll make love."

"But first finish the story. When last we left poor Harold, the chap was unhappy because he wasn't famous."

"You really want to hear about Harold?"

"If I do, I'll know you better. I'll do anything to know you better, Bronwyn." He touched her body gently, and she trembled. How could life be this sweet without any help from those precious little pills she hoarded?

"You make it difficult to concentrate," she said.

"Want to phone in your remarks?" he teased.

She laughed. Even dumb jokes sounded wonderful coming from Terry.

"Okay," she continued, "Harold was annoyed because he wasn't famous, so he was always looking for what he called the Big Deal. I think he expected me to lead him to it, but, of course, I didn't, and he always felt I'd let him down. I got what I wanted from marriage, which was Gwyneth, and he was getting nothing from the marriage. Then, as happens with men of money, a deal was offered him one day by a Wall Street firm. He could get control of Driscoll's, the biggest department-store group in the United States, and even though he didn't know beans about department stores, he wanted it. I think the biggest reason he wanted the group was that it owned Polly's on Park, and that's where all the rich ladies who are our friends do their shopping. So, let's dissolve to his first meeting with the store principals, his management group. It was scheduled for the night before last. He wanted to begin the meeting at eight at night, but I got him to start the meeting at seven, and I thought I could get out in time to come to you—well, for starters his children and I were all at the store in the auditorium on time. Everyone was there except Harold. I still don't know where he was, but everyone was sitting there, and some dreary pianist was playing Cole Porter and George Gershwin badly. This was all going on for fifteen minutes. Gwyneth, who's not easy, was cranky as the devil, and his two monstrous children by his first marriage were glaring at Gwyneth and me because there we are, all forced to sit together on a stage. Finally, fifteen minutes late, Harold walks in, strides up to the microphone, and says first to a group of executives who've never before seen him, "Nobody is allowed to be late. I will not tolerate it. Of course, no rules apply to me."

"Then what happened?"

"I think the audience went into shock. They didn't know whether he was kidding or whether he was for real. I think some of them thought he was an actor who'd come in to play Harold Ashter. Anyway, he rambled for twenty minutes about his life and his dreams."

"And meanwhile my life and dreams had to wait for you, Bronwyn. I hate that man."

"So do I. But what can I do?"

Terry held her. "I'll think of something. We need a story, too. He can't keep us apart with his ridiculous meetings."

"I tried to fly here after the meeting, but Pumpkin Corners was fogged in, and I couldn't take off."

"Oh, my darling, what we missed."

"But look what we've gained. Would our love have been this sweet if I'd arrived on time?"

"I think so. But first I think it's time to love again."

"Are you in love with love, or are you in love with me?"

"I am a man who's made to love, darling. Like Dostoyevski, I believe that if you love everything, you will perceive the divine mystery in things."

"The divine mystery." She rolled the words on her tongue like a delicious secret.

"We could write it," he whispered. "We could explore and write the divine mystery, the secrets of Harold, the story of Suzette—"

"Suzette? You're not joking, then. You're really interested in stories about people like Suzette."

"Yes, oh yes."

"Then, like Fitzgerald I should tell you to draw your chair up close to the edge of the precipice, and I'll tell you a story."

"You have a rare gift for storytelling, Bronwyn."

"Maybe because I've been nothing but an observer all my life."

"That can't be true."

She pulled back from the man who knew so little of her and to whom she was ready to give so much. She put her hand to her face. No, there were still no telltale bumps. She did not want a friendly 'lude. She did not need Seconal. She had never felt so whole, so perfect. Dare she try for love with this man? Drugs and money did not seem to be saving her. Could love?

"You don't really know me, Terry."

"I know enough to know that I can't live the rest of my life without you in it. What role do you want?"

"I don't know," she hedged.

"Of course you know," he said, his voice strong and deep. "Do you want to rent a life the way we're doing now, or do you want a down payment on a real life? Come on, Bronwyn, let me put it in your basic real-estate terms. Do you want to rent or to own the body you're walking through life?"

She touched his face gently. "At this moment I am living life intensely, Terry. I'm not a visitor to my life now; I'm a participant. You made this happen, here in this dumpy motel in this pea-size bedroom that's smaller than the maid's room in my house. Until today I've been an observer of Bronwyn's life. I stand by and watch me doing deals and ordering dinner. I look on as I buy a ring I like or a painting or a coat. The only time I've participated is with my baby, and I'm ruining her. I don't know why, but I am. Somehow I think that if I take my chances with you, I won't ruin anyone anymore."

"Do you really mean that?"

"I do."

"We're wonderful one times one." He smiled.

At last it was happening. She understood it all. Her body was ready, and her mind was clear. She would leave Harold Ashter, and she would take Gwyneth. Never mind about this ridiculous date for telling Harold the story of the accident. She'd put that out of her mind. Only Terry could occupy her heart, her love. He would understand the accident. He'd love the story. Yes, he'd love it. She'd have to tell him one day. Not now, of course. Now was the time for them.

50

DIANDRE WATCHED AS THE LINE SNAKED SLOWLY TOWARD THE buffet luncheon table at the von Steubens'. Everyone was here, absolutely everyone, all of New York's social over-forties, with their faces pulled taut, noses bobbed, and long blond hair banded with black velvet, these older women with their sleek young bodies (tucked, exercised, and liposuctioned), carrying back to the living room plates dotted with salad, a bread stick (no butter), and a small spot of seafood risotto. Seafood risotto had become the luncheon food of choice after Virginia Payne North served it to a group of balletomanes the previous fall. Now Mrs. North herself was standing in line for society grub. Diandre had to admit that Virginia was some piece of work. She wanted to get her school built someplace up there in God-knows-where, so she had gone to Wilhemina von Steuben and persuaded her to have a buffet lunch at her Park Avenue apartment. The Very Socials had all turned out in their little look-alike suits and their little me-too afternoon dresses. Why not, Diandre thought. What woman in her right mind would turn down luncheon at the von Steubens'? It was New York's most photographed apartment, its long living room throbbing with rich, red damask walls, the copper-colored foyer where fifty royals could mingle without touching, and the dark green dining room (where, the hostess assured them, the painters had left only minutes before). Now the photographers were snapping the ladies in line, and perfect ladies that they were, no one interrupted a phrase to turn her best side, smile, or indicate in any way that she was at the moment being captured by a cameraman whose greatest worry was "Will these people feed the photographers, or do I have time to grab a burger on the way back to the office?"

Diandre had found her way here with Topsy Turvee, the second-best columnist on the city's third-best paper. Still, an invitation was an invitation, and she knew that in her present role of the Other Woman, there was no way Virginia herself would extend an invitation.

Virginia, standing in line just a few women ahead of Diandre, her face glowing with that famous smile, was turning now to greet friends as they came back through with their filled plates.

Diandre looked to the left and right and then decided to assert herself, step forward, and pay homage to Mrs. North. "Hullo, Virginia, so terrific to see you," Diandre trilled, her English accent tightened to its most British cast.

Virginia turned slowly. That accent . . . was it? No, she wouldn't have the audacity to come up to her. But yes, it was. It was that Englishwoman. To think that she had once invited her to a dinner that had brought this mini scandal to Anne. The unbridled audacity of this interloper! How dare she think she could harm one of her beloved Seconds. Virginia looked at Diandre squarely for at least sixty seconds without speaking.

Diandre drew her eyebrows together in puzzlement. Didn't Virginia recognize her? "Diandre Devon," she reminded Virginia. "I'm Diandre, Lady Devon."

Virginia drew herself as tall as she could. "Oh no, you're no lady," she answered. Then, without speaking further, Virginia turned and took her luncheon plate and linen.

Diandre, palms upturned, shrugged her shoulders, and the photographers clicked merrily. Tomorrow the headline over the picture would read "S(n)ubstitute: The Story of the Lady Who Thought She Was a Lady."

≡

Casey listened without hearing.

"Casey, did you hear what I'm telling you about that woman? She acts as if I've stolen you from Anne. She acts as if you're some piece of *property* that belongs to someone else."

"What property?"

"Casey, I don't believe you've heard me."

"Why hasn't Anne called? What's she doing over there?"

Diandre sighed and walked to the bar in her apartment to mix a fresh drink. Casey had the attention span of a newborn flea. "Just like a man," she muttered, "you're able to listen only when the conversation centers 'round you."

"Where's Anne?" he repeated.

"Still in London, luv."

"What does she think she's doing there?"

"P'raps she's seeing the Queen."

"She wouldn't."

"Oh, darling, you're so tiresome. That's a joke."

"I'm not laughing."

"Well, I'll give you a toddy to cheer you and then turn on the telly. There's a story due on the five o'clock news showing you taking a bunch of foster kids on your boat."

"Yacht. My yacht. When did I do that?"

"Yesterday. Remember? I had you stop by the boat—excuse me, yacht—and the bankers brought the papers for the California winery."

"Those other guys haven't bought a winery yet, have they?"

"Other guys?"

"You know, Anne's friends. Peter what's-his-face, the one who wants to be the ambassador, and that idiot Ashter."

"No, no they haven't bought any wine or spirits yet. You'll be the first. By the by, Anne doesn't have very good taste in friends, does she?"

"She says she works too hard to have friends. She says—oh my God." He stared at the TV screen. "There's Anne. Hold that station. Who told her she could be on television when I'm going to be on?"

Diandre stood back in surprise. How indeed had Anne managed to get on television—and with a story obviously originating in London?

"And so," the announcer droned, "as we said, it's finally America's turn. Tired of watching the influx of British, Japanese, German, and Australian money in New York, the rich and powerful Anne Burrows—"

"Rich and powerful?" Casey screamed. "She's not rich. She's not powerful. I am."

"Hush," Didi cautioned, "I can't hear." She fiddled with the dial and now Anne's big, blond presence filled the screen. Anne was nodding and smiling in a conspiratorial fashion at the interviewer.

"It's not a question of chauvinism, I promise," Anne said with a little wink. "It's just a matter of good business. Everyone thought that I was coming over here to announce the redecorating of our old hotel. Well, it's hard to surprise you British, but I am announcing the formation of the Anne Burrows Company and our first project, which is the purchase of the Knights Hotel in Knightsbridge."

"The Anne Burrows Company?" Casey choked.

"The Anne Burrows Company," the announcer repeated. "And where does that financing come from?"

Anne shook her finger impishly at the reporter. "I've not told anyone but Fudge."

"And who, pray tell, is Fudge?" was the reporter's rejoinder. "Is that a code name like Deep Throat?"

Anne threw her head back and laughed a long sensuous laugh just as the news reporter cut back to the desk in New York. "And that, ladies and gentlemen," announced the five o'clock anchorman in New York, "was a replay of that fabulous American Anne Burrows, who's taking London by storm. Where is the headline-hungry husband of the world's newest hotel empress? We sent our reporters out to find Casey Burrows this afternoon, and all his office would tell us was that he was in conference. We'll bet he is, and we wouldn't want to be on the other side of the desk. The irascible Mr. Burrows, known for his quick temper, fires letters off to reporters he doesn't like, smashes lenses of photographers—"

Casey Burrows, big Casey Burrows who had once played college football, lunged at the Chinese lamp next to his chair and threw it with the force of a pass into the end zone directly into the television set, which responded with an electrical hiss and sputter. Then he scooped up the George II chair he'd been sitting on and, with the wailing cry of a man gone mad, threw it through the plate-glass window onto the terrace.

Breathing heavily and sobbing, Casey Burrows stood in the middle of Lady Diandre Devon's once-perfect apartment now reduced to a sea of glass shards and splinters.

Lady Diandre Devon stood by silently. The passions of men no longer surprised her. Just as Casey indulged himself, and only himself, in love, she recognized that his hatred was yet another self-indulgence, a frenzied fever that would burn for these moments and leave him spent, bewildered, and in greater need of her than ever. Then she would give him the comfort he wanted, answer the questions he wanted asked.

But who was going to answer her questions?

How did Anne know about that hotel in Knightsbridge?

51

THEY HAD REACHED THEIR CRUISING ALTITUDE WHEN THE CAPtain came back to the sitting room. Ordinarily Mr. and Mrs. Burrows were deep in papers and conversation at this point of the trip, and he was accustomed to standing respectfully in the doorway until an appropriate break in the work allowed him to announce the weather on the return trip, request the time for meal service, and remind his passengers to tell him if anything should be needed.

But tonight was different.

He knew the minute he opened the cabin door and saw Anne holding her son, Kip. "Poor baby, poor baby," she was crooning. She looked up and saw the captain and smiled. "He's teething," she whispered. "No fun, is it, darling?" she cooed.

Miss Patch was holding the little girl, Fudge, and the older girl, Cissy, was coloring, her crayons and paper spread on Mrs. Burrows's desk.

The captain shifted uncomfortably. He could handle the Burrowses at business, but signs of domestic life always kindled the guilt he felt at being away from his family, a guilt that surfaced only when he saw other families. He had to admit, however, that on the way over to London, it had been kind of fun to help Mrs. Burrows and Miss Patch with the kids. He'd taken Cissy up to the flight deck to show her the instruments and introduce her to the crew, and when he'd brought her back for the rest of her night's sleep, Mrs. Burrows had invited him to sit down for a cup of coffee. It had been fun talking to her that night; she'd seemed so different, sort of real. He even told her about some of his experiences flying for the airlines, and she'd asked about the last time he'd flown to London. That was when he'd told her about Lady Diandre Devon and the Knightsbridge people; he'd remembered all the plans for the Knights Hotel. Mrs. Burrows had taken notes, and she'd told him that he'd been helpful, and he was really proud of that. Sometimes these people just took their captains for granted, a little like their furniture or their investments, all the things that they wanted to have as long as they didn't have to think about them.

Still and all, he'd better stop thinking about that trip and tell her now what he wanted to say. He wanted to get back. "The weather, ma'am," he began tentatively. Mrs. Burrows was always keen to know the weather. Nobody liked flying through or around storms, but she had an almost pathological fear. He liked to reassure her calmly with what he called "my John Wayne voice" before each trip.

"This poor little fellow isn't going to be much concerned with the weather, Sam," she said. "He has his own problems."

"Yes, ma'am, but I wanted you to know there's a big storm over the Atlantic. We'll do our best to go around it, but it may add some time to the flight, so don't be concerned—"

Anne looked up at the captain, and she said words she had never said before. "I'm not worried. No storm can scare me." Then she looked at the children around her. Here at thirty-five thousand feet above sea level she had finally planted her feet firmly in reality.

The captain opened his mouth to speak, then decided against it.

52

I N THAT DREARY LITTLE MOTEL ROOM TERENCE BELL HAD TOLD Bronwyn Corcoran that she was his Maud Gonne, and then, after that night of long lovemaking and short sleep, when they'd awakened the next morning entwined in each other's arms, he had whispered to her:

> *"What were all the world's arms*
> *To mighty Paris when he found*

> *Sleep upon a golden bed*
> *That first dawn in Helen's arms?"*

The whispered words caused Bronwyn to burst into tears, and when Terry'd tried to comfort her, she'd explained that the beauty of the moment had touched her soul as nothing in her life ever had. Even her adoration of Gwyneth, she'd confessed in a halting voice, was naught compared to this love.

The overwhelming and consuming passion of the twenty-four hours filled both Terence and Bronwyn with what Bronwyn called "our sad joy."

The first telephone call after their tryst Bronwyn spoke of "our sad joy." Terence knew what she wanted to hear, and he wanted to reassure her, to cheer her, and promise that still he was that man who "loved the pilgrim soul in you and loved the sorrows of your changing face," but those words would not come. Instead, with delicious quotations and intimations of passion too great for words, he teased her, tried to please her, and made light of their love, letting it float like a feather above them. Whenever Bronwyn turned a telephone talk to questions about next steps in their life together, he turned not to answers but to his own needs, that strange need he had for her, the need to hear her stories.

≡

"It's been two weeks since your lady love was here," Sean remarked to Terry one evening. The two men were seated in their cramped kitchen drinking beer and sharing a pizza. Terry, his mouth full, nodded. He wasn't anxious to eat quickly; the longer his mouth was full, the less reason he had to talk about Bronwyn.

At last he spoke. "I'm glad you're back, Sean. It's been lonesome here without you."

"I don't believe that for a minute," Sean answered.

Terry looked up and smiled knowingly. In the eighteen months of their shared living, Sean—despite his frequent travel—had come to know Terry better than anyone had ever known him before. Tonight, as the cousins sat in their sparse kitchen, Terry found something extraordinarily companionable about their bonding, this closeness rooted in genes and nourished by propinquity. He didn't want it spoiled by business talk just now, so with affection he said, "We're a good combo, cuz."

"Then why didn't you build a decent fire in the living room tonight?" Sean teased.

"Ah, dear cousin, the wood was green as the shamrock," Terry responded with a heavy brogue.

"Good thing you're not so green," Sean answered quickly.

"Meaning?" Terry felt his scalp tighten and a familiar heaviness in his chest, sure signs that his body knew that criticism was forthcoming.

"I mean, Terry, that I hope you're shrewd enough to get everything together for the bookshop. The word is that Pumpkin Corners is going to be a winner, and if you can make the place work, it could be the beginning of a very big business."

Terry felt his hands grow cold. "Big business?"

"Sure. Bookstores can be a big business. We could create a national chain based on what you do here—"

"No. No," Terry insisted. "That's not what I want."

Sean stood and pounded the table. "Man, what *do* you want? You want to stay holed up in this dump for the rest of your life and play telephone tag with a rich New York landlady?"

"We don't play telephone tag."

"Right. You don't even telephone her. No, you're a real Don Juan, aren't you?" he asked sarcastically. Without waiting for an answer, his sarcasm turning to barely disguised annoyance, he asked, "Why would you take her to that motel? This cottage of ours is no palace, but at least it's better than that hole. Hell, I went away for two days so you could have this place to yourself."

"How could I bring her here? She thinks I really live at Innisfree, where 'midnight's all a glimmer, and noon a purple glow.'"

Sean wiped his mouth with the back of his hand. "I swear by God's justice that even though we're blood, I don't understand you."

Terry spoke slowly as if the pace would make his strange reasoning understandable. "If she never sees this place, then I can keep telling my stories. Don't you see, Sean, that it's stories that make the world bearable?"

"Stories? What about women, especially rich women? I've even met a few poor girls in my time who make things bearable."

"My life is spun with my own silk. Don't you see? I live on

stories. They're my—my beer and pizza." He pushed his plate toward Sean.

Sean shook his head in disbelief. "You just like to sit and make up stories?"

"Yes," Terry said quietly.

"You don't want a lady's shoes under your bed?"

"No." Now Terry's tone was emphatic.

"Why not? It's not so bad unless, of course—"

Terry caught the innuendo. "Don't worry, cousin. It's women I want. *That's* not my problem."

"Then what is?"

"I don't want to be trapped by my passions. I want to be set free by love, not walled in. When I lived in Boston, there was a girl who used to come into the bookshop all the time. She was a college student who played the guitar and sang sweet songs, and she did have the heart of a poet. She took some of the things I wrote and set them to music, and sometimes we did little performances for our friends, and when there was enough wine and enough pot—well, sometimes it worked."

"When didn't it work?" Sean asked.

"When she slept over one night and left her shoes under my bed. Then the next week she decided she really ought to have a robe at my house. The next thing I knew she needed to have her shampoo and her razor and her toothbrush and—get the picture? At the end of three months she was in my closets and in my life. She thought we ought to get married. Remember now? First we had to spend Christmas with her family, and then I had to let her sister come to visit. Pretty soon she wanted to cut my hair and pick my friends and tell me what music to play, and it all started with her shoes under my bed. The day we divorced I decided I'd never let another woman sleep in my house. No matter where I live, I'll live there without a woman until I want to have a woman with me forever."

"How will you know you want her forever if you won't even give her a shoe under the bed?"

"I'll see a woman once, maybe twice—and then decide what's next."

"Okay. You saw this one, this Bronwyn, once. Have you seen her twice? I mean, have you two made it—gotten together—seen one another—since you went off to that crummy motel?"

"No."

"Well, why? Why haven't you seen her? Won't she take your calls?"

"Oh, she'll take my calls. In fact, she makes the calls."

"And?"

"And I don't take the calls."

Sean crumpled the beer can in his hand. *"You* don't take the calls?"

Terry leaned back in the rickety chair and put his feet on the table. "It would spoil things."

"You really make me crazy. How would talking to that woman spoil things?"

"Talking is too real. It's too much like shoes under the bed. If I talk to her, before I know it I'll have her here again; and for me the romance will be gone. But as long as I write to her, I can keep the romance going."

Sean turned around and threw his beer can into a brown paper bag that stood in the corner of the kitchen. "Well, with you, I guess writing is as good as talking."

"Better," Terry admitted. "It's much better."

≡

When the telephone rang, Terry didn't hear Sean answer. He was startled when his cousin walked into the kitchen. "It's her," he said in a matter-of-fact tone. "Shall I tell Miss Bronwyn Corcoran that the Irish prince will deign to speak to her?"

Terry lifted his head. "I can't talk now," he explained.

Sean shrugged his shoulders. "She seems pretty anxious."

Terry put his head back, closed his eyes, and said nothing.

Sean pressed for a positive answer. "Are you sure, Terry? Won't you just say hi to her?"

"No."

"She sounds as if she's crying."

Terry shook his head sadly and frowned. "That won't do." A moment later he looked up. "Tell her I had to go out, but I sent a message. Tell her this: 'I have spread my dreams under your feet; Tread softly because you tread on my dreams.' "

"Will she know what that means?"

"Oh yes. It's Yeats."

"Won't she be upset? It's as if you're telling her to leave you alone."

"No," said the erstwhile poet, "she won't be upset. She'll be fine. I know her, Sean. She's strong."

53

JUST AS SOME MEN ARE BORN TO SCIENCE, OTHERS TO THE ARTS, and still others to commerce, Gregory Sawyer had found his natural niche in life. For almost thirty years now he had made a living out of being sensitive to rich women's needs. It was not too difficult to know how to be acutely aware and respond to the cash-and-carry ladies because most privileged women had the same need, the need to have a man at their beck and call, a man who didn't disappear behind a financial paper or in front of a television set, a man who was tuned not only to the deal on the telephone, but to them. Early on Gregory had learned that once a woman had a man in her life to pay the bills, what she most wanted was a man who was—well, fun. She wanted a man to gossip with her, to accompany her when her chief money-maker was off making money; a man who would meet her for lunch and not just eat, but dish; a man who cared about the newest designers and the latest plays; a man who'd read the new books and who could condense them so that she could dismiss or praise the author of the week in one sentence without having to crack a book herself. Often these men of convenience were homosexuals and often they were simply asexual, men who got their sexual thrills from hobnobbing with the people who made headlines. What Gregory understood well was that his particular brand of titillating toadying was a sexual substitute in the lives of his women, too. Long tired of seeking satisfaction in bed, most of Gregory's women had learned instead to find pleasurable ripples in lunching with the right people, dining in the right homes, and playing charity queen for well-photographed events. Years ago he had heard Marlene Dietrich hold an audience in thrall as she told the secret of being successful with women. "One thing only," she had said in that famous throaty voice. "When a woman speaks, look at her and listen as if she were the only person in the world." Gregory had followed that advice. From time to time it took him precariously close to bedding a woman, but still he could tell himself proudly he had never had to do more than comfort a woman in bed. No man really had to do more if he didn't want to; really, all these women wanted was a man who would listen. He had been privy to a thousand secrets, but it all boiled down to one secret: men who make a lot of money get their sexual satisfaction in business, and women are a convenience to be used when the markets are closed. Ergo, rich women need companions and can afford the best. As far as Gregory was concerned, he was the best.

Nothing reflected his ability to excel at his chosen profession better than the room where he lived. It was one room in a rent-controlled building and had what Gregory prized most: a chic address. The ladies all knew the address; it was where their drivers came to pick him up and deliver him, but no woman had ever seen this room, this perfect jewel box where he had created his own dream-world setting. He did none of the foolish things that New Yorkers always did when they lived in one room; they somehow made it seem like three rooms, with sofas that converted into beds and broom closets that became dressing rooms. No, Gregory took the one room and made it a sensual, sumptuous bedroom. The walls were covered in dark green velvet, and the two windows that looked into a dark alley were covered by beige, brown, and green taffeta balloon shades. On the floor was wall-to-wall faux leopard carpet. In the center of the room stood a canopy bed, and on either side were a pair of nineteenth-century hand-painted commodes. A jade figurine lamp on each gave the room much of its rich light. Gregory's work—his sifting of invitations and calls—was done at the black lacquer ormolu-trimmed desk between the windows. A nineteenth-century desk lamp with fat candles gave the necessary glow to that side of the room. Gregory's dressing table outside the white bathroom held his ivory collection, and over the dressing table hung a gilded Louis XVII mirror. Gregory loved his room as much as his women loved their jewels and houses and clothes. He smiled as he thought of clothes—ah yes, clothes. His closets were full of them, his clothes that he wore with his ladies and the clothes that he wore with his men. He opened the closet door and felt the sweet silks of the dresses there—the dresses from designer friends. Did they know what he did with them? Perhaps. But even if they did, each pretended to acknowledge his charity in sending the clothes to impoverished people wherever the latest tragedy might dictate—a coal mine cave-in in West Virginia, an earthquake in South America, a volcanic eruption in Europe.

Now Gregory reached in his closet for the small dotted tie. Yes, it would look right with the black suit. He had been summoned to Virginia's for dinner. She hadn't told him who the guests would be. Maybe Juliet Caesar would be there; yes, that young woman he'd met at Virginia's for the Rosabelle School luncheon. He'd been meaning to call her, that ex-stripper who needed a few lessons in Basic New York. He crossed to the desk and made a note. Better get to that woman soon. That old goonybird she'd married could kick off any day, and he'd better be certain no one beat him to the widow's side.

BOOK SIX

"The end of all our exploring will be to arrive where we started and know the place for the first time."

T. S. ELIOT

54

PUFF, UNDER THE BED, WAS SQUEALING HIS HIGH-PITCHED, FEAR-ful squeal.

Sienna, in bed, her eyes open and her body trembling, echoed her small dog's fear of the day to come.

She had thought that Sidney's confidence in her would make the anticipation of today's confession easier.

But it didn't.

The cold sweat, the shaking were proof of that.

Even the rain foretold the kind of day this would be.

Yes, even the gods on high were sending the furies to pour down yet another punishment on the Seconds.

But there was no turning back now; the three of them had agreed.

Today each would tell her husband, rid herself forever of the terrible secret that had haunted them most of their lives.

Sienna wanted to telephone Anne and Bronwyn; no matter the time, weren't they—like her—lying in sleepless beds awash in pools of fear?

Twice she put her hand on the telephone.

Twice she withdrew her hand.

She looked at the dial on her bedside clock. Two thirty, still hours before Peter would get out of bed and go into his dressing room. She closed her eyes; she would use those hours to renew, refresh, and remind herself that no matter what Peter said, no matter how great his anger, how deep his disappointment, she had done her best.

She had even found a sense of family love.

Love, she sobbed, love—she'd pretended she could live without it all her life. First she'd substituted sex for longtime love. She'd had no relationships with her parents because they were unfeeling and uncaring toward her. And now, now just when she thought she might have found love, the furies—those old gods—were all going to take it away.

Sienna, still sobbing, pulled a part of the comforter still warm from Peter's body close to her.

Outside and inside the storm raged.

55

I T CAME SHARPLY TO ANNE AS SHE AWAKENED ONCE MORE IN HER own bed in New York that rain, thunder, and lightning were the precursors always of the decision days of the Seconds.

Hadn't it been the torrential rain and accompanying hard-rock sounds of thunder and flashes of lightning that had provided the built-in video track for the Accident?

And now, outside the windows of the Dome, trees were bending with the wind, and rain was beating against the casements high in this aerie. Today, the day the Seconds had promised one another to tell their husbands of their secret past, the city was reeling under a wild electrical storm.

But there is to be no more calling of the game on account of rain, Anne said to herself, and then she smiled a small, satisfied smile to think how far she had come.

Today the storm did not ride her.

Today Anne Burrows rode the storm.

She knew last night that she was a different woman, that rain would never again dampen her life plans; she knew it the moment she'd heard the captain predict a bumpy flight, and she'd felt no fear. So they'd tossed a bit in the air? So what? That was the price you paid for getting around the world quickly.

And once she'd felt that certain calm, the children, too, had sensed her peace and had all slept the night away not only on the plane but in the car coming home from the airport.

Casey wasn't there to greet them when they came home, of course. Well, why should he be? She hadn't told him when she was returning, and he probably didn't even realize that she had taken the children with her.

Anne pulled the covers tight under her chin. How many days

ago was it that she, too, would not have known where the children were? How strange life was. No matter what you did to make things happen, in the end life took its own course. Look at Gregory. He'd come back into their lives to make mischief, and instead of letting him turn her into an angry, ferocious tiger, Anne had turned herself into another kind of forest creature, the protective mother shielding her cubs. She sighed. How had it happened?

And what was to happen next?

No way to predict.

All she knew was that today was the day, the day Anne would confront Casey with the truth.

But would the truth set her free?

She'd soon find out, and so would Sienna and Bronwyn. She reached for the telephone and pulled back.

No, this wasn't the time for support from the Seconds.

This was the time to be strong alone.

And now there were to be no more delays, no more excuses.

She pushed the covers back and sat up.

Time to go to work. The disciplines of a lifetime did not change with the weather.

She'd go to the office this morning. There were calls to make and people to see. And then there was Casey.

No more delays.

No more excuses.

She repeated the words like a rallying cry for her life.

I'll go. I'll go, she promised herself, but only after I play with the children for an hour.

56

B RONWYN AWAKENED AT SIX TO THE SOUNDS OF THE STORM. Harold, beside her in the bed, silenced thunder with his snores.

But today she could not hear him, for she knew that her heart had stopped beating.

Yes, her heart was not beating.

What a strange sensation this was.

She was choking, silently choking, as the noisy world closed in
on her.

Obviously she must spread her wings—aah, yes, that was it!
Hail to thee, blithe spirit.
Bird thou never wert . . .
Air.
The bird needed air.
She went to the window and knelt next to it in her gown.
Then she threw open the window, and a gust of wind and rain
knocked her back.

She blinked and shook her head sadly.
In that moment she remembered she was not a bird.
She was a woman, earthbound and dutybound to tell her hus-
band a secret.

First, however, she would make a telephone call to Maine.
Oh, Terry, she whispered, you have the power to save me.

57

SIENNA WATCHED HIM TOWEL DRY HIS STRONG BODY. SHE TRIED
to say something, but the words would not come. Maybe it
would have been easier last night. No, that wouldn't have been fair,
she told herself sternly. She was long past the days when sex was a
weapon to use instead of love and brains.

Then, as he reached for his shirt, she found her opening words.
"Peter," she said, her voice pitched a little too high for early morning, "Peter, I've never told you all the truth about me."

"Are you sure you need to?" he asked teasingly. Inwardly he
groaned. Oh no, not before the office.

"I have to talk to you before you go."

He'd make a stab at keeping it light. "Remember me, baby?
I'm the fellow who was in that bed with you a few hours ago. Wasn't
that all I had to know?"

"No," she said soberly. "I must talk now."

He shrugged. "All right."

"I must tell you something."

She led him to the two chairs that faced the terrace where

the rain streamed against the French doors. Yes, she would tell in the face of rain and thunder and lightning. She would tell with the strength and the courage that love would give her. And as she told, she would pray that he would be able to separate the old fear from the new love.

"Peter," she began softly, "you've always wondered about my relationship with Anne and Bronwyn."

Peter looked at her with some annoyance. "Well, certainly I've wondered why you have this incessant need for two women who are so different from you."

"It goes back to that summer we spent together," she said. "I'd had another one of my terrible times with my parents, and I was happy to go away. I *think* I was happy, although I also think I wanted a house like the kind I saw on television, one where the mom made cookies, and the dad made jokes."

"So does everybody," Peter interrupted, a half smile on his face. "That's why I got married. I was going to be Daddy Perfect, and she was going to be Mrs. Perfect. Only she turned out to want to be Ms. Perfect, and she wanted me to pretend to be one half of whatever—God, I'm sorry, Sienna." He reached over and squeezed her hand. "Sometimes I look at you and wonder how I ever got so lucky. I had a wife who made me feel like an imitation man, and now I have you, and you make me happy every day."

"Peter, I need to explain something." She had to say it now or she knew it would never be spoken. "Peter, it's about Gregory Sawyer."

Peter gasped. "You haven't fallen for him, have you?"

"Fallen for Gregory? Oh, my darling—I can't believe what you're saying. Gregory Sawyer is the man we hate."

"*We?*"

"We. The Seconds. We. Bronwyn and Anne and I have had a kind of threat over our heads ever since he came back into our lives. Once there was a girl named Rosabelle, and we were involved in a camp prank that ended with Rosabelle's death. It was an accident. I swear it was. We weren't guilty really, but I suppose someone could be persuaded to dig it all up and make a case once more about the three of us, especially because we have some money, and our husbands are all well known. I know you've worked hard all your life, and with the possibility of Washington and the FBI looking into every corner of our lives—I knew it was just a matter of time before it all came up. I've—we've all been sick about it ever since Gregory showed up. Now the three of us have all decided to tell our husbands so that Gregory can't. We've been terrified that he'd go to the three of you and tell you we're murderers. And now I've told you," she cried, "and that's why I'm going to leave you before you have to leave me—" And with those words the tears that had knotted her fears and worries into a dark package within her heart burst from her, and she could not speak.

Peter leaned forward. "You're going to do what?"

Her mouth could scarcely form the words. "Leave you, before—"

"—I'd leave you? Oh, my darling, how could I ever leave you? How could I leave the only satisfaction, the only happiness I've ever had in all my life? You can't leave me. I won't leave you. Look, I don't want you hurt any more than you are now. I'll never tell anyone—"

"But people will know, Peter. This story with Gregory is going to come out, and people will think I've lied, and everything you do is so honest."

"Darling girl, don't you know that honesty—like love—is highly subjective? How honest are any of us with ourselves? How honest can we afford to be? Do you think I can really accept any guilt for my first marriage? I find it more—more honest—to blame Judith. And I sometimes find it easier not to talk to you at all than to try to explain the ways I feel about you. Look, Sienna, I've had a hard time finding my comfort level in this marriage. When you've been married a long time to someone else, it's difficult to think of yourself with another woman. Even when it's preferable, it just doesn't seem normal. I even had trouble remembering your name. For a long time I kept wanting to call you Judith instead of Sienna. It's strange to think that there's another woman who answers to Mrs. Peter Marvell—not that Judith was ever willing to have anyone know her by that name. My only fear has been that you'd leave me."

"Leave you?"

"I know it's not glamorous to be married to me, and I know that I'm remote, and I know I do everything by the clock. I know that women like a certain intimacy and a feeling that they come first.

I've never given you that. And I realize what you've done for me.
Sidney and I had lunch yesterday—"

"She didn't tell me."

"I asked her not to. I wanted to be with her and to see just what
her feelings were for you because you seemed so—so taken with her,
and I wondered if those were genuine emotions, and when she talked
of you, and her eyes filled with tears—oh, Sienna, I realized how
lucky I am. I don't care what you did when you were a child. I don't
care what your mother did to you and your father didn't do for you.
I don't care about anyone in this world except you. You are the best
woman who ever happened to me, and all I want is your happiness."

"But, Peter dear, Gregory Sawyer may come to you and want
money—"

"If you want me to give it to him—"

"I don't. Don't give him anything," she pleaded.

Peter stood and pulled her to him. Together they stood framed
in the French doors and watched the rain. Peter said nothing for a
few minutes. Together they watched the lightning, heard the thunder, and Sienna felt no fear. She had no secret from her husband.

Finally Peter spoke. "I've had something on my mind these
past days, too. Frankly, it came about because you sent me over to
Anne's new exercise place, and Casey—"

"That creep," she interrupted.

"No editorial comments, please," he said, squeezing her shoulder. "Anyway, Casey made a crack I didn't like, and I had to think,
do I really want your whole past washed in the press once more? And
then as I thought about whether I could be really selfless or not, I
said to myself, Hey, wait a minute. They're not only going to dig up
your lawn, Sienna; they'll investigate everybody in my life. And do
I want my life played out on the nighttime news? What about my
ex-wife when they start hinting she's a lesbian? Then somebody will
ask if the children are gay? What am I doing to Gene? I think he's
straight, but he is in his twenties and not married. What he is is his
business, but questions can hurt. And we both know how new Sidney
is to self-confidence. Let a few reporters get hold of her, and who
knows if she'll even have the strength to go through with her marriage. So this is what's been on my mind. And I've pretty much come
to the conclusion, Sienna, that I'm not meant for public life. I don't
want a lot of snooping and prying into my private life. I liked the

idea of being an ambassador. Hell, I didn't like it, I loved it. I was even studying Spanish on cassettes while I rode to the office. I was so flattered I couldn't see anything but the honor and the glory. But what's beyond isn't worth it for me."

"Oh, Peter," she whispered, "what did I ever do to deserve you?"

"You gave me love," he said quietly, "and that was more than any other person in my life ever offered."

Slowly he turned, took her hand, and led her back to their bed.

"It's not Wednesday," she whispered.

"Can't you pretend it is?" He smiled.

When she awakened, Peter had already left for the office, and still the rain was beating against the terrace windows. A nice, friendly rain, she thought.

It was the telephone that brought her back to the world of appointments and challenges. "Dear," Virginia began.

"Yes, how are you feeling, Virginia?"

"All right but not perfect, and that's why I need you today. I'm having tea here with Gregory today, so do something for me at noon, please."

"What is it?"

"I've told Juliet Caesar you'd take her to lunch."

"Virginia! How could you?" she blurted.

"Because my darling little Seconds all seem to know that charity begins at home, but they have a little trouble extending it. Now stop being a stuffy little snob, and help that woman. She's smart, and all she needs is someone who'll point her in the right direction. I'll do what I can, but I'm not as young and strong as I was with you girls."

"But, Virginia—"

"Don't 'but' me, darling. I don't care where you take her, but give her a few tips on choosing friends. She seems to think Bonnie Brickmaster is the queen mother, and since I know that Juliet's not going to buy the co-op Bonnie wants to sell her, Bonnie is going to drop Juliet so fast that poor Juliet may be forced to talk to her husband, Old Shopping Centers, if you don't come to her rescue."

"All right. I promise I will," Sienna said. Virginia was right. She had to think of others . . . others.

The other Seconds.

Those others—had they told yet?

58

A NNE LEANED AGAINST THE SOFT LEATHER OF THE CAR. THE accoutrements of power were spread before her: the pull-down desk, the telephone, the fax machine. Once, when she was a little girl, she'd watched the rich old men leave the apartment house where her mother worked and where they'd both lived. Through the heavy draperied windows she'd watch as the men—reduced to sameness by their look-alike dark suits and purposeful stride—greeted the doorman and went into their limousines. Now here she was, another kind of executive, in her own limousine traveling her own route. Anne closed her eyes. It had been a long ride to today. She thought about Casey. Had he always been so cocky, so overbearing, so—so impossible? No, really he hadn't. She could remember him as a brash young man sure that he'd get ahead, but somehow his youth and inexperience had made him lovable. Now his heavyhanded manipulation of people and events, his overwhelming sense of self had caused her to question the reasons for all his actions. Was he helping people, as he claimed, or was he just trying to lengthen his shadow over the City? More and more she was convinced it was the latter. "And I don't want you darkening my life any longer, Casey," she whispered. "I've had enough."

"Where are we going, Madam?" her driver asked. She smiled. Yes, *her* driver. Not Bellamy, Casey's driver. That idiot Bellamy still hadn't found out one thing about Gregory. But maybe he wasn't such an idiot. Maybe Casey paid him. Anne waved her hand as if to discard Bellamy, Gregory, and maybe even all men. Why not? After today she wouldn't need any of them.

"Where, Madam?" the driver inquired once more.

Anne looked out the tinted windows of her car. The rain pelting the streets looked blue from behind the glass. And somewhere out in that rain two other women were preparing for their freedom, too.

Yes, last night she'd read Fudge a funny story about a lion who lied, a story that ended with the lion telling the truth and becoming the king of the beasts once again. That was when the whole idea came to her. And now it was going to start—

"Take me to the public-relations office for the hotels, and wait for me. No matter how long it takes, no matter how many traffic tickets you get—stay there and wait."

From her office on the sixtieth floor of Casey's newest building, Lady Diandre Devon watched the skies open. Only in New York did it rain with such intensity. London rain was a gentle rain, almost a mist; it never seemed so violent as this kind of storm. Yet she felt no danger in the midst of this peculiar kind of American violence. She felt protected for the moment, safe in an aerie that was chrome and glass and filled with every high-tech communications device known to man. She could call in the world with the flick of a button, and she could get to the man she needed with a flick of her finger, for Casey had secretly moved his office to this private floor with hers.

Diandre crossed her arms and shook her coppery head. Casey had a temper to match this day. Yet all this violence, these outbursts of weather and temper, were short-lived. Casey's madness last night, his insane rage, had cooled within fifteen minutes. And this storm, too, would end by tomorrow. Funny about last night. It was as if he wanted to rage, unchecked, with no self-possession in order to be claimed and calmed, for once he had finished his fireworks, she had been able to work her own special magic, and by morning she had persuaded him that Anne was an ungrateful wife whose only goal in life was to be him.

But was that true?

As Diandre Devon watched the storm beat against the triple-thick windows, she wondered—what is Anne Burrows really like?

Then, through the currents of thoughts and through the soft music that filled the office, Diandre heard a cool voice. "Remember me? I'm Anne Burrows."

Diandre wheeled. And there, rain-soaked, but somehow with a royal dignity, Anne, like a proud Valkyrie, was fixing her bright eyes on Diandre. Diandre started to shiver and hugged herself to allay her fears. "How—how did you get in here?" she managed to ask.

"I guess you forgot, Lady Diandre, but I own the place."

"This is *my* business," the Englishwoman answered briskly.

Anne tossed her briefcase on a chair and threw her rain-soaked coat on a table. "Oh my, didn't Casey ever tell you? What he owns I own, and this business is a part of Burrows Enterprises. So, being a watchful corporate executive, I thought it was time I paid a visit to my public-relations firm, and, incidentally, to my husband. By the by," Anne asked as she looked about the room, "where is Casey?"

Diandre reached for a cigarette and then remembered she had stopped smoking. She bit her lip and said finally, "He's out to lunch."

Anne clasped her hands in delight. "So he is, Lady Diandre. In every way my husband is out to lunch. I'd so hoped he'd be here because I want to talk to him."

"You can tell me anything, and I'll tell him," Diandre countered.

Anne laughed. "Any other wife would resent that remark, but I like you for it. You know something? Basically I think we're very similar, and there are those who say that men keep marrying the same woman over and over. Well, we'll see."

"What's that supposed to mean?"

"Let's not play games, Diandre. I'm going to tell you why I'm here because you can make the whole thing happen. I told you we're alike, and I do believe that what I want is exactly what you want."

"How do you mean that?" Diandre asked.

"Sit down," Anne commanded. "I mean, *please* sit down, and let's do a deal."

Diandre, her black cashmere dress clinging tightly to her full body, backed toward her glass desk.

"No, no," Anne said with a wave of her hand. "No hiding behind desks. We're going to do this like big girls, face to face." Anne pointed to the two metal chairs on the guest side of the desk. "We'll sit here," she said, "and I'll do the talking."

"May I take your hat?" Diandre asked.

"No, thanks," Anne answered. "I think you've taken enough from me."

A small smile played on Diandre's lips. "You're too smart for him, Anne."

"So are you," Anne said, "but let's not tell him, not yet anyway."

"Why are you talking to me like this?"

"Because you are going to go to my husband and tell him that if he doesn't ask me for a divorce today, you are leaving, going back to London."

"I—I—"

"Good, you're speechless."

"But why do I want him to divorce you?"

"Silly girl, you know the reason. You want to marry him. I don't know if you're pregnant yet, but you have a big enough body to convince him that you could be, and he's frightened enough of his image not to want any children out of wedlock. So while it may be all right for rock singers and movie stars, well—let's face it, Diandre, you know illegitimate children aren't for corporate America just yet, and no one is more image-conscious than our dear Casey."

"But why do you want to divorce him, Anne? Don't you like being Mrs. Casey Burrows?"

"I did. It worked very well for a very long time, and it gave me enough confidence to be Anne Burrows. I like that even better. But we know that Casey has to have a wife. It sort of goes with the territory, and if he has you waiting, a real lady instead of a maid's daughter, I think he might like this new ending to the fairy tale."

"There's something you aren't telling me, isn't there, Anne?"

"No, but there's something I'm not telling him. I thought I had to tell him a long, sad story before it was distorted and told to him, but I've realized—"

"You've realized that if you can get rid of him, you won't have to tell your story."

"Not to him anyway."

"But I'm not sure I want to marry him," Diandre said quietly.

"Of course you want to marry him, darling," Anne assured her. "Because if you don't, what is there for you? I am now in a position to make life uncomfortable for you in your very own London, and here in New York we both know it's much more profitable to be Casey's ex-wife than Casey's ex-lover." Anne paused. "I understand that Casey is here now. We won't tell him just yet that I'm here, but you're going to go into his office, Diandre, and you're going to give him his ultimatum—it's marriage or nothing—and then to remind him of your many charms, you will take off all your clothes.

Along the way you'll make sure that Casey has his clothes off, too, or at least enough clothes off so that when I open the door—so unexpected, such a shock, tsk tsk—Casey will somehow or other decide that he's leaving me for you."

"You're very shrewd, Anne, very shrewd. The wronged wife always gets the big settlement."

"But think what you'll be getting, Diandre. After all, my ending is your beginning."

Diandre looked at Anne for a long minute. "I don't see what anyone has to lose with this deal."

"Right. You get a husband. I get rid of a husband, and Casey saves face. Now, you have thirty minutes before I open the door to that office where I know Casey is and where I will soon find you two *in flagrante delicto.*"

"I didn't know you knew Latin," Diandre said.

"Just the necessary phrases to get a girl through important dinners," Anne answered.

Diandre picked up a notebook and pencil from the table next to her. "If you'll excuse me now, I think I hear Casey calling. I think he wants to discuss—ummm—futures."

Anne smiled and nodded, and when Diandre left the room, Anne picked up the telephone. "L. D. Sothern," she said to the operator. And then Anne took a deep breath, her first easy breath in days. L. D. Sothern was the best divorce lawyer in New York, and he was going to be at her side when she opened the door to Casey's office thirty minutes from now.

How perfect.

Casey would ask for a divorce before he ever had a chance to learn about the accident, and her future would be set. And if Gregory were ever to come to her in the future, so what? As a single player, a woman not afraid of hurting her marriage, she could strike back. There was Gregory's hidden transvestism as her weapon—and who knew what else?

How really perfect this all was.

She'd leave Casey with the only person tougher and more ambitious than he, and she'd leave herself free.

Free at last!

59

BY MIDMORNING THE NEED FOR AIR, GREAT GULPS OF FRESH AIR, and the need for Terry were making Bronwyn feel a sense of desperation. So, despite the heavy rain and the backed-up traffic sounds of auto horns and driver epithets that echoed down Fifth Avenue, she decided to go out. At eleven o'clock she threw a black slicker over her trousers and jacket, put on a pair of rubber boots, and, bare-headed, opened the door to walk out in the heavy downpour.

Harold's valet, Cargill, was coming in with packages just as she was leaving. "Madam, best put something on your head. It's raining out there," Cargill advised.

"Oh," she responded vaguely.

Why is he telling me? she asked herself. *I know. Of course I know it's raining. Why is he telling me how to dress? Doesn't he know I don't want a hat?*

Instinctively she had gone bare-headed, for in the sober, windy darkness of this day, the rain and tears could mix, and she could cry out for rescue.

Rescue me, she sobbed. *Terry, come and save me. Drop into my life tonight. Give me a signal, a clue. Call me, and say you are waiting, and then I won't have to tell Harold about the accident. Say that you're coming to take me to Pumpkin Corners, and we'll scoop Gwyneth into your pumpkin coach or pickup truck or whatever it is that princes ride in today.*

Block by block she spoke to herself and made the promises she wanted to keep. *Take us, Terry, and we'll never have to see New York again, never have to pretend to be the best and the smartest and the greatest everything. Because I'm not. I'm not the best.*

The few pedestrians did not stop to talk or wonder—they simply shook their heads. The streets were full of women who talked to themselves. Bronwyn, unaware of any destination, circled her block. Turn the corner. Walk, walk, step, step. Turn the corner. Walk, step, walk, step. She had no idea of the hours as she walked, stepped, and continued her monologue. She sloshed through the heavy puddles at the curbs and looked for the deepest water.

That's what I deserve. I'm the worst, so I should get the worst. All I wanted was money so I wouldn't be poor and ugly, and now I have money, and I'm still the poorest and the ugliest. Anne is bigger and better, and Sienna is, too. And I'm nothing. Terry, why don't you take my calls? Why did the operator say you've moved? It must be a mistake. Because you love me, Terry. I know you love me. You love our poems and our stories and our romantic whispers. You do, don't you? Don't you? No, no you don't. No. No. Even you don't want me. Oh, Terry, Terry, where are you?

Then through the sound of the wind and the beat of the rain, through her own pleas for help, she thought she heard someone call her name.

"Bronwyn . . . Bronwyn."

Terry. Terry's come at last, she sobbed. She turned and flung her arms to embrace—

Harold.

It was Harold who had spied her in the street as he was being driven home in his long stretch limousine.

"Where are you going alone in the rain?" he called from the lighted warmth of the car.

She stood in a puddle on the sidewalk and looked at him, her eyes glazed and her mind playing tricks. But they were nothing compared to the trick Harold had just played on her. He—Harold—had pretended to be Terry. Hadn't he? Hadn't he driven up and spoken her name? Well, now was the time to tell him where she was going. "I—I—" She wanted to explain that she was walking to Pumpkin Corners, going to meet Terry, and then she was going to gather Gwyneth into her arms and take her, and they would go away, far away, and leave New York and him forever. Harold could buy companies and buildings and hate everybody, and she wouldn't care because she would love and be loved. But the terrible choking had come back; a sensation of little valves inside her throat closing and shutting off life kept her from talking. She tried to make the valves open, to fight the choking, to answer, but no—no words would come.

Give in, she said to herself. *Give in, and relax. Let it all go.* She must be able to talk; tonight was the night she had to tell the truth.

Ah—she was startled now by a new voice within her that spoke up and answered with a logic so strangely like her own. If you can't talk, the voice said, if you can't speak, then how can you possibly tell Harold where you are going?

Yes, she argued. *But even before I tell him where I plan to go, I must tell him about the accident, and then I'll be able to say I am leaving. Yes, that would be the proper order.* But now she couldn't speak. *Mustn't break my promise and change the order.*

But you will be breaking your promise to Anne and Sienna, the voice warned, because—well, if a woman couldn't even say hello, how could she tell of her transgressions, her old sins and her new ones?

Harold opened the door of the car, and the driver came around to lead her into the back seat with her husband. "Get in," Harold commanded. His big bulk intimidated her. She nodded and let herself be led into the warm, dry limousine. Without speaking, she curled up to make herself as small as possible in a corner of the car.

"Look at you," Harold admonished, the corners of his mouth turned down. "You're soaked to the skin."

But she did not hear the words, only the staccato rhythm of his speech reached her.

Boom boom boom boom.

Beat beat.

Yes, that was Harold talking—*Boom boom boom boom*—he had seen Anne on TV—and did she know Peter's daughter was getting married? But the words she heard did not translate into thoughts—only the rhythm of his speech reverberated in her head.

The car slowed in front of the Fifth Avenue mansion.

"What's the matter, Bronwyn? Cat got your tongue?" Harold asked.

She shook her head but said nothing. She felt such peace, a kind of self-hypnosis induced by the mesmerizing rhythm of the cadence of his speech.

The driver opened the door and helped her gently from the car. She thanked him with her eyes. She felt like a forlorn child as she started up the stone stairs, Harold's heavy steps following her.

Cargill opened the door. "Madam," he announced, "Mr. Terence Bell called as you left. He'll call back again tonight."

She lifted her rain-splashed face and smiled.

The *boom boom boom boom* had stopped.

"Thank you, Cargill," she said softly.

60

JULIET CAESAR TAPPED HER LONG RED NAILS NERVOUSLY ON THE restaurant table.

Why this dump?

What was the idea of meeting at this dumb little Tex-Mex place when everybody knew the big girls ate at Sylvan's? "It's raining," Sienna had said, "and I thought it would be fun if we did something—oh, kind of down and dirty." What was that supposed to mean? Hey, maybe Sienna wanted to hear more stories like the ones she'd told that day at Virginia's. They all seemed to like that stuff. Maybe Sienna didn't want the others to know she liked to dish. Because as far as this rain went—hey, maybe that was just a line, because any wife worth her husband's insurance could see it was raining. Juliet looked down at the tapping fingers and stopped to finger the big ring. Not a perfect D, but so what? It was a family heirloom, and which one of Mrs. North's Seconds could say that? She'd have to stop thinking that way. Like Mrs. North told her at lunch the other day, "Marriage is not a contest, dear. You're all winners now. Don't act as if you've ever been a loser." Mrs. North—oops, Virginia—had suggested she put away the diamonds for daytime, so she'd started leaving the headband, the daytime choker, and the bracelet at home. (Lolly Little had written of her diamond bracelet: "Some of the ladies are wearing tennis bracelets, but not the new Mrs. Juliet Caesar; her little string of diamonds look more like hockey pucks.") But the ring? Forget it; that was going to go wherever Juliet went. She smiled a satisfied, catlike smile, put her hands on her lap, and happily polished her big stone with her napkin.

Rich sure was more fun than poor.

Juliet sighed deeply, folded her hands, and lowered her eyes. Mrs. Marvell had just come in the door, and she didn't have a raindrop on her. Oh yeah. That was another thing. Rich means never having to look for cabs in the rain.

"Juliet." Sienna extended her hand—none of that cheek-to-cheek stuff—and said the name with more friendliness than Juliet had ever seen her exhibit. She really must want to gossip.

"Sienn-ah," Juliet answered with just the same upper-class cadence. Her natural choice would have been *Sienn-er*.

"I picked this place," Sienna confided, "because I didn't want to go to a restaurant where we'd spend all our time saying hello to everyone in the room. This is our lunch." Sienna leaned on the word "our" so that it had a kind of intimacy that thrilled Juliet.

Juliet wiggled contentedly against the stiff banquette.

"Oh, I see you're wearing your ring," Sienna said. "I'm so glad because I've always wanted to see it up close." Sienna smiled broadly. Why not admire it? Why not make Juliet proud and happy when she was so happy herself? Was this Virginia's secret, too? The knowledge that when one is secure in one's self, it's possible to be interested—even more than interested, to care—about others.

"It's a family heirloom," Juliet announced.

Sienna nodded appreciatively.

"That's why I can't take it with me."

Sienna did not ask if that meant after death or divorce. "Well, it's the most beautiful ring I've ever seen. How do you think it will look holding a taco?"

"Honey," Juliet said, "I've held more tacos than most people in Mexico. That's the kind of food I lived on for years."

"Oh, I thought this place would be different for you, kind of fun, informal."

"It is. But if you want down and dirty, Sienn-ah, I'll show you."

"Oh well, it's still a good place to get to know one another, and obviously we're going to see a good deal of each other if you're going to chair the benefit for the Rosabelle School." Strange, but it was now so effortless to say the name. She felt so free, so light without a secret.

"Well," Juliet began, "since we're going to get so friendly and everything, let me ask you something I'm too nervous to ask Virginia. What's with this Gregory Sawyer?"

"He ran the school where Anne and Bronwyn and I—"

"I already know that," Juliet said. "What I want to know is where's the lady in the wheelchair he was pushing when I saw him in Vegas?"

"You just saw Gregory Sawyer in Vegas?" Sienna trembled in anticipation of the answer she sensed she would hear.

"No, I didn't just see him, and he wasn't Gregory Sawyer. In 1986 this guy was in Vegas, and his name was William Deedle, and he was very attached to a lady with a big wheelchair and a bigger pocketbook." Juliet paused. "I guess you don't understand, Sienn-ah, but that means she was very rich, and she bought him clothes and his boys—"

Sienna grabbed Juliet's arm. "Are you sure? Absolutely sure?"

"As sure as I am that in 1982 his name was Rip McCoy, and he came on to one of the chorus boys in the line, took him for seventeen thousand dollars."

Sienna pushed the table away. "Juliet, forget lunch. You and I are going downtown to see a lawyer named Wilson Tibbitt, and then we're all going to see Virginia. Our dear, dear friend Gregory is in for a very surprising tea time."

61

THE YOUNGER YOU WERE, THE MORE FASHIONABLE IT WAS TO lament the good old days, those years just after World War II when American dreams were framed by white picket fences, men took the corporate job for life, and women longed for better babies, 'burbs, and burgers. New Yorkers, however, wished to recapture a world unlike that of the rest of America, for their world wasn't just a physical city; it was a state of mind, a city where kids arrived daily by plane, train, and bus to await the big break, where those just starting could live a lot on a little, where being rich meant long white gloves, your grandmother's pearls, and your daddy's money. It was Manhattan that the New York people longed to recapture, a sense of city best summed up in the old-time good-time feeling they had whenever they saw Gene Kelly tapping on rain-soaked streets and singin' in the rain. In many ways it was the New York Virginia Payne North had first known when she went to work for her future husband. Virginia was among the first of the born-poor-but-married-rich smart women who by century's end would control the social and cultural life of the city.

Virginia accepted her power as a kind of right to rule. She exercised her unique position with both authority and dignity, and in time her leverage gave her the pick of the parvenus, those newly minted CEOs, lawyers, and money-market merger managers who sought the benediction of a social empress in order to validate their

dollars. Virginia had, long ago, decided to give her favors and guidance not only to women who—like herself—were to the log cabin
born and had worked hard to make their own money before marrying rich, but to men who put grace before greed. Certainly Gregory
was in the latter category, a man who made a woman feel—well,
good about herself. At first Gregory had made Virginia herself feel
so good that she'd overlooked the little things—where had he spent
the last ten years? Who really knew him? Where did his money
come from? Who were his friends? Now she sensed it was all coming
to an end. Sienna had called; she and Juliet had to see her. An
attorney was coming with them. That did not bode well. Attorneys
always unmade the world that men and women with imagination
created.

≡

Virginia was sitting in her library when they came to call.
Sienna embraced her. "I—we—"
"What have you found about Gregory?" Virginia asked quietly.
"You knew?" Juliet asked.
"I know nothing," Virginia answered, "but I sensed that one
day someone would come and tell me Gregory's been just another
fantasy. Dreams like this don't come true for women like me at this
time in life."
Sienna shook her head. Maybe Virginia should have her
dreams. Why was she doing this? For Virginia or for herself and the
Seconds?
Virginia shook her head sympathetically. "You look terrible,
Sienna. Don't be afraid to tell me. I've been suspicious, but I haven't
wanted to confront my suspicions. Now, who is this young man
you've brought, and what does he want to tell me?"
"My name is Wilson Tibbitt, ma'am, and I work at the law firm
where Hedda Anderson—"
Virginia nodded and waved her hand impatiently. She wanted
none of the preamble.
"Just tell her," Sienna urged. She had never seen Virginia less
than calm and in control of all her emotions.
"Mrs. Marvell was concerned that Gregory Sawyer might be—
well, might be taking advantage of you because you're rich and
have—"
She interrupted and asked briskly, "What did you learn?"

"Mrs. Caesar and Mrs. Marvell had lunch today—"

"Young man, didn't anyone ever tell you there's a bottom line to all stories? Now, let's get to the bottom line."

"All right, Mrs. North, but you won't like it."

"Tell me anyway."

"Better yet, I'll show you. We've been checking Gregory Sawyer for a while, but Mrs. Caesar gave us our break today when she actually confirmed some of the aliases we've suspected him of using."

"Aliases?" Virginia asked cautiously.

"He's not what he seems," Wilson Tibbitt said righteously.

"Few of us are," Virginia admitted, "but we manage to stay within the law, but if a man uses aliases—"

"Chances are he's outside the law. Your instincts are right, Mrs. North. He's outside the law."

"Did you know this, Sienna?" Virginia asked.

Sienna shook her head. "I—we—we were all suspicious. I guess today's my day for honesty, Virginia. You see, we carry our own guilt about Gregory, too, because he's a part of our past, and something happened that summer at school, something terrible happened to us—"

"Not just now, dear," Virginia murmured. It seemed that a part of her life was ending, a sunshine part, and the future lay ahead as rain-filled as this day. "I knew I'd have to hear this someday, and I think I'm thankful that it's coming now and from you. Now give me the details."

Wilson Tibbitt spread a computer printout in front of Virginia. She read it slowly and calmly, and when she finished she folded the paper and turned to the three. "Gregory is coming here for tea. I think we should greet him together. All four of us. Now we have several hours to make our plans. And you can all be on hand when I ask Gregory if he wants one lump or two."

62

THERE ARE WOMEN WHO CAN LOOK BACK AND IDENTIFY THE DAY and place and time when innocence was lost, but Bronwyn Corcoran was not one of them. For Bronwyn there never was an innocence to lose. In her father's drugstore, and in the two rooms above the drugstore where the family lived in the forced closeness of middle-class poverty, the real facts of life began the day she was born. The smells and sounds of family began in the cramped bedroom where her parents' bed and her crib were so close they touched. Later she would move to something called an in-a-door bed that folded down from a living-room closet. To open the bed she had to move the heavy mohair twin chairs that matched the bright blue mohair sofa. "Don't soil the antimacassars," her mother would warn, as if those crocheted arm protectors somehow made the furniture more valuable. Early on Bronwyn learned there were only two places where she could be alone, safe from the inquiring looks and heavy breathing of her parents. They could not see her in the tiny storage area behind the prescription counter at the drugstore or burrowing deep into her chair in the far corner of the children's reading room at the neighborhood library. As a toddler she had found the secret place behind the drug counter. Even as a preteen Bronwyn was able to fit her body into the compact space, and there, with her own peculiar treasures to amuse her, she would sit for hours. At first the treasures were candy and magazines from the store—piles of chocolate bars that she savored while she read the magazines her mother said were not for "good girls." After a while she realized the magazines all had the same story with different headlines. There was always a two-headed baby, a child born to an eight-year-old girl in Venezuela, a sex ring made up of suburban housewives, and a man who saw Jesus revealed while riding on the subway to Avenue B. By the time she was eleven, Bronwyn had graduated to the women's magazines, and soon she learned that these magazines, too, always had the same articles, with a slightly different lure. There was the requisite article instructing a woman on how to get a man (act as if he's smarter than you even when he's not, act as if he's stronger than you even when he's not, and so on and on and on). Then there was an article about how a woman got her man ("I let him think he was smarter," "I let him think he was stronger," etc., etc., etc.). Finally there was an article on how to lose fourteen pounds in a week and keep it off. Bronwyn knew what the stories would be, but they were her only glimpse into the life she expected to live when she finally got out of the drugstore. She knew there was a better life, a much better life. Books taught her that, the real books, the books she found in the life she lived at the library. It was at the library that she finally learned to put aside the drugstore reading for what she instinctively recognized as the real dream world. She also learned to put aside the candy for what she found to be the real dreams to sweeten life—the pills her father dispensed. Sometimes she couldn't remember when the acne began—was it before or after she replaced the magazines with books?—but hiding behind the pages of a book either in the back of the drugstore or the back of the library became a way of not facing the world, not with her face anyway. Bronwyn noticed that whenever she had an important exam, her skin flared with new pustules, but when she took the pills that calmed her fears, they seemed to soothe her raging skin as well. And the pills, contrary to what the magazines wanted you to believe, didn't dull her intelligence. Indeed the pills were yet another spur for that active mind, that keen inquisitiveness and mathematical brilliance—so unexpected in those days in a girl whose love for literature thrilled all her English teachers. The result was excellent grades, which led to that summer as an assistant teacher, then to a college scholarship, and finally to the business that let her earn a million dollars a year. Bronwyn, at forty, was no innocent. She had known poverty, rejection, and drugs. The only thing she had never known was love. And then, when she was forty-four years old, she had met Terence Bell.

≡

When Bronwyn stumbled into the house, dazed and dulled by her day walking the rain-filled streets, and heard Cargill tell her that Terence Bell had called and would call back, she blinked and lifted her face expectantly. And from that strange place, that little storeroom at the back of her mind where she often heard sounds and words, she began to put the pieces of her life together. "Terence Bell," she mumbled.

"Who's that?" Harold snapped. "Name sounds familiar. Isn't it for me?"

"No, no," Bronwyn answered, her voice shrill with the fear that Harold would take her call just as he had taken her world. "He's mine."

Then, as if a divine presence had entered her life and permitted her to see the future, she raised her head and with a lightness of spirit began to run up the steps to her room.

"You only have fifteen minutes," Harold said.

She stopped midstep. "What?"

"Remember? We're going to the museum to that party for the store tonight."

"You didn't tell me," she said.

"I did."

"No," she insisted.

"Yes, I did. It was last week. Listen, we don't have much time, so don't give me any arguments. Just go and get dressed."

Bronwyn now took the steps slowly, and then, remembering Cargill's words, recalling her vision of moments before, she walked with dignity to the landing at the top of the steps. She put her hand on the antique cherry dresser that stood beneath the portrait of Gwyneth. She felt a sense of security unlike any she had ever known. She had Terry a phone call away, her daughter a picture away—and now all she needed was to get this man far away. "I am not going with you, Harold," she said coolly.

He laughed. "Oh, where are you going?"

"I'm leaving you. I'm going away with Terence Bell."

"Terence Bell?"

"Yes, the man who called, the man who's calling again. You just heard Cargill say it."

"You can't leave until I say you can leave."

She threw her head back, her wet hair clinging to her face, her eyes burning with the possibilities for life, and then she brought her head down slowly and said deliberately, "I said I'm leaving."

"You stay."

Now her mouth twisted, and she remembered today was the day. Yes, today. This was the day they would all tell their husbands about Gregory. Yes. Today she would say all the words that would make her free forever. She breathed deeply and then said without hesitation, "I'm about to be blackmailed by a vicious, cruel man because—"

"What? Are you queer or are you crazy?" he screamed.

But his words overlaid hers. She had begun to talk, the frenzied speech of someone who continues speaking no matter what anyone says. It was not a conversation. It was a speech, a revelation, and she would tolerate no interruption. "Once I got into trouble, Harold, once when I was a kid, and I played a prank, and someone got—"

ummmm, uh—hurt. It was all of us, Sienna and Anne and me."

"I knew you were queer for those women."

She blinked at his words, waited a moment to digest the mean-ing, and then said in a level tone, "Harold, you're the one who's crazy."

"Crazy? Me, crazy? Who's the one who's getting blackmailed? Not crazy me, I'll tell you. It's crazy you. Well, you go ahead with your fags and queers. I'm not standing around here waiting to be blackmailed."

"How touching, darling," she said with irony. "But frankly I don't care where you're standing around because I'm leaving, and you're on your own from now on."

"On my own?"

"Oh, don't worry, Harold. You won't be on your own for long. Some poor girl who's never had two cents will find a way to get your money. All the single women in New York, all those old divorcees and new widows and never-marrieds, they're all going to chase you, Harold. And I promise I'll never tell them what you're like, because I want to see you get just what you deserve. And what you deserve is a real old-fashioned gold digger, a nice old-timey girl who'll marry you for your money and take you for every last cent. I don't want a penny of yours. All I want is out. Out. Away from you. So just move aside and let me go."

"Let you go? I want you to go. Get out of here, you cheap piece of trash. And take your kid with you."

"I figured you'd say something loving like that about Gwyneth."

"I never wanted her," Harold growled.

"I want her. I want her," Bronwyn repeated, "and so does Terry."

"My God!" Harold shouted as he looked at his watch. "I only have five minutes to get to the museum."

When she dialed the little house where Terry lived, she knew there would be an answer on the first ring. Wasn't Terry sitting by the telephone waiting for her? Still, if he was, why was she trembling so? Trembling . . . like an aspen leaf, she thought. What book had that line?

Second ring—and still no answer. *If love were like the rose is/And I were like the leaf.*

Third ring—*Leaf . . . . leaf.*

Fourth ring—*Leaf . . . leaves . . . leaving.*

On the fifth ring she heard the phone lift at the other end, and she sobbed out loud in relief.

"Hello," said the strange voice.

"Terry?"

"No, Sean."

"Sean?"

"Terry's cousin. Is this Bronwyn Corcoran?"

"Yes, yes." Thank God he knew who she was.

"I called you, Bronwyn, because I wanted to talk about the bookstore."

"You what?"

"You know, the bookstore at Pumpkin Corners."

"The bookstore? What about the bookstore? Who are you?"

"Terry's my cousin. We're partners."

"But I want Terry. Terry called. Where's—where's Terry?" Fear squeezed her heart.

"Well, that's why I called."

"You called?" Terry was dead. She knew it. No one had to tell her. Weren't their hearts joined forever? Wasn't her heart stopping?

"Yeah. Terry left, but I still want to do the bookstore."

"Left?" *Leaf leaf.* "I don't know what you're talking about."

"Well, before Terry went to Europe—"

"Europe?" *Leaf . . . leaves.*

"Umm, well, like Terry got tired of everything here."

"Tired of everything?" *Left.*

"He gets like that. He always has. You know, he has this weird imagination, and he does things until he gets tired of them, and then he needs to do something new, and so he goes away until—but I guess you figured that out about him."

Left . . . gone . . . Tell me more. "I don't understand what you're saying."

"Well, here's what I'm saying. I called you and said I was Terry because I figured you'd never know what I was talking about if I gave my name. I want you to know that Terry went to Europe, but I still want to be your partner in the bookstore. I think you can build a whole chain from this, and you can make a hell of a lot of money, Bronwyn."

Left. He'd left. Terry left. No good-bye poem. No last sad songs for me. "But you mean it was you who called and said you were Terry?" She did not wait for the answer. "But you're not Terry." No indeed. He wasn't Terry. Terry, darling Terry, her light and her hope and her life, hadn't called. This strange cousin who wanted her money had called. But Terry didn't want her. In the end he hadn't even wanted her money. He'd wanted only himself and his dreams. No, it wasn't Bronwyn he'd wanted at all. He'd wanted that dream of Bronwyn and Terry, that sweet Irish song of love that only he could hear. He didn't want to share the love. He wanted it just for himself. And in that room—in that hall not twenty feet from here— she'd just thrown her whole life away on a phone call Terry never made. "When is Terry coming back?" she asked finally.

"We never know with Terry," Sean answered.

The telephone dropped from Bronwyn's hand, and she shook her head in disbelief. The years in the drugstore, the years of study, the years of work had led to—to what? To this road to nowhere. She felt her body grow rigid, a physical protest against—against what? Against whom?

There's no one who wants me. I disgust Harold. Terry can't stand me. He ran away from me. Maybe he had the answer. Yes, that's it. The thing is to run away from me.

Bronwyn stood slowly and walked in a stiff, robotlike movement toward her bathroom.

She knew where she was going. *Yes, yes, Terry, hold your dream. I will join you "into the eternal darkness, into fire and into ice."*

63

GREGORY SAWYER DID NOT SIMPLY WEAR HIS CLOTHES; HE shared a history with them. Now, as he walked through the rain to Virginia's home, he wore the black suit that he'd had made by a Saville Row tailor. This suit was known as the Winkle suit, for it had been paid for by Lurette Winkle, the Atlanta—or was it New Orleans?—widow he'd danced across the Atlantic with aboard the

QE2 three summers ago. The shoes, hand-made and English, had been the gift of a rich young lover, a darling boy really, who'd collected ambergris and older men. Gregory's shirt had been custom-made some years and a shirt size ago, and he'd paid for it himself—it was just after he'd sold that stock in a nongushing oil well that managed somehow to pay off for him. The dotted tie, however, was a gift from Virginia. He patted the tie through the old raincoat he wore. That was the real sign of a gentleman, he told himself, the ability to wear old clothes and make them look better than new. This old coat had been in his closet for, oh, maybe twenty-five years, but it looked better than anything men bought today. It had that worn patina of George III silver or an English country table. Gregory liked the feel of all his clothes; he loved to press his body against them, feel the rich wool and touch the beautiful hand stitching, run his fingers through the silks, and sniff the fragrance of real leather. There was comfort in knowing that one was always dressed like a man of worth. Gregory knew that clothes do make the man. Yes, he smiled as he walked up Park Avenue and through the deluge, yes, he grinned knowingly as he heard the thunder and saw the lightning—even the gods applaud a man of quality. And I, Gregory Sawyer, he assured himself, am definitely a man of quality about to have tea with one of the richest women in New York.

Who would ever have dreamed of such possibilities?

Life could be filled with such delicious surprises. Who would—who could have dreamed this chapter in his life? And to think—he shuddered slightly now—he'd almost missed this turn in the road.

He thought now to that long-ago night . . .

≡

. . . Sheriff Joe Fennick was at home in bed when the call came. It wasn't so special to get a middle-of-the-night call from Gregory, but tonight Gregory's usual soothing voice quivered with an unspoken uneasiness. "This is Dr. Gregory Sawyer—"

Joe sat upright in bed.

"Please come immediately, Sheriff. There's been an accident. Oh, and I will meet you in my living room," Gregory said. There was a special emphasis on the words "my living room." Something was up. Usually Gregory wouldn't let Joe near the school. Instead he'd

call, use the code name "Greta," drive to Joe's, and walk directly into the unlocked bedroom.

Joe put the phone down and ran his fingers nervously through his thinning blond hair. Although he was only twenty-nine, he'd inherited the Black family tendency toward baldness. "You won't have a hair on your head when you're thirty-five," Grandma Black had promised him when he was just a toddler. Maybe that was why the girls had always scared Joe—get one now, and she'd leave when she learned he'd be Old Baldy just when other guys were getting their acts in gear. He put his jeans on over his pajamas, the way he figured a cop would, and then he went to the garage and mounted his motorcycle.

The minute he walked into that living room Joe felt as if he were walking onstage to act his part in the senior play. "Sheriff," Gregory said, sounding more like the hero in the play than a school director, "these girls have had a dreadful accident."

Joe blinked at the three girls huddled in the middle of the room. One, a kid with a terrible complexion, was biting her lips. A little one was sniffling, and her wet hair was streaming down her face; he could see her eyes were filled with tears. Was it fright or sadness? The third one, a big blond girl, seemed the most ready to talk, although her breathing was fast and irregular.

"What's going on here?" Joe asked. He hitched his pants just the way those cops did on television.

"It was an accident," Anne said softly.

"We were playing. It was all kind of a—sort of a game, and Rosabelle was in the backseat."

"Rosabelle?" Joe asked.

"The girl who was drowned," Gregory said abruptly.

Joe took a shocked step backward.

"The girls took my car without my knowledge," Gregory said slowly, and then he repeated the words to make sure his excuse was reaching the addled brain of the shocked sheriff.

It was at that moment that a fragment of memory seemed to sweep Bronwyn's mind, and she saw the women's clothes in Dr. Gregory's car. In the sweet, simple voice of a young girl, and with the mind of an accomplished reader who read books to understand life, she said, "When we took the car, we emptied Dr. Gregory's clothes from the back."

Gregory raised his eyebrows slightly. "Oh yes, I dumped a few old slacks and shirts of my brother's there."

"No," said Bronwyn slowly and deliberately, "we took out your women's clothes, the ones you wear."

Her words triggered fresh fears in both men.

Joe wanted to scream and tell her no, no, I wasn't the one who was in them. No, no, I wasn't the one you saw when you peeked through the windows—had she peeked through the windows? Had Gregory been followed? How much did the girls know?

Gregory turned and looked at Joe. Everything about the sheriff was soft and sweaty and smelled faintly of motorcycles. Gregory sighed deeply. He watched as Joe rubbed the wet palms of his hands against the oil stains on his jeans.

Gregory clucked sympathetically. "Obviously those weren't clothes I wore. Did you look at the size? Why, they'd be too small for me." Slowly and deliberately Gregory murmured, "Who knows, Joe? They just might fit you—or your mommy. But I never wore those clothes, did I, Joe?"

Bronwyn thought the sheriff was going to cry. Her literary mind, her exploratory thoughts that linked plot and characters, had worked for them.

Anne, herself involved in fantasy, was not ready to give up her newly invented life, and even though she didn't understand the full import of Bronwyn's insights, Anne felt her breathing go low and regular as she said, "Sheriff, we had an accident," and then just as she thought she would be able to tell their story, there was a constriction in her throat and a terrible knot in her stomach. She doubled over and began to cry. "Oh, Rosabelle, come back. Please come back, Rosabelle."

Sienna's shock and sadness over Rosabelle now got the better of her fear for herself, and she, too, began to cry.

Bronwyn put her arms around Sienna and rocked her gently. "I'll take care of you," she murmured in an almost motherly tone. Sienna flung her arms around Bronwyn's neck.

The young sheriff looked at Gregory.

"Obviously this was an accident," Gregory said. "Step outside, and I'll give you the details."

Outside, Gregory leaned against the little cabin and outlined the facts with no hint of emotion. "I'll burn the clothes, Joe, and tomor-

row at Parents' Visiting Day, you and I will meet with all the parents. They'll all need some reassurance, and I see no reason to mention—umm—anything of anyone's private life. Not the girls' or mine. And certainly," he added, his eyes narrowed, "not yours."

The next day the coroner conducted a brief inquest; the tearful girls, with Gregory acting as a sober-sided and solemn father figure, told the story of the accident. Once or twice Sheriff Joe Fennick almost interrupted to ask again why Rosabelle had been in the backseat. Each time he wanted to ask that question, he signaled his concern and hitched his pants, but before he could pose it, Gregory interrupted to press the girls' story more firmly into the mind of the coroner. He knew that by the time the inquest ended Joe wouldn't be sure how much he'd dreamed, how much he'd seen, and how much Gregory had told him. The inquest went just as Gregory had scripted it.

But Gregory did not script the next chapter. It was sometime during the following winter that Gregory heard that Joe had been killed in a motorcycle accident. And, as Gregory knew, that meant that no one could ever question Rosabelle's death again.

Indeed Rosabelle and the three girls were far from Gregory's thoughts after that night. Gregory never again so much as flirted with a lawman, for there were far more fascinating names and women—and boys—to serve his life and plans.

And then one day, in the midst of a dull social season and somewhere between a countess and a midwestern widow, Gregory saw a picture in The Fashion Daily, *a picture of the fabulous Anne Burrows with Virginia Payne North.*

So Anne had grown up and become that Anne!

Interesting indeed.

Under ordinary circumstances Gregory wouldn't have given a faux pearl to meet Anne again, but as a friend of Virginia Payne North she might be very useful.

Virginia was certainly his kind of woman, and he knew that all he had to do to be gathered into her rarefied social circle was to volunteer to serve as a fund-raiser, for if there was one thing that was worth cash in New York, it was an attractive male willing to have afternoon meetings with women and help them with their charity boards.

But that's how it always was with charity.

You worked on behalf of a lady's favorite charity, and she'd work on behalf of yours.

Of course, in this case Gregory Sawyer's favorite charity was Gregory Sawyer.

≡

Gregory deposited his very wet coat and hat with the butler, slicked his hair in front of the mirror in the gallery, and strode down the hall to greet Virginia. He always liked being the first to arrive, and to assure that he generally arrived at the appointed hour. Everyone, of course, did the proper New York thing of arriving fifteen minutes after the requested time. As he moved gracefully through the gallery, he anticipated their meeting. She would be seated prettily in her cozy library, the bar open and some kind of hors d'oeuvre—caviar perhaps—waiting. He'd have champagne, he thought. Yes, instead of the proper glass of wine he usually drank with Virginia, he'd have something more festive. He didn't know the reason, but somehow he felt as if this afternoon was—well, special.

"It sounds as if Gregory has arrived," he heard Virginia say even before he reached the library.

He patted his hair and squared his shoulders. Who could be there even earlier than he?

Gregory walked into the room.

A slim young man, only slightly shorter than Gregory, stood to greet him. The young chap pushed his horn-rimmed glasses up on his long nose and blinked curiously. His curly brown hair was in need of barbering, and he was wearing one of those disgusting off-the-rack suits that pretended to have English ancestry. Gregory frowned as he realized that this man looked unlike anyone Virginia would entertain in her home. What was this interloper doing here?

Gregory looked at Virginia.

She did not speak.

Then he looked at the young man.

"I'm—I'm Gregory Sawyer," he said, the hint of English accent shining through his name.

The young man blinked. "Gregory Sawyer," he repeated slowly. "Oh yes, and also known as William Deedle, also known as Slim Babbitt, also known as Rip McCoy, also known as J. Prescott Towers, also known—"

Gregory had stopped listening.

Standing there in Virginia's library wearing his fine English clothes and excellent hand-made boots, Gregory Sawyer had been stripped naked by a blinking young man in an off-the-rack suit.

64

"VIRGINIA, WHAT KIND OF—OF GAME IS THIS?" GREGORY ASKED indignantly.

"That's precisely what I was going to ask you," she answered.

"Do you believe this—this impostor?" Gregory had recovered his old aplomb and, his haughtiness reasserted, he posed the question with anger.

Gregory now looked around the room. There was Sienna. What was she doing here? And not with—oh, this was too much—Juliet Caesar.

"Listen, Rip," Juliet said coolly, "you don't remember me, do you? See, when you knew me I was shaking it at Vegas. One of the Bal de Masque dancers. Remember when they brought that show over from Paris? The girls all wore great headdresses, hid their faces, and all you saw was their bodies? Well, I was one of them. You never looked at us. You wanted all those chorus boys—"

"That's enough for Gregory to get the authentication we need," Virginia said. "Thank you, Juliet, for coming. Please leave now."

Juliet stood, shook her family heirloom diamond to make it sparkle in the late afternoon lamplight, and waved, saying, "Ta ta."

Gregory turned to Sienna. "You did it, didn't you? You went running to tell about me, but how about you? Did you tell what Rosabelle is really about? Did you tell about the—"

"Stop. Enough," Virginia said. She could not bear humiliating Gregory further nor did she want any more disclosures and further despair. "Gregory," she confessed sadly, "you gave me a good time for my money, but the ride is over."

Gregory breathed deeply and said with bitterness, "Who started this? I'll bet it was Anne. Yes, Anne the Killer Whale," he added coldly.

"No." Virginia shook her head. It wasn't Anne. It wasn't Bronwyn, and it wasn't Sienna. It wasn't even Juliet. Dear Gregory, it was you. You see, you were just too good to be true. I do—I did—fancy you, and I can't say I'm happy to burst the bubble. I'd like to keep this all quiet. It's not a story that I'd care to have bandied about New York. I've been a little silly, and no woman my age likes to have others know that. You see, you came to me because you knew my girls, my Seconds as I affectionately call them. I never really asked them about you, and obviously they volunteered no information. But now that I know the—the history that I do, it's obvious I can't support a school in which you're involved."

"But you've already bought the land, Virginia."

"So I have, and you can keep whatever money you made on that real estate because I *will* get the school built, and I know the Seconds will help me. You'll have nothing to do with it, Gregory. In fact, you will go home, pack your bag, get your passport, and be on a plane to Rio at midnight."

"But I don't know anyone in Rio."

Virginia threw her head back and laughed. "You will soon enough."

"I don't think I can go there, Virginia."

"Too bad, Gregory, because if you don't, then this excellent lawyer here is going to call the police."

"The police?"

"You misrepresented yourself to me and to my friends, and—" She shrugged. "You know how it is, Gregory, when you tussle with a woman like me. I don't like to be humiliated, and the only reason I'm sparing you public ridicule is that you, like me, were born poor. And we who have achieved a certain place must help one another keep our dignity. It's all right for the born rich to lose it every once in a while with their own in-fighting, but we money-come-latelys can't afford to lose anything but money. So before you lose anything else, I think you'd better pack your bags and get out while the getting's good, Gregory."

"I really cared for you, Virginia," he said.

"I hope so," she whispered, "and I will believe you because I want to. But frankly, Gregory, I think I'm being as good to you as you ever were to me."

Gregory nodded, turned, and walked briskly from Virginia Payne North's home and life.

Sienna watched him leave and put her arms around Virginia.

"I don't know," she said softly. "I don't know about winning and losing anymore. I thought I was going to lose everything today. Nothing is ever the way we expect it to be."

"No, it isn't," Virginia agreed. "Now please leave, my dear, because I want to talk about my school with Mr. Tibbitt."

≡

Virginia sighed. "Do you think I'm an old fool?" she asked Wilson Tibbitt.

"No, I don't," he said thoughtfully. "I think you did what any woman who's alone would want to do; you put a little romance in your life. My mother's a widow, and all the time I was working on this, I kept thinking what I'd do if you were my mother, and I was torn. I think about my mother making her frozen dinners each night in her microwave oven or playing bridge with other widows, and I wish she had a man to kiss her and tell her she's still lovely. You and my mother, Mrs. North, you women are all alone through no fault of your own, so why not try to make life a little better for yourselves?"

Virginia stood and walked to Wilson slowly and said in words that seemed to come from the very heart of her, "You're a very fine young man, Wilson, and now we're going to redo my will. I'm going to set up a foundation to start the school, and I'm going to make the Seconds the trustees. You'll be the executor of my estate, and we will make the school happen. We'll get a good administrator, and we'll do our best for some young people."

"I hope, Mrs. North, you'll see the project through yourself," Wilson said.

Virginia shook her head thoughtfully. "No," she answered, "I cannot tell the water to run uphill and the sands of time to stop. Thanks to modern medicine, I'm still here, but even medicine has its limits."

"Mrs. North," Wilson said, extending his hand, "I'm proud to know a real lady."

≡

She was having dinner alone on a tray in the library.

Such a long day.

Such a difficult day.

Suddenly she was aware of someone else's presence. She looked up. "Holmes, have you been standing here long?"

"A few minutes. Madam, Mercy Hospital emergency room just called. Miss Bronwyn has had an—an accident, and they thought you should know."

"An accident? But why call me? Where was her husband?" Virginia asked quickly.

"I don't know, Madam, but they said they called because you are listed on her identification as next of kin."

"My God," Virginia gasped. "I must get to her."

"I'll take you," her butler said quickly.

Virginia turned, and the shadow from the lamp fell across her face. "No," she whispered from the half-light, "that just wouldn't be right. You're not—family. I'll go alone. But you can do something for me," she said. "Mrs. Marvell, I think, went back to Bedford, but try to find her, and also try to reach Mrs. Burrows. Tell them both to meet me at Mercy Hospital. As next of kin, I know that at times like this the family must be together."

65

LATER, VIRGINIA COULD REMEMBER ONLY THE POLICEMAN WHO stood guard at the emergency room. Although she knew that ambulance sirens were screaming around her, that attendants with worried looks were running in and out through the constantly swinging doors, that there was a rustling sea of white—nurses, nurses' aids, paramedics—the only night face that imprinted itself on her was the policeman's. He was a boy young enough to be her son, his blue figure bobbing in the sea of white, his doughy face flushed with the excitement of being a man of authority at the center of the action, and then, so that no one might see what lay behind his mask of importance, the young man wore dark glasses that acted as mirrors. When Virginia tried to see his eyes, she saw instead her own. What kind of man would try to fool you by making you look at yourself? A frightened man, Virginia thought. But I am more frightened, she wanted to tell him. It was a night to be feared, just like that night so many years ago when she had brought Calvin to this same hospital emergency room. That night she had ridden in the ambulance with

Calvin, and all the way she had known that she was going to Mercy
Hospital a wife and would leave a widow. Memory, that old friend
Memory, which makes heroes and villains of us all, now made her
shiver with the remembered fear of that time. But she must concentrate on tonight. She blinked. The officer had trained his mirrored
glasses on her, and with a brusqueness in his voice she hadn't heard
since she was a young secretary, he asked what she was doing there.
She looked in the mirrored eyes and wondered, too.

"Lady," he repeated, "I wanna know what you're doing here.
Who ya want?"

She paused. Who was it she wanted? She wanted Calvin. This
was where they had taken him; isn't this where they'd bring him
back?

The boy blew his breath through the puffy cheeks. "Lady, who
ya want?"

She came back to reality with a start. "I am looking for Mrs.—"
No, she thought, Bronwyn won't use his name tonight. "For Miss
Bronwyn Corcoran."

"You a relative?" Mirror Eyes asked.

Yes, Virginia nodded. Yes. Then she wet her lips and said
slowly, "She is my daughter."

≡

Soon after—or was it just then?—Anne arrived.

"Holmes called me and said he'd also called Dr. Bradley,"
Anne explained, "and I called Sienna in the country. She's on her
way."

Virginia swayed slightly, leaned against Anne, and knew in that
instant that the past was over, and she must respond with Anne to
the present, to whatever faced them. Sensing Anne's anxious scru-
tiny of her, Virginia shook her head as if to exorcise the old demons.
"I'm all right; it's Bronwyn who needs us now."

Anne nodded. From the moment she received the call, Anne
had feared the worst. Mercy Hospital was another way of saying
Something Really Bad Has Happened. Mercy, with its legendary
emergency room, was the hospital you chose only when the patient
was in extremis; it was no country-club hospital with gourmet
menus. This was a serious big-city hospital whose history was written
in the street stabbings, rapes, murders, child beatings, and traffic

accidents of the day and night in New York. "Have you found her here yet?" Anne asked Virginia.

No. Virginia mouthed the word, but no sound came.

Anne looked for a chair. If she could just seat Virginia—but no. Virginia was clutching her arm; Virginia would not be downed just now. All right. Anne tucked her arm under Virginia's and said, "Stick with me. We're going to find her." A woman in white pushing a gurney with a patient anchored to life by tubes and overhead bottles tried to move Anne aside, but Anne stood in her path. "Where's Bronwyn Corcoran?" she demanded of the startled nurse.

"Out of my way," the nurse responded through her mask. "Can't you see I'm busy?"

Anne grabbed her arm. "Can't you see I'm desperate?"

"Move it," the nurse snapped. "I'm taking this kid to surgery. If you want somebody, go to the desk. See?" She indicated the direction with a shrug of her shoulder. "There. In the middle of the room."

Anne took Virginia, wheeled, and walked briskly to the podium at the center of the White Sea. Would they ever see Bronwyn again? "I am Anne Burrows," she said with authority to the woman behind the desk.

"Fill out your form," the nurse answered in a weary voice.

"I said I'm Anne Burrows," she answered in her best New York voice.

The woman looked over her half-glasses. "So?"

"So help us," Virginia said crisply before Anne could answer.

Anne turned and looked at Virginia with surprise. She'd thought she was holding Virginia up, helping her maintain her composure while she, Anne, looked for Bronwyn. Now Virginia was acting with that inner authority that made her the doyenne of society. With three words spoken calmly, she had asserted her right to rule.

"My daughter is here, and I must find her," Virginia said. "If you don't know where she is, then ask one of the other women behind that desk with you." Now Virginia raised her voice, and her tone was sharp and clear. "Who knows the whereabouts in this hospital of my daughter? Her name is Bronwyn Corcoran."

From the other side of the podium a woman with springy gray curls and wearing a white uniform turned to them. "Are you Mrs. North?" she asked.

"Yes," Virginia responded, but there was no relief in her tone.

"I've been waiting for you. I took the call from Dr. Bradley. He told me you're his friend and patient and asked me to help you until he's able to get here. I checked, so I can tell you where she is. Bronwyn Corcoran is over there, over in that cubicle with a woman whose husband just tried to strangle her."

"And Bronwyn?" Anne asked. "What's happened to her?"

"Didn't anyone tell you?" the woman wondered.

Virginia shook her head.

"Suicide attempt. Pills. Probably alcohol. They think it was a pretty sophisticated mixture. She obviously had access to all the best designer drugs. She's having a tough time. She's over there, but—" Now the older woman looked with sympathy at Virginia—how much do women have to see before they know it all?

"I will go there," Virginia answered without hesitation.

"She's hooked up to a lot of hardware, and she's being monitored. And," she called as they crossed the room, "she won't know you."

Virginia strode ahead purposefully, and Anne—despite her height and athletic build—rushed to keep up with her. When they came to the curtained area, Anne pulled back the sheet and looked in. She expected to see a room, a place with beds. Instead she saw a small portion of space—how big was it? Perhaps six feet by two feet. She shook her head in disbelief.

Virginia looked at her precious Second, now hidden by a network of tubes and beepers, wrapped in science as if electricity could keep the light of life burning. And as she looked, Virginia's eyes filled, and then she began to weep uncontrollably, sobbing for Bronwyn, for that barely breathing form that lay under the sheet in front of her. Oh, this child. This poor child who had walked so many miles, climbed so many steps. What terror had made her believe that lying down in this last six feet was better than standing up to fight? Didn't Bronwyn know that no matter how bad any moment was, life is still the best of what we are given? Bronwyn, Bronwyn, she wanted to cry out, no matter how desperate life looks, it is at least life. Life is what you have; it is all you are given. It is a blank page whose scribbles and scrawls are made in the hearts of men and the souls of women. How could you give it away? "Oh God," Virginia cried out, "give her another chance! Don't let her die. Let her know she matters. Life matters.

"Doesn't she understand how important she is?" Virginia asked, her tearstained face turned to Anne. Then, bending over the still form on the narrow bed, she said softly, "I love you, Bronwyn."

Anne, her arm tightly around Virginia, now bent over the small, still form. "I love you, Bronwyn," Anne repeated.

And then in the never-ending tumult of the emergency room, with the body-laden carts careening wildly, the shouts and the moans behind the curtained partitions, the police and the nurses and the forms and the questions—from a distant place Bronwyn's eyelids fluttered open.

≡

The sirens were still screaming the news of fresh tragedy, and the white sea of uniformed attendants was still rolling rapidly through the emergency room when Sienna and Peter arrived to join Virginia and Anne standing at the entrance of Bronwyn's area. Sienna was wearing blue jeans and a turtleneck sweatshirt; her hair was tied back, and her face with no makeup looked very pale and white.

"We were in bed, but we came as soon as Holmes called," Sienna said in a low voice. "They told me it was a suicide attempt. Do you think she tried to tell—?"

"We don't know," Anne answered, "but the *wonderful husband*"—she grimaced as she emphasized the words—"isn't here. The one who found her was the maid. Thank God she had the presence of mind to call an ambulance and then get to Virginia."

"My dears," Virginia said, "you never know how much someone in Bronwyn's condition can hear and know, so why don't we move from here and find a place—there has to be an all-night cafeteria somewhere in this hospital—and let's have a cup of tea. I've done a lot of thinking this past hour, and we need to talk together."

Peter walked behind the three women. Strangely, this had been the most wonderful night of his marriage, the time when—for reasons he didn't yet know—he'd felt that at last he'd found his place in life, and his place was with Sienna, the warm-hearted woman whose love made his blood flow, his heart beat. He had made a family decision, not a business decision. Perhaps that was why he felt so alive at last. Today he had been given not just a sense of marriage but a sense of family. He and Sienna had both made decisions today that would unite them with each other and with his children in ways that would last all their lives. How sad that this, the most married moment of their life, should be interrupted by—by life. He shrugged. He remembered what someone once said. Life is what happens to you while you're busy making plans.

≡

Virginia traced the spilled sugar on the table with her finger. How to start? The way she always did—with honesty. "You probably think I've been a fool."

Sienna and Anne exchanged glances. "I told Anne," Sienna said. "I told her about—about today."

"I knew you would." Virginia smiled. "That's what sisters are for. But, my dear, if I've been foolish, at least I'm going to try to do something about it all." She pushed the sugar aside, took a deep breath, and looked directly at the two women. "Gregory Sawyer," she said in a low, level voice, "is on his way to Rio."

Anne dropped her coffee cup with a clatter. "Then you did it? I couldn't believe I—I—"

"I've never seen you at a loss for words, Mrs. Burrows." Virginia laughed. "My," she said shaking her head, "but it feels good to laugh, doesn't it? Gregory Sawyer was gallant, but he wasn't good for many laughs. I don't know if Bronwyn's escapade tonight was related to Gregory, but I suspect his shadow was cast over this night some years ago."

"You know more about us, then, than you ever admitted?" Sienna asked cautiously.

"No." Virginia shook her head. "I know no more about you now than I did when I first adopted my darling Seconds. I don't know how or why Gregory came into your lives except for the stories you three have told me."

"Today was our day to tell the truth," Sienna said, "so let me tell you, Virginia."

Virginia reached over and touched Sienna's lips with her fingers. "Hush, dear. I don't need any more stories. I'm much too old for more tales. Besides, if you love someone, the truth just gets in the way of the fantasies you need to keep you comfortable. Please don't disturb my truths; I've grown accustomed to them."

"But Bronwyn couldn't handle her truths, could she?" Anne asked.

"I think her fantasies did her in," Sienna said. "She dressed Gwyneth like a toy—"

"Gwyneth!" Anne gasped. "Who will tell her that her mommy's sick?"

"And what's to become of the child?" Virginia asked. "I think that her mother has a long recuperative period ahead of her. She has to—to recover from this physically, and I think our darling Bronwyn needs to have some good therapy. She needs a place like Pembroke."

"Pembroke? That's for addicts," Peter said.

"Ugly word, Peter," Virginia said, "but let me ask where you'd send her? I've known for a long time that Bronwyn has been taking pills, but I didn't realize how serious it really was. If I did—" She shrugged and shook her head. "No, even if I knew, what could I have done? This was her cry for help; this was her way out. I'm beginning to understand. And now that she's called for help, we must send her to the best treatment center, something not too far from here, a place where Gwyneth can, in time, visit."

"You're right, Virginia," he agreed. "That's the place for her."

"Certainly they won't take the child, too," Virginia said. "I wish I were younger and stronger; I'd take her with me if I could."

"Harold Ashter mustn't keep her," Anne said.

"He wouldn't want her," Sienna reminded them, and then she looked at Peter.

Peter smiled and put his arm around his wife. "We'll take her," Peter said. "We'll take her to live with us until Bronwyn's feeling herself."

"Do you mean it, Peter?" Sienna asked.

"I think it might be fun to have a child around for a while," he said.

Virginia nodded approval at Peter, and then she looked at the women sitting with her; she looked at the tiny Sienna, who'd come to her bruised and broken in spirit, a woman who'd thought love was something her mother traded for houses and cars. She looked at Anne, Anne who acted strong to hide weakness, and she thought of Bronwyn lying under this same roof—Bronwyn, who tried so desperately to write her own ending.

I love you, Virginia tried to say. I love all of you, she wanted to shout, but she did not. Instead she let the love flow through her body. She let her blood run with love, and she let her thoughts overflow with love, for she knew in that moment what she had given the Seconds and what they had given her. The real gift they had exchanged was love. Forget the people she'd helped them meet, the doors she'd opened, and the secret words she'd whispered.

Through the years, past life and past time, what they would have, what the Seconds would have—first, last, and forever—would be a family of love that would loop them for their generation and the generation of their children.

Virginia closed her eyes. She felt very tired. It was the end of such a long night, such a long life. A merry ride in some ways, wasn't it, Calvin? So many sweet times, and yet so difficult, too. But then, no one had ever promised her that love was easy.

66

NEW YORK DOES NOT SLOW DOWN FOR THE OLD, THE SICK, OR the despairing. It is a city always ready for those at the ready. No matter the condition of the old players, the curtain goes up all over the city each night, and the entertainments are nonstop. The opera, the Broadway theater, off-Broadway, and off-off Broadway. Restaurants open noisily and close quietly. People rush off to Southampton to see the same people they see in the City, and they jet off to London to see the people they may have missed in Southampton. Designers have showings, and photographers take the pictures of next year's ladies in this year's clothes. Charities are run like businesses—but in New York no business is run like a charity.

One of the first women to come on the charity scene with a firm knowledge of business was Virginia Payne North. In the 1950s and 1960s when she made her name as Mrs. Calvin North, women in society did not do what they called "work." "Work" was what men and single women did. Virginia, however, having been in the business world for many years before her marriage, knew what "work" was about. She was the first of the society women to know how to read a balance sheet, to question expenditures, and to apply business pressure to raise charitable funds. Further, she performed all her jobs with dispatch and grace. She was what her contemporaries and the press termed "a fixture" on the New York social scene. Yet when Virginia, weakened and tired, took to her bed for days at a time and all but disappeared from events other than her own special charities, only a few columns made mention of her absence.

Each morning Sienna and Anne checked with each other before calling Virginia, for over the past months Virginia had become testy when both called her within the same hour.

Those calls from her Seconds had once started her day. Now she thought her Seconds were spying on her, checking to see if she was still alive. She wanted their concern; she resented her need of them.

Still, she knew that as much as she needed them, Bronwyn needed them more. Bronwyn, now at Pembroke, was making progress. She had come through the physical horror of that night; now the long road back to a kind of health she had never known was beginning. Gwyneth had become a part of Sienna and Peter's household, and the little girl was looking forward to her mother's return.

Yes, that was something to plan.

Bronwyn's return.

Virginia thought about it a great deal, but she hadn't been ready to discuss it.

She hadn't wanted to talk about Bronwyn or the school the several times that Anne had come to see her, bringing her children. Somehow it wasn't an appropriate subject in front of little Fudge.

And she certainly couldn't talk about Bronwyn when Sienna came to visit with Gwyneth.

It was very sweet of them to bring along the children when they came to call, for only in the past months had she come to know the second generation of the Seconds. Dear children they were, and Virginia was touched, for they now called her Gammy.

And then one winter day, one cold, bleak day a call came from Virginia's butler, Holmes.

Sienna recognized his voice and froze. Did this mean—

But Holmes was calling with a pleasant surprise. "Mrs. North is feeling very good today, and she thought it would be delightful to have both you and Mrs. Burrows join her for lunch at Sylvan's. Usual table. Usual time."

"I'll call Mrs. Burrows, and no matter what she has scheduled, I'm sure she'll be there. We'll both be there," Sienna added hurriedly.

≡

Virginia arrived first in order that her beloved Seconds not see that her step had slowed and her breath had shortened in the weeks since they'd last seen her in public. She sighed. It just took so much more out of one to dress and go out.

Sylvan hovered in his customary way. "A glass of champagne with my compliments?" he inquired.

"Not a glass, but a bottle," she answered. "We're celebrating Mrs. Marvell's pregnancy. To think she'd been told for years she could never have a child, and then this miracle." Virginia paused. "You know she's having a baby in just a few months."

Sylvan nodded. Only a blind man would not know about Sienna's pregnancy. Her tiny body had grown enormously, and her new clumsiness was a parody of her former delicate movements.

"Oh, and here she is," Virginia exclaimed, clapping her hands in delight. "Hello, dearest Sienna."

Sienna, more short of breath than Virginia, kissed the older woman firmly on the cheek and landed even more firmly on a chair opposite Virginia, who was seated on the banquette. "I'll never be able to fit behind a banquette again," Sienna moaned.

"Nonsense," Virginia said, "you'll be the same skinny little thing in no time at all."

"I feel like a little piggy. Matter of fact, I feel like all three little piggies," she said with a smile, "and I want to tell you this is the happiest complaining time of my life."

"Babies are a miracle," Virginia agreed.

"None so much as this one. I've had all the tests, and everything seems very good," Sienna added, crossing her fingers.

"I wanted to invite Juliet today, but she's in Tokyo this week."

"Tokyo? For the benefit?"

"Oh, my dear, she's traveling the world to make this the most successful benefit in the history of benefits. She left yesterday morning, very unexpected—"

"I don't know whether you heard about the pledge she got from the German prince," Sienna said excitedly. "Wait until you hear that whole story—"

But before Sienna could begin, there was a palpable turning of heads at every table in the room.

"Anne has entered," Virginia said dryly, "and the room has practically saluted."

"It's that way everywhere Anne goes now," Sienna explained. "See? Instead of all that white she used to wear, Anne now wears red, and instead of looking like an ice queen, she looks like the Queen of Hearts."

"My dear, all your symbolism seems to come from the nursery."

"I guess it does," Sienna admitted sheepishly.

Anne deposited her red cape at the coat-check desk and walked regally and slowly toward her friends. She did not stop along the way to do the hellos and little air kisses that had once characterized her. Nor did she come in showing emotion as she had that day so many months ago when she'd first read the item about her husband in Lolly Little's column. Today her measured steps and interest in reaching her destination, not dominating a room, had the reverse effect. By her indifference to those who lunched, she dominated their view and their thoughts.

A small buzz went through the room.

"*Smashing.*"

"*She doesn't look like the leftover wife.*"

"*Why didn't she always wear red?*"

"*Does she have a boyfriend?*"

When she reached the table, Anne put her arms around Virginia. Sienna would have sworn there were tears in Anne's eyes.

Anne was struck by the obvious change in their friend. Virginia seemed pale and thin, two things no makeup artist, not even Hugo, could hide.

"We're having champagne," Virginia announced brightly, "so settle back, Anne. You seem to have this room in an uproar over your dramatic look."

Anne smiled. "I have a new clothes adviser."

"Oh?" Sienna asked.

"Ricardo Monte," she said with a smile.

"Is he a new designer?" Virginia asked.

Sienna laughed. "You've been away too long. He's the new genius on Wall Street. Evidently our Anne has him telling her how to budget her considerable money. Good for you, Anne. Peter wondered who would bag him."

"He's not bagged," Anne said, "but you're right; he's handling my investments these days, and my clothing allowance—"

"He's single and attractive," Sienna persisted.

Anne shook her head. "Don't overdramatize it. I'm just out of one marriage, and I'm not planning another for a long while."

"Casey didn't wait, did he?" Virginia asked. "You know, dear," Virginia confided as she leaned across the table, "when I'm at home I just don't ask the same questions. The things that seem indecent to ask at home seem so—so appropriate here. So, do tell me what really happened with Casey."

"What really happened," Anne explained, "is that Casey actually believed he was Superman. No, I guess he thought he was Superdeal. I can understand it a bit. Besides, I don't hate him any longer. I've cooled in all my feelings for him. It's wonderful what divorce can do. You know, it can force you to stand back and admit that you were wrong. Well, I was wrong. I thought Casey was a fantastic man. Honestly, I once did. I knew he was competitive, of course. He was proud of me in front of other people and competing with me intensely when we were together. So long as I reflected well on him, all was fine. But he didn't want me to have a singular identity. When I started being known as Anne Burrows instead of Mrs. Casey Burrows, he became very nervous. But when Lady Diandre came into his life, he really climbed some invisible mountain, and from the top of that whipped-cream dream, he thought he was the supreme being. Through circumstances"—now Anne laughed— "circumstances I don't dare repeat in polite company, I'm out of that marriage. Oh, let's simply say that I found Casey and his English friend in a rather embarrassing situation, and that made me the wronged wife. Casey may think he can get away with anything, but he really didn't want his romance—his dirty little romance—in the tabloids. Basically he's old-fashioned, and besides, his mother would have been furious. So we divorced quickly, quietly, and with a very big settlement for me. And he really backed into his marriage with Diandre. I thought that would be the icing on the cake for me. Sort of like answered prayers."

"How's it working?" Sienna asked.

"My best information comes from the office," Anne answered. "She's pushing him hard to be an English gentleman, and since he never learned manners American style, he's hopeless. Their marriage so far has been marked by three very public quarrels, but I've got so much of the business that"—Anne looked at both of them and fluttered her eyelids in mock innocence—"he can't afford another divorce."

"You know," Virginia reminded them, "I always said the ladies at lunch didn't come to eat; they came to dish. I hope you both will continue to see Juliet Caesar. It's strange, isn't it, that she was the key to our finding out about Gregory. Mr. Tibbitt came up with a lot of stories even after Gregory left for South America."

"You probably know a lot more about Gregory than we do," Anne said.

"But he can never come back into our lives and threaten us," Sienna said. "The truth can't hurt us now."

"Once I learned about him, I realized that obviously he knew something about you that he was holding over your heads—but I really don't want to know the story," Virginia added hastily as she saw the look, the old look of fright, come into Sienna's eyes. "I like only those stories that don't touch the ones I love."

"Did you love Gregory?" Sienna asked for the first time. How many times the Seconds had wondered, yet had lacked the confidence to pose the question. With Gregory gone, all barriers to their full relationship with one another were removed. And so she wondered if indeed this man had betrayed their beloved Virginia with promises of love he was incapable of giving.

Virginia shook her head. "Infatuated perhaps. Delighted certainly. But in love? Never. I had one love, and I lived my love. I still do. You see, love never dies. People leave, but love doesn't. My love for Calvin is there every day of my life. It's in the papers I read—silently I turn and wait for his opinion—and because I knew, rather, know him so well, I can hear his laugh or his words of derision. Calvin is still in my bed, at my table, and always in my heart."

Sienna, her heart too full to speak, nodded. She knew that same kind of love for her husband. How precious it is today, she thought. How precious it would be for all time.

Anne, concerned that the conversation was going to result in a good old-fashioned cry between her two companions, raised her glass. "Since you ordered champagne, Virginia, I propose a toast to you."

Virginia raised her glass. "Perfect," she answered, and then with a twinkle in her eyes said precisely, "To you, to Bronwyn—and yes, to me. And most of all, to our school."

"The school?" Anne repeated nervously. "Then you're going ahead? You said you owned the land in New Hampshire where the school was—"

"That's why we're here," Virginia announced firmly, her voice now sounding like that of the energetic woman they had always known.

Anne and Sienna looked at each other in silent communication, pleased to see hints of Virginia's old energy and displeased at the thought of having to reorganize their lives around yet another charity.

"I do want the school to be built. I do want to leave something behind." This last Virginia said very gently, with just a tinge of tremor in her voice. "Will you help?"

"I am having this baby—" Sienna began, her words trailing. Then realizing that she could never refuse Virginia something she wanted, she sat as straight as she could. "Yes, Virginia. Yes, of course. I will do anything I can."

"I'll make the first pledge," Anne said simply.

"No, you can't," Virginia said. "In truth I am leaving enough money to build the school. The money Juliet is raising will go for scholarships. We won't need any dreary charity balls or selling tickets to Broadway shows no one wants to see or buying of tables for dinners no one wants to attend. I've plenty of money for this, and I've decided it's what I want most to do with my money. But the real reason for our seeing one another today is that I have an idea. I understand that there's a house on the property, and I think it would be wonderful if Bronwyn had it as her place to go when she's ready to leave Pembroke. It would be a wonderful place to take Gwyneth, and she could set up headquarters there and, as a superior real-estate developer, she could be in charge of building the school."

"Oh, Virginia," Sienna said, her voice cracking with emotion, "you are the most generous, the most giving—" and then she lowered her head and began to cry. She cried for the mother she hadn't had, this mother she did have, for the women who were in every sense her sisters, for little Gwyneth, whom she now loved, and for her unborn child.

Anne applauded, and everyone in the restaurant turned to see what had happened at the table.

But all they could see were three women, three well-known women who had come to Sylvan's, where everyone chose to be visible, and had instead wrapped themselves in their own invisible love.

67

I T WAS SPRING, THE SEASON OF REBIRTH, YET IT SEEMED TO VIR-
ginia that instead of feeling new, she was feeling unaccountably old, almost as if parts of her were breaking down.

Not since the day two weeks before when she had met the Seconds at Sylvan's had she ventured forth for lunch. She did manage to work at her desk some hours every day, but now that the arrangements for the school had been made, she did not have the same kind of dedicated energy that had once characterized her. "It's the kind of rootless and pointless way that I felt the first two years after Mr. Calvin died," she confessed to Holmes, who had been her husband's butler. "No matter where I am, I don't feel comfortable; I don't feel I belong, and I can't put my finger on an illness. I'm just not at home in me. I feel as if I have my mind in a stranger's body."

"What does the doctor say?" Holmes asked with devoted concern.

"What doctors always say, 'There's nothing wrong. You're not as young as you used to be, and you have to get used to living with a lot of physical changes you never thought about.'"

"Do you believe him?" Holmes asked.

"Let's say I want to."

"Madam, if you thought a change of scene would help, I would be happy to make arrangements for you to go to London. You could stay at the Connaught as usual, and my sister who lives there would come to stay with you. Or, if you wish, I would be pleased to accompany you, and she and I could run things for you there."

Virginia smiled appreciatively, yet this momentary glimpse of kindness served only to remind her how dependent she had become on those around her. It was not a situation she found appealing.

"Let's say I'd like to, and I appreciate your offer in the devoted spirit it was made, but no. I just can't seem to keep my mind on any serious subject. I keep drifting off to inconsequential things, and mostly I drift back—back in time. I keep thinking of reasons to do nothing. I look out the window, and I look inside me, but I can't seem to look anywhere else."

Holmes frowned. He knew his mistress truly was ill.

Virginia turned and faced the windows in her drawing room. Below she could see the trees beginning to bud, and even the dirty waters of the East River did not seem so uninviting as they had the previous months.

The seasons changed, and life did, too.

≡

Virginia opened her eyes, and the room, the landscape of her familiar room, swam dizzily before her.

Sienna? It was Sienna, wasn't it?

"Virginia, we're here. Virginia, can you hear me? It's us. Anne and me, Sienna. We're here. We're with you."

Virginia fingered the white duvet. "Aaah, it's so white, so clean." Virginia knew it was cleaner than anything she'd ever seen in West Virginia, but somehow she couldn't explain to her dear little Seconds. Their beginnings were so different—so different.

"Don't leave us, Virginia," Anne whispered.

Virginia was floating above them now. Didn't they know that? Oh, but she must say this to them. She would have to come back and tell them, promise them what they needed to know. She stopped the—what was it she stopped?—and spoke softly to her girls. "I won't leave you. Don't you know yet, darlings, that I will always be there each time you need me? I will come quietly, very quietly, through the terrible noise of your lives, and whenever you want, you will be able to hear my small, nagging voice. Of course"—she smiled now at Anne—"I know you won't always listen."

"I will, I will," Anne protested.

"Sometimes you will." Virginia held out her hand.

Both young women grasped it.

"Sometimes," she assured them, "is good enough for me."

And then Virginia smiled, for this fleeting series of events, this small moment called life, had produced this moment she had awaited so long.

She looked up and saw not her Seconds. They were far, far behind her. Now walking toward her, straight and tall as he had once been, was Calvin.

She closed her eyes.

Life had been worth the wait.

Epilogue

T HE EXES.

 All of their husbands had had at least one, the wife before
the Wife, but somehow the Seconds had managed to put those
women into the back room of their marriages, that dark place in
memory where husbands rarely dared—and second wives never
chose—to look, save for holidays ("Will the children go to our house
or *hers?*"—the word *hers* always said after one measured beat and
with a sibilant *s* so that the question ended with a hiss).

 Family occasions—birthdays, graduations, confirmations, and
marriages—presented the real problem, for the family occasion provided No Way Out. The ex-Mrs. had to deal with the present Mrs.

 There were countless stories among the Seconds about ex-
wives, those first mistakes made when their husbands were young.
Second wives relished those stories when present friends who knew
the first Mrs. Whoever confided that no one had ever seen the
Husband as happy as he was now. How wonderful that the first Mrs.
Whoever had been swept away by drugs or drink, boredom, circum-
stance, or one of the Seconds. When in public, the Seconds clucked
sympathetically at stories of the Original Wife and her continuing
failures. Successes of the First Wife were greeted with silence or a
forced smile and the words "How nice," and the never-expressed but
often-thought question "Will that reduce the alimony?"

 But the situation was somewhat different in the Peter Marvell
household. He had not been the one to leave; Judith had. He had
not ended the unhappy chapters of their marriage; she had. A true
feminist, she demanded no alimony. Still, despite Peter's protesta-
tions of love for Sienna, the fact that he'd met her after he was
divorced from Judith, and his promise that he had never been so
happy as he was with her, Sienna felt uneasy as Sidney's wedding
approached, for she knew she would have to deal with Judith for the
first time.

 Despite Judith's willingness to leave the planning of the wedding to Sidney and Sienna, Sienna knew that the day would come

when the second Mrs. Peter Marvell would come face to face with the first Mrs. Peter Marvell.

It was just that she hadn't expected that day to come today. Not today when she and Anne were to bring Bronwyn from the hospital, reunite her with Gwyneth, and start the two on their new life in New Hampshire. Not today when the effects of her pregnancy left her feeling clumsy and uncomfortable. "Pregnancy does nothing for a short woman," Sienna complained to Peter as she moved slowly and gracelessly to get out of bed.

"That's a woman for you," Peter chided. "Complains when she can't get pregnant, complains when she does."

"I'm not complaining," Sienna sighed, "just reporting. And I don't look forward to today's calendar."

"But you're bringing Bronwyn from the hospital, aren't you?"

"Anne and I are. It's strange, Peter, but at the inquest after Rosabelle"—it was such a relief to be able to talk freely about the event that had shaped so much of her life—"Bronwyn held me and said, 'I'll take care of you.' Isn't it a wonderful turn of life that now I was able to take care of her?"

"I think it was great for us; I liked having Gwyneth here," Peter said. "I'd forgotten how sweet a little girl can be."

"Well, think about how sweet little girls grow up," Sienna said with a deep sigh. "I'm meeting your ex-wife for lunch today to discuss the seating for the wedding lunch."

"Oh," Peter said dully.

"That's how I feel about it, too," Sienna said.

≣

Today's luncheon had been Sidney's idea.

"Please, Sienna," she had begged, "my mother wants to be at the wedding, and she thought that you should plan it because my father's giving it, and she really can't afford to do a wedding, and I wanted you to do the wedding with me because my mother's so antimarriage, but I know we all have to be together, and someone has to take the first step, and my father won't, and my mother won't, and you're my friend—"

In the end, of course, the words "my friend" moved Sienna more than any other argument advanced by Sidney, so now Sienna—in the last month of a pregnancy that was bigger than she—sat awkwardly at a table in the restaurant of the Royal Hotel.

"Why the Royal?" Anne had asked when Sienna told her about today's luncheon.

"I don't want to eat at the Dome where I know everyone," Sienna explained. "I don't want to do a number. If I go to the Royal, there won't be any other diners in the room except three ladies accompanying their convention-bound husbands, and that suits me fine."

Sienna had arrived early in order to be spared the discomfort of being seen first by the chic, thin woman she assumed Judith to be. She sat at a table facing the door, waiting for the elegant woman she expected.

Judith would stand apart from this crowd. Sienna was sure of that. The women now filling the room were part of the traveling wives Sienna expected, ladies who wore the precise little three-piece knit suits with the skirt slightly bagged in back, designer handbags strapped to their shoulders, and their short hair colored various shades of blond and coiffed in tiny, tight curls.

No, Judith would not be one of them. She would surely stand out in this group. But where was she? Sienna frowned and looked at her little watch—she wore an inexpensive watch today, no point in displaying wealth before Judith.

It was seven minutes past the appointed meeting time. Where was Judith?

It was just when Sienna had turned to speak to the captain to order some mineral water that Judith appeared almost without notice.

"Judith here," a voice said abruptly.

Sienna, startled, almost jumped from her seat. Indeed she wished she were agile enough to rise, but she wasn't.

And even though she was sitting there awaiting Judith's arrival, she was not prepared for her appearance.

The woman who stood before her, unlike Sienna, was large. She was tall, even taller than Anne, and she was large-boned. But the surprise was that she was *old*. Somehow Sienna had expected Judith to be frozen in time, to be a belligerent forty-year-old marching to a feminist beat. Instead there was a woman in her mid-fifties, her gray hair pulled into a bun with wisps of hair falling unattractively over her face. She was wearing a black suit, no makeup, and no jewelry. Still, despite the plainness of her appearance, she exuded a vitality, a kind of energy.

Sienna masked her surprise with a quick, nervous smile and invited Judith to sit down.

The formalities took only moments, and in that time the two women judged each other in the all-knowing, yet unknowing, way that only two women who have shared a name and a life with the same man can regard each other.

Judith the Horrible, Judith the First was not what Sienna expected. "I want to thank you for being so good to Sidney," Judith said.

Sienna nodded. Wasn't Judith supposed to be an angry first wife?

"You're not at all the kind of woman I expected Peter to marry," Judith said coolly. "I thought Peter would marry someone out for his money, and I know you're a rich girl from the Midwest, so I've wondered why you'd want an older man."

"I wondered about you, too," Sienna said quietly. She didn't add that she'd wondered why anyone would give his freedom to Peter, a man who obviously enjoyed marriage and a regulated life, a man willing to give a wife a long leash and a comfortable one at that. Judith obviously was not a rich woman.

"Let's talk about the wedding. Give me the facts and your questions," Judith commanded. Obviously she was taking control of the conversation and the lunch. It may have been Sienna's invitation, but it was Judith's agenda.

Briefly Sienna outlined the plans, the menu, and the guest list. Did Judith want to add names? As many as she wanted, of course. Did Judith want to have her family Bible carried by the bride? Did she want her lace hanky?

Judith shook her head. No, she wanted no other guests. No, she didn't have a family Bible. Matter of fact, she didn't believe in God. And, as for lace hankies, she gave those up with ladies' teas.

"Wouldn't you like to—ummm—order some lunch?" Sienna asked.

"No," Judith answered. "Some coffee black, and then I have to get back to court."

"Court?"

"Yes, I'm involved in a case where a woman's rights were

violated. Interesting. She was fired because of an office romance. Married man. He tossed the woman aside of course. So she has no job. No man."

"Is there a lesson in that for me?" Sienna asked impulsively.

Judith laughed. It was a hearty, real laugh, not one of those polite lady-to-lady laughs. "Maybe."

Sienna was surprised. She liked Judith. "From the way you're looking at me, I suppose you're wondering why I married Peter."

"He's a nice man," Judith volunteered, "but he never made me happy. Now that I think about it though, I don't think anybody could have made me happy. You see, at that time in my life I believed that marriage violated a woman's rights."

"Do you still think so?" Sienna asked softly.

"Sometimes, but then that's what I always expected. Until I went into analysis, I really believed that I was the one who should take the broken cookie, the cracked cup—I really thought that was what I deserved, so you see, the broken marriage was what I expected. I never thought I'd be a successful wife, and in the end I proved me right. I wasn't a successful wife."

"But if your attitude had been different, would your marriage to Peter have worked?" Sienna asked earnestly as she looked at Judith's face, imploring her to say—to say what?

To say that the marriage would have worked, and there would have been no chapter two, no Sienna? Or did she want her to say that the marriage was never destined to work? Judith shrugged. "I don't know. That's something we'll both wonder about forever."

And then Judith stood. "I have to get back," she announced. "I'll see you at the wedding."

"There is a rehearsal dinner—" Sienna began.

"The wedding will be enough for me," Judith said, turned, and strode from the room.

"Wait!" Sienna wanted to call out, but she said nothing. She said nothing as she watched the purposeful, tall woman leave. This meeting had been so abrupt, so unsatisfying. Had Judith walked away from Peter, too, leaving more questions than answers in her wake? For Judith had been right, of course. Both women would wonder forever just why and how their lives had turned out this way.

Sienna would wonder, as she sat self-consciously at Sidney's wedding, what events and quirks of life placed her at Peter's side.

Were there memories she would never transcend, ways she could never really belong to the present because her husband—no matter how much he loved her—was still locked into a past he'd never escape?

On days when she held her new baby, filled with thankfulness for the life and love she now had, she would wonder if this new life had been created by her, Peter, or—in some strange, long-ago way—Judith.

She would wonder, alone, in the dark corners of the years to come and through the days of joy that would be hers.

And on days when Peter's preoccupation with business and attention to Gene, to the son that he and Judith shared—that relationship that never admitted her—on those days when Sienna's peace of mind was threatened, she would wonder if Judith in the mean and lean days of her marriage to Peter had uncovered a solemn truth that caused her to leave, that made Judith into the woman she was today. For Judith had not been ugly, mean, or shrewish toward Sienna; she had been unemotional, yes, but with it all practical and straightforward. Had she always been that way? And had memory sharpened her edges for Peter? Had memory and his own sense of self altered the truth to fit Peter's image of himself?

Yes, she would wonder always if Peter's easy explanation for the ending of his first marriage were Judith's as well. What was Judith's story? What was Judith's complaint?

In the end, of course, Sienna would look at the homes and the family and the serene life she was creating for Peter, and she would remember that although he had once loved another woman, those days were gone.

But now, for the first time, she realized that the memory of Judith and his own desire to have been the Right One in the marital wars had enhanced Peter's appreciation of her.

Peter wanted Sienna to believe that Judith was the villain in the marriage, and she wanted to share that belief. But could this old, odd woman have hacked the marriage to pieces all by herself? Hadn't it taken some kind of action on Peter's part, too? Was he truly as blameless as she—and he—wanted to believe?

Sienna sighed deeply and sipped the water in front of her. She was surprised to see her hand shaking.

That's only natural, she reminded herself. Judith has already left this room, and still she is on my mind.

Why should it be different with Peter?

Why should I think that any second marriage—even a good one—is a vaccination for memory?

≡

Anne awakened to the sound of heavy rain and the rumble of thunder, but when she looked from her bedroom window across the park, there was no rain.

It keeps raining in my head, she thought. I still can't get accustomed to sweet sunshine days.

"Mama, Mama," came a husky little voice.

Anne knew that voice; that little baritone girl could be no one but Fudge. Anne leaned over and scooped up her daughter—her daughter, scruffy blanket in one hand and stuffed Ducky in the other—into her bed. "Do you know something, Fudge?" she cooed. "You have a voice that matches your name. You have a chocolate voice."

Fudge laughed her funny little rumbling laugh.

"Fudge. I wonder if anyone will ever call you Virginia."

"That's Gammy. Where's Gammy?" the little girl asked.

Anne's eyes filled. A few months earlier Anne had taken Fudge to visit Virginia, and as Virginia, pale and weakened, greeted them in her library, Fudge asked if Virginia was her grandmother. Anne began to say no, but Virginia said yes, in a clear loud voice, and from that day Fudge called her Gammy. Now the child was looking for Gammy.

"Let me tell you something," Anne said softly. "Gammy has gone away. We didn't want her to go, but she had to leave. She wasn't feeling well, you see."

Fudge's eyes were wide. "I don't see."

"Some day you will," Anne promised, "and someday you'll hear about your other gammy, too. She was Mommy's mommy."

"Was she a princess?"

Anne paused. "Yes, she was a kind of princess, and she would have loved you very much."

≡

The foliage was full and lush.

Like me, just like me, Bronwyn thought as she walked up the long hill to the house. Was it only four months since she had come here? No, of course, it had been longer, but she remembered best these past four months, the sweet long days of spring, that time of growth, of planting and watering through her garden variety of moods and changes.

When she'd first awakened, after such a long sleep, she'd had a vague sense of—of who? Oh yes. The Seconds and Virginia. Dear Virginia, birdlike, had fluttered over her with soft wings brushing her arms, healing her heart. Later Bronwyn had awakened in a strange, dark place, and Sienna—it was Sienna, wasn't it?—had been touching her and murmuring, "No, no, we mustn't tell her yet."

Tell, Bronwyn wanted to say through the parched lips and dry tongue, but the words would not come forth. Only her eyes, her large eyes, spoke.

"She wants to know," she heard Anne say in that crisp, commanding voice.

Of course I want to know, Bronwyn cried silently. God, why couldn't she tell them what she wanted to say?

"I can't tell her," Sienna said, her voice quivering with sadness.

"If you don't, she'll think something's happened to Gwyneth," Anne cautioned.

At the mention of her daughter's name, Bronwyn had pushed up on one elbow, pursed her lips, and faintly, ever so faintly, cried, "Gwyneth." Then she'd dropped back totally exhausted, her blanched complexion matching the white pillow.

"Gwyneth is fine!" Sienna had shouted. "Please hear me, Bronwyn darling. All Gwyneth wants is her mommy."

"Mommy," Bronwyn whispered and slept peacefully through the dark days and nights of the hospital.

Now, at the top of the hill, Bronwyn sat on the little bench under the tree, but Bronwyn could not see the tree, for her eyes were closed, and in her mind's eye was her child. How wonderful it would be to see her daughter again, to be a woman once more instead of a person tied to a regimen in a place tied to nothing from the world Bronwyn knew.

"Bronwyn." It was Anne. She always knew Anne's voice.

She sighed, opened her eyes slowly, and, standing in front of her, were—yes, Sienna and Anne.

Bronwyn rose slowly from the bench and put her arms around Sienna, then patted Anne on the arm.

"No more kisses?" Anne asked.

Bronwyn shook her head. "I'd kiss you, Anne, if I could reach you. But to tell the truth, you're so tall, I've always felt as if I needed a stepladder to have a conversation with you."

"Oh no," Sienna moaned, "are we going to have to deal with a new you now who always tells the truth?"

"No," Bronwyn promised, "I'll still tell social white lies."

"Then we can still be friends," Anne assured her and put an arm around her and squeezed her shoulder. "I'm glad you're not going back to the City," she added impulsively.

"So am I," Bronwyn admitted. "You couldn't stay away though, could you, Anne?"

Anne shook her head. "New York is what makes my blood flow. It's ugly and dirty and full of angry, disappointed people, but it's where the winners are, and—oh, I'm sorry, Bronwyn," she said quickly, her eyes filling with tears at her gaffe. "I didn't mean—"

"You didn't mean to say I'm not a winner? But I'm not," Bronwyn said, her voice calm and controlled. "I'm not a winner in the New York sense. But I do know I can't handle that big scene, so in that way I am a winner. I know what I can and can't do. I'm lucky that my real-estate business could be sold, and I'm lucky that Virginia decided she wanted to create the school. Bad as he was, at least Gregory conceived this, and then Virginia went ahead and made all the plans—"

"The Virginia Payne North School. She never would have chosen that name, but we're the trustees, and that was our unanimous decision," Sienna reminded them. "Virginia endowed the school; she caused us to help create it. It must be our tribute to her." Taking Bronwyn's hand, she said, "And as trustees, Anne and I are lucky that we have you to see us through the building and the staffing. You know, I think Gwyneth will love living up there. She's enjoyed living in the country so much these past months."

"And who knows," Bronwyn added, "Gwyneth and I just may move up there for good. I could always teach, maybe poetry," she said softly. "Yes, I could teach now that I can separate fact and fantasy."

"If you can do that, you may be the only one of us who can." Anne laughed.

Bronwyn touched her face, and it felt smooth. No beneath-the-surface poisons waiting to spoil her looks and her sense of self. "If only Virginia could see us now," she whispered.

"She does," Sienna said firmly. "You don't think this sunshine today is an accident, do you? Virginia is still taking care of her Seconds."

"Think of what we've been through together—all these years, all these times," Bronwyn said softly.

"No," said Sienna, "think of what we're going to go through—all those good new years, all the good new times."

They looked at one another with a look as old as the conspiratorial look of their teens, a look as new as the sorrows of their past year.

"I think Virginia would be proud of the Seconds," Sienna said.

The other two women nodded, and then, their arms looped around one another, the three walked slowly down the hill.